FORGOTTEN WITNESS

A Josie Bates Thriller
Book 6

By

REBECCA FORSTER

Forgotten Witness
Copyright © Rebecca Forster, 2013
All rights reserved

ISBN: 0615928072
ISBN-13: 9780615928074

Though certain elements of this novel were suggested by actual events, it is a work of fiction. All characters, whether central or peripheral, are purely products of the author's imagination, as are their actions, motivations, thoughts, and conversations, and neither the characters nor the situations were invented for them are intended to depict real people.

For

Annemaire Boehm-Forster
my mom who inspires me in more ways than she'll ever know
&
Meriam Helen Czuleger
my mother-in-law who is greatly missed

Special Thanks to:

Stephen Kyle (English Steve) and Ian Francis (and daughter Amelia's sleepless nights) for providing fertile ground for my imagination. I'm honored that you allowed me to channel the core of your marvelous persons into the two heroes of this novel, with liberal creative license.

Jenny Jensen, my muse and incredible story editor who understands my vision before I do.

Bruce Raterink for your unfailing confidence, superb eye, amazing brain, and way too cheery attitude.

Marianne Donley and Sandra Paul, novelists whose opinions I respect and friendship I cherish.

Author's Note

Some writers find inspiration in their hearts, some in their souls, and some because they are inquisitive. I am the latter. I truly believe that nothing I can imagine is stranger than what happens in real life. Whether it was a child being tried as an adult for murder (*Hostile Witness*) or a blood feud impacting the lives of Josie, Hannah, and Archer (*Eyewitness*), I build my stories on real legal, social, or emotional foundations.

Forgotten Witness is no different. I was challenged and inspired by recent science, politics, and modern history. This was a fascinating book to write; I hope it is an entertaining one to read.

CHAPTER 1

WASHINGTON, D.C.

In his State of the Union address, President Obama cited brain research as an example of how the government should "invest in the best ideas," one of which was brain mapping. The details are not final, and it is not clear how much federal money would be proposed or approved for the project in a time of fiscal constraint or how far the research would be able to get without significant federal financing. – Los Angeles Times

ॐॐ

Can't get you off my mind. Wish I was there. Give 'em hell today. Stay warm. – Voice message from Archer to Josie

ॐॐ

"I see that we are coming upon the three o'clock hour. I would like to thank the new members of the Foreign Relations Committee – Senators Johnson, Klupec, Garner and Abel – for sitting in before their confirmation to this esteemed body.

"I would also like to thank those who have come so far to testify here today. A rise in factional tensions in Eastern Europe has been the focus of this committee for some time now. While our State Department has kept us apprised of their diplomatic efforts, we are cognizant of the fact that our citizens can also be affected adversely in their everyday lives by world events. To that end, it is the charge of this committee to be aware and proactive..."

With that, Josie Bates zoned out.

Senator Ambrose 'Pat' Patriota, lion of the senate, White House bound unless the electorate suddenly turned fickle, and chairman of the Foreign Relations Committee of the United States Senate was doing exactly what everyone in a position of power did when they wanted to reaffirm their importance: they pandered for the cameras, the record, and the public. For the most part, Ambrose Patriota had a rapt audience. Anyone who bothered to glance Josie's way would assume she was also spellbound by his rhetoric.

Those people would be wrong.

Josie was doing what every good lawyer did when cross-examinations, opening statements, and testimony dragged on: filtering and compartmentalizing information and tagging buzzwords. It was a skill that allowed her to react appropriately on a moment's notice and appear as if she had hung on every word opposing counsel uttered. At this point she doubted she would be called upon to respond to anything, but old habits die hard.

She had spent two days in this marble-floored room staring at the carved, curved, gleaming walnut bench that could accommodate fifteen senators. That bench sat on a dais wide enough and long enough for three times as many aides. Before she was invited to Washington, Josie assumed a chamber like this would be cavernous. In reality it was cramped and utilitarian, the human equivalent of an ant farm. The only difference was that not all these humans were engaged in work of any discernable value whereas ants labored selflessly for the good of the colony.

She, however, had done what she had come to do: testify about her experience with Eastern European cultural justice and the terror it had wreaked upon Hannah Sheraton and Billy Zuni, Archer and her. Sitting on a hard chair at a long table, Josie spoke into the microphone in front of her and tried to ignore the phalanx of photographers crouched on the floor between her and the committee. She had been the last of three witnesses and the least interesting. The Albanian girl who had been trafficked at the age of fourteen and rescued by the pastor of a local church was the star of the day. She spoke about her ordeal in halting English that made her tale even more poignant. Now twenty, she was a poised, brave, and exotically beautiful young woman who was in college and studying to become a psychologist. Taking second place was a Serbian immigrant who had built a solid business in the U.S. only to suffer economically and personally at the hands of Eastern European organized crime. The photographers had salivated when he held up a fingerless hand and told of the nightmarish extortion and torture committed against him. His adult son sat behind his father, wiping away tears as the older man spoke.

Josie pulled up the rear, telling the senators about Gjergy Isai and the ancient code of justice that cost three people their lives in Hermosa Beach and put her ward, Hannah, and Hannah's friend, Billy, on the run. Josie had told the senators of the one phone call she received, a message from Hannah reassuring her that they were alive. She was a smart girl and had called in the dead of night, leaving a message on the office machine, unwilling to hear Josie's voice for fear it would draw her home before it was truly safe to come back. Josie told the committee of the very real threat that others from the Isai clan would come for Billy and that the cycle of retribution would be never ending unless they intervened. Sadly, without Hannah and Billy, without pictures, without wounds, Josie's urging of reconciliation of ancient laws with modern justice made little impact.

"And lastly, we want to thank Ms. Bates for coming all the way from California to enlighten us about the very real threat stemming from Albanian cultural justice known as blood feud, a practice that both the Catholic Church and Albanian government have denounced..."

Josie acknowledged the recognition with a slight inclination of her head. In turn, Senator Patriota graced her with the kind of smile one might give an old friend. That was a good trick since they had never met. Minions had orchestrated this event and lavished attention on the witnesses in an effort to make them forget that the man in charge hadn't even so much as shaken their hands. Now he owned a piece of them. Their stories, their pictures, and their sworn statements were in the public record. Josie had no doubt that all of it would be used in Patriota's upcoming campaign. Washington was a well-ordered machine when it wanted to be.

Then Josie's attention was caught by something other than Senator Patriota's acknowledgement, and it wasn't the first time it had happened during the proceedings. For the last hour she had been the object of someone's scrutiny. Now, as the hearing came to a close, her sense of unease intensified.

She cut her eyes left and scanned the people standing against the wall. She looked right and did the same. No one showed any particular interest in her. She resisted the urge to look behind her, to look people in the eye and see if they suddenly averted theirs. Instead, she rubbed the nape of her neck, working out a kink as she tried to convince herself that she was simply tired. Away from the beach, the sun, and the surf she was the proverbial fish out of water. As beautiful as fall was in the nation's capitol the chill in the air, the weight of her coat, the gloves in her pocket made her itch for Hermosa Beach. She was also aware that the memories of her kidnapping and imprisonment in a cement hut could blindside her and paralyze her when she least expected it.

"PTSD", the doctor had said.

"I'll deal with it," Josie assured him.

Sometimes that was easier said than done. Now was one of those times. Josie looked back at Ambrose Patriota in the hope that focusing on him would quell her anxiety. The strategy was no hardship since the senator was an exceptionally good- looking man for his age. His jaw was still square and strong despite the softening that came with age. His eyes were sharp, bright, green, and spoke a language all their own. He wore his thick hair fashionably long and the waves were marbled with shades of steel grey and glinting silver. Patriota's People, as his constituency was known, adored him and their ranks had swelled to include voters across the country. The man usually said what he meant and stood by his principles when push came to shove. Josie didn't always agree with his politics, but that's not what this was about. This hearing was about Hannah. If anyone could help Josie bring her home it would be this man.

Yet her interest in him was more personal than she liked to admit. Seeing Ambrose Patriota in the flesh had a strange affect on her. She was bothered by the notion that she knew him, or, at the very least, that they had met before. But details about where and when that might have been were elusive. She had run in some high-powered circles early in her career but never with Washington elite. And wouldn't he have remembered her and mentioned it in his correspondence if, indeed, they had crossed paths? She almost laughed at that last bit of arrogance. A politician met thousands of women; there had to be more than a few who stood as tall as she did. Still, in profile, viewed from a lower vantage point, his bearing militarily precise, Josie could swear that she had been this close to him before…

Suddenly, Josie's daydreaming came to an end. Patriota was wrapping things up. For the witnesses this exercise in politics was excruciatingly personal, but for the senators it was simply an item to mark off their calendars. Everyone started to move at once. Aides picked up their bosses' files and whispered about the next appointments on their calendar. Staff received their marching orders in return. A few of the senators socialized but most fled the room. Reporters leapt from their seats, photographers pushed off the floor. Half of them turned their lenses on the retreating politicians and the other half converged on the witnesses. One in particular wanted to chat with Josie.

"Ms. Bates! Hannah Sheraton was tried for murder in California. Could you address her legal problems? Do they have any bearing on her current situation?"

Josie picked up her coat, eyeing the man as she put it on. Her first instinct was to tell him to take a flying leap. Hannah had been acquitted of murder and there was no reason to discuss that history. Her second thought was to keep it simple and direct the conversation in the hopes her message would reach a larger audience.

"Hannah is a hero. Billy Zuni is alive because of her..."

Josie lost her train of thought, distracted momentarily by a disturbance in the back of the room. She smiled slightly, thinking that the people smashed together near the exit looked like a school of fish panicked by a predator swimming among them. But Josie was the only one who seemed to notice. The blond girl who was her guide for the day touched her elbow and whispered her name.

"Sorry," Josie apologized to the reporter. "You were asking?"

"Hannah's mother is in prison. Have you kept her apprised of this situation?" he asked.

"Yes, I sent word to the prison where Linda Rayburn—"

Josie's eyes went back to the commotion by the door. A man was pushing through the crowd, bobbing and weaving. His head came up. His head went down. He bumped into people, careened off a chair, and froze like a prairie dog catching the scent of a coyote. Josie's alarm was immediate and debilitating. A sick, sinking feeling washed over her just before she grew cold and an instant later flushed hot. Her instinct was to run and hide, but she couldn't seem to move. She tried to make eye contact with other people, but no one looked back. Why didn't they see what she saw? Why-

"Ms. Bates?"

She blinked and zeroed in on the reporter again. He had a gap between his front teeth and his teeth were clenched in irritation.

"Yes. Sorry. I've sent...." Again she faltered. Again she couldn't remember her point. She laughed a little. "I forgot the question. It's been a long day."

Josie wiped her brow with the back of her hand. Her mouth was dry. The blond girl stepped in.

"Maybe we can give Ms. Bates some breathing room. Senator Patriota's office will have contact information on all the witnesses for your follow-up."

Expertly she started to ease Josie past the reporters. Just then the man who had been so intent upon getting into the room while everyone else was trying to get out raised his head, locked eyes with Josie, and went into high gear. Using his clasped hands like a wedge, he cut a path through the throng.

Josie turned into her escort just as the reporter shoved his microphone closer. She flinched. Her heart thundered. Her head pounded. She couldn't breath. She couldn't speak, but the girl was still talking as if nothing were wrong; she was still guiding Josie into danger and the reporter was still spitting questions. Josie looked back at the man. He hadn't taken his eyes off her. He hadn't slowed his pace.

This was not her imagination.

She wasn't wrong.

The man in the blue suit was coming for her, she was the only one who knew it, and there wasn't a damn thing she could do about it.

કૈ૦ન્શ

Ian Francis had not been a man to be reckoned with for many years. He had never been of much consequence even before the dark time. He had not been wealthy or famous; he had not been a rake or a rebel. But all that was about to change because he had changed. Ian didn't know why or how this had happened, he only knew that one day he woke up in the light. When the light blessed him he knew he must run through it, making the most of the hours during which he could think rationally and act decisively. Thinking was good; acting on those thoughts was heroic.

That was success, was it not?

Even as he asked himself that question, his mind winked out. When it was back on line it was filled with terror. People were pushing him, turning their backs on him, looking at him as if he were vile.

Who were they?

What were they saying?

He couldn't make out words but he saw their angry faces bouncing on the meniscus of the dark that floated at the edge of his brain. He was frightened they would stop him before he did this one good thing, so Ian fought the only way he knew how. He recited the rules.

Rule one: eat, drink, sleep, and pray you wake up still in the light.

Rule two: write things down so if the dark comes you will know what happened when you were last in the light.

Rule three: When the light comes, run.

Now he was running toward the tall woman with the short hair. He saw her blue eyes widen with fright. That was bad. If she was scared she might not listen. Still, he couldn't wait any longer. He was lucky to have found her at all. She was the proverbial needle in a haystack, a ship in the night, a –

He began again.

He was lucky to have found her at all…

He forgot.

Eat. Drink…

Tears came to his eyes.

He was slipping away.

A ship…

He sniffled in sorrow. He panted with determination. Ian Francis clasped his hands ever tighter around the treasure he brought for her. He threw himself at the two men in front of him. One had a microphone. It clattered to the floor when Ian pushed him aside. The man cursed as he toppled into an older woman. She fell sideways.

Ian did not stop.

He ran for the tall woman. He was so sorry, but it had to be done. Just as she made a sound that seemed to deny the inevitable, Ian threw himself at her, his clasped hands hit her breastbone, and he fell upon her.

His face was so close to hers that he could see her long lashes, the golden tan of her skin, and the flecks of dark in her blue eyes. Josie looked into Ian Francis' flat brown eyes, felt the heat of his breath, and noted the fine structure of his face. His wide mouth moved so quickly he didn't seem to breathe. The veins at his temple pulsed as if they were struggling to push his thoughts forward.

Josie had braced herself for an assault but when the man went limp, she couldn't stand her ground. She grasped his hands in both of hers as they fell: Josie landing on her hip, the man dead weight on top of her. The blond girl screamed. Journalists scattered. Spectators fled. A photographer snapped a picture and, in the second before the security guards hauled Ian Francis off Josie Bates, he put something in her hands, his lips touched the edge of her ear and he whispered:

"I know where she is.

CHAPTER 2

"Where are you taking him?" – Girl
"Do you know who he is?" – Capitol Police
"He just seems sick. He shouldn't go to jail." – Girl
"We'll take care of him. You sure you don't know him?"
– Capitol Police.
"No. No. But where are you taking him?" – Girl

❧

"Pick up! She's here, Archer. Call me back." – Voice mail,
Josie to Archer

❧

Eugene Weller was a pain in the butt because he wouldn't
take no for an answer. That proclivity also made him
invaluable to Ambrose Patriota.

They had met when Eugene interned in Patriota's
office during the senator's second term. That term was a
mere shadow in the senator's memory, but it was as
bright as the Big Bang in Eugene's. The moment Eugene
walked into Ambrose Patriota's chambers, the second he
touched the politician's hand, Eugene Weller became a
true believer, an apostle, a follower of a man he
considered no less than a political god.

Fresh out of a college that had no claim to fame and
was planted in a town in a fly-over state that was equally

without color or celebrity, Eugene had graduated nearly friendless. That was fine with him. The people he hung with were of no real interest to him in the same way Eugene did not inspire them. Having served their purpose to one another, they scattered like seeds. Most of them would root, grow anemically, and die the predestined death of the mundane middle class. Eugene would be the exception, not because of any specific ambition but because he had a keen self-awareness, a crystalline understanding of his role in life. He would never be a king or a kingmaker, but he would be a hell of a king's minister. That was not to say Eugene Weller was a sycophant; he simply longed to be an apostle to a worthy prophet. He had talents to offer a person of worth but his ungainly appearance and his inability to grasp the subtleties of social interaction kept many people from recognizing his intelligence, his potential for unwavering devotion, and his keen strategic sensibilities. Eugene was convinced, in the way that some people can be, that a great and true destiny awaited him and that he would recognize it when he saw it. Six months before he graduated, Eugene spied a notice on the placement office bulletin board announcing internships in Washington D.C. He was enthused enough to mention this to his long-widowed mother.

Unbeknownst to Eugene Weller, his mother was not only tired of her wraith like son taking up space in her home, she was also screwing her married congressman whenever possible. During a particularly satisfying encounter with the congressman who had been a fairly successful pig farmer before his entry into politics, Eugene's mother determined the time was right to ask for a favor. Her request that he help Eugene get the internship was one that pleased the congressman to no end. First, he could actually accomplish the task and second, the local press would eat up the story of a local boy going to the Capitol. Add all that to his paramour's deepest gratitude and it was a win/win. The pig-farmer-turned-politician didn't know it at the time, but Eugene's appointment would be the last favor he ever did. He would lose the next election to a pretty housewife who stood on an inane platform that would, nonetheless, capture the voters' fancy.

But the stars aligned for a moment and Eugene Weller arrived in Washington as one of six interns assigned to Senator Patriota's office. Four of those interns left Washington never to return, one committed suicide in the bedroom of the Secretary of Education, and Eugene found his prophet. Like Saul blinded by the light of God, stricken off the back of an ass, Eugene Weller fell figuratively at the feet of Ambrose Patriota and embraced the city that would be his Damascus. Eugene was not particularly religious, but he was so fond of the analogy that he would often expound on it at cocktail parties, fundraisers, and the occasional White House dinner where he was a placeholder due to his GSA seniority and affiliation with Senator Patriota.

Eugene never noticed attention waning and smiles freezing as he spoke of this because he was a true believer and there weren't many of those in Washington. Most people were there for the freebies, to bask in the light of power, secure a government job from which it would be almost impossible to get fired, or wrangle a contract they could milk. Yet, people listened because in his official capacity Eugene Weller was a person of power. He carried out Senator Patriota's wishes, anticipated his every need, and proved himself worthy of the man's patronage every day in every way. At that moment, Eugene was doing what he did best: following up, checking a loose end, heading a problem off at the pass, chasing a dot that might need connecting.

He walked with a brisk step down the long hallway in the basement of the building, passing closed doors behind which men and women labored to feed the bureaucratic monster that was Washington. These people made no decisions, they analyzed nothing, they simply processed and programmed, never questioning their work or their worth. The closed doors were marked with numbers and discreet designations. Room 1201: Senate Accounting. Room 1224: Senate Janitorial. Room 1310: Senate publications and communications.

Eugene made a sharp right and found himself in another even longer, long hall. Fewer doors pocked the walls and the ones that did had numbers but no indication of what lay behind them. Eugene did not slow his appropriately measured pace when he approached the door of the room at the end, his eyes did not flick to the cameras at the top edge of the door frame, he did not smile for the person monitoring the screen on the other side as he punched in the code that would open the door. There was a two second lag before the lock clicked giving him just enough time to grasp the handle and push the door open.

Once inside the door closed, locking him in a rectangular space that was exactly six feet long and four feet wide. There was a door directly in front of him and more cameras above him. He took three steps, paused as his fingers performed another digital tap-dance on another keypad, and listened for the lock to give way. When it did, he walked into the offices of The Sergeant at Arms and Doorkeeper, Chief Law enforcement officer of the Senate and overseer of U.S. Capitol Police whose power encompassed the right and charge to arrest and detain anyone interfering with Senate Rules. Certainly the man who had thrown himself at Josie Bates, a guest of and witness for Senator Patriota, had interfered grossly with senate business.

"Good afternoon, Mr. Weller."

The receptionist smiled at him. He smiled back perfunctorily as was his habit. He had no idea what this woman's name was, nor did he care. What he did know was that she had been a receptionist for over five years. She would never go further than the GSA level in which she found herself and would never leave her mark on anything. Eugene could spot the middling folk a mile away. However, if the security doors were ever breached she would be the first one taken out. He wondered if she ever considered that.

"Which room?" he asked.

"Six," the woman answered.

"Thank you," Eugene responded and off he went.

He passed rows of grey desks where information specialists tapped away at their computers, inputting data, pulling up images and graphs and statistics, interfacing with other agencies, and basically doing a fairly decent job of keeping everyone in the building safe. Eugene went by two offices separated from the fray by glass walls. In one, a woman wearing pearls and a dark sweater set spoke quickly into her headset. Her face was a bloom of red and purple. She was a prime example of the perpetually angry, frustrated women who lived in this city where sexual and power scales tipped heavily in favor of men. He wondered why women stayed here, banging their heads against a ceiling that would probably never crack for them much less break.

In the other pseudo-office a man unleashed his rage on a kid in a cheap green shirt and dark pants who eventually slunk off clutching a stack of papers. Eugene would hate to work in such an environment but he presumed anger and frustration were the nature of the security beast.

On he went, considering that it was much more productive to let people know what you expected and then take nothing less. In the tangle of government people looked for surety, consistency, and assurances that their decisions were correct and valued. That's how his senator conducted business. Eugene almost laughed at that familiarity. His senator, indeed.

"Hey, Genie! Didn't take you long to poke your nose in!"

Eugene stopped abruptly and turned stiffly, knowing who hailed him even before he saw the man's lumbering mass coming down the hall. Eugene disliked Officer Morgan because he was disrespectful, out-of-shape, and generally base. Sadly, Morgan was of sufficient rank that Eugene could not complain about his slovenliness and his reasonable requests that he should be addressed as Mr. Weller by all security personnel had only resulted in the Genie moniker being picked up by others in the department. Most had the courtesy to call him that vile nickname behind his back. Morgan was the exception. Eugene originally thought this rudeness was a form of social Tourette's and the man did not understand how unseemly it was. He was wrong. Morgan knew exactly what he was doing. Eugene, though, knew when to pick a fight. The right time was when you knew you would win.

Morgan pulled to a stop and put his hand on the wall as if to keep from tipping over once he came to a standstill. He was an oddly shaped person who carried his weight in his barrel chest. His head was comparatively small and his legs bowed. He was an inverted triangle of a man whom Eugene knew to be unattractive and yet there was a Mrs. Morgan out there somewhere who thought him decent looking enough to marry.

"Figured you'd be down here," Morgan chuckled. "Hate to tell you, you wasted a trip. Poor guy's just a loon off the street."

"If he came in off the street how did he get into chambers, Morgan? Everyone is supposed to have a pass. Could it be your officers can't even handle something as simple as a vagrant?" Eugene cut his eyes to the man's hand still splayed against the wall. That hand bothered him immensely. He didn't like the way Morgan's cheap wedding ring cut into his fleshy finger, or his ragged nails, or the dark hair tufting at his knuckles.

"I didn't say he was a vagrant." Morgan found his center, let loose of the wall, splayed his legs to balance himself, and passed over a slim file. "And my officers handled everything just fine. The guy had a pass. Officer Craven tagged him when he walked in 'cause he looked like he hadn't slept in days. Hell, we all look like that half the time," Morgan laughed. "Anyway, since he was quiet while he was watching, there wasn't anything to worry about."

Eugene flipped the folder open. Inside was a picture of the man in custody. There was also a computer run on his name. The capitol pass was clipped at the top.

"This information is ancient. And the pass!" Eugene was annoyed. "1990? How did he get by with this?"

Morgan shrugged. "It's still valid. The computer says so. It's a pass issued to personnel."

"Personnel? That man works here? In what capacity? I want to talk to his supervisor," Eugene snapped.

Morgan pointed to the read-out. "He was an adjunct to the Department of Defense out of Texas A & M. We're running it down. He says he's a scientist. I don't have a lock on it, but '90 is the last year he was on the payroll."

"Then why was he here today? Why does he still have a pass?" Eugene closed the file, terribly annoyed by what he considered systemic ineptitude.

"It's the government, Genie." Morgan stuffed his hands into his pockets. One had a small tear at the corner. "When are you going to learn we are only 4.8% efficient? I read that in that magazine they send around here. Weird they even wrote about it. Usually, they spin all the news so it sounds like we're goddamn geniuses. Guess it was hard to put a good spin on that little statistic."

One hand came out of his pocket and he flicked the pass clipped to the file.

"There's a zillion of these floating around. Maybe he kept it as a souvenir. You should bring it up with Patriota. Somebody should invalidate these things, especially these days. Anyway, he's in there. You can see him, but I don't know what good that's going to do. He's just some wonk off his rocker. Still, if you want to see how harmless he is be my guest."

Morgan went around Eugene, opened the door to room six, and gave Eugene a little nudge.

"Always nice to have a second opinion from the guys who make the laws, Genie. Down here, we just try to enforce 'em."

"I wouldn't make light of this, Morgan," Eugene warned. "That man disrupted a senate hearing. He accosted a witness. I'm sure someone got a picture. This is no small matter, and if you think it is you're in the wrong job."

Eugene walked into the interview room and closed the door knowing that Morgan probably found all this fuss delightful. At least he had been truthful. Ian Francis appeared harmless lying on the couch, one leg on the floor, one arm mashed between him and the back cushion as he slept. Eugene walked over to the sofa, stood above him, and when the man didn't open his eyes Eugene pulled up a chair and sat down.

"Wake up, sir. Mr. Francis," he ordered. "I'd like to talk to you."

Ian Francis' eyes opened on command, but Eugene was not prepared for what happened next. With startling speed, the man grabbed Eugene's lapels and wrapped them in his fists.

"Don't touch me! What are you doing?" Eugene stood up abruptly, knocking the chair to the floor as he tried to extricate himself, but Ian Francis' grip was tight and he was pulled up like a fish on a hook as Eugene threw himself backward.

"Chatter," Ian whispered frantically.

"Morgan!" Eugene screamed even as he grappled with the man's hands. Still Ian held tight.

"Chatter. Artichoke. Marigolds." Ian hissed and spittle sprayed over an ever more terrified Eugene Weller. "Chatter. Marigolds in the house. In the house!"

"Morgan!"

Eugene screamed again just as Morgan hurdled through the door. The cop took hold of Ian's shoulders but the man clung like a barnacle, pulling himself closer and closer to Patriota's aide.

"My girl," Ian sobbed. "Marigold."

"Get him off me, Morgan!" Eugene cried out, knowing there were mere seconds before he peed in his pants. "Help anyone!"

Eugene's head whipped around to look for reinforcements since Morgan was proving useless. Then everything changed. When he looked back again Eugene saw a different man. Ian's fingers loosened, his knees gave way, and he slumped. Eugene threw away his hands as Morgan scooped the man up before he hit the floor. With surprising gentleness, the cop settled him back on the rock-hard sofa.

"Told you, Genie," Morgan said quietly. For Ian he had an even kinder voice. "Poor guy. You're just not all there, are you?"

"Harmless. That man is not harmless." Eugene huffed, embarrassed that he had needed rescuing and that he had panicked like a woman. "He could have killed me."

"Well, he didn't," Morgan pointed out. "I'll stay with him for a while and see if I can find out where his home is."

"I doubt he has one," Eugene muttered as he tugged at his jacket and then swiped at his lapels. He would have to have this suit cleaned. It felt like the man had left crazy all over him.

"Everybody lives somewhere." Morgan stuck his hands into Ian's pockets and came up with a key attached to a piece of white plastic. Morgan smiled and Ian Francis mimicked him. "Is this yours, buddy? Where are you staying? You want to go home, dontcha?"

"Yes. Please. I need to get back to my girl. It's cold here," Ian muttered.

"Yeah, you should have a coat. Is she there? Your girl? Will she take care of you?" Morgan glanced at Eugene. "The guys who brought him in said some girl was asking about him. Maybe she'll be back."

"Good grief, your *guys* are inept. This man just spooked a hundred people in a hearing, assaulted a witness, assaulted me, and you let the one person who showed interest in him leave? The inmates are running the asylum, Morgan."

"My thoughts exactly," Morgan deadpanned.

On the couch, Ian Francis shook his head, nudged his glasses up his nose, and beetled his brow as if trying to hold on to one cogent thought. He looked up at the two bickering men. If they had bothered to look, they would have seen tears in the crazy man's eyes. Instead, as Ian sat up Morgan clapped him on the back and rubbed it hard, rattling his brain.

"My brother's kid has some problems. He gets agitated and such. You give 'em a rub and everything's good," Morgan said to Eugene.

"Artichoke? You know? A few marigolds still..." Ian spoke to his clasped hands.

"Guess he's hungry."

Morgan laughed but Eugene wasn't listening. He was staring at Ian Francis. Slowly, he put his hands on his knees and brought his face close to that of the befuddled man.

"Artichoke. Chatter. Marigolds," Eugene said.

Ian's eyes snapped up and brightened with gratitude, "Yes. Marigolds. You remember?"

Eugene shot up, scowling at the man on the couch.

"Fingerprint him. Run him through the entire system. Everything. If he had that pass, he was vetted at some point. It shouldn't be a great chore to pull his records."

"Jesus, Genie, really?" Morgan moaned. "I have no reason to hold him."

"Figure one out, Morgan. I'll expect to hear from you today. No more than a couple of hours."

Eugene headed for the door with his brain on overdrive. Ian Francis' words triggered an elusive memory that made Eugene nervous. Of course, this could all be in his imagination – though most would agree Eugene had little of that – but he had a feeling that something important had transpired.

Morgan called after him. "The woman he ran into isn't pressing charges is she?"

"No." Eugene paused in the doorway. "But you never know. People want to hold someone accountable for the smallest things."

Eugene glanced back at the pathetic man in the old blue suit, but when he inadvertently met Morgan's eyes, he couldn't hold the man's gaze. Eugene Weller did not want his compassion questioned by the likes of Morgan. As he left the room, he muttered: "Get me the information."

Outside the door, Eugene took a moment. He rotated his neck aware now that his muscles had tightened to the point of pain. He pulled at his jacket as he concentrated on loosening the ones that locked his jaw. Retracing his steps, he passed the glass offices where the man was no longer yelling at anyone and the angry woman was staring at her desk, exhausted by whatever had upset her. He went past the receptionist who was fielding phone calls with a voice so expertly modulated that Eugene wondered if she was able to shake it when she got home. He went down the short hall, opened the door to the longer hall and walked out of camera view. It was only after he was back in the main building, stepping briskly through the crowds of people doing business there, that he realized his shirt was wet under his arms and he stank like a common man.

CHAPTER 3

...the defendant named judges and United States covert government agents including Attorney General Eric Holder claiming he was a victim of voice-to-skull mind control technology at the hands of the U.S. government. The judge dismissed the case promptly, stating Banks was "wholly incredible and delusional". — TruthStream Media

"Tea, or something stronger?"

Ambrose Patriota sat easily in a regency style chair upholstered in gold satin and exquisitely embroidered with brown unicorns. Josie sat opposite him on a couch with rolled arms, covered in burgundy fabric shot with golden threads. The upholstery was pulled so tight it looked like a bad facelift – all sheen and no shadow. There was a low mahogany table resting on claw and ball feet in front of her. Inlaid occasional tables were scattered around the office. The focal point of this political man cave was an impressive desk whose ancient origins Josie couldn't begin to imagine.

The walls of Senator Patriota's private chambers were covered with black-framed citations and photos of a career that spanned four presidents, one English queen, ten prime ministers in various countries, and an untold number of dictators. There were a few well-chosen pieces of art: one Chagall and two Picassos. This opulence would have been suspect had Josie not checked him out after being invited to testify.

Ambrose Patriota was to Greek-Americans what John Kennedy was to the Irish. Money, ambition, and PR fairy dust were all it took to turn a young, Greek, son-of-an-immigrant into a powerful senator. As a young man he had spent a number of years turning a once modest family shoe company into money with a capital M before stunning the business world by joining the military. Ten years, one honorable discharge, and one perfectly orchestrated campaign later he was the governor of Texas. In the next blink he was the go-to-guy in the senate. Soon he would be president. Josie couldn't help but be intrigued by him; charmed was another matter. Men with this much power made her nervous, but her wariness was a precaution not a prejudice.

"I'm good, thanks."

Ambrose Patriota raised his index finger and the young woman awaiting Josie's pleasure faded away. The senator sat back, unbuttoned the jacket of his dark suit, and lamented: "Always a drama around here, I fear. If it's not someone trying to kill us, it's someone trying to touch us, talk to us, sway us, or degrade us. I apologize for what happened."

"I'm not sure what you have to be sorry about," Josie suggested.

"Our lack of security for one. Our people are better trained than that. I'm sorry you were the one in the way."

"Senator, I wasn't in the way. That man came at me for a reason." Josie moved, itching to be out of the office, eager to talk to the man in custody. Sadly, the rules of this place were as unforgiving as the couch she sat on and Ambrose Patriota was kindly dismissive of her desires.

"I'm sure it seemed that way, but I fear you are indulging in wishful thinking. You came to talk about a personally horrifying experience, anything people say to you here will be interpreted in that light."

Josie returned his smile, but it was not as practiced as his. Her expression clearly indicated she did not like to be patronized.

"What he said was very distinct. I did not mistake it. He knows where Hannah is."

"Truly?" One heavy brow rose to challenge her. "That man told you specifically that he knows where Hannah is?"

Patriota hit Hannah's name a little hard and Josie realized that he was trying to put it in context. It both amused and frustrated her that the essence of her testimony was forgotten so easily. Before she could point out that it seemed his hearings were an exercise in futility, she saw things click into place like lucky sevens.

Hannah.

Albania.

Hearings.

Jackpot.

"Ms. Bates – Josie – please, don't get your hopes up that this man knows anything about your ward," Patriota said.

"That man pushed his way through a hundred people and came directly to me. His exact words were, 'I know where she is'. That statement is specific to my testimony. This isn't about hope. This is about follow-up," Josie insisted.

"Of course, of course," Ambrose assured her. "My chief of staff is doing exactly that, but your faith is misplaced. That man has no answers for you."

"I'm not talking about my faith in him but in you. I believed your promise to do everything you can to help the victims of Eastern European crime. Unless, of course, this has all been a waste of time and you were pandering."

"I only pander on Wednesdays," Patriota teased. "In all seriousness, the authorities are interviewing him. However, as an attorney, you understand that what people say they know is often very different from what they do know. That man may have been moved by your testimony so he made something up thinking he could make you feel better."

The Senator leaned forward slightly, raising his palm as if to show her there were no tricks up his sleeve.

"In Washington, as in a courtroom, people can become fixated on their fantasies. They believe they have the singular ability to expose a great and important truth. They show up in any public forum: at schools, at rallies, and especially at political gatherings. They will speak to anyone who will listen. They are adept at choosing just the right words that will make someone as passionate as you clutch at the straw they are holding.

"They believe in atrocities and conspiracies. They come here to save the world by speaking out and sometimes by threatening those of us who serve the people. Washington is its own unique and not always logical world. It takes an old hand like mine to steer through it."

"I am not naïve, Senator, but I am not going to turn a blind eye to a possible informational thread," Josie argued. "I simply want proof one way or the other that he wasn't talking about Hannah."

Patriota leaned back in his chair, seeming both annoyed and amused by her tenacity.

"When I was a young Senator I thought as you. I wanted to listen to everyone. But I learned quickly that this job is like triage. I must weed through all the problems, and the broken people, and the desperate tragedies until I find the one thing that is possible to save and nurture."

He sighed at exactly the right moment. He gestured just emphatically enough as if this would prove his dismay.

"It used to be there would be a handful of these poor souls running around, getting it into their heads that they had something to contribute to the process or a solution to a problem. In reality, they are the problem."

"It must be difficult to deal with concerned citizens," Josie noted, her gaze even and her smile small.

Patriota's eyes flashed. He was unhappy to be challenged in this way but too practiced to lash out.

"I am not easily shamed, Ms. Bates, because I am a realist. People like that man are not your concerned and curious American citizen. If he were, he would have gone through channels. He would have engaged the services of someone able to articulate the problem and manipulate the system appropriately. He might have sought out a lawyer, don't you think?" His eyes crinkled as if he enjoyed calling ever so politely on to his personal carpet. "Although if he had done that there might have even been more drama. Politicians and lawyers, we are cousins, are we not?"

"I suppose the difference is that a lawyer gives the benefit of the doubt," Josie pointed out.

"Often for a price higher than a politician's." Patriota threw back his head and laughed, pleased to make a joke at his own expense. "I find a lawyer's outrage is often equal to either her billing hours or the interest of the press. I am not being disrespectful, but we in Washington can't be as democratic as a lawyer. I applaud all who step up to the table, but I know not everyone will get to sit down. There simply aren't enough places."

"And you decide who gets a chair?" Josie asked.

"This is what I am elected to do," Ambrose said candidly. "Government has limited resources. Most constituents are happy if their lives are not disrupted. However, some human beings are sensitive to outrage. The right voice raised at the right moment is as combustible as an open campfire in a dry wood. That person will get my attention, and I will determine how to best deal with him or her. Your gentleman was only crying wolf. Wolf criers, I dismiss."

"If I did that, I would have dismissed half my clients. I would have dismissed Hannah when I first met her and she would have been railroaded into jail."

"Apples and oranges, Ms. Bates. These folks, the ones who burst in looking like they haven't slept or eaten for days because they are so consumed with the import of what they alone know, have only nonsense and noise to offer. That detracts from the real business of our government."

"Which is what?"

"To maintain and protect the state. It is not about the individual, Ms. Bates. If it were, we would spend our careers ineffectual, broken hearted, and despairing."

Suddenly he smiled broadly and the effect was nothing short of glorious. Again, Josie was stung by the idea that she had known him. Before she could grasp the memory, he maneuvered the conversation toward a conclusion.

"You've drawn me in, Ms. Bates. If we had all the time in the world we would debate the purpose of the constitution, the intent of the founding fathers, individual freedoms versus the good of the whole. But we don't have that time and we are really only talking about a slight ruckus." Patriota touched the arm of the couch as if assuring her that they were friends again. "You're far too young to have had enough experience to accept the fact that almost all things truly are what they seem."

"That's cynical, Senator," Josie suggested.

"No, no, no." He sat back again, waggling his finger. "That is an honest assessment and an efficient use of both my brain and my time. But that doesn't–" The office door opened, interrupting him. "Ah, our debate is about to be settled. Eugene. What news have you brought us?"

Josie looked over her shoulder. Sounds of a busy office skittered through the open door only to be silenced when Eugene Weller closed it again.

"Everything is taken care of, Senator." Eugene paused beside Josie and shook her hand. "Eugene Weller, Ms. Bates. Senator Patriota's chief of staff."

Josie took his hand thinking he looked a bit like a Wyeth painting. Eugene Weller could have been the corner grocer, the town pharmacist, or an insurance salesman were it not for his well-cut suit and obvious influence.

"Eugene is one of the most competent staffers you will find on the hill," the Senator announced proudly. "I hope he is also the most loyal."

"Always, Senator."

Eugene slid his hand from Josie's grasp. His palm was moist; his smile disappeared too quickly. The man was not as confident in his position as Ambrose Patriota gave him credit for.

"Eugene is quite modest. I know ten senators who would steal him away from me given half a chance. Luckily, this is government and no one can entice him with more money. Though I fail to see why he hasn't fled to the private sector. With what he knows about the goings on here he could command quite a salary and probably add to it with a few bribes to keep him silent. Isn't that so, Eugene?"

"I'll write a book someday, Senator," Eugene answered.

"You'll wait until I'm dead and buried, I hope," Patriota countered. "So, tell us what you have found out."

"The gentleman's name is Ian Francis, sir." Eugene paused as if waiting for a reaction. None was forthcoming. "He holds a Canadian and American passport. He worked as a consultant to the Defense Department at one time and he was a professor at Texas A & M many years ago. Mr. Francis is not drunk. He is confused. It appears he has fallen on hard times and, perhaps, suffers to some degree from mental illness."

"Drugs?" Patriota asked.

"No. Nothing was found on him."

"Weapons?"

"No, sir. He had a senate pass. It had not been renewed since the early nineties but security sent him through. A misunderstanding," Eugene assured him.

"You see. It is as I said." Patriota was pleased.

"But did you ask specifically about me or Hannah?" Josie pressed.

"I'm sorry, I don't have anything more to tell you."

Josie was fully aware that his was a non-answer but there was no time to pursue it further. The senator planted his palms on the arms of his chair and pushed himself up. He buttoned his jacket. They were done.

"There. Taken care of. I believe there is a reception where we are expected. A small thank you to those who have put themselves out to enlighten us."

"You'll only be able to stay ten minutes, sir." Eugene moved in on Patriota. "This has set you back twenty on the schedule and you're due at–"

"We'll make it. We always do, Eugene." His attention turned to Josie. "It was delightful to spend time with you. Shall we?"

But Josie still sat, looking intently at Patriota as he stood over her. She got to her feet slowly.

"Senator, I have to ask. Have we met before?"

"I'm sure I would have remembered."

He stepped back and swept his hand toward the door. When she hesitated, when it seemed she would press the matter, Eugene Weller held her coat out.

"Perhaps I could talk to Mr. Francis," she suggested as she took it. "If you could get me to your security offices, I'll take it from there."

"I'm afraid that's not possible," Eugene answered. "Protocol is being followed. And, of course, we must be concerned with Mr. Francis' rights. You are a guest of Senator Patriota and have no official capacity here."

They moved in unison, Eugene holding open the door of the senator's inner sanctum. Patriota went first. Josie followed only to take one step back for the two she had taken forward.

"What will your people do with him?" she asked Eugene.

"If everything checks out, he'll be escorted out of the building. His pass will be revoked."

"Will they take him out the front of the building?" Josie prodded.

"We leave those decisions to security."

Eugene muttered an apology and went around her, quickening his step so that he could beat Patriota to the doors that lead out into the main hall. Josie admired the choreography and the dodge. She had no choice but to follow them. In the hall, the senator shook her hand once more and took his leave easily. He wouldn't remember her name in another ten minutes but in that moment she was the focus of his attention.

"It has been a pleasure, Ms. Bates. I do hope that Hannah will find her way safely home."

"I intend to see that she does," Josie answered.

"I doubt there isn't much you want that you don't manage to get," Ambrose said.

"That is a true statement, Senator."

"You see, even politicians tell the truth once in a while. I will keep you in my prayers. We will do what we can."

Josie took his prayers and his promise with a grain of salt. She didn't need either. Government's wheels turned too slowly to help and if God were smart he would watch over Hannah like a hawk. If he didn't, Josie would make sure there was hell to pay even in heaven.

The senator withdrew his hand but Josie clasped his in both of hers, feeling the need to keep him close. For the first time, Patriota seemed to see her in all her complexity. There was something in his expression – something so fleeting Josie would be hard pressed to describe it – that told her she was not imagining this nagging deja vu. But he was impatient so she said the first thing that came to mind in order to keep the dialogue going.

"I could help that man."

Ambrose Patriota's countenance turned brittle. Like a children's game, his left hand came atop hers. The senator, she was sure, always made sure his hand was on top. It was that person who made the rules and dominated the play. With a slow smile, he let her go.

"Security will do anything that is necessary. Isn't that correct, Eugene?"

"Of course, Senator." Eugene didn't so much as blink but Josie could feel his distaste for her.

"And we would provide him with counsel licensed to practice in the District, should he need it," Ambrose went on.

"Advocacy is advocacy," Josie countered. "And it doesn't have to be in a professional capacity."

"So it is. In Washington, though, that word takes on a new meaning. We must protect the government and those who make it work."

"My mistake, I thought government existed to protect the people by whose grace it stands," Josie responded lightly, but there was no mistaking her meaning.

"I love a woman with a quick mouth," Patriota said.

"I believe that's quick wit, Senator," Eugene Weller suggested.

The senator looked Eugene up and down, seeming to lament the man's lack of it.

"English is my second language. I sometimes confuse words. Thank goodness Eugene is here to watch over me. And now, the time. I'm afraid Eugene was right. We will have to miss the reception."

He put one a hand on Eugene's shoulder and pointed to a young woman coming down the hall with the other.

"There is Sarah going back to the office. Sarah," he called out. "Will you be kind enough to escort Ms. Bates to the reception? You know where it is?"

"Yes, sir. This way."

Sarah waited, hand outstretched but Josie didn't take her up on the invitation. She was looking after the senator and his chief of staff as they walked away. Finally Sarah grew impatient, so Josie relented and went with her to the reception room even though all she really wanted to do was go home. She was tired of the cold and of people who thought *outside* was the distasteful corridor that connected one government building with the next.

Behind them Ambrose and Eugene walked and talked. Just before they turned a corner, Patriota looked back at Josie's retreating figure. Eugene followed his gaze to see what had caught his boss's interest.

"Don't worry, Senator. She's scheduled for the red eye."

"Eugene, if I were to worry about everyone like her I would have been in my grave long ago."

CHAPTER 4

"No. No, they aren't taking it seriously." – Josie

"Do you want me to see what I can find on this guy?" – Archer

"I've got a few hours before I have to be at the airport. I'll check him out." – Josie

"I got a call from the trucker who saw the flyer on the kids. He says he picked Hannah and Billy up and dropped them up north near Sanger. I figure they're headed to San Francisco. After you get home, I'll head out that way." – Archer

"You should go now." – Josie

"Not a chance. Max and I have a homecoming planned." – Archer

"It will be late." – Josie

"But you'll be home." – Archer

"Unless I find Hannah here." – Josie

"Up north is a better bet. I picked up your mail." – Archer

"Anything urgent?" – Josie

"You got a letter from Chowchilla." – Archer

"Great." – Josie

"You want me to open it?" – Archer

"Or burn it." – Josie

"How about I open it and then burn it? Just in case." – Archer

"Whatever. Linda and I have nothing to talk about." – Josie

"I'll take care of it, babe." – Archer

"Thanks. See you soon." – Josie

"Not soon enough." – Archer

৵৽৶

Josie lingered exactly two minutes after she hung up with Archer and then she opened the door of the reception room, walked into the hall, and out of the building. She left behind the other two witnesses, their families, Patriota's staffers, and various hangers-on who drank cheap wine while nibbling cheese cubes and celery sticks. If any of the people in that room could have brought Hannah back home Josie would have nibbled cheese cubes until she turned orange. Since they couldn't, she took off to find a private place to check out the one lead she had; the one she hadn't mentioned to anyone.

By the time she got outside the day chill had turned to night cold. She walked a few blocks with her coat collar turned up and gloved hands pushed into her deep pockets. A breeze ruffled her hair, the cold stung her nose and made her eyes tear. Despite the weather and her worry and her homesickness, Josie was not immune to the majesty of Washington D.C. One could not help but be inspired in this city of symbols and monuments to war and sacrifice, freedom, justice, and determination against all odds. From where she stood the White House looked otherworldly, lit up as it was against a blue/black sky. The Washington Monument watched over the National Mall. A wise and weary stone Lincoln sat in perpetual contemplation. The black wall of the Viet Nam Memorial glistened, the names of the fallen etched in ghostly white on Death's marble ledger.

It was October. Thanksgiving would come too soon and Christmas on the heels of that. Time was running away with her and even the inspiration to courage and wisdom that this city offered could not erase the emptiness she felt. Josie would never despair of finding

Hannah, but she was sad that the future wasn't clearer. Archer admitted that the trail he followed was sometimes more intuition than anything else and that Hannah was proving more resourceful than he expected. He conceded that they might have to wait for the girl to come home in her own good time. Josie had been ready to accept that until now.

She wiped at her eyes, shook off her self-pity, and let her melancholy go on the fog of her breath. Longing for something was never productive. If it were, her mother would have come back long ago.

Josie walked until government buildings gave way to restaurants and stores. Those melted into brownstone neighborhoods and then apartments. Soon she would be out of the mainstream altogether. She paused to look at a menu posted in a restaurant window but the place was too lively for her to concentrate properly. She had already checked out of her hotel, but her bag was still there. She could work in the lobby while she waited for the shuttle, yet for some reason she didn't want to be predictable. Josie settled on the familiar and walked into the first Starbucks she came upon. Grateful for the blast of warmth, she peeled off her gloves, unbuttoned her coat, and waited in line.

"Coffee," she ordered when she reached the counter.

"Just coffee?" The barista seemed disappointed.

Moments later, Josie's coat was draped over a chair at a table in the back corner of the L-shaped room. The coffee was good, her phone was charged. She took a drink and then Googled Ian Frances.

The first page listings brought up a racehorse's website, a few guys who had written novels, an artist in

Australia, and a reference asking her if she meant Francis of Assisi. She cleared the phone and typed again: *Ian Francis.*

More authors.

She typed Ian Francis, Canada. She got a haberdasher and a mathematician.

The next time she tried Ian Francis, A&M University and found what she was looking for. Ian Francis was a professor of forensic neurology and imbedded in the article Josie found was a formal headshot showing a much younger and very much healthier man. He was intelligently posed, his gaze honest, and his demeanor temperate. The accompanying article was dated 1981 and entitled *Effects of Sleep Deprivation on Neural Functioning.* She found references to his published writings in 1978, 1983, 1989, and 1994. That didn't mean other information didn't exist, it only meant she was eager to get on with the real task at hand. Josie took the thing Ian Francis had thrust into her hands out of her pocket before it burned a hole through it.

It was a piece of white plastic, cylindrically rolled and secured with a thick blue rubber band. It was no bigger than a stogie and wrapped with origami precision. She ran her fingers up and down the length. She couldn't feel anything inside; there were no wires along the skin and there was no discernible smell. She peeled off the rubber band. The plastic was so tightly wrapped that it didn't immediately come apart. She picked at the triangular end with her nail, unrolled it, paused to pull out the folded ends, and rolled again.

When she was done, Josie was staring at a cheap plastic bag measuring five-by-eight and heat-stamped with the crude image of a tall building of no particular architecture. There were no words, numbers, or symbols on the outside but she could clearly see that there were things inside so she opened the bag. It yielded a very small clear plastic bag of white powder with a numeric code written on it, a lock of hair wrapped round with yellowing scotch tape, and a little torpedo of rolled paper.

As much as Josie would have liked to think the lock of hair was at least proof of Hannah, she knew it was not. Hannah had shaved her head before she spirited Billy out of the hospital. This hair was smooth and chestnut colored, not black and curled and kinked like Hannah's. This was something a mother kept of a child or a man kept of his lover. These things made no sense and yet the man's voice rang clearly in her head. He was so sure; so specific.

I know where she is.

He had forced this package into her hands with purpose.

I know where she is.

For one brief moment there had been a spark of relief in his eyes. That was why she believed in him. She believed because he had worked so hard to get to her. She believed in Ian Francis because he was all she had.

Josie picked up the cigarette roll of paper.

There was a fringe of chads on one side as if it had been torn from the spirals of small notebook. A rubber band was wrapped around this, too, but it was delicate, fraying in places, and wound like a Cat's Cradle. The minute she touched it the thing disintegrated. It was a little bit like her hopes that Hannah would be found.

❦

Ian Francis walked down the street, his arms ridged by his side, palms flat against his thighs, his steps minced, and his gaze fixed. His thoughts were surprisingly clear: he was angry with himself for being clumsy. He had frightened that woman. That was the last thing he wanted and the last thing he remembered.

Ian stopped, his interest suddenly caught by the reflection of a man in a window. Two times he did this and the second time he touched the glass. When he understood that this was his own reflection, his chest grabbed and his heart hurt. How had he come to this? He was pathetic. He paused a third time at a boarded up store and this time he peered through wooden slats covering dirty glass to see if he was any better. He wasn't. Ian clenched his jaw tight to keep from crying out in shame.

He moved on again and then Ian stopped for a final time. In this window he looked past his reflection at the mannequins dressed in cheap and unattractive clothes. A tear came to his eye. He shuffled forward by an inch and another and put his nose against the cold glass. He forgot everything as he looked at the dark haired woman made of plaster. Her face was turned upward. He could see the joint where her head was attached to her neck. One arm dangled longer than the other. She had no shoes. Her feet had no toes.

"My girl," he whispered.

Ian took one step back, put his hands up, and cupped them over his mouth and nose. He breathed out, warming the space he had made. He spoke words inside that space and they echoed back at him. Words would keep him in the light as he walked. He didn't want to leave her in that window with no toes and her arm hanging loose but he must. And why was she looking for him in the heavens when he was right there on earth? Since he didn't know the answer to that, he talked to himself about the things he knew.

"There is a connection between the cerebral and the...the...Keep an imprint of recently acquired memories. It is known to..."

The knowledge that had once belonged to him was broken into shards as his brain misfired.

"There is a connection..."

It was too hard.

"The cerebral..."

It was impossible.

"My girl is broken..."

He began to tremble. The train of his thoughts derailed in favor of memories of her: dark haired, dark haired, dark haired.

What else?

Please, what else?

The trembling reached his hands and then his fingertips. Ian Francis dropped them away from his face. He turned one click. He stared at the street. This was so different than the place he shared with his girl.

His chin lowered.

His lips went slack.

He was listing.

He was forgetting.

Then he did not tremble. He did not cry. He did not think.

Ian Francis was gone, so Ian Francis' body moved on.

☙◆❧

The paper was so old and rolled so tightly the sheets seemed laminated. When Josie finally managed to flatten it, the paper simply rolled back in on itself. With nothing to weight it, Josie reversed the roll on the edge of the table. Finally, she spread it in front of her and what was on it was splendid to look at.

The pages were filled with exquisite, near-microscopic letters so uniformly formed that they appeared to be typeset. The space between each letter was the width of an eyelash, between words maybe two. The writing stretched from edge to edge, top to bottom. There was no hint that the author had penciled in guidelines to help his hand stay straight on the once-blank paper and yet every line was arrow straight. Josie knew only two sorts of people wrote this way: convicts because resources were precious and mental patients because they herded their words together so they wouldn't fly away. Ian Francis, she assumed, learned his craft in the mad house.

She squinted at the writing. It was English but that was about as close as she could come to making sense of it. The neatly printed words were a jumble leading nowhere and numbers adding up to nothing.

Rememberrememberememberemembermk
Poor thingpoorgirl isamarigold.
Ultraartichokechatter!Marigold.
194519531976SWGBS1986EB.

Stars and flowers punctuated the missive at intervals, tiny little fairy drawings, delicately adorned the narrow edges at the top of each page.

Josie turned the first page over only to find more of the same on the back. She would Xerox this, magnify the pages, and analyze them properly with Archer when she got home.

She turned the second page front to back and then the third. There was no writing on the back of the third page, only a drawing of a woman in a chair obscured by a pattern that could have been bricks or bars. Josie squinted but couldn't make out who the woman might be. She looked even closer and saw the intricately drawn picture was actually made up of pinhead printing even more amazing than the notes. The woman looked like a prisoner. Her arms were bound.

Sitting up slightly, Josie dropped her forehead onto her upturned palm. The bottom of the paper curled up but didn't completely obscure the picture. If the situation hadn't been so weird, Josie would have laughed at herself. The bag was new and maybe even the small bag with the white powder in it, but this paper, the tape around the lock of hair, and the rubber bands were old and fragile as if they'd been stuck away in a drawer for years. The person in the drawing, the person whose curl of hair had been so neatly kept was probably real but none of it had to do with Hannah. More than likely, whoever this woman was, she was real only to Ian Francis.

Suddenly, the paper rolled up and spun off the table. Josie lunged for it but succeeded only in knocking everything else to the floor. Heads turned and a guy in a well-worn khaki jacket and jeans got up to help.

"Hang on. I got it." He plucked the little roll of paper from under his table. Josie picked up the plastic bag.

"Thanks," she said as she put the paper in her bag.

"No problem," he answered.

When he didn't move she gave him what he wanted: her attention.

"You okay?" His brow furrowed making him only slightly more handsome than any twenty-something kid should be.

"I'm good," she answered.

"I mean, you really okay? 'Cause if you're staying there you must have some heavy shit weighing on you. I've got a pad. You can come with me. My friend won't mind. It would be better than going there."

"How do you know where I'm staying?" Josie asked.

He pointed at the plastic bag. "The Robert Lee, man. Bad news. Looks good on the website, but it's a dump. I've seen hostels in Russia better than that place. You really shouldn't stay there. I don't think it's safe."

Josie looked at the plastic bag and the picture stamped on it. It was a hotel that didn't meet the standards of a kid who stayed in hostels.

"I'm not staying there. I'm just looking for someone who is." Josie folded the bag into a packet and put it in her pocket as she asked, "Is it close?"

"Five blocks maybe. City blocks, though. You've got heels." His smile brightened. "I could go with you just to make sure you're okay. There's a party later. It would be cool if you want to go."

"Thanks for the invitation, but I'm leaving on the red eye."

She stood up. He stepped back to really get a good look at her. She shrugged into her coat and tried not to laugh. It had been a long time since someone tried to pick her up. She would tell Archer about this kid, Archer would kiss her and say 'the man obviously has good taste' and then they would make love.

"Yeah, well. See ya."

The guy gave up graciously and went back to his table. He kept his eyes on the very tall woman, with the very short hair until the door of the coffee shop closed. He went back to his iPad, and Josie went on to find The Robert Lee Hotel.

స్ౕౕ

Across the street and down about thirty yards Morgan sat in his car watching Ian Francis. It had been a long time since he had a call from on high giving him marching orders, but when it came Morgan didn't ask questions. He knew exactly what was going on. Weller was interested in this schlub for some reason so he had thrown his weight around. That was cool even though this kind of surveillance was a little beneath Morgan's pay grade. Still, no skin off his nose. It was kind of nice to get out of the office for a change. Besides, following the guy was a piece of cake. Ian Francis wasn't exactly a sprinter. Even if Morgan ran over his feet the guy probably wouldn't notice. The only problem was that the cop found it painful to watch him. It would have been so much easier to just pick him up and drive him where he was going because that was all the information his supervisor wanted – that and who the man might meet up with once he got there.

While he watched Ian, Morgan reached for his stash of jerky. Teriyaki turkey. His wife picked up double packs at Costco. Costco was maybe the greatest contribution the United States ever made to civilized society. You couldn't beat double packs of jerky anymore than you could beat the buck-fifty hot dog with a refillable soda.

Sinatra crooned on the radio while Morgan daydreamed about hitting Costco on the weekend with the old lady for a few of those dogs. That was why he almost missed it when Ian Francis started walking ahead of schedule. It was like someone flipped a damn switch. Ian Francis lurched toward the corner and turned with purpose. Morgan chawed on the jerky as he eased the car back onto the street and turned the same corner slowly. Just then the phone rang.

"Morgan, here."

"Eugene Weller."

Morgan raised a brow. Weller's request had gone through the supervisor but now he was on the horn personally.

"It's been over two hours. Where is he?" Eugene demanded.

Morgan swallowed a spearhead of jerky and almost choked. He managed to say: "Still walking."

"Do you think he's living on the streets?" Eugene pressed.

"I'll let you know when he stops. So far he hasn't stopped." Morgan immediately regretted his tone. Eugene was a pain in the ass but he wasn't stupid.

"I would suggest you take this a bit more seriously. Call me if he makes contact with anyone."

"Hansen told me to call him." Surely mentioning the supervisor would be enough to remind Eugene that he had been the one to set the ground rules. It wasn't.

"Call me first," Eugene snapped and the line went dead.

"Yes, sir." Morgan muttered this to dead air and turned his phone off. "You friggin' twit."

Morgan stopped the car, draped his arms over the steering wheel and watched Ian Francis wobble before he become mesmerized by the sight of his reflection once more.

"Why is Genie so interested in you, you poor schmuck?"

CHAPTER 5

A Washington Post exposé on domestic surveillance reveals massive FBI databases keeping tabs on Americans not even suspected of criminal activity; costly fusion centers that threaten privacy but produce little intelligence of value; and insufficient and inaccurate intelligence training for analysts serving in the almost 4,000 different counterterrorism organizations across the United States.
– ACLU

ॐ

Eugene Weller had made his excuses to Senator Patriota and sent him off to his next appointment in the fairly competent hands of one of the staff; a young man whose name Eugene could never remember but who distinguished himself by writing exceptional letters that captured the senator's voice beautifully.

For the last two hours Eugene sat in his office, dark save for a small lamp on the far wall and the light of his computer screen. Three windows were open, each with different references to Ian Francis and his work for the government. More information on the man, his work, and ancillary personnel had been printed out. Certain references had been written down and would be checked elsewhere rather than commit additional searches to the computer's memory.

Ian Francis was neither a major player in the grand scheme of things nor did he participate at a particular critical time in the project he had referenced, but the fact remained that he had been a part of it. Senator Patriota would be impressed that Eugene had recognized this to be more than a common security breach, too. Of course, there was more to be found but it wasn't necessary to pursue the matter immediately. Eugene hit print, closed the open windows, and relaxed.

Feeling as if he had been smart enough to decline desert after a fine meal, Eugene was left satisfied but clear-headed. He marveled at the efficiency of government on the micro level. There was a plethora of information in the system and yet, more often than not, it was input and forgotten. In a few short hours Eugene had put together a very clear picture of an intricate spiral of dominoes that had stood for decades. Ian Francis was the finger that flicked Josie Bates, a latecomer who had inadvertently placed herself first in the chain. Thankfully, the blow the man dealt her had been glancing. She wobbled, Patriota held her upright, and that gave Eugene time to move her out of the queue. In a few hours the woman would be home and trying to put all this out of her mind. Now here he was, Eugene Weller, domino two; stable and aware, he was not only in the queue, he was master of it.

He paged through the information again slowly, unaware that he was smiling. He checked the clock and saw that he was late for the meeting at the senator's house. He called and left his apologies with Lydia: business at the office, he explained. She said she would pass along the message but that they were all getting along fine. Eugene hung up having read between the lines.

They were all getting along fine without you, Eugene.

He smirked. If she only knew how much the senator needed him she would treat him with a little more respect. No matter. Eugene needed no accolades, only the satisfaction of knowing he had served well. He looked at the phone and felt a little tug in his groin, a response to the almost giddy excitement that was building as he waited for Morgan's call.

Eugene Weller couldn't wait to find out where a dead man went when he visited Washington D.C.

❧

The streets Josie walked were eerily silent. She passed alleyways, stepped around cigarette butts outside a smoke shop, and crunched over a trail of broken glass that lead to a liquor store where a glassy-eyed clerk watched television.

To her left, in the shadows of a storefront, a pile of trash moved. Josie glanced toward it expecting a cat to dash away. Instead, she found herself looking at the craggy face of an old woman. A knit hat was pulled low over her brow and her bottom lip was pulled up over toothless gums. The woman didn't blink and Josie passed, painfully aware of the imbalance of life. She could not right all wrongs anymore than Ambrose Patriota could.

Behind her the woman rolled over again in the dark, disappearing herself. Josie pulled her collar tighter. She turned the corner and saw The Robert Lee Hotel a block ahead. The neon sign atop the building needed repair but other than that it didn't look too bad at all.

Then she opened the door.

❧❧

Initially, Josie didn't notice any one thing about the place because she was overwhelmed by the general sense of decay.

The lobby was impressively large and at one time had been majestic. Above her, two meticulously crafted barrel vaults came together at right angles to form a groined ceiling. Once that ceiling had been covered in gold leaf to catch the light of the huge chandelier that had lit both whore and ambassador as they made their way down the grand staircase. Now the gilt was flaked and spotty like a fancy manicure picked down to chips. The chandelier was missing crystal fobs and candle bulbs and what was left hadn't been cleaned in a decade. Instead of sipping Vodka Gimlets at the bar on her left, two men in pajamas were taking slugs out of a bottle while they sat next to a piano that probably hadn't been played since the Eisenhower era.

Josie went the other way, treading on wall-to-wall carpet that was threadbare in patches and in others intact enough to see that there had once been a floral pattern of pink mums on a brown background. This path led her to the front desk that had been built to accommodate a crowd of guests. Those crowds had stopped coming long ago. She ran her gloved hand along it as she peered behind. There were no computer consoles which she found interesting since the hotel had a website. There was an open pack of gum, a stack of magazines, the remains of take-out Chinese, and some towels that didn't look all that fresh. At the far end, there was an office. The window was covered with mini blinds. Three of the slats had been bent at the ends and the middle ones sagged as if someone had worn them down, constantly peering out, hoping to spy a guest. Light flickered behind the blinds in the predictable pattern of a television. Unable to tell if there was anyone in there or not, Josie leaned over the counter and hauled a huge ledger up and over.

Five people had checked in that day and two had already checked out. None of them were Ian Francis. She flipped the page back. Two days earlier business was stellar. Twenty people had signed in over the weekend. She scanned the names. Half of the signatures were illegible and the others were easily dismissed simply by their length and fancifulness. She flipped back another page and her eyes were caught by the name Frances but this was a first name and the signature was sprawling. Nowhere did she see an example of the cramped, bizarre writing she had in her possession.

Josie turned the pages again and ran her finger down all the names once more. Bingo. There was an entry for a guest with a last name of Francis. The initial was A. She had missed it the first time around.

"You want to check in?"

Not quite startled, just surprised to find anyone in the place with enough energy to call her out, Josie looked up. A man of medium height and maximum girth had propped himself up in the doorway between the lobby and the office. He wore a button down shirt and pinstriped pants. The pleats fanned out under the weight of his stomach. There was a nod to propriety in the shape of a black knit necktie improperly knotted so that the bottom tail was longer than the top. He was looking over his shoulder at the television but had spoken to her.

"No. Thanks," she answered.

"Didn't think so." He guffawed at something he saw on the tube before he looked at her. His left eye was lazy and kept swinging toward his own nose. "Restaurant's been closed for about four years. Bar, too. I gotta bottle if you're looking for something to warm you up. Or Mulligan's is open. 'Bout a block down if you want something to eat."

"I just had some coffee, but I appreciate the offer. I came to visit a friend. Ian Francis. Can you tell me what room he's in?"

"You already looked in the book. I saw you. You're not a PI. You'd be better than that if you were. You his wife? Maybe you're a spy. You look like one of them Bond girls. They weren't too smart neither but they were lookers."

"Promise. I'm not a spy." Josie crossed her heart.

"It's the way you got your coat, you know." He made a circle around his neck. "Spies turn up the collars on their coats like that." He ambled to the end of the counter, stopped and crossed his arms on the edge. "So, did you find him?"

"I found someone with the same last name, but the initial is wrong," she said.

"Sometimes people do that. Stupid just to change your first initial." Josie heard the last trill of a Viagra commercial. Whatever he was watching would start soon so she pressed on.

"This man is about five-ten. His hair is close cut and brown. Stubble on the face. Greying. Glasses. Mid-fifties. Maybe older. He was wearing a blue suit when I saw him."

"That the best you got?" the man asked.

Josie shrugged, "He's a nervous guy. Kind of stops and starts."

The clerk raised his chin and two more came with it. "Him. Yeah. I know him. Odd duck. He ain't drunk."

"Could he have signed in as A. Francis?" Josie asked.

"Yeah, but he didn't. It was a kid. A girl. She signed in. I didn't figure out he was with her until a day later."

"What did she look like?"

"Like a kid in a coat and hat. What do I know?"

"Is she black? Pretty? Did you see a teenage boy with them?"

"Lady, I told you I don't know," he moaned and then that lazy eye of his managed to straighten for a suspicious second. "You sure you're not here to make no trouble?"

"Nope. No trouble." Josie's heart beat hard. Once, twice, three times, like Hannah tapping out her anxiety. She gave it a minute to calm down. "Are they still in room 720?"

"Unless he bolted and didn't pay. That would be a bitch. I gotta cover the room when that happens. They don't pay me enough to do that, and how am I supposed to see everything. Can't stay up twenty-four-seven."

"If he's gone, I'll cover it." Josie turned away.

"Want me to call up? Maybe the girl is there and you can talk to her."

"No." Josie was already retracing her steps. "Where's the elevator."

He pointed to the lobby. He had no time for anything more. He was already in his office. Josie found elevators in the back of the building. She pushed the button three times before she heard a whir. The numbers above the doors stayed dark. She was about to head for the stairs when a bell finally dinged. She pivoted, getting back just as the door opened. She stepped inside then out again. A rat was nestled in the corner, dead and destined to ride the elevator for eternity. It would be better to take the stairs than to get caught between floors with that thing. At least that's what she thought until she opened the exit door.

The stairwell reeked and she had seven flights ahead of her. She blessed the hours on the beach playing volleyball. Seven flights would be a piece of cake; seven floors were nothing if it got her to room 720, Ian Francis, and the girl who was with him.

Ian jumped a little. He shivered. He wrapped his arms around himself and took the cheap phone out of his pocket. The people in the building had taken it away and then they gave it back. That was nice because the girl had given it to him and told him it was important that he keep it. Good, good girl. She was there no matter what time he needed her. Sometimes he didn't sleep and she didn't either. Of course she might sleep and he might forget that he had been watching her. He also might forget that he had slept. Oh, life was strange and he was so tired.

Ian pushed a button, remembering that a button must be pushed. A number came up and a picture next to that. He pushed the number next to the picture he recognized. The phone rang. He said hello. She spoke quickly, a habit she picked up when she realized how fast the dark came. She almost had what they needed, she said. She would be back soon, she said. She asked where he and reminded him how to go back to the room. That was good that she reminded him because he was unsure.

"Are you okay?" she asked again.

He mumbled and nodded even though she couldn't see him.

"You shouldn't have gone alone. I'm sorry. There was the time to consider."

He didn't tell her she was right. He shouldn't have gone alone. He forgot to tell her that it was getting harder to stay the course. His arm simply fell to his side. He still clutched his phone. Muscle memory. He had been so used to holding things: pens, pointers, his sweet girl's hand.

Ian Francis continued walking, concentrating on the words pulsing inside his brain.

Hurry. Hurry man.
Hurry for your girl.

CHAPTER 6

"Just checking in. Max is fine. A little off his food, but I think it's just because he misses you. We all miss you." – Voice Mail, Faye Baxter to Josie

❧❧

Upstairs at The Robert Lee Hotel was no better than down. The guest floors were aged, grimy and clinging to their old glory by a fraying thread. The seventh floor smelled like a stew-pot of dirt, bad plumbing, mold, bodily fluids, and food. The plaster ceiling crumbled in places where melting snow and driving rain had leaked through a roof that needed replacing thirty years ago.

At the end of the hall was a window and icy air blew through the broken glass. Josie could make out the shadow of a fire escape past that. She walked slowly, noting the silent butlers outside each room, the grime on the doors, the torn carpet. Josie measured her steps, staying alert but she heard nothing until she knocked on the door of room 720 at the end of the hall.

"Mr. Francis?" she called. "Mr. Francis. It's Josie Bates. From the hearing?"

She knocked again. The sound her fist made on the door was hollow and swallowed by the room beyond. Josie took hold of the knob, ready to break the door down if necessary. It wasn't. The door was unlocked so she pushed it open slowly.

"Mr. Francis? It's Josie Bates," she called. "I'm coming in to talk to you. Don't be afraid."

Josie wished she could take her own advice, but she couldn't. She was terrified. Her heart beat harder, sweat formed under her collar, her coat weighed her down, and her gloves seemed to constrict around her hands. She strained to hear a response. She heard nothing. Josie had heard this kind of nothing in Billy Zuni's house where death kept its quiet, cold counsel. She had heard this silence in the concrete prison where she thought she would die. Josie had heard this silence in her home when she was thirteen and her mother deserted her. She wasn't sure she could walk into that void again and alone. But this time it was for Hannah, so she threw the light switch.

The overhead fixture was out but there was enough light coming from the hall to let her see the layout of the room so she left the door open. In front of her was an entry that was no more than five feet long. To the right was a partially closed pocket door. Flat-palmed, she slid it back to reveal a small bathroom. Josie turned on the light. There was a hairbrush on the counter, a glass with two toothbrushes, and a small bar of soap near the sink that had been opened and used. Two towels hung neatly on a bar. The mirror was glued to the wall and plastic clamshell brackets held it in place. It looked like the bathrooms in the base housing where Josie grew up. The mirror itself was cracked on one corner and the silver backing was showing through and turning black in another. The shower curtain was drawn over the tub. She pulled it back with one finger. There was a bar of hotel soap and bottle of cheap shampoo. A woman's shampoo.

Josie went to the main room. It was standard: two beds, a low bureau, a chair, tall and narrow french doors overlooking the street. Those doors were framed by chiffon sheers yellowed with age, sagging where the drapery pins had come loose. They rippled like the hem of a ghostly gown.

Convinced she was alone, positive she wasn't going to trip over a corpse, Josie walked to the window and looked out. What she assumed to be a balcony was only an illusion. A railing had been bolted to the building outside the window as a safety guard for sleepwalkers and drunks. Summers in D.C. could be brutal and there was no air-conditioning when this place was built. Tonight the doors were closed. She pulled the drapes aside and put her hand up to the glass. Cold air was seeping through cracked caulking and yet the room was relatively warm. She touched the radiator. It was cool but not cold. Someone had been there to turn it on and off.

The spreads on the full-size beds were thrown over the pillows but the sheets were un-tucked. She walked between them, fumbled with the switch on the lamp that sat on the table between them and finally managed to turn it on. The dim bulb under the fringed, grey shade shed light that made everything look like it was floating under dingy water but it was better than nothing. She opened the narrow drawer in the bedside table and found a bible. Someone had written a profanity on the cover and misspelled it. Josie closed the drawer. There was no iPod, tablet, book, or notepad. There was nothing in the room that a normal traveler would have. There was no loose change, no pen, and no keys. There had been no medicine bottles in the bathroom. There was nothing to indicate that someone had eaten here. The bureau was clean, too. She pulled back the sheets and stuck her hand under the pillows of the first bed and then the other. No nightclothes, books, or treasures. She lifted one mattress and then the other and wanted to wash her hands when she was done.

Josie opened the top drawer of the bureau.

Nothing.

She opened all six drawers.

Nothing. Nothing. Nothing.

She swept the room again with a sharper eye and was rewarded for the effort. A small, wheeled bag was tucked into the corner of the room, half hidden because it was black and the sheers had blown over it. A case could be made that she had already broken a passel full of laws just by walking into this room and searching it. Josie, of course, could argue an exception. The door was open and she was concerned about the occupant. Searching a closed, partially hidden suitcase was another matter and it should have given her pause.

It didn't.

ॐॐ

The girl poked at the numbers and letters of the keyboard earnestly and yet she still made mistakes. Little sounds of frustration bubbled up between her lips but she was careful not to be too loud. The last thing she wanted to do was bring attention to herself. Not that anyone in this Internet café had given her a second look.

She reentered the numbers and this time she got it right. Behind the coffee bar a printer whirred. She logged off and went to the counter where a young man with a short beard and long hair took her money. He paused when she put out her hand for her change.

"Man, you've got a short lifeline." He touched her palm with his pointer finger.

She grabbed back her hand. "Can I have my copies?"

"Sure." He looked sheepish as he realized it probably wasn't a good thing to point out that she was doomed. He looked at the boarding passes. "Sweet. Wish I was headed that way."

"Can I have them?"

"Sure." He handed them over along with her change.

"Thanks." She pocketed the money, folded the passes, and didn't bother to look at him when she said: "And that's not my life line. It's my heart line. One true love."

"Yeah? Well, good luck with that," he snorted.

She left with a scowl on her face, striding through the crowded café full of people no older than her, people who didn't have a care in the world, who thought love was sex and sex was worth something. She knew better. Real love took over your soul, it guided your life, and it fed on your heart and mind until all you could see was the person you loved. When you were in the grips of true love, nothing else mattered. She had been taught about true love by an expert.

She pushed through the door and left behind the smell of coffee, the sound of conversation, the clicking of computers and hurried on through the cold night knowing that she would only feel safe when they were back home again – or at least back to the place where they started – and that was just plain sad.

൭൸െൟ

Josie grabbed the case and swung it onto the bed. It was light and cheap. The zipper jammed when she started to open it. Working her finger through the opening, Josie felt the fray of lining fabric that had caught on the teeth. Patiently, she worked it free until the zipper gave.

Inside, neatly folded, were clothes held tight by a strap. The plastic buckle unsnapped easily and Josie lifted out each piece as she found it: a man's T-shirt, clean but worn thin, two pairs of men's underwear, a woman's long sleeved T-shirt. She held it up and knew instantly it wasn't Hannah's. This one was medium and Hannah wore small. This one was the color of sherbet, cheaply screen-printed with a riot of flowers and fruits. Hannah wouldn't be caught dead in it. Josie left it on the bed and pulled the rest of the clothes out of the suitcase: a plain bra and equally plain panties. Josie put the clothes back as she found them. The list of what she knew was getting longer than what she didn't.

She knew that Ian Francis was not a citizen of D.C. or he wouldn't need a hotel room or a suitcase. Ian Francis had not traveled here alone unless he was fond of women's clothes. And, finally, Josie knew that Ian Francis and the woman he traveled with must be wearing almost everything they brought with them because it was cold outside and the case was nearly empty.

She clicked the buckle back in place, flipped the top up, and unzipped the outer pocket. Empty. Still, she felt she was coming up short. Ian Francis was fond of puzzles, hidden things, cyphers and it was up to her to figure this out. Josie opened the case again and this time ran her hands around the sides stopping when she found something deep in the lining. Pushing her hand inside she found a map of D.C. The Russell Building and the Capitol Building were circled, the metro stops marked. She tossed it aside and reached into the pocket again. This time she came up with gold: four small bags of the same white powder Ian Francis pressed upon her. These had markings, too, but the codes were different than the one in her bag.

Cupping her palm, she swiveled to hold them up to the weak light only to stop mid-turn. Slowly, her fingers curled around the packets and her hand fell to her side.

"Hello," said the man standing at the foot of the bed.

CHAPTER 7

"Hey, Archer, what's shakin?" – Burt

"Josie thinks she's got a bead on Hannah." – Archer

"No kidding? That would be a helluva thing finding her half way across the country. Sit down. I'll get you some chow. How about a beer?" – Burt

"Just the food. Jo's taking the red eye. I've got to pick her up." – Archer

"It'll be good to have her home. Max still at Faye's?" – Burt

"Yeah. I'm going to pick him up and head on over to the house." – Archer

"I swear, you're turning into a husband and you aren't even married." – Burt

"There's worse things to be." – Archer

"Did you tell her what Linda wanted?" – Burt

"No." – Archer

"I wouldn't go to that prison. If Josie does, you better go with her." – Burt

"Depends on what she finds out in Washington, I guess." – Archer

"I'm betting she won't go. That's where my money is." – Burt

᨝᠊ᡐ

Ian Francis looked at Josie without surprise or anger. His arms hung at his side, his jacket was open. His glasses caught the light at an odd angle so that it appeared shades had been drawn over the lenses, but it was only a

67

reflection of the drapes He tipped his head, the curtains parted and she saw his eyes were no longer frantic or fearful. There was – and here Josie paused just to make sure she had the right word – affection in his gaze.

"I came to see you," Josie whispered. "I hope you can help me."

Ian Francis' head tilted again. He looked like a puppy hearing the steps of its master on the walk. Josie swallowed hard and her grip tightened on the small plastic bags.

"You said you know where she is," Josie said. "I'll do anything. Give you anything. Just tell me."

His brows beetled. He pushed at his glasses with one finger. They went askew because his hand was trembling. Before she could show him her treasures and remind him that he had given them to her for a reason, he hopped the train of a mind that refused to stay on its tracks.

The quiet was different now. Calmer. Non-threatening. It was the same lack of sound Josie heard lying in the ocean, ears under water, arms out, face turned toward the sun. The rocking of the gentle swells and the warmth deprived the senses. Stay too long like that and you sank, dying because you didn't have the sense to know you were drowning. At that moment, though, Josie was fully aware she was drowning because she filled the silence to bursting with her anticipation.

She slipped her hand into the pocket of her coat and dropped the plastic bags inside. She didn't want to lose them if she had to fight him off; she didn't want to leave them in case she had to run. Josie also didn't want to kid herself that all would be well because he was so serene. She had seen calm turn deadly in an instant, so she fought the anxiety that was coming in the only way she knew how. She tried again to engage him.

"When you said you know where she is, did you mean Hannah? If you know where Hannah is, please tell me."

Josie stood still, overly aware of her height, the broadness of her shoulders, the boyish hair that left her neck bare to the cold, the heels on her shoes that made her taller than Ian Francis. In the face of this man's serenity, Josie felt diminished.

"I don't understand what you've given me." She withdrew one plastic bag from her pocket. "Show me the way. She's like a daughter."

Josie barely whispered the last word, but it was the one Ian Francis heard. His head fell forward, and his shoulders drew up as if a great weight had been lifted. When he raised his face again he was transformed and he was beautiful. From the corner of his eye, a tear fell and tracked his cheek. He let it go, either unaware of it or relieved to finally let it fall.

"You didn't lie, did you?" Josie whispered.

"No, my girl," he said back. "My girl."

Ian Francis stepped toward her. Josie trembled with an emotion more profound and unnameable than anything she had ever experienced. He lifted his arms, but she was not afraid. He took one more step, but she did not recoil. He embraced her, but she didn't resist because his touch was sweet and familiar. It seemed as if he had held her this way before. Her cheek met his. His skin was warm; the stubble of his beard was surprisingly soft. A car drove by on the street below. Somewhere someone screamed in anger. Josie only heard the sound of Ian Francis' breathing. He cupped the back of her head with one palm. A second passed and then two. When the third ticked away he stepped back, took Josie's face in both his hands, and looked at her as if he could look at her for eternity.

Reverently, Ian Francis kissed Josie Bates.

"My sweet girl," he whispered against her lips.

Letting her go in the next moment, he went to the french doors. He opened first one side and then the other. Ian Francis took one step and rested his hips against the railing of the false balcony. He breathed in the cold air, smiled, and crossed his arms over his heart. Then Ian Francis leaned forward and fell on to the street below.

の∞๑

"Holy crap," Morgan barked into his phone.

"What? What?" Eugene screamed.

"He took a dive. He took a dive. Holy shit, Genie. Gotta go."

"Is he dead?" Eugene screamed some more, but Morgan broke the connection.

How in the hell was he supposed to know if the guy was dead? He was dialing for emergency services and ordering an ambulance in case he wasn't. People were looking out windows – not that there had been any noise – people in this neighborhood knew when stuff like this went down. Morgan kept his eyes sharp on everything as he talked especially on the kid rushing down the street. Then he saw the person hanging out the window where Ian Francis had stood not two seconds ago.

Holy hell, what a mess.

❧

Josie realized what was happening too late. There was nothing she could have done to stop him and nothing she could do to save him. She reached the open doors seconds after his head broke open on the sidewalk. She was horrified. Stupefied. A man had taken his life and the way he had taken it defied reason. He had not cried out in despair. He had not made demands. He had not threatened to kill himself. He had just done it. He had given no reason for the kiss, no reason to hold her, no reason to leave her. He had not raised his arms as if he thought he could fly but crossed them as if he were simply finished.

But he hadn't accomplished a damn thing. Josie still didn't know where Hannah was; she still didn't understand the things he had given her or the things she had found. He could have waited just a minute more, an hour, a day. She would have sat with him, walked with him, coaxed and cajoled the answers out of him. Was it her fault he couldn't wait? Had she intimidated him? Violated him? Disappointed him?

Had she?

Josie grabbed the railing. Her knees wobbled. She sank to the floor, her face thrust against the ironwork as she gulped in the cold air. Still, her stomach heaved and hurt. It didn't matter why any of this had happened; it mattered that it had. It didn't matter what information this man possessed; it was gone. Josie heard a car door slam and the sound of hard shoes running from down the street. A man was coming from the left but someone else was coming from the right. Bundled in a car coat, wearing jeans, and gloves and a hat, was a slight girl. She got to the body first and threw herself over it. Stunned, Josie pulled herself up and peered through the dark, hardly believing what she was seeing.

"Hey!" she called. "Hey!"

Down below the person clutching Ian Francis looked up and Josie saw the face of a young girl, a young woman. Her features were obscured by the dark and her pain; Josie's vision was obscured by shock and wishful thinking.

"Hannah?" Josie murmured, and then she screamed: "Hannah!"

The girl's head snapped toward the fat man running toward her as if she thought he had called her out. She swooped down and put her face next to the dead man's and in the next instant she was running away, gone into the dark, taking with her the one thing Josie wanted: information. That girl knew what Ian Francis knew.

Josie turned to run for the door. She didn't make it seven steps much less seven flights of stairs before her legs gave out again. She fell hard across the end of the bed and slid onto the floor.

"Damn!"

Hope was severed and faith was next on the chopping block. Josie had no hope of finding Hannah without Ian Francis and her faith in his promise wavered. But there was one thing left and that was determination. Josie had plastic bags of white stuff, a lock of hair, and the almost indecipherable notes written in an insane hand on old paper. She had the memory of his face as he searched hers, his touch, his kiss, and his whispered endearment:

"My sweet girl."

Still shaken, Josie turned toward the bed, dragged the cheap suitcase down, and ripped off the tags. Her pockets were getting full. She staggered to her feet just as the sirens sounded in the distance. She stumbled down the stairs and by the time she walked through the front door of the Robert Lee Hotel Eugene Weller's government issue car was there.

❧

Eugene was close enough to see what was happening and far enough away that no one would notice him.

An ambulance had arrived in record time. Paramedics rushed out to assist the man on the sidewalk. When it was clear that no assistance was needed, the body was covered with a sheet to await the medical examiner's van.

As if not to waste a good call, Josie Bates had been coaxed into the back of the ambulance where a young paramedic knelt down, took her blood pressure, and waved his finger in front of her face. He spoke to her for a long while, stepped down, and let Morgan in. Morgan talked to her another good long while. His stomach hung over his pants and his cuffs were pulled up so far Eugene could see that he didn't have the sense to wear black socks with black shoes. Josie Bates on the other hand still looked as chic as she had at the hearing. Every now and again she punctuated what she was saying by stabbing the air or slicing through it to make her point. Eugene couldn't wait to hear what her point might be. He would get the report the next day but at least now he had seen for himself that there was nothing to worry about.

Eugene started his car just as the medical examiner's van arrived. He made a U-turn as they were taking out the stretcher. He looked in his rearview mirror once more and saw them cart the body away. He stepped on the gas, working out in his mind exactly what he was going to say to Ambrose Patriota. More importantly he imagined what Ambrose might say to him. Whatever it was, Eugene knew he would sleep well that night. He always did when a day wrapped itself up so nicely and put itself away.

Still, just to be sure, he made one more call despite the fact that it was too late for anyone to be in the office of public information. The woman he was calling was excellent. She would pick it up first thing in the a.m. and put the wheels in motion.

"It's Eugene," he said, not bothering with a last name. "Contact every media outlet that covered Patriota's hearing today. I want all pictures of Josie Bates culled from their archives. Push the other witnesses. They were more interesting. Also, any mention of – or pictures of – the man who disrupted the last few minutes of the hearing need to go. Any questions, call me."

He signed off and, as he did so, saw the clock. It was late but he would still make it for the better part of the meeting.

As he drove, a smile came slowly to his face as he thought about Morgan. Perhaps he had been too hard on the man. Perhaps Morgan wasn't mocking him, but admiring him when he coined that nickname. After all, he was a bit of a genie. Ambrose Patriota's wish was his command. Sometimes, Ambrose didn't even have to make a wish for Eugene to grant it.

Magic.

CHAPTER 8

"I'll come get you, Jo. I can catch the next plane." – Archer

"Don't come. I'll make my flight. I'm at the airport now." – Josie

"Call me when you're on the ground. You have carry on, right?"
– Archer

"Yes." – Josie

*"We'll leave Max with Faye. I'll have her cover your stuff at the
office for the next few days. Just take it easy when you get back."*
– Archer

*"No. I need to work. And I want to see, Max. I want to see you.
Do you think that girl was Hannah?"* – Josie

"No, Jo. She wouldn't have left you." – Archer

"She did once." – Josie

"She didn't have a choice then. Get some sleep on the plane."
– Archer

"It could have been Hannah." – Josie

"I don't think so." – Archer

"But he said…" – Josie

"Don't cry, babe." – Archer

"I'm not. I'm not." – Josie

❧❧

Josie put her phone away, finished her drink, and sat
staring at all the things she had collected that night. She
didn't know how long she sat like that or what prompted
her to snap out of it. At some point she realized there was
not going to be an epiphany sitting in a now closed bar at

Dulles in a stupor. Josie did the only thing she could think to do: she dug in her purse for the tags she'd taken off the suitcase in Ian Francis' room, shoved away from the table, hitched her bag, and took them to the first United Airlines counter she came to.

"Excuse me. Could you tell me where this flight originated?" She passed the luggage tags across the counter. The woman in the uniform started typing. A minute later, she had the information Josie wanted.

"Really," Josie muttered. Then she said: "Can you book me through from LAX?"

"When would you like that?" The woman asked.

"What's the first one going out tomorrow?"

"It leaves at seven in the morning. You won't have much time between flights."

"It doesn't matter." Josie handed the woman her credit card. When she was done, Josie dialed Archer again.

"I need you to meet me at the airport with a few things," Josie said.

"Sure. What's up?"

"I'm going to Hawaii."

෧෧

"Ambrose?"

Lydia Patriota opened the door of the den smoothly, making her presence known with that one perfectly modulated word and a hint of extraordinary perfume. Although she called to her husband, the other men in the room immediately acknowledged her with admiring looks. She rewarded them with a quick and winning smile.

Lydia Patriota was a lovely woman many years the senator's junior but blessed with a grace and carriage that belied her youth. She was the second Ms. Patriota, the first having passed on some fifteen years earlier leaving behind Ambrose and two children who were now grown, successful, and above reproach. Of Lydia's many charms, the fact that the second Mrs. Patriota did not want her own children despite being of childbearing age was high on Ambrose's list of things he liked about her. He had no desire to be the butt of jokes about his virility, nor did he wish to leave a child orphaned should life not bless him with immortality, neither did he have time to spend with a little one. That he and Lydia loved one another as perfect, powerful, pretty people can was just icing on the cake. He had no doubt that, at his passing, she would be a most lovely widow and that she would truly mourn him. Luckily, she would not be wearing weeds anytime soon.

"Is there anything else you gentlemen need for the evening?" Lydia asked.

"Thank you, dear, we're fine." Ambrose answered for the four men in the living room.

"I'll be going upstairs then," she said. "Don't keep my husband up too late. And Woodrow, I don't care who you are, honey, don't smoke in the house. Standing next to an open window does not draw the smoke out on a night like this. You've only succeeded in making the room chilly and stinky."

With that, she left the men to their confab and went to her bedroom thinking how interesting it would be when the stairs she climbed were those in the White House. Behind her, the men chuckled their appreciation. There was something quite nice about a beautiful woman who wasn't afraid to slap their wrists. Ambrose, as Lydia's husband, took great delight in their delight. For Lydia, after all, belonged to him.

Then Ambrose's eyes fell on Eugene. The boy – for that was how he always thought of Eugene Weller – had not enjoyed Lydia's interruption. Pity. Eugene would do well to hook his horse to a woman. At least then he would have someone to concentrate on besides Ambrose and somewhere to release his nervous energy. Tonight he seemed even more preoccupied than usual and his intensity was wearing. Perhaps it was because he had come late to the meeting; his normally unflappable demeanor had been disturbed by the breach in his scheduling. Annoyed, Ambrose finished his drink, and set aside the glass, missing the marble coaster and landing it hard on the fine wood.

"Better watch it, Ambrose. Lydia is going to have your head tomorrow if she sees a water ring on that wood," Jerry laughed.

"Lydia's displeasure is a thing to be feared, Jerry," Ambrose agreed as Eugene swooped toward the glass.

Ambrose waved him away and rectified the situation himself. His impatience with the boy was starting to feel like the pangs of old age, a speculation he would keep to himself. Age was going to be an issue in the coming election, and it was up to Ambrose and his team to minimize it. His next thought was that his response to Eugene was something else altogether. It might be the itch of familiarity; the feeling a man who has risen to a certain status gets when he looks at the wife who had been his rock but has become his millstone. Perhaps his disappointment was simply a reflection of his belief that the greatest sin was to be reactive. The world was filled with Eugenes waiting to clear up messes and when they finally got the chance, their actions were out of proportion to the need. Case in point, the simple act of misplacing a glass required only that it be put onto the coaster. There was no need for Eugene to lunge for it as if he were saving Ambrose from an assassin's bullet.

Ambrose wiped the watermark slowly as he considered that small men with myopic vision populated the world. His observation was not an arrogant one; it was objective. The three men in this room – four if one counted Eugene, which no one did in this context – were different. They were Ambrose Patriota's peers of a sort. If not visionaries, they were powerful men of patience who could accomplish things quietly and effectively.

Woodrow Calister, Chairman of the Armed Services committee, was by far the most like-minded in this very private caucus. He understood the global implication of Ambrose's ambitions. He was a patriot at heart and possessed a marvelously analytical mind. He believed all things were possible; he knew beyond a shadow of a doubt that the things he wanted were probable.

Jerry Norn, a member of the subcommittee on Intelligence was a close second on Ambrose's list of those he admired. What Jerry lacked in patriotism – for he was an opportunist by nature – he more than made up for in enjoying the challenge of keeping the wheels turning. He truly believed that there was no better governing or economic system than that of the United States.

Mark Hyashi, a Senator of Japanese/American decent, had joined them only a few months ago after more than a year of careful investigation on the part of the other three senators. He sat on the Homeland and Government Affairs committee. Such an appointment was coveted and that the seat went to a freshman senator was a testament to Mark's intelligence and passion. Hyashi's insight into the ability of the Japanese political social and military culture to mesh and create a complete and selfless consciousness provided Ambrose a counsel that was invaluable.

Mark drew parallels between the Japanese people willing to die in the service of their god-emperor and the more contemporary mindset of terrorists. If only, he had been heard to say, there was a pill that people could take to clear their minds of prejudice. There would be no more warlords, no more religious fervor, and no ideological pressures. People would act for the common good. Ambrose agreed but argued that such a pill would be a moral challenge for scientists and ethicists. Woodrow pointed out it would be better than a wet dream for the military. Jerry added economists to the list. The only thing scientists and ethicists would agree upon is that government had no business in people's brains; military men and economists, on the other hand, believed that's exactly where government belonged. Ambrose knew that neither camp had it right. Such power needed oversight and only those who ran the government, the military, and the economy could provide it and those people were the politicians: the right politicians, naturally.

"Now that I've been scolded, too, gentlemen, shall we get back to it?" Ambrose directed. "Eugene, if you would."

"Of course, Senator."

Eugene raised the remote and pointed it at the huge television behind a frame of carved mahogany. The familiar TED logo came up on the screen and faded in favor of a young Asian woman speaking to a casually dressed man wearing a tightly fit headpiece that looked like the interior strapping of a bicycle helmet.

The senators knew every word of her presentation by heart so the sound was muted. Still, they were glued to the set as the woman typed on the computer keyboard. The camera cut to the computer screen revealing a white circle inside an orange square. The woman stepped back, the man focused on the orange cube, and seconds later that cube filled the screen. In the next instant the man made the cube shiver and retreat just by thinking it so. The senators had seen him do this four times that night and still they reacted with anticipation and then excitement.

"There. Did you see it? A millisecond and that orange thing was gone. Vanished." Jerry fairly bounced on the sofa cushion and then threw himself back, clapping his hands as he kept his eyes on the screen. "Can you imagine what could be done with that technology? Medicine is one thing, but I bet those two never thought of defense and intelligence applications. With the discipline our troops have, you take a battalion and get them all thinking on one target. Boom. Done. The enemy is thought out of existence."

"It didn't disappear completely." Woodrow, arms resting on his knees, narrowed his eyes at the paused image. He was not as impulsive as his colleague but he was impressed. "I'll grant you it was damn close. This could usher in a whole new generation of warfare."

"Or peace," Ambrose reminded them.

"You're all reaching," Mark Hyashi interjected. "That man wasn't manipulating a solid object. We're a long way from medical or military relevance without that."

"I wasn't serious," Jerry snorted. "If this could be applied that way, I'd be the first to invest. We've never even considered that any of these people are close to physical manipulation. What do you think about it, Ambrose?"

"I think we're fighting wars with drones and robots. Soon everyone else will be, too." Ambrose said. "If our people could interfere with our enemies' software programs, drone controls, perhaps even the minds of the operators, we would change the landscape forever. Engaging in war would be futile."

"Speaking of our enemies – or even some of our friends – they'll have this as soon as we do if not sooner. They'll steal it or pay for it and they'll have us over a barrel," Woodrow noted. "We'd do the same if they had anything close to workable."

"Nothing is ever simple," Ambrose pointed out. "Nor is it foolproof. We already know that governments around the world are watching that young lady, but she is our citizen and that gives us an edge. She and her intelligent friends think they will cure cancer, feed the starving, and change the climate. We see that it can be used for so much more. Unlike Miss America, we will not just hope for world peace, we will some day assure it by wiping a brain's ability to hate. It is doable. We must take steps to make sure this and other advances are not left in the hands of brilliant idealists and their tunnel vision."

"But it's bulky, Ambrose. Granted, the headpiece is a far cry from the early net caps and electrodes, but it's hardly subtle," Woodrow pointed out.

"Except," Mark Hyashi countered, "once a technology breakthrough is made, improvements follow in months, not decades. Mainframe computers used to fill rooms. Now a woman carries an even more powerful computer in her purse. Fifty years in the making and yet everyday someone builds on the pioneering science. I agree with Ambrose, this isn't a parlor trick."

Mark Hyashi wandered toward the television. He tapped the screen.

"Ten years ago that thing he is wearing cost tens of thousands of dollars, but she said this one was manufactured for a few hundred dollars. Two years from now it will cost pennies and the technology will be hidden in the earpiece of a pair of glasses or buried in that guy's head." He turned back to the men, his handsome young face clouded with conscience. "The question is what part do we play?"

"We fund it with enough caveats to assure that it belongs to us for as long as possible," Woodrow answered.

"We can attach funding to any number of bills," Jerry agreed. "Most of our colleagues don't even read the darn things. We'll probably be the only four who know the funds have been requested or allocated."

Woodrow played devil's advocate and pointed out the obvious.

"Homeland Security is the place for this kind of thing but it isn't going to appropriate funds for anything like this, Mark. You guys are being watched like hawks. The country has sunk a ton of money into virtual border fences that don't work, TSA is inept and—"

"Yes, yes. We know. All outdated. All ridiculous programs." Ambrose waved away the obvious. "Billions have been wasted because no one looked ten steps ahead. We boasted about achievements before they were achievable. We all look like fools and aren't trusted because of it.

"Did you know our government conducted experiments in psychic driving at one time?" Ambrose glanced over as Eugene quietly took his glass and refilled his drink.

"That was 1965. Someone saw the possibilities of controlling the mind of a driver of transport trains, airplanes, or cars. That was the original vision and what we just saw is the result of that."

"Who funded that one with the brown paper bag and subliminal messages way back when?" Hyashi chuckled, missing the point or, to give benefit of the doubt, lightening the mood.

"That would be Intelligence." Jerry Norn raised his hand and pretended to be chagrined.

"I see a certain poetic justice there."

Woodrow's laugh was accompanied by the clink of ice. He had gotten up to refresh his drink and when he turned around he was holding the bourbon decanter as if it were a tarnished crystal ball.

"'62. Operation Northwinds. That was my favorite. Or how about False Flag? There was a friggin' great idea. Hijack a few of our own planes, bomb a few of our own citizens and blame it on Iran. Thank goodness the president saw the light on that one."

"He had to have some convincing before he gave it up," Ambrose winked.

"Ambrose. Ambrose," Woodrow lamented as he put the decanter back. "According to you, you've been responsible for half the good decisions every administration made since George Herbert."

"You wound me. I will take credit for at least ninety percent. However, I fear I was in no position to counsel anyone back then. I'm old, I'm not Methuselah."

"I doubt there was ever a time you didn't make sure you were pulling some strings, Ambrose."

Jerry barked his signature laugh. It was easy to see why he was re-elected time and again. Big and jovial, he could kiss a baby and a call girl with the same aw-shucks aplomb. His PR was so good that only a handful of people knew that he was the biggest skirt chaser in D.C. and that handful didn't included his wife. Ambrose didn't like that, but he did like Jerry's smarts. The man could remember everything: every detail of testimony, every statistic, every word uttered in his presence. He was driven not by power but by the puzzle of politics; a puzzle of how people fit together, why certain ones were pivotal and others passed through life without notice. Of course, Jerry wasn't Woodrow. Woodrow was the real deal; he was Ambrose's moral compass.

"I only take credit where it's truly due, Jerry," Ambrose said magnanimously. "And when it is to my advantage."

"Next year you're going to be elected president," Hyashi interjected. "Then you will have to take credit or blame for everything. It won't matter if you make the decisions or not."

"If I was reluctant, I wouldn't run," Ambrose noted. "I don't want eight years to go by and—"

"I think you better figure four, there, Ambrose. No need jinxing things," Woodrow warned.

"Eight years. Four is not enough," Ambrose insisted. He was speaking to the choir but sometimes the choir forgot the tune. "My friends, there are those inside our country who believe our borders are not sacrosanct and that our country belongs to anyone who wishes to claim a part of it. In the extreme, there are those who would like to make us disappear like a little cube on a computer screen. I'm not talking about our troops. I'm talking about all of us. Wiped away. Gone and forgotten."

Ambrose's eyes clouded as he thought of the things that pained his heart more than he could say. People who did not understand the exceptionalism of this country, of everything its people had accomplished in a few hundred years, appalled him. But even these realities were nothing compared with the one that cut him deepest.

"More importantly, gentlemen, there are those who believe in nothing: not hard work, not morals, not intellect. My grandparents would be ashamed. I am ashamed."

"As we all are." Hyashi truly believed as Patriota did, but Hyashi was more practical. "Still, no matter how much you want it, Ambrose, even eight years is not enough time to change the way our citizenry thinks or for this science to reach its full potential. The most we can hope for is that technology can be used to keep us safe until our collective thinking changes again."

"This isn't the only technology." Woodrow took his seat again, sobered by the turn of the discussion.

"It doesn't matter what technology we're talking about, none of it is ready. We're going to have to fund the testing quietly, and we'll have to be patient. Same as we're doing with the nonlethal weapons testing," Jerry pointed out. "I think we're all agreed on that."

Ambrose raised a hand shoulder high. Behind him Eugene Weller engaged at his signal.

"Eugene. How many grants has this young lady applied for?"

"Thirteen. Seven federal applications, three with her home state, California, and three private."

"Where are the private funds?" the senator asked.

"Google, Apple, and The Universal Group."

"Fine. Let's have The Universal Group handle it since they have the lowest profile and are the most dependent on government contracts. They can approve her funding with one of our own people on the oversight committee," Ambrose decided.

"Senator Norn, could you also get to someone at Health and Human Services to approve her grant?" Eugene asked.

"I can. There is a most lovely and influential undersecretary who will assist," Jerry chuckled.

Eugene ignored the senator's boast. "We also have access to private donors who will only need a slightly revised prospectus and, perhaps, a phone call from Senator Patriota to get on board."

"Very good, Eugene," Ambrose said. "And with that, I think we'll call it an evening. We have a full year, my friends, but the convention will be upon us before you know it. It is a symbolic exercise and nothing more. Polls say the general election is also assured, but I will still have to campaign. That will be grueling. I'm not a young man, but this program and others like it will define my presidency. I want results by the end of the first term."

Ambrose stood. The others set aside their drinks. Woodrow smiled as Jerry clapped him on the back and made small talk as they moved toward the door. Coats were found, buttoned up, scarves draped around necks although it was doubtful they would get chilled on their short walks to the chauffeured cars awaiting them. Ambrose, ever the good host, saw them out. Mark Hyashi hung back, wanting one more word with the next president of the United States.

"Ambrose, I just want you to know that I am willing to do my part in all this, but I don't want political speak between us. We are talking about cultural manipulation not guidance, and we have no idea what the unintended consequences of that will be – economic not being the least of them. I want your assurance that research and application will be transparent from the start to those of us who sign on."

"My only concern is the safety and prosperity of this country, Mark." Ambrose grasped the young man's hand. "We want to be left in peace. What I propose is enlightenment. Permanent enlightenment."

Ambrose shook Mark's hand and clapped him on the shoulder, following him onto the doorstep. Woodrow had paused beside his car, his driver holding open the door. He caught Ambrose's eye and a question passed between them. Ambrose lifted his hand and waved him off without anyone else seeing. Woodrow ducked into his car. Ambrose went back inside where Eugene lingered.

"Ah, Eugene, it's time you go home. It seems you've had a long day."

Ambrose took the last coat from the hall closet. He was tired but he still had an hour or two of reading to do. It bothered Ambrose that the boy was breaking protocol in so many small ways this evening. He passed the coat to Eugene who took it but made no move to put it on.

"Eugene?" Ambrose prodded.

"I was late because of the man at the hearing today. Ian Francis?"

"Yes?"

"He's dead." Eugene blurted.

"Really?" Ambrose was less than curious.

"Senator, he jumped out of the window of his hotel," Eugene insisted.

"That's tragic. Poor man." Ambrose shook his head and opened the door wider. Eugene missed his cue.

"His name is Ian Francis, Senator. Perhaps you'll remember him from this."

Eugene took three sheets of paper from his breast pocket and gave them to the senator. It took a moment for Ambrose to understand what he was looking at. When he did, the silence stretched even further. Because the senator still stood at the open door Eugene did not imagine that the shiver that ran through the great man was anything but a reaction to the frigid air. Finally, he spoke.

"I didn't realize. I didn't know him personally." Ambrose refolded the paper.

"But you were a part of it. You were the one who..." Eugene began, only to stop when Ambrose closed the door and came close.

"It is history, Eugene," he said quietly, "and I was a very small part of that history, I assure you."

"Given the discussion this evening, I thought it relevant. This could be devastating to the campaign, not to mention this new program. If the press gets wind of this, it would be a scandal, sir." Eugene insisted.

"I have no enemies in the media," Ambrose insisted. "The opposition is considered fringe, not me."

Eugene shook his head, unconvinced. "Times are different, Senator. The media can change from one minute to the next. I think we need to be ready."

"What I think is that it is very late." Ambrose left no room for dissent. "We'll talk later if you really think we must but as you said the poor man is dead. That rather ends the matter, I believe. No one will come asking questions. Trust me."

"We're heading into a national campaign." Eugene tried again to engage the senator, hoping that he would at least acknowledge his brilliance in putting two and two together. That wasn't going to happen.

"And that's what we should be concentrating on." Ambrose opened the door again and stood aside to give Eugene a clear exit path. "It sounds like everything is taken care of. Good night then, Eugene."

Eugene hesitated still. He had never questioned Ambrose's judgment but alarm bells were sounding in his head.

"Josie Bates was in the room when he jumped."

Eugene was finally rewarded with Ambrose's undivided attention. Ambrose's brow furrowed, his mouth turned down, his head tilted as if he could now hear the call to action.

"She knew him all along then? Do you think Ms. Bates was laying the groundwork for something? No, no," Ambrose shook his head, answering his own question. "To what end? There's no connection between this man and Eastern Europe. There would be no reason to disrupt a hearing on a subject that was so personal to her."

"I don't think it's anything like that." Eugene was quick to reassure him. "I was thinking that Francis possibly came there for you. It was unfortunate that he ran her down and that his rambling could be construed as pertinent to her problem. It was my fault not to recognize how determined she was to follow-up. I could have mitigated the outcome by monitoring a meeting in controlled circumstances. I'm sorry. I let you down."

"Nonsense, Eugene. I wouldn't have thought it of her either. I believed we had sent her on her way. We miscalculated, that's all. There is no fault. It was a fluke," Ambrose assured him but the senator's mind was still working on the permutations of possible problems that could come from that woman's curiosity about Ian Francis. "If Josie Bates did have an agenda of some sort, we would have had reporters on our doorstep by now. Did you speak with her?"

"I thought it best not to connect your office in any way outside of the hearings. I was in touch with Officer Morgan throughout. Morgan was following Francis to see where he went. He didn't even know Bates was in that room until the incident. Then he interviewed her. Francis didn't say anything to her about his work. He never spoke to the desk clerk or other residents. Morgan and Ms. Bates agree that he purposefully fell from the window. The girl who was with him has disappeared."

"Then it sounds as if you have things well in hand, Eugene." Ambrose squeezed Eugene's arm. It was done.

"Would you like me to take that?" Eugene's hand was out. Ambrose looked at the sheets of paper in his hand.

"No, but thank you," he said. "You need to be off. We have an early morning."

"Good night then." The younger man took the outside stairs slowly, pausing on the last when Ambrose called out to him.

"It really was a long time ago, Eugene. Intentions were good. We learned from it."

"Yes, Senator," Eugene said.

"Thank you, Eugene. I'm blessed to have you. I trust that you won't speak of this to anyone."

If Eugene responded Ambrose Patriota didn't hear. The door was closed but the chill remained, so Ambrose went to the dying fire and stood in front of it. It did nothing to warm him so he threw the papers onto the embers. They curled at the edges, singed, and then caught in a quick burst of flame. It was a silly thing to do. If Eugene had found this information anyone could, but watching it burn made Ambrose feel better.

So many people came and went in a man's life one couldn't remember them all. But he remembered the time, the mission, the high hopes, and the ignominious fall of those powerful men who had since gone to their rest. Now he was in power and he would do things differently. The paper was ash, so Ambrose packed away the memories, flicked away the speck of guilt that had landed on his shoulder, and went upstairs. This time the outcome would be very different.

This time no one would get hurt.

ॐ∞ॐ

Woodrow Calister dialed Ambrose's private number but disconnected the call before it rang through. His chest expanded as he took a deep breath, but he made no sound as he let it out again. He felt like an old man after one of these evenings with Ambrose. The senior senator, the party's pick for president, was a rare individual to be sure. To have Ambrose's energy, to believe so surely in one's own destiny, was a gift. Or a curse. Or just plain stupidity. Woodrow couldn't decide which it was. Still, he admired Ambrose greatly and was honored to stand beside him. They would make a good team when it was the two of them running the country.

His eyes wandered from the view of a city he had long ago stopped admiring. It was all show, every last bit of it. A great show to be sure. Still, to those who knew it well, there was no comfort to be found in it.

"Matthew?"

His driver indicated that he was listening by the merest motion of his head as he made a clean and sweeping curve through an intersection at a light that was questionably more red than yellow.

"Did you ever see that movie *Westworld*? You know, Yul Brenner is some kind of robot and people go to this place for vacation and they can live in any time period they want for a week. The robots act like roman slaves or Greek gods. Yul Brenner is a gunslinger robot in the old west and he goes berserk and then all the robots go berserk and kill everyone. You know the movie?"

"Sorry, Senator. I don't think I've seen that one," he answered.

"Too bad. Good movie. Mindless people doing outrageous things to please themselves because the robots can't feel anything. Of course, all the robots look like people and they are all beautiful. Anyway, it was a statement. Eventually the things you abuse or try to control will turn on you. At least that's how I took it." Woodrow spoke to the back of Matthew's head, longing for a bit of conversation, and hoping to coax it out of the man whose job it was to see and hear nothing.

"Wish I could help you, sir," Matthew said. "I'm not sure I know who Yul Brenner is, sir."

"*The King and I*? *The Ten Commandments*? Yul Brenner."

Delighted that the chauffer was interested, Woodrow was ready with a bio of the great actor but just then the car passed under a streetlight. Woodrow saw that Matthew was smiling and it wasn't a good smile. It was the kind Woodrow's kids gave him when he was showing his age. It was the smile his wife gave him before she had enough of the political life and left him. Those smiles never bothered him, but this one did. This was his chauffer humoring him and that just ticked Woodrow Calister – distinguished leader of the Armed Services Committee, respected senator, soon to be vice-presidential candidate – off in the worst way. It angered him so much his eyes burned with it but he stayed silent. In the grand scheme of things Matthew was nothing. Woodrow wasted no energy on him. Instead, he dialed Jerry.

"It's me. I was just wondering, do you think Hyashi's really on board here?"

Jerry assured Woodrow that he had no doubt Mark Hyashi was one hundred percent Patriota's man.

"Look, I'm only a few blocks away. Let's have a nightcap. Something happened with Medusa today. It's been on my mind."

"Not a good time, buddy," Jerry said. "I'm not exactly at home."

Woodrow heard a woman giggle and his heart went cold. He didn't care who Jerry Norn screwed, but he hated that Jerry Norn didn't either. They were, after all, senators. Woodrow hung up knowing Jerry wouldn't give a second thought to his terse goodbye. Woodrow, though, was doing a little soul searching.

It wasn't like him to feel this way: a little depressed, a little dissatisfied, a little powerless. He just couldn't put his finger on why. Was it that Ambrose was the chosen one and he was destined for the number two spot? Could it be as simple as jealousy? Or was it that the game had become too predictable? Perhaps what was on that television screen bothered him. That lady scientist was so delighted that she had invented something that could make a man's mind more powerful than any weapon in the world. That scared him? Why didn't that scare her?

"Matthew?" Woodrow said from the dark.

"Yes, Senator?"

"Two soldiers were killed today. We were testing a new weapons system. It was supposed to just make them incapable of moving but it killed them."

"That's a pity, Senator." Matthew said and then without changing his tone he asked: "Would you like to go home?"

"Yes, Matthew. I would like to go home."

Woodrow Calister turned his face to the window and wished he had someone to talk to.

CHAPTER 9

MAUI, HAWAII

WOMEN'S CENTRAL PRISON
CHOWCHILLA, CALIFORNIA

"This is a surprise. We don't get much eye-candy here." – Linda Rayburn

"Prison's a bitch." – Archer

"Yeah, well, much as I appreciate you driving all the way out here, the invite was for Josie." – Linda Rayburn

"She's a little tied up looking for Hannah." – Archer

"I know about those hearings. Lot of good they did." – Linda Rayburn

"I didn't know politics were your thing." – Archer

"Hannah's still my kid. It's not like I could just forget her." – Linda Rayburn

"I doubt she'll ever forget you, either. So what's with the visitor request? I didn't think Josie was your favorite person. " – Archer

"I have an idea where Hannah might have gone." – Linda Rayburn

"You could have put that in the letter." – Archer

"That's it? How about thank you. Or, really? Where?" – Linda Rayburn

"Where?" – Archer

"Oregon. There was a guy who took us in a few years ago. She might go to him if she's looking to lay low." – Linda Rayburn

"Why would he help her?" – Archer

"I was very good to him." – Linda Rayburn

"What's his name?" – Archer

"First, a little business. I've been doing some reading." – Linda Rayburn

"How to Live a Purposeful Life?" – Archer

"Funny. Penal Code. I may have grounds for an appeal." – Linda Rayburn

"You think Josie should handle it?" – Archer

"I could sign off on the parent thing with Hannah." – Linda Rayburn

"You already signed off." – Archer

"Maybe I'm rethinking. It's not a done deal." – Linda Rayburn

"Just so I'm straight, you're bargaining with Hannah?" – Archer

"Just an exchange of information. You talk to Josie about an appeal, and I'll tell you all about Sam in Oregon." – Linda Rayburn

"You give mothers a bad name. I'm outta here." – Archer

"Sam Idle. He called himself Damn Idle, you prick." – Linda Rayburn

☙❧

Because Stephen Kyle sang badly, he sang loudly. He also spoke loudly, laughed loudly, loved loudly, and basically lived large. He had lived this way in many a place and his current place was Maui, Hawaii, which for a fair skinned, well-fed, and bald Brit seemed an odd place to end up, indeed. He had also done many a thing before taking to Hawaiian life, all of which had brought him something he craved: money, women, adventure, and notoriety. At that very moment, he was craving a pulled pork sandwich with a healthy serving of slaw on the side and a cold beer. He would, of course, settle for a nice bit of Mahi-Mahi caught fresh for Mama's Fish House and a martini. The day was coming upon the time when it was perfectly acceptable to have a cocktail; perhaps even share a cocktail with interesting company of the female persuasion.

Sadly, interesting company was not to be had at the moment save for his own, of course. Nor did it seem that there would be a beer or a martini in his future anytime soon since the rain had begun to fall in earnest. England had its share of the wet stuff so he was no stranger to it, but in Hawaii one must pay attention when it fell like this. Fickle as a mistress, it was. Sweet and gentle one moment, raging with fury the next. And, like a mistress, it was always beautiful but could be dangerous if one didn't give it one's full attention. In fact, no one in their right mind would keep driving on the road to Hana in this weather. Stephen Kyle was often accused of not being in his right mind, so he kept driving.

"Damn bloody stuff," he muttered as a particularly dense curtain fell from the sky.

"Bloody idiot." Stephen cursed the weatherman who had predicted rain but not torrents, not tempests.

When he was done with that, he began to sing Royal Blood's *Out of the Black* with gusto, loving that his voice sounded quite good in the cab of his truck. His singing was so excellent that he forgot the rain, drummed his beefy hands on the big steering wheel, and gave the old trolley of his a little wiggle just as he hit a perfectly acceptable high note.

Unfortunately, in the next minute he hit something else.

ॐॐ

It was all over in seconds: the crunch, the spin. The frantic attempt to keep the rental on the road failed. The car bumped down the incline just under the bridge and landed sideways in a tangle of ferns, hibiscus, and banyan tree roots. Josie's hands were still clenched tightly on the wheel minutes after the crash. That was the first thing she was aware of, the second was the sound of the rain, and the third was her ragged breathing.

She let her head fall back, closed her eyes, and did a quick inventory. Her head was spinning, but she hadn't hit it. Her stomach was clutching, but only because her seatbelt had done what it was supposed to do: grab and restrain. She had gone cheap on the rental so no airbag deployed. Her arms would hurt in a few hours because she'd braced against the fall by pushing out on the steering wheel even though she knew better. Go with it. Roll with it. Finally, she relaxed her fingers, extended them, and let go of the wheel as she opened her eyes. Her purse was dumped on the passenger side floor and that window was cracked. So was the back window on the passenger side. To her left there didn't seem to be anything different than the right: forest and more forest. Above her the rain went from sounding like a machine gun to a car wash. Water slid off the windshield in sheets. Though she wasn't hurt, she was darn ticked. Josie couldn't imagine what she'd hit but whatever it was it felt like a brick wall.

She turned off the engine, unsnapped her belt and nearly tumbled to the other side of the car. Stabilizing herself with her feet, Josie leaned over and gathered her things. Reaching behind her, she grabbed the steering wheel and pulled herself upright and then tried the driver side door. The angle made it nearly impossible to push it open with her hands so she leaned back and put both feet against it. With a great heave she shoved until the hinges caught. At exactly that moment, the wind whipped through the mountains and drove the rain horizontally, drenching her in the process.

"Damn! Damn!"

Josie turned her head as she slid off the seat and took the short drop to the ground. One foot hit a bush and the other slid in a river of mud. Muttering, cursing, wet to the skin, she slung her purse across her body, took one last look at the car, and started to hike. The incline wasn't much but she was shaken and the terrain was sodden so it was slow going. She slipped, grabbed onto a tree, and pulled herself up a few feet toward the bridge before slipping again and sliding all the way back to the beginning. She set to it once more with a grunt, choosing her footholds, pushing the rain out of her eyes, spitting it out of her mouth, and clutching at any plant that seemed to have deep roots. Josie almost reached the top before she felt herself going backward again but this time she was ready. She grabbed for a root that wove in and out of the ground like the hump of a sea serpent. It held strong. Hanging there, her feet buried in mud, her arms stretched taut, and her grip weakening, she heard:

"Hello! Hello there!"

Just as Josie looked up, the rain stopped, the sun broke through and the short, wide man standing on the narrow bridge above her threw arms out and splayed his hands on the railing. He was grinning at her, his face nearly hidden by a hat that was half beanie, half mini-umbrella.

"Good God, I've found me an Amazon!"

"I don't believe it," Josie muttered and then called back, "Can you give a hand?"

"Delighted." He came around the edge of the bridge railing and positioned himself solidly with one hand on the rail and his other out to Josie. "You're going to have to step up a bit more. No sense both of us getting muddied."

Josie looked down, saw a rock that would give her a boost, and planted her foot on it. She looked back up to see his fingers wiggling. She put out her hand and grasped his. A second later Stephen Kyle hauled her up to the road.

"There you go. There you go. I fear your sandals will never be the same. No worries. We have plenty where those came from. Don't you know enough to honk before you go 'round these twists and turns?"

"Maybe you could have honked. That thing's a monster," Josie complained as she eyed Stephen's truck and then the man himself. He had swiped the silly hat off and was rubbing the top of his head like it was the belly of a Buddha, unfazed by her pique.

"Ah, but I have the right of way. That's what you didn't count on. I dare you to say otherwise. It's in the rule book."

When he laughed Josie wanted to deck him. This had not been her best day for a lot of reasons, not the least of which was that she had to admit that Archer was right. She was on a fool's errand looking for Hannah in Hawaii.

"There's no rule book."

Josie sat down on the side of the road and put her head in her hands. She took one deep breath then treated herself to another, dropped her hands, rested her forearms on her knees, and gazed at the car. Stephen Kyle sat beside her.

"Sorry, didn't mean to be flip. You just looked so magnificent hiking up that hill I thought you were uninjured. Any blood? Anything broken?" He poked at her arm and then brushed at her hair.

"I'm fine. Don't worry about it." Josie brushed right back, swatting his hand away.

"Well, someone needs to worry a bit. You're far from everything and that car of yours is going nowhere." Stephen looked skyward. This time he patted an ample middle that was covered with a lime green Hawaiian shirt. The man's hands were like his mouth, unable to stay still. "Ah, I love it when it stops raining. Breathe in, my girl. Nothing like the scent of paradise to make you feel better. Would that we could package the stuff. That's why God made rain, you know, so that you can appreciate the glory of his other creations when it's cleaned them all up."

"How far are we from a tow?" Josie peered down the road, first one way and then the other.

"A good distance. Never fear, I'll get you where you're going. Come on then. Be a good girl. Can't leave you out here by yourself." He stood up and dusted off his board shorts.

"I'll call for a truck." Josie started to dig in her purse for her phone.

"You can do what you like, but there's no reception out here. Nothing but highway. Six-hundred and twenty curves. Fifty-nine bridges. Half of them are that way." He pointed north. "And the other half are that way." He pointed south. "You're right in the middle. It's going to rain again and, much as it would be a pleasure to continue seeing you wet as a guppy, I think it better that we get you dried off just to make sure that you're not mistaken about the state of your impressive body. Best hurry."

He offered his hand. She took it. She knew enough about Hawaii to know that rain and sun came and went. Today rain was winning.

"Josie Bates," she said.

"Keoloko," he answered.

"Right. All Hawaiians talk like they went to Oxford."

"Oh, you want to be formal. Stephen Kyle. I go by Stephen to those who love me."

"Got it."

Josie pulled at the t-shirt suctioned to her midsection as they walked to the big truck Stephen had pulled to the side of the one lane bridge. She reached for the passenger door handle but he stopped her before she opened it.

"Not there, my darling. You'll get a face full of pineapples. Come on around back."

Josie did as she was told, checking out the artwork on the side of the paneled truck. It was a veritable explosion of Hawaiian art: flowers, surfers, waves and *wahinis* in rainbow colored grass skirts. In curlicue fonts painted in pink, the truck screamed *Shave Ice! Pineapple by the Slice! Mango Cola!* In the center of it all, was a huge picture of Stephen Kyle dressed in the plaid shorts and a Hawaiian shirt and hoisting a pineapple in each hand. A wreath of flowers encircled his head and emblazoned like a manic psychedelic halo over that head was the word Keoloko.

"Nice," she said as she joined him behind the truck.

"Pays the bills." Stephen Kyle cranked the handles down simultaneously and pulled open the huge double doors in the back of the truck. He threw out his arms like a ringmaster.

"There you are."

Josie looked inside. The cavernous space was packed with things: boogie boards, boxes of umbrella beanies, a hanging rack of clothes, and a bed. Everything, including the spread on the mattress was emblazoned with the Keoloko logo.

"You live here?"

"Hardly. Come on. Up you go. I'm not a masher."

She was barely inside when he slammed the door. The truck went dark except for the light coming through a small window that looked into the cab and through the front windshield. A moment later, the engine came to life smoothly and the truck lumbered back on to the road just as the rain began to fall again. For the next two hours Josie laid on the mattress drying out, counting the twists and turns on the Hana Highway, and listening to the man up front channel Don Ho and the Beatles at the top of his lungs.

❦

Michael Horn arrived at his office at 6:00 a.m. He handled four client conferences, two meetings with the administrative staff, and reviewed countless claims at the large insurance office that carried his name. He then spent another four hours reviewing the new government regulations that were going to make him crazy at best or put him out of business at worst. His concerns were a well-kept secret because nothing ever seemed to rattle Michael Horn. Some saw him as robotic and apathetic but the truth was quite the opposite. Michael Horn was a man of such deep feelings that if he did not simply get on with business he would dissolve into a puddle of doubt and fear, he would be paralyzed by the sheer enormity of the battle life had thrown at him, a battle no one at work knew he waged.

At the end of the day, he left the office and drove through downtown Cleveland to his favorite burger joint. There he picked up dinner and resisted the urge to dig into the french fries as he drove home. Once there, he took off his suit jacket, draped it neatly on the back of the dining room chair, loosened his tie and made space for his dinner on the table that was littered with files and papers, pictures and maps, legal briefs and bills. The house was quiet as a tomb because no one lived there anymore but him. His wife had left over a year ago taking their twelve-year old son with her. Intellectually, Michael understood that his fight was not hers. He also understood things like honor and ethics and morals and the rights of the individual. He couldn't understand why her righteousness had limits. She thought he was titling at windmills; he believed he must slay Goliath. She insisted all he needed was to give in to his grief and all would be better.

Michael told her she was wrong.

She told him goodbye.

He took a bite of his burger. It was excellent as always. Just enough meat, a tease of pickles, and the secret sauce that he was sure was nothing more than Thousand Island dressing. Still, he liked the idea that somewhere there was a safe that protected the recipe for secret sauce. He took a french fry, ate it, and then reached for the television remote. He should have wiped his hands first. His wife hated grease on the remote. Then again, his wife would have hated that he moved the television into the dining room. Then again, his wife didn't live there any longer so he stopped worrying about the remote as the news came on.

...the head of the NSA has once again been called upon by congress to explain why more than eighteen million citizen communications have been monitored on a regular basis for years. This disclosure comes on the heels of the administrations vehement denials –

The phone rang before Michael could enjoy the latest rounds of denials by the government on any given subject. You probably couldn't get a straight answer if you asked them what day it was but they wanted to know every time you took a leak. He waited for the answering machine to pick up. He had no desire to fight with his wife, or decline an offer to buy new siding, or address an office crisis that his managers were hired to deal with. Michael took another bite of his burger and smiled. A pickle. The pickle bites made him the happiest. The answering machine engaged and his wife's voice announced they were not at home.

"Well, half of us aren't," Michael muttered and made a mental note to change the announcement. The machine beeped. There was a hiccup and then he heard:

"Michael. It's Sheila. Do you have *The Post* from a few days ago? Look at page–"

Michael Horn forgot the burger, his fries, and his greasy fingers and picked up the phone.

"Sheila. Don't hang up."

"I'm glad you're there," she said. "Are you still getting *The Post?*"

"I am. I just haven't looked at it lately. I've been busy. Hold on." He put her on speaker as he rummaged through the newspapers that were stacked on the chair at the far end of the table. "Can you hear me?"

"Yes. Find the tenth."

"Got it," he called.

"Page thirty-six. It's buried; only a few lines. Headline is: Robert Lee Suicide." Sheila said.

"I've got it." Michael switched on the overhead light and shook out the paper and read:

"The Metropolitan Police Department responded to a nine-one-one call on Wednesday night when a resident of The Robert Lee Hotel jumped to his death. Officer Morgan of the Capitol Police was also on scene. He confirmed that earlier in the day the victim had been detained after disrupting a Senate hearing presided over by Senator Ambrose Patriota. The man, Ian Francis, was an expert in forensic neurology who, at one time, worked for the Department of Defense. One witness, Josie Bates of Hermosa Beach, California, was questioned at the scene and released. Anyone with information regarding relatives of Ian Francis is asked to call Officer Morgan."

"That's it," Sheila said.

"Thanks. Anything else?"

"No, Ernie's home soon. You know how he feels about this," Sheila said. "He's so worried we're going to get in trouble especially with the NSA stuff going on."

"He shouldn't worry. We're small fish," Michael assured her.

"That's what I tell him, but you know how it is. Can you believe it? Ian Francis, the little twerp. I thought he was in hell a long time ago," Sheila said.

"He is now."

There wasn't much more to say after that. Michael heard the click on the other end of the line. He tossed aside the newspaper and sat down in front of the larger of the two computers he had at the end of the table. He typed out a note to the lawyers telling them about the death notice but held off asking them to research. It was costing a fortune to see this thing through and Michael could do the preliminaries as well as they could. He would hand it over when he had as much information as he could get.

"We're closing in, grandpa. Yes, we are. This is just too good."

Michael was grinning when he stood up and gave his grandfather's picture a wink. Then his smile faded. He was talking to a dead man while he stood in an empty house.

❧

"Anuhea! Cool and Fragrant. That's what her name means. No people on earth have names like the Hawaiians do. Pure poetry."

Stephen Kyle pointed to a young girl lounging on a rattan sofa petting a Siamese cat. She looked at Josie with beautiful dark eyes that registered no surprise at either her presence or her appearance.

"Aloha." The girl said. The cat purred.

Like a dust devil, all whirling motion, kicking up dirt and sand along his narrow path, Stephen went on to the next woman.

"And this is Aolani. Her name means heavenly cloud. Their mother named them well." An identical girl sat at a table reading. She looked up and graced Stephen with a lovely smile and raised her head so that he could plant a kiss in the middle of her brow.

"Aolani is studying to be a nurse. And a fine one you'll be. Who wouldn't want a heavenly cloud by their bedside? Who, I ask you? We must find a Hawaiian name for you, Josie."

"I think I'll stick with the name I've got–" Josie began, fully intending to cut this hospitality short but the man wasn't done.

"Ah, and there's Malia. That means beloved. Not by me, of course," Stephen guffawed. "Far too young, even though she adores me. Don't you, dear thing?"

"You betcha," Malia said just before she disappeared into the back of the house.

"She's not Hawaiian, you know." Stephen offered this aside confidentially.

"The Brooklyn accent was a dead giveaway," Josie assured him.

"A good ear you have. Puerto Rican. Her real name is Maria, but you put a grass skirt on her and crown of flowers and she's Malia, beloved of the gods of Hawaii, arrived on this earth on the back of the great turtle or some such. Drink?"

Josie smiled because it was hard not to. She had slept in the back of the truck despite, or because of, Stephen Kyle's singing. It had taken her a few minutes to ground herself after she woke up. Now here she was, a guest of an English Mad Hatter in a tropical rabbit hole. Still, there were worse places to be than this house and were it not for Stephen Kyle she would be walking the road from Hana.

"There's a bathroom over there for you to wash up. You'll feel so much better if you do. Glad you're dried out. Anuhea." Stephen called to the reclining girl who looked at him with a smile. "Could you get Josie here a shirt from the cabinet and see if you can find a pair of flip-flops from the shipment that was going over to the Royal Lahaina?" To Josie: "I'm thinking you wear a nine? Yes?"

"Yes, I'd be grateful for the flip-flops, but I'm good with my shirt. I'll change when I get to the hotel."

"Suit yourself, darling. Off you go."

Ten minutes later she was back and renewed. The flip-flops outside the bathroom door were orange with pineapple shaped jewels on top. She put her muddied sandals and purse by the front door. When she got back, the girls were where she had left them and Stephen was behind a Tiki bar. The wood was dark and the front was covered in rattan. Josie had seen one like it at a vintage shop on Pacific Coast Highway and the store was asking a pretty penny for it. This one was longer and in better condition.

"This is amazing." She slid onto a bar stool and ran her hand along the smooth, dark wood.

"Koa wood; the most precious of all precious woods; the revered tree of the gods. It's ancient. The tree is protected now. This was a doorway in King Kamaiama's palace. I came to it by a trade from the man who was the son of the man who carved the piece out of an ancient tree. What will you have?"

"Do you have a beer?" she asked, marveling at how long he could speak without a breath.

"We have whatever your heart desires."

Stephen grabbed two glasses, uniquely fashioned with thick rounded bottoms, an air bubble floating inside. Next came a glass decanter blown by the same artist. He popped the stopper and Josie smelled the distinctive scent of Scotch whiskey. He poured and pushed one glass toward Josie.

"Fine stuff."

She was about to decline when he reached below the bar and came up with an ice-cold bottle of beer, twisted the cap and set it in front of her. That was followed by a can of Macadamia nuts.

"There you have it. What you want: a beer. What you don't think you want but you really should want: my very best scotch. And what you need: sustenance." He drew up a stool opposite her, picked up his glass and toasted: "To your health and the health of every beautiful woman who walks the earth."

Josie picked up the scotch and touched his glass. They grinned at one another. It was a better start than their first one. He took a drink, smacked his lips, and looked directly at her.

"Now, in all seriousness. Are you well, or do I need to call for a physician?" Stephen asked.

"I'm good, really. I'll be a little sore tomorrow," Josie answered. "And I do appreciate the help."

"Least I could do." He downed another generous portion of his drink. "I've got a tow going out to where you went over. We'll get it all sorted out, but I'm not sure you should get back on the road. Wouldn't want you to hit anyone else." Before Josie could point out that she believed he hit her, Stephen called: "Anuhea. Aolani. Get your lovely arses in gear, darlings. The show starts early tonight. You must dance as never before."

"It's raining, Stephen," Anuhea complained sweetly.

"It won't be when the curtain goes up. Go on, now, sweeties." He shooed them away, continuing his discourse seamlessly with Josie. "You get to know the weather patterns. I can tell to within ten minutes when it will clear. Not many can do that. And, you, where do you hail from?"

"Hermosa Beach. It's a small town in Southern California."

"Ah, I'm not a fan of Los Angeles, but I do like Big Sur. Lovely place."

"You've never seen Hermosa. You wouldn't even know it was close to L.A.," Josie said and took a sip of her beer. "Look, I appreciate your hospitality and your help with the car, but I really need to get back to my hotel. It looks like you and your ladies have some plans tonight, so if you could call me a cab I'd appreciate it."

"You're here alone? No husband waiting for you?" Stephen raised a brow.

"Not with me. My fiancé is in California. "

"Pity you're spoken for. He should have bought you a big diamond so the rest of us know you're taken."

"I'll wait for the gold band."

"Are you a darling angel from heaven? No diamonds and you're still faithful to the bloke? I hope he knows how lucky he is."

One of the girls stuck her head out from the hall and asked Stephen if they were working with the fire sticks that night. He answered in the negative and she disappeared once more.

"Do you let all your employees live with you?" Josie asked.

"I'd never let an employee live here! Those are my protégées who also happen to work for me. They are amazing girls and each of them needed just a little leg up." He spoke fondly of the twins. "Their father worked for me. Fine man. When he passed away, he asked me to watch over them. No hardship since they are good girls and lovely as you can see. And Malia, my tough little bird? She had a sad life, but a great heart. I can afford to help out, so why not? Sadly, each will be off in their own good time." He grinned at Josie. "Ah, I'm going on. What was it I had my mind set to do?"

"A cab?" Josie reminded him.

"Nonsense," he answered. "We'll drop you on the way. Where are you staying?"

"The Grand Wailea."

"Perfect. We're showing at the Four Seasons and that's right next door. Meanwhile, Shall I entertain you with a little Keoloko hospitality?"

"I doubt I have a choice," she laughed.

"Right you are," Stephen answered.

Josie didn't mind. There were worse places to be. When she had first stepped out of the truck and seen the overgrowth and the rickety fence, she had assumed she would find a modestly livable place but Stephen Kyle's house was an island palace. Behind the bamboo stands and bushes, behind that rickety fence, was an exquisite home made of glass and wood, furnished comfortably and elegantly. There was art on the walls, statues in niches, books on the low table. It was clear that Stephen loved his house and that made Josie homesick for hers.

"So you probably want to know about me," Stephen bellowed, making this a statement rather than a question.

When Josie looked up all she saw was his grin. All she heard was his bark for attention. She missed the kindness and curiosity behind his eyes.

"Or, perhaps you'd like to say a little something about yourself. What brings you to Hawaii looking like you have the weight of the world on your shoulders? It's not divorce since you haven't even tied the knot yet. One last fling, perhaps? If so, then I am your man, indeed."

Josie shook her head. "I was looking for someone. I thought she'd be here in Maui. She isn't."

"It's a small place," Stephen said. "What's her name?"

"Hannah Sheraton."

"Anything more?"

"She just turned seventeen," Josie answered, reluctant to give this man too much information. Nice as he appeared to be, she had no desire to be steamrolled by his good intentions. Stephen raised his chin. He pursed his lips. Josie took a drink of her beer and listened to him wax poetic.

"Ah, a runaway. A boy is involved, more than likely. Romeo and Juliette?" He raised his glass, emptying it in between inventing his fiction. When he was done, he revised his story. "No, an older man. That's it! You're the mum on the hunt. I see it, of course. Terrible stuff. Terrible."

Josie took a handful of nuts and resisted the urge to point out that he was of a certain age and sharing his house with three young girls.

"I'm not her mother. I'm her guardian. It's a long, complicated story that is almost unbelievable. This girl is incredibly resourceful and she's scared, but she would never admit it. She is probably with a boy. His name is Billy Zuni. If they're together it's better than if they're apart," she said. "It would all be absurdly ridiculous except that it's very serious."

"Truth is often hidden under a mountain of ridiculousness. You just have to know where to put your hand in the pile of manure to find it."

Stephen raised his glass again only to stare sadly into the abyss when he saw there was nothing left but ice. Josie noted the pinky ring. There was no stone and no engraved initial, just an exquisitely fashioned oval of gold. At his throat was a necklace of Puka shells, on his right wrist a stack of braided leather. His nails were manicured. He was master of all he surveyed. He put the glass on the bar and splayed his free hand on the wood.

"I haven't heard of anyone by that name on the island."

"Do you know everyone on Maui?" Josie asked.

"I do," he answered. "If by some chance I have forgotten who someone is, they know me." Then he changed again, the happy host was back as Aolani emerged from the back room. "Isn't that so my darling? Is there a soul I don't know on Maui?"

Josie looked as Aolani came back in the room. A crown of flowers circled her head and sat low over her brow. She wore a long skirt but carried a grass one. Her midriff was bare and buff and under her open work shirt she wore a bra made of fake coconut shells. She looked into a mirror framed by pink shells as she adjusted the straps on her costume but she spoke to Josie's reflection.

"Yes, it is true. Everyone knows Stephen."

"There you have it," Stephen cried. "If I haven't heard of Hannah coming to the island, then she hasn't. The question is why do you think she has?"

Josie pushed aside her drink, got off the stool and went to the front door. When she came back, she had the luggage tags that she had carried from Washington.

"I took these off the suitcase of a man who said he knew where she was. I was able to track the flight number on this one from Maui to Los Angeles and on to Washington, D.C., so I reversed the process and here I am."

"That is a trek for sure," Stephen muttered as he took the tag.

"This man went all that way to find me to tell me about her." Josie got back on the barstool.

"Then why didn't he tell you exactly where she was?"

"Because he killed himself first."

Stephen's eyes flicked up. She offered a little shrug that seemed to say 'how about that'. He responded with: "I hope you don't have that affect on all the men you meet."

"He's the first one. I don't think you have to worry." She handed him the second tag. "This was on the case, too. I went to that street but there's no such address. I was headed back to Lahaina when you ran into me."

Before Stephen could respond, Anuhea wandered out dressed in a short, sky blue sarong. Anklets of flowers were fastened above her bare feet. Stephen looked up.

"Lovely, Anuhea. That's a good girl. Where's Malia?"

"She's coming, Stephen."

"Excellent," he answered offhandedly, distracted by what Josie had given him. "You are right about one thing. The address doesn't exist because this isn't a house on a road and that is not a house number. This place isn't even on Maui. I know what it is. I know where it is. I do, indeed."

But Josie wasn't listening. She was looking at Malia who was ready for work. She carried a grass skirt and a crown of flowers but she wore a pair of jeans and a t-shirt the color of sherbet, emblazoned with cheap silkscreen in a riot of island flora. Josie had seen the same shirt in a freezing hotel room in Washington D.C. But this one was newer and there was a part of the design Josie had not seen before. Woven into the design was one word: *Keoloko.*

She was in the right place.

To the casual observer, Officer Morgan was a pretty simple man. He got a haircut every six weeks, he shined his shoes every night, he and the missus messed around on Saturdays and sometimes they didn't even wait for the sun to go down. He had planned for his retirement and had a nice nest egg, not to mention the pension that twenty years as a government cop earned him. He had a son in Alaska and they were on good but not close terms.

He played cards with a group of guys who he called his brothers. It would seem Morgan was living the dream.

To anyone who knew him well, and pretty much that was limited to his wife who was a saint, Officer Morgan was not a simple man. He often thought deep thoughts. He wondered about life, death, right, and wrong. What he was wondering about as he sat behind his desk was the envelope that held the possessions of one Ian Francis. Deceased. Dead as a doornail. Pitiful in his last moments of life and probably a long time before that. There had been something about the guy that just sort of made Morgan's heart grow big and sad. Ian Francis had not been your everyday, run-of-the-mill nutcase.

"No, Siree", Morgan thought as he poked at the stuff with his finger.

Actually, it wasn't all the stuff in the envelope he had collected the night Ian Francis died that intrigued Morgan, it was the guy's cell phone. He had found it in the bushes a couple feet from the body, collected it, and forgotten about it for a while. When he found that phone, his first reaction was to do what he always did: mark it and send it on over to the morgue to be handed over to whoever came to claim the body.

He didn't do that. He kept it and now he fiddled with it. He turned it on. He checked the contacts list. There was just one number. No name came up, only a picture of a serious looking young woman. He had put his thumb on the call button twenty times and twenty times he had taken it off. Any other time he would make the call, find out who was on the other end, offer his condolences, and ask if they had any interest in claiming a body. But this wasn't any other time. His supervisor was clear: no time on the clock for this one. Period. It came, he said, right from the top. God knew what top he was talking about, but Morgan backed off.

Still, Eugene Weller was interested in this guy who had seriously disrupted Senator Patriota's hearing. The lady lawyer who had been in the room when he jumped was no slouch as he had found out when he checked up on Josie Bates. It was all feeling a little too over his head and the last thing Morgan wanted to do was get on the bad side of Patriota or his geeky goon, Weller.

Finally, he put the phone back in the evidence bag, took the bag, and left the office. The cameras caught a picture of his ample posterior walking down the hall, his equally impressive stomach when he turned to go back from where he came, and the moment after that when he turned around once more.

It took Officer Morgan a while but he finally made it upstairs and over to the Russell Building where he checked in with Weller's secretary and asked to see the man himself. Genie left him cooling his heels for ten minutes. One minute longer and he would have left, but Eugene's timing was good. Morgan had no choice but to do what he came for.

"Brought you something, Genie. I logged it, but I didn't call the contact." Morgan handed over the phone. "I'll be happy to if you want. This is probably the girl that was with him. Just thought you might need to do something first. I don't know what."

Eugene looked at the picture of the blond girl. He smiled a true and genuine smile that gave Morgan the shivers.

"Thank you, Officer Morgan. You did the right thing."

Officer Morgan didn't smile. He was kind of surprised that doing the right thing felt so crappy.

"Okay. So, just sign for it. Then we're good."

Eugene Weller looked at the paper. There were ninety-five signatures on the darn thing. People took responsibility for evidence all the time. He picked up his pen. What could it hurt?

CHAPTER 10

"Do you know what time it is, Jo?" – Archer

"You never complained when I woke you up before." – Josie

"All right. I'm awake." – Archer

"This guy says the place I'm looking for is on Molokai." – Josie

"It takes a lot of money to get all the way to Hawaii, but you're there, check it out. If it's a dead end, stay a few days and relax. I'm going further north." – Archer

"What's up there?" – Josie

"Following a tip, same as you." – Archer

"The trucker in Sanger?" – Josie

"The mother in Chowchilla." – Archer

"Hannah would never contact Linda." – Josie

"She didn't. Linda thought you might like to handle her appeal in exchange for a lead on Hannah. I told her it wasn't going to happen." – Archer

"So she sent you to San Francisco?" – Josie

"Oregon. Just figured it couldn't hurt to stop and see if there was anything going on in San Francisco." – Archer

"And?" – Josie

"No one in the morgue matching their descriptions. No one arrested for prostitution. Negative at soup kitchens and shelters." – Archer

"I think Linda's just getting her jollies. I wouldn't trust her."
– Josie

"We'll see." – Archer

"I wish I could sleep." – Josie

"You will. When you get home. When we're all home." – Archer

"That will be nice." – Josie

"You wouldn't have done it, would you, Jo?" – Archer
"What?" – Josie
"Handle Linda's appeal." – Archer
"What do you think?" – Josie
"I think maybe. To get Hannah home." – Archer
"I think it's a tough call. Goodnight, Archer." – Josie
"Night, babe. Love you." – Archer

శ్వా

So long as the memory of certain beloved friends lives in my heart, I shall say that life is good. – Helen Keller

శ్వా

It didn't take Josie long to realize that Stephen Kyle hadn't exaggerated. Everyone on Maui did know him. That was because he owned everything that wasn't bolted down. Keoloko Enterprises owned the biggest chain of souvenir stores on the islands. They were found in every shopping center, strip mall, and on every highway. His stores sold beach towels and shot glasses etched with volcanoes, dashboard dolls that would hula for eternity in pickup trucks from California to Kentucky, Tiki gods, hang loose key chains, plastic leis and ukuleles, taffy, Macadamia nuts in all their incarnations, shirts, and skirts, and salami. If you couldn't find what you wanted in a Keoloko store, it didn't exist in Hawaii.

But Stephen Kyle was an expansive kind of guy and the stores just weren't enough for him. He employed half the local teenagers and housewives to ply his wares from inside fake grass shacks set up outside parks and along roadsides. They sold slices of Keoloko pineapple, cones of shave ice, sunscreen, and more leis. Their husbands, boyfriends and brothers were employed by Keoloko car and tour services and fishing boats. He ran another boat out to Molokai regularly to bring provisions to the three bed and boards on the island and one place that few knew existed and fewer still knew had a name. This was the place Stephen believed Josie was looking for: Ha Kuna House on Molokai, not Ha Kuna Road on Maui.

"Sure you don't want me to call over first? That might be a better idea then just popping in."

That was the last thing he had asked her the night before and the first thing he said when she got in the car on the way to the harbor. Both times her answer was the same:

"No. I don't want Hannah to run. I want one shot at convincing her that the two of them will be safe at home."

"And how would you go about doing that?" he asked.

"I'd tell her I would die before I let anyone hurt her or Billy," Josie answered.

"If she thought there was one chance in a million it would come to that, she would never come home," Stephen countered. "I haven't met her, but even I know that."

No response was called for. In a short amount of time she had learned that Stephen Kyle wisdom was a thing to be reckoned with. She and Hannah would never put the other one in jeopardy and that was why Josie needed to see her face to face. That's how she would know Josie was telling the truth.

They drove twenty minutes from the house to the harbor where he commandeered one of his fleet, a sightseeing boat called *No Problem,* for their journey across the way to the island of Molokai.

Stephen's chitchat was punctuated with expressions of gratitude that the day was calm. One thing he could not bear was a choppy sea. His brother, Stephen said, drowned in a choppy sea. Of course, the sweet bastard had been drunk which might have had something to do with the unfortunate accident. Still, the sea had been choppy that day. And chilly as the English seas were, there was hypothermia to consider. And, Stephen added, his stomach – not his brother's – was sensitive to motion. Always had been since he was a child. This caused him a great deal of derision at boarding school.

Josie basked in the warmth of the sun, relished the taste of sea salt in the spray, and caught half his stories as they cut through the water heading toward Molokai. Her new best friend amused her in the best possible way. She seldom ran across people like him: curious, magnanimous, accommodating, brash, and smart. The phrase, 'he would give you the shirt off his back' seemed coined just for Stephen Kyle. She imagined a third of his stories were true, a third had basis in fact, and a third were the product of his raging imagination. Josie reciprocated with stories about Faye, Max, and Archer. Stephen countered with more stories of his mum, his ex-wife, and his favorite goat that, sadly, had been lost in a tragic accident atop the roof of his historic country home in England. He quieted as they closed in on Molokai, a magnificent, awe-inspiring bit of nature that was at once fearsome and beautiful.

Sparsely populated, Molokai was home to the highest sea cliffs in the world and every inch of them was covered with the most brilliant green. Those cliffs rose from a sapphire sea and into a cobalt sky so bright it hurt the eyes to look at it. By the time they tied up the *No Problem* and got the car, Stephen was back in true form and giving her the two-dollar tour as they drove. That eastern part of the island where they were headed was cut off on three sides by the Pacific and bordered by the Kalaupapa National Historical Park. Deep in a canyon at the foot of the mountains was the leper colony founded by Father Damien. Leprosy was gone; the buildings where lepers were nursed and museum that documented their suffering were the island's only tourist draw.

"Have you ever seen the place?" he asked. Josie shook her head. "Well, then we'll come back another day. You must take a mule down miles of switchbacks to get there. They took quarantine of those poor buggers quite seriously. I'd have to send you alone though. I don't care for those mules. Riding a mule is like being in a boat on a choppy sea. Upsets the tummy. Malia likes it. I'll send her with you."

That, Stephen said, was for another day when they had no chore to do. The place he was taking her was reached by car on a narrow road through some of the most beautiful terrain she had ever seen. The Molokai uplands were cool and he took great care on the roads that sometimes skirted the edge of the cliffs. Finally, Stephen stopped at a turnout.

"Here we are," he announced.

"I don't see anything."

"It's not far. Deliveries are made from a different entrance. There's a wider road and all. We'd have to drive too far around. Besides, this affords us a lovely walk."

They both swung out.

"Might be best to take it slow," he suggested.

"Is there a problem?" Josie asked.

"If Hannah is being held prisoner here as you suspect, I'd be disappointed to walk into some den of crime and find a knife to my throat. You're a pretty thing, but no one is worth that and, while I am dashing, I cannot be mistaken for James Bond."

"I didn't say she was kidnapped," Josie pointed out. "Besides, I thought you worked with these people. How long have you been delivering supplies here?"

"Six years, but it's not like we're gossiping around the water cooler with the folks. They fax their orders and my boys over here meet the boat and deliver the supplies. I don't have what you'd call a relationship really," Stephen muttered.

"Has anybody ever pulled a knife on one of your guys?"

"There's always a first time for such a thing," he complained.

"I promise, it won't be today." Josie patted his hand, slid it off her arm, and headed down the path that cut through the tropical forest.

"Could be that you're crazy," Stephen grumbled as he followed. "Maybe you have a knife." He raised his voice. "It dawns on me that could be the case." He lowered his voice to grumble some more. "They won't be happy if I bring a crazy woman here. I'm just saying that it would have been polite to call."

They walked that way for a bit and then he took a hop and a skip and came along side her.

"In for a penny," he sighed, but Josie wasn't paying attention any longer.

She was tuned to the turn of the earth, seduced by the place in which she found herself. Whatever was going to come, she was glad it would come here where the plants had leaves made of satin and flowers of velvet, where the perfume in the air was blown on trade winds, the ground was dappled by sunlight sifting through a canopy of exotic trees, and the silence was the stuff of cathedrals not tombs.

"I'm glad she's been here," Josie said.

There was no need for Stephen to answer. Such, his silence seemed to say, was the power of island magic. Here Josie could be convinced that wishes came true and that all intentions were benign. He did not point this out anymore than he would mention that Josie was talking as if she had already found the girl. If her bubble were to burst, it would do so in its own good time with no help from him. Besides, Stephen Kyle was in no hurry for this walk to come to an end. He fancied himself a bit of Adam in the garden with Eve by his side. Pity this Eve kept her clothes on, but one couldn't have it all.

The road rambled through the forest revealing signs of human intrusion as it pleased: a small greenhouse just off the path to the left, a bench on the other side, a hoe that had been left leaning against the tree and, ahead, the first glimpse of a two story, white clapboarded house.

Ha Kuna House.

The architecture was Victorian, a reminder of the days when well-meaning missionaries nearly destroyed the

Hawaiian culture. The juxtaposition of formal architecture and the riot of unbridled landscape were astoundingly beautiful.

The windows on the ground floor were tall and overlooked a wrap-around porch. Six rocking chairs were lined up on one side of the front door. On the other side there was a single wheelchair. Just beyond the house Josie could make out the edge of another building. She leaned a bit and saw that there were two.

"It's a compound," Josie commented. "How many people live here do you think?"

"Figuring what we bring over in provisions, six or seven. Mr. Reynolds is the man who does the ordering. They keep to themselves." Stephen's gait changed to an amble, his voice dropped a decibel. "I'd forgotten how lovely this place was. I was only here once to secure the account."

"Some hands on businessman you are," Josie drawled.

"No need to be when things run smoothly. They order, we deliver, and they pay like clockwork. Would that all the world worked that way," Stephen answered.

"Do you ever bring anything unusual?"

"Such as manacles for young girls held captive?" Stephen caught himself before he laughed aloud because Josie's expression indicated she was not amused. "Sorry about that. No, is the answer. Food, toilette and cleaning supplies are always on the list. Once my boys brought a doctor from Maui."

"Would your men let a couple of kids hitchhike on one of your boats?" Josie asked.

"No. My boys are good workers. They know the rules." He paused to consider the building. "I've often expected to have one of my men come back one day and tell me the place is empty. It has that feeling, doesn't it? Like your granny's house, you know. You go every Sunday when you're a child and then one day you're older and forget to go and the next time you see her she's in a coffin. That's what this place feels like to me. Pretty but lonely and all worn down. It's as if it has lingered past its time."

Josie thought he was wrong. This looked like a place where two scared kids could feel safe. She gave his arm a tap.

"Today isn't the day granny's going to kick the bucket." Josie took the porch steps with Stephen Kyle right behind her. Gentleman that he was, he hurried around to open the screen door.

Josie walked through it and into a time warp.

❧

Eugene Weller had his finger on the pulse and it was a healthy beat he was hearing.

He was well ahead of schedule planning for the convention. He had a short list of vice-presidential candidates who had been put forth by the senator's personal caucus even though they all knew there was little reason to vet them. Woodrow would be the nominee. Ambrose hadn't said as much, but Eugene could read the signs. They all could. Still, their 'just-in-case' list was interesting.

They unanimously liked Sam Hemsly out of New Hampshire: a fine, upright man who was a little left of Patriota but loyal. He could be counted on to adhere to the platform, but Eugene could make a case that he was not the prime pick.

Sam Hemsley had not been blessed with Patriota's good looks, nor had he aged well. That alone would not have been of concern to Eugene, but he was now in possession of medical files that, in the hands of an astute strategist on the other side of the aisle, could compromise a Hemsley/Patriota ticket. Any hint of difficulty dealing with stress, any spin that Hemsley might be on death's door even if it wasn't true, might give the voters pause. Patriota was the oldest candidate ever to seek the office and statistics being what they were, he might die there. If Hemsley were seen as vulnerable, Patriota's popularity would take a hit, too. An electorate perceiving the demise of two older men in the highest offices which would open the door to a possible accession of the Speaker of the House who no one, save her own constituency, could stomach was something to consider.

The governor of California was a possibility and one Eugene would accept. As was the ex-governor turned senator for the great state of New York. He was young, energetic and good-looking. Eugene was quite taken with a picture of him and Patriota at the Kennedy Center during the awards ceremony. They were perfect foils. Patriota, aging and still virile looking, the young senator, blonde blue eyed giving off the boy next door vibe with a CV that included Harvard and Yale.

There were also the recommendations from the head of the party, various donors who thought they had bought Patriota and, of course, Lydia. She shouldn't even have had a voice but even Eugene had to admit that her suggestion of the governor of Alabama was not a terrible one.

Of course, they hadn't quite finished screening any of them and, as Eugene knew, that always turned up a few clods of earth that a politician wished had stayed tamped down. Although with these three, he doubted anything major would come up. Thankfully, Ambrose had been around long enough to know how to gracefully handle anything out of the ordinary, but it would be better if he didn't have to.

"Mr. Weller?"

Eugene looked up as Ann came into his office. The woman had the most annoying habit of knocking and opening the door simultaneously. How she managed with a stack of reports in her arms he would never know. He did appreciate her talents though. She was an insanely organized person.

"I have almost everything you requested yesterday." She started to flip folders with the most impeccable rhythm, giving him just enough time to look at the routing slips, open the top folder to glance at the overview and judge the extent of the reading that would be required. "This is the EPA report on the fracking issue and I've included the rebuttal from The University of Oklahoma and J.P. Goodings. I took the liberty to cull it down to three talking points that meet the Senator's agenda."

Thump.

"Blow back from the State Department regarding the Eastern European crime hearings the Senator conducted. Albania was not thrilled and has made their displeasure known. State suggests no action on the part of the senator but our ambassador has contacted their ambassador and is smoothing things over. You'll see that I added a few notes on projections regarding trade with that country in the next few years, extrapolating to cover the senator's transition to the White House."

Thump.

"This is today's correspondence from home. I've separated it into fan mail – just as an FYI since I've already taken care of answering those with the general letters – complaints, donor letters, and local issue reports. I broke the last into issues that might have national importance so you can start drafting an address and those that are purely local to Texas."

Thump.

"Excellent as always, Ann," Eugene said.

"And, finally, here's the ISOO list you requested of the Defense Department's declassified documents. These correspond to the dates and search parameters you requested but it looks like they went back a little further because it popped up some older stuff that seemed relevant. If you want to let me know what you're looking for, I'll cull it down for you."

"No, thank you. I can manage," Eugene answered.

"Okay, but you're going to be up all night with this monster."

Thump.

Ann was out of folders. She left the same way she came with a flip of the door. Eugene didn't notice. He was already running through the list of declassified documents that carried any mention of Chatter, Artichoke, and Marigold. Ten minutes later he picked up the phone again. This time he connected to the ISOO and asked that copies of specific documents be sent to his office immediately with cross-reference to any groups or individuals who had requested similar documents under the Freedom of Information Act. Finally, Eugene opened his drawer and took out the cell phone that he had put away so carefully.

He hit call.

৵৵

The house in which Josie stood was true to its architecture and purpose. There was no front desk, no receptionist, no sign-in for visitors, nothing to indicate that this was anything other than a private home. A wide-blade fan turned lazily above them, moving the still air in the entry. The wood floors were dark and polished. A straight staircase ran to the second floor and the railing matched the color of the wide floor planks. The stairs were not carpeted but a blue runner led down the long hall that ran parallel to the staircase.

"Kitchen's back there; Reynolds' office, too. I'll see if I can scare him up." Stephen started on his way, hesitated and put one finger to his lips as he thought out loud. "Don't be disappointed if Hannah isn't here. Once people start to run, it's hard for them to stop."

Josie tucked in her bottom lip as she inclined her head. He saw by her posture that his warning had come too late. Josie's hopes had been up since the minute she heard Ian Francis whisper in her ear. Since there was nothing to be done about that, Stephen took off leaving Josie to wait.

She didn't do it very well. She never had.

To her right were wide doors that opened to reveal a comfortable drawing room. Deep chairs were covered in chenille; there was a sofa with rolled arms and an old television console. The windows looked out onto the porch. She closed the door and went to the other side of the entrance hall and opened those. The room was identical to the first except this one had books on dark shelves built into the wall, a game table surrounded by four chairs, and another wheelchair. An old black man sat in the wheelchair seemingly asleep with his eyes open. Josie was careful to be quiet even though there was probably nothing short of the end of the world that could distract him. There was a buffet with a silver urn on top. Josie took a look at the books: classic fiction, Hawaiian history, and a full encyclopedia. The man in the wheelchair hadn't moved so Josie went back to the hall. The time dragged on and still Stephen did not come back. Josie was about ready to follow him when she heard a noise upstairs. She listened harder and heard it again. Without a second thought, Josie went toward it, taking the stairs lightly.

The first.

The second.

She took the third and fourth and paused.

The sound was slight, even, and it was directly above her.

She went up three more steps and then four until she was on a wide landing. There was another shorter flight. She went up to the next landing that opened on to yet another hall. The walls and the three doors on either side were painted bright white. The sound must have come from behind the door at the end of the hall, discernible only when Josie had been directly beneath it downstairs.

She went straight to it but stopped before she went in. After all these months it couldn't be this easy no matter how much she wanted it to be. A crazy man had pointed the way, after all. And it was only a sound that had come from this room, not the sound of a voice she recognized. Yet, she couldn't turn back without knowing. Josie opened the door and found herself in a two-room suite.

The floor was the same dark wood that ran through the entire house. The main room was painted white but the light that came through the leaded glass windows made walls shimmer like silver. There was a bed covered with a blue and white Hawaiian quilt. To her left was a set of french doors, the glass panes covered by white lace curtains. The doors stood slightly ajar and through the lace Josie could see a woman rocking in the high backed chair. She could just make out the delicate shape of her head and her short, dark hair.

"Hannah?"

Josie pushed the doors open a crack. The woman stopped rocking. Josie stopped breathing. Her disappointment knew no bounds; her sense of emptiness expanded until it was bottomless. It took only a moment to realize that this woman was too tall to be Hannah. Her hair wasn't black like Hannah's but dark grey. This woman's skin was not the color of cocoa but pale as if she had never been in the sun.

Not wanting to disturb her, Josie backed away only to stop when the woman turned and looked over her shoulder. Their eyes met through the narrow opening and when they did Emily Baylor-Bates smiled at her daughter.

CHAPTER 11

"What's your pleasure?" – Bartender

"Beer." – Archer

"You got it." – Bartender

"Are you serving food at the bar?" – Archer

"Name it." – Bartender

"Calamari and a bowl of chili. Can you turn up the sound on the TV?" – Archer

"Most people prefer the view of the Golden Gate to the tube." – Bartender

"Just want to hear what the talking heads have to say about Patriota." – Archer

"He's a slam dunk. I don't even know why they're going to bother with an election." – Bartender

"It would put too many advertising people out of work if they didn't." – Archer

"You a political type?" – Bartender

"My lady testified at one of his hearings." – Archer

"That and two bucks will get you a cup of coffee." – Bartender

"I hear you, but she still believes in miracles." – Archer

"She's better off going to church. Calamari coming up." – Bartender

ॐ

"Bullocks! What have you done to yourself?"

Stephen Kyle and Bernard Reynolds had been coming up the stairs when they heard an anguished cry followed

136

by the sound of breaking glass. Both of them had sprinted the rest of the way, Stephen pushing Reynolds aside and getting to the room at the end of the hall first. Now they were standing in the doorway, paralyzed at the sight of Josie kneeling on the floor in a bloom of broken glass, her hand a bloody mess, and her complexion ghostly. One pane of the door was shattered but she still had hold of it. Reynolds reacted first. He moved Stephen out of the way and rushed past Josie to the woman in the rocker.

"Emily? Emily! Are you all right?"

He fussed over her but she seemed not to notice. Instead, she looked at Josie, mildly interested and hardly concerned.

"Get that woman out of here. There's a first aid kit in my office, back shelf of the closet," Reynolds ordered.

"Yes. Good idea. Come on then, Josie." Stephen reached for her.

"Don't touch me," she growled.

"Josie, come on. Stand up. Your hand looks bloody awful. It must hurt like hell. We don't want to upset this lady anymore, do we?"

He took her shoulders but she yanked away again. Again he tried. Again she pulled back, lifting her head slowly to glare at him. Bernard Reynolds stopped ministering to the woman, fully aware now that there was more of a situation here than he originally thought.

"Kyle. Move this woman away now," he warned as he put himself between Josie and Emily.

"And just how would you expect me to do that if she doesn't want to go?" Stephen snapped. "Maybe you should move your woman there. Maybe that would do the trick because it seems mine doesn't care if she bleeds to death right here."

The air in the room crackled. Josie seemed to neither hear Stephen's warning nor notice Reynolds' anger. She had planned for this moment since she was thirteen years old. The script had changed over the years because a girl would react differently than a woman, but the outcome was always controlled.

How stupid.

How idiotic.

How predictably unpredictable.

This was a visceral moment, a blinding, gut-wrenching explosion of emotion that rendered her helpless.

"Josie. Come on up," Stephen cajoled.

Josie looked at the hand he tentatively put on her arm. She heard him speaking but couldn't make out the words. For a second she thought it was Archer come to help her. It should have been Archer. It wasn't.

"That's my mother," she muttered.

"Ah," was what he said, and then: "You can't keep holding to the door that way. See. Look. You've got hold of a shard of glass. Got to hurt, don't you think? It's damn awful. You're making a mess of Mr. Reynolds' nice floor."

He had one hand on her shoulder as he put his other firmly around her wrist. Josie seemed to understand. She looked at her hand. She saw what he saw: the glass, the blood on the floor, her pants, her arm, but she couldn't connect it to pain.

"This wasn't how it was supposed to be," she said.

"I imagine not."

He pried her fingers loose and the minute he did so the blood flowed more freely. He could see two major gashes, one across her palm and the other on her thumb. He pinched a shard of glass from between two of her fingers, tossed it aside and put his thumb flat and hard over that wound.

"Hold your arm up. That's a good girl."

"I want to talk to her." Josie struggled to her feet, holding onto Stephen only long enough to get her balance. She yanked away from him as she pulled up her t-shirt and wrapped it around her hand to stop the bleeding. "I need to talk to her now."

"Kyle!" Reynolds barked. "Do you want me to call my security?"

"Now is not the time to fight me, Josie." Stephen watched Reynolds and whispered a warning. "Later, my girl."

He put an arm around her and tightened his hold when she resisted. Josie's eyes flashed, but his gaze deepened and his expression gave warning. She didn't heed it. Her head snapped toward Emily. She pulled and pulled some more trying to get away from Stephen as she cried to Emily.

"Why did you leave? I want an answer. Why?"

Stephen dug his fingers into her ribs. Josie started to pull back, she was ready to fight him if she had to, then the realization of what had happened hit her broadside. Confusion, nausea, anger, fright, and the voice of reason collided and Josie was caught in the eye of the storm, suspended and paralyzed in the silent core. Sensing he had the upper hand, Stephen steered her toward the door, raising his voice for Reynolds' benefit.

"Here you go. I have you well in hand. I served in her majesty's army. Didn't wait for a medic when one of us took a shot. Tough boys, those. You would have done well," he blathered.

"I deserve to know," Josie began, but Stephen had her well in hand.

"Shhh, love. You've got a tiger by the tail. We will figure this out bit by bit."

"Wait in my office," Reynolds called after them. "I'll be down as soon as I have Emily taken care of."

"Excellent," Stephen called as he walked Josie through the door. Once they were in the hall she pulled away.

"I don't need your help," she said.

"Yes, you do if you want to see your mum again," Steve assured her. "Reynolds is none too happy. He could have us tossed out of here in a snap and then where would you be?"

"You don't get it. You don't," Josie whirled and tried to go past him but he caught her around the waist and pulled her close.

"You'd make a good dancer if you had any hips on you." Josie struggled but he held tighter and lowered his voice. "Don't try it. You're not up to the fight."

Josie caught her breath in a way that could have been construed as a sob and then she melted into him. Stephen gathered her up as she buried her face in his shoulder.

"You're a strong one," he soothed. "You have to be if you're still standing after seeing your mum brought back from the dead or wherever she's been."

He gave her hair a pet and when she didn't cry he led her down the hallway and to the stairs. They took them slowly and carefully all the way down to Reynolds' office.

Josie didn't resist because Stephen was right. She wasn't up to a fight. She didn't even know she had stumbled onto a battleground until she was face to face with the enemy.

৵৽৹

Michael Horn ran five miles, fixed a broken light fixture in the house, and closed a deal to insure a town of three hundred thousand souls when he got to the office. At noon he determined it was an appropriate time to call California again.

He dialed and waited. And waited. Even California couldn't be that laid back. It was after nine. There should have been a body in that office by now. Just as he thought that, he heard a breathless woman say:

"Baxter and Baxter, how can I help you?"

"I called a few days ago. I need to speak to Josie Bates, please."

"She's out of town, and I don't know when I expect her back. This is Faye Baxter. Can I help you?"

"No..." Michael began before he had a change of heart. "This isn't a legal matter in the normal sense. I need to talk to her about Washington."

There was a definite change. Michael could feel it and it felt good.

"Do you have information on Hannah?" Faye asked.

"Who?" Michael asked.

"I thought you wanted to talk about the hearings," Faye said.

"I want to talk about Ian Francis. Could you just tell her I need to talk to her about Ian Francis as soon as possible." The winds changed again. This time it didn't feel so good.

"I'll give her the message. What was your name again?" Faye asked.

"Horn. Michael Horn." He recited his phone numbers again. Three of them and hoped that this woman was taking them down. "It's very important that I talk to her."

"I'll give her the message. But she's in Hawaii on personal business. I honestly don't know when she'll be back," Faye answered.

"I have to talk to her. You give her that message."

Michael wished he could take that back the minute he said it. It wasn't what he said; it was how he said it. Even to his own ear his anger and frustration seemed to be at the boiling point. The woman on the other end went on the defensive.

"I'll let her know. She'll call you when she can. Have a good day."

"Wait. I'm sorry. Can you tell her I'm going to send her some information? It's about Ian Francis."

But Faye had hung up. Michael Horn held onto his receiver just a little longer. Any lifeline, no matter how tenuous, kept his hope afloat. Finally, he got a glass of water and went back to the living room. There he started rifling through his research but his heart wasn't in it. At least not until he picked up the information he had downloaded the other night. Once more, he read through the list of documents made public and then again. Finally he started to make sense of the information that had only been an impression before. He circled one entry over and over again with a red pen.

"Hawaii," he whispered.

Michael Horn sat down and started to compose a letter to a woman he had never met. If Josie Bates was following Ian Francis' trail then they must have something in common.

&ps&

"She deserted me and my father twenty-seven years ago. If you're interested, I can tell you how long she's been gone down to the hour. She never tried to contact me or my father or anyone. Now I find her here? You better believe I have a helluva lot of questions, and I'm not leaving here until I have answers."

In the corner of Bernard Reynolds' office, Stephen rolled his eyes, crossed his arms, and assumed that he would be losing Ha Kuna House business before the day was out. It was never a good idea to destroy your client's place and now there was this: a tirade, a history lesson, and a therapy session.

When Josie found her voice she couldn't stop talking. Not while he cleaned up her hand, butterflied the deep but narrow cuts in her palm, slathered antibiotic ointment on the scrapes on the side of her hand and wrapped the whole thing in gauze.

She kept talking while he searched Reynolds' office for a bottle of booze. In lieu of a tranquilizer dart, he thought a drink might slow her down a bit. If that didn't work, he'd take one to dull the pain her incessant chattering was wreaking in his skull. But there was not a drop to be found. He did find a bottle of aspirin. That wasn't going to make a dent in the pain Josie would eventually feel, but it couldn't hurt so he gave her four. When they were back on Maui he would give her something stronger and pack her off to her hotel if he could get her off this island by nightfall.

"How are you two doing?" Reynolds was back, giving perfunctory lip service to his concern. Stephen answered:

"Her hand will be fine. No stitches needed. We apprecia–"

"I want to see her. I want to–"

Josie made her demand as she started to get up but Stephen pushed her back down. Her head whipped toward him, but he would have no more of her lip.

"You've waited this long, you can wait a bit longer I think. Let's hear what the man has to say."

"I'm fine. I am. I don't want any trouble." As if to prove it, Josie swung her head toward Reynolds as she made a show of settling.

"Neither do I," Bernard Reynolds agreed. "But you have already made a great deal more than you know. I can't imagine what Mr. Kyle was thinking bringing you here like this. This is a private facility. People visit by appointment. What you've done is against all protocol and I will hold Mr. Kyle personally responsible. We will certainly be rethinking our business relationship with Keoloko Enterprises."

"It isn't his fault. I asked him not to call. I believed a young girl I've been looking for was here. I thought if she knew I was coming, she would run away again." Josie put her hands out to plead with him. "And if we had called and I asked you about Hannah, you would have said she wasn't here. We never would have come. I never would have known about my mother. Tell me everything. Why is she here? How long has she been here? Was she in an accident?"

Mr. Reynolds went around his desk and sat down. He was shaken but to his credit he kept himself in check. He clasped his hands and bounced them lightly on top of the desk.

"Before I answer any questions, I want you to know that I am not your enemy. I am Emily's advocate. You aren't the only one with questions, nor are you the only one who is upset. I understood she had no family. I have never had anything happen like this, and I am not happy about it."

He unclasped his hands and adjusted the picture frames on his desk. It was him with two grown ups she imagined were his children, obviously sired by a *Haole* and a Hawaiian. There was a baby picture in a frame that was hand painted with the words 'for grandpa' but there was no picture of the wife, nor did Reynolds' wear a wedding ring. He did wear the typical uniform of an island professional – khaki pants and a Hawaiian shirt – but hadn't left behind his mainland habits of hard soled shoes, dress socks, and a watch. Now that the picture frames were attended to, he seemed at a loss on how to address his distress. Stephen helped him out.

"Mr. Reynolds. Perhaps I can get you something for your nerves?"

"Nerves?" Reynolds repeated.

"By God, man, we all need a drink. Where do you keep the booze?" Stephen barked.

"We don't keep alcohol in this house," Reynolds said. "Maybe we should start."

Josie interrupted. "I will be happy to give you any information about me that you want, but right now I really need some answers. First, what is this place?"

"We are a private home for people with memory disorders like Alzheimer's and such," Reynolds answered.

Josie shook her head. "She wasn't sick before she left. I would remember something like that. My father would have said something."

"She might have been sick," Stephen interjected. "Parents don't like to visit their worries on their children. Don't forget, you were only a child then."

"Believe me, I haven't forgotten anything," she assured the men. "My father was deployed. He was hardly ever home in the years before that. It was her and me and she was perfectly fine the night before she vanished. She hadn't been forgetful leading up to that night. Her speech was normal. The only thing that was odd was that I heard her crying in her bedroom. My mother never cried. And then she was gone. Her clothes were still in the closet. She didn't take anything. She went to bed and in the morning she wasn't there. Do you think I could forget that?"

"No, I don't," Mr. Reynolds agreed.

"How long has she been here," Josie asked.

"At least fifteen years. That's when I signed on to administer the facility."

"And before that?" Josie pressed.

"I don't know. I would have to go back through the records."

"Then let's just do that," Josie said.

"Josie, be reasonable," Stephen wailed.

"No, it's all right," Bernard Reynolds held up a hand. "I know that this must have been extraordinarily traumatic for you, but it is no less traumatic than what happened to Emily. She is a sweet woman, and I will make sure no harm comes to her."

"I wouldn't do anything to hurt her," Josie insisted.

"Confusing a resident like Emily can be hurt enough. She's had episodes over the years and we finally have her on an even footing. Her reality is this minute and little else. You're going to have to accept that."

It was obvious that Mr. Reynolds believed that would be the end of it; Josie knew this was just the beginning.

"I will accept that when I am personally convinced of it," Josie answered. "I am her daughter. She looked straight at me. She smiled. Whether she consciously knows who I am or not means nothing in the face of the fact that there was something there. Medicine is not an exact science, Mr. Reynolds. Even if it were, you are not a doctor. I would bet that each of our assessments of her condition has about a fifty-fifty chance of being correct. I'd lay money on my fifty percent."

"And my staff and I have cared for her for many years," he countered. "I believe we have the advantage. I am sorry for it, but that is the reality."

Josie steeled herself. She knew he was telling his truth but she also knew that this was no different than a witness on the stand in court. Her job was to keep them testifying until they spoke the truth she wanted to hear.

"How many patients do you have?" she asked.

"Four residents at the moment. Quite frankly, though, I don't need to answer–"

"This is an expensive property to keep up with only four people. Exactly how exclusive are you?"

"Very."

Clearly there was a change of attitude. The shock of what had happened was wearing off; his empathy for Josie's plight was wearing thin. The consequences of what happened that day could be much farther reaching than the injury to Josie's hand or her heart. Mr. Reynolds no longer fidgeted and color was returning to his face.

"I am not at liberty to discuss our residents or the particulars of this home. And I resent the cross-examination."

"It was just an observation," Stephen piped up. He straddled a chair back to front and draped his arms over the top rung as he tried to get into the conversation. He grinned at Josie who had no humor to spare. He tried the same trick on Reynolds who ignored him, too.

"Not true, Mr. Reynolds," Josie said. "This is a grave situation, and I would like to know everything starting with how she is paying for this kind of facility. I would like to talk to everyone who has contact with her now and for the last however many years she's been here. That would include the other residents. I want to see her commitment papers. Who is her guardian? I will need her medical records. Most of all, I would like to arrange to transport her as soon as possible. I'll be taking her back to California. A referral by your doctors would be appreciated, but isn't necessary."

"Is that all?" Reynolds asked and Josie missed the ice in his voice.

"Yes, for now." She got up, tugging at her long knit shirt with her good hand. The shirt and her pants were ruined, covered in blood.

"You'll have a long wait, Ms. Bates. Not only will I not allow you access to any of our people, I wouldn't tell you what Emily had for breakfast." Mr. Reynolds looked at Stephen. "If there is legal action by this woman, there will be counter suits and you will also be named. This is a private institution and as such—"

"I believe this institution sits on Federal land and is, therefore, under the jurisdiction of the Federal courts," Josie pointed out and his attention swung her way again. He was more formidable than she first imagined.

"And the buildings and the people who run this institution are private. We hold a ninety-nine year lease on forty acres within the confines of Federal parklands. I believe that clarifies our status."

"Yes," Josie answered. She would not leave it at that but Reynolds didn't have to know. The good thing about a legal standing was that exception was the rule. If anyone could find it in this case, she could.

"Good. Then you will also understand that there is nothing I can do for you personally. I have no proof you are who you say you are." Bernard Reynolds voice was flat but it quivered just a bit.

"I can give you a birth certificate, driver license. I'll give you…"

"You could have twenty driver licenses," Reynolds stopped her, unwilling to listen. "I have no doubt your names are the same, and that there is a resemblance, but none of that does me any good. Ha Kuna House and its administrator is legal guardian for Emily. How am I to know if Emily is your mother and not an aunt or a sister? And even if I took the mother/daughter relationship at face value, I have no independent corroboration that you are a sympathetic party. Given what you've told me and your behavior here today, I could argue that you are not here to help Emily at all. Perhaps you are looking for payback for something."

"Reynolds! Please. No need to be insulting." Before Stephen could finish, Reynolds turned on him.

"Then let me point out that you are pretty much a name on an invoice to me. I should have thrown you both out."

Josie talked over him, "My mother's disappearance is a matter of record."

"I only care about what happens now. I am not at liberty to discuss anything about Emily without her express consent. She can't give it, and I choose not to answer any questions about this institution."

Bernard Reynolds stood up. Stephen did the same, twirling the chair and putting it back where he had found it.

"Josie, come on. Let's catch the tide. We'll think on this." Stephen touched her shoulder and gave the administrator a glance as he got up. "And I'm sure Mr. Reynolds will check with his people. We'll sort it out, won't we?"

"I will definitely be talking to my superiors," Reynolds answered. Stephen didn't think that sounded hopeful at all.

Josie got up, too. She was suddenly exhausted. Her hand was beginning to throb, her heart was battered, and her brain was as close to befuddled as it had ever been.

Her entire adult life she had been both decisive and persuasive. Now she was reduced to this: no clear choice, no defined course of action, and no argument that would sway this man. Josie did the only thing she could think to do: she begged.

"Let me see her one more time. Give her a chance to tell you who I am."

"Ms. Bates," Mr. Reynolds said her name like he was reading it off a list of people who perished in a tragic accident. "Emily doesn't even know who she is."

"She'll know me. Please," Josie whispered.

Reynolds looked at Stephen whose shoulders rose as he chucked his chin up and added his two cents. "If what has already happened didn't upset the woman, I doubt Josie going up to say a few words will."

Reynolds looked at him with contempt but he couldn't deny Stephen was right. Still he warned: "The minute you are anything other than conversational, you will be removed. Is that understood?"

Josie nodded. She and Stephen followed the director up the stairs to the top floor. Emily still sat quietly in her chair. Reynolds whispered to her while Josie and Stephen held back and strained to hear what he was saying.

Are you up to it?

Visitors

You can say no

Emily looked at Reynolds as he hunkered down next to her chair. She smiled at him and watched his lips as if that would help her understand what he was saying. She wasn't impatient or confused, engaged or curious. Emily Bates was simply there like the chair in a room or a window in a wall. She brought no energy to it, nor did she take any away. The light had passed from golden to pale as a peach as the sun went down. The glass had been swept from the floor and the jagged pieces removed from the broken frame. The lace panel had been removed to be cleaned of Josie's blood. The missing curtain made the two rooms feel naked as if the resident had moved on.

Josie had that same feeling of emptiness when she stood in her father's house after his death. It wasn't a personal void, just a physical one. Without her father, the house was nothing more than walls, a patch of lawn, and a roof. Someone else would eat in the kitchen, and someone else would sleep in the bedroom and watch television in the living room. Someday they would be gone too and the cycle would start again.

Reynolds patted Emily's shoulder just before he stepped aside giving Josie permission to approach. Josie cleared her throat, fearful that her voice would catch on the first word she uttered. Emily kept her eyes on Bernard Reynolds the way Max might watch Josie, with utter trust that she was safe in his presence.

Emily had nothing to fear. Josie wasn't a lawyer, she wasn't a woman about to be married, and she wasn't guardian to a girl with too much courage for her own good. Josie Bates was thirteen again, in awe of her beautiful mother, shy in her presence. Emily was the woman Josie had wanted to be. She prayed her mother wouldn't find her lacking. She refused to believe that Emily would not recognize her at all.

Josie went around the chair and stood in front of Emily. Their first encounter had been so swift, so staggeringly brutal, that Josie had only registered an impression of the woman. Now she saw her as she was:

aged but still beautiful, regal, and elegant. How Josie had always wished the sum of her parts were more like her mother's, but Josie's height, the cut of her cheek, the broadness of her shoulders, her slim hips made her a handsome woman, not a stunning one. Josie's movements were purposeful and athletic; Emily's were strong but fluid and ladylike. And yet there were changes that underscored how much time had been lost. Deep lines fanned at the corner of her mother's eyes, her skin was almost colorless making her appear luminescent, her bones were small and fragile. That was not what Josie wanted. She wanted Emily to stand up to her and explain herself, but then Josie saw her mother's feet and wondered if Emily could even walk any longer. Every disappointment Josie had suffered, every flash of anger, every resentful moment she had experienced over the years disintegrated at the sight of her mother's feet covered by the soft slippers. Josie had the fleeting thought that Emily could no more have stood up for her all those years ago than she could stand up to her now.

Josie bent down and hooked the fingers of her good hand over the arm of the chair to steady herself. Emily's eyes flickered away from Bernard Reynolds and rested on Josie's hand. When Emily looked up, Josie saw that the color had faded in her mother's eyes like a blue pinafore left too long in the sun. Emily smiled. She inclined her head and then raised one hand. She cupped Josie's face.

"You are so pretty," Emily said.

"Tell them who I am," Josie whispered.

Emily titled her head to the other side. Two of her fingers moved as if to test the mold of Josie's jaw. Josie could not resist that touch. She nestled her face in the palm of her mother's hand, she let her shoulders give up the great weight she had carried so many years, she let her eyes fill with tears that had never been shed. Josie sank to her knees and closed her eyes.

"Tell them."

In what seemed an eternal moment, Josie waited to hear her mother speak. Instead, she felt Emily's hand on hers, Emily's breath against her cheek. Josie opened her eyes just as Emily leaned forward. They were closer than they had ever been, but Emily was smiling at someone else.

"Here's my daughter. She can tell you who you are."

Josie followed Emily's gaze. There, in the doorway of the bathroom, clutching a broom and a dustpan was a young woman. The last time Josie had seen her she was wearing a hat, a heavy coat, and bending over the body of Ian Francis.

లోతో

"Amelia. I didn't expect you for another day." Mr. Reynolds moved forward and motioned her into the room. "This is Ms. Bates and Mr. Kyle."

The girl nodded to Stephen, but her eyes skated over Josie as if she were a patch of thin ice to be avoided at all costs. Slowly, Josie got to her feet. She moved her hand to the back of Emily's chair as if to prove possession was nine tenths of the law.

Josie couldn't believe that she had ever thought this was Hannah. This girl was at least twenty-five. Her skin was gorgeous, pale and clear with a hint of pink on her cheeks. Her long blond hair was fine and pulled back in a ponytail, her bangs caught off to the side with a barrette. Her face was heart-shaped and her grey eyes would be beautiful if you could look past the dark circles underneath them. She wore a pair of jeans, a long sleeved t-shirt, and tennis shoes.

"What are you doing here?" Josie demanded.

"I was cleaning up the glass." Amelia locked eyes with Josie and pulled her lips together in a tight, hard line. Josie imagined she was being defiant, but on second glance she realized the girl was being cautious, pleading with Josie to remain silent.

"This is one of our aides. Amelia Francis." Mr. Reynolds said.

"You're a nurse?" Josie asked.

"Amelia is one of our *lawehana,*" Mr. Reynolds said. "In Hawaiian that means a woman who helps."

"It means a servant," Stephen grumbled.

"Not here," Reynolds corrected him. "Here it means a woman who helps. Without her, Emily would not be as healthy as she is now. Emily didn't like the woman from the agency, Amelia. She missed you."

Emily swiveled in her chair and both hands clutched at the arm. She looked at the people around her, her expression concerned, her movement agitated.

"I would like to see Ian. I think I haven't seen him. Have I seen him? Have I? Because I'm afraid..." Her head went left; it went right. "I'm afraid..."

Josie started to move toward her mother but Amelia put herself between the two women.

"Don't. She doesn't like to be touched, especially by strangers."

Again there was a flash of something in those exhausted eyes, but Amelia looked away before Josie could figure out what it might be. It was the girl's touch and whispers that settled Emily.

Emily whispered back but loud enough for everyone to hear. "I don't want people looking at me."

Amelia whispered again as she smoothed Emily's hair. When she righted herself, she pivoted, retrieved her dustpan and walked away, speaking to no one in particular.

"I need to get the trays ready."

Before Amelia could make her escape, Reynolds raised his arm and blocked her. "Where is your father, Amelia? I'll bring him up for her."

"I left him with our relatives. I couldn't do it on my own anymore," Amelia mumbled.

"I wish you had come to me. We should have talked about it," Reynolds answered, obviously annoyed.

"I didn't think I needed your permission," Amelia said.

"No, of course you don't." Reynolds took a quick look around. All eyes were on him. "I'm concerned about his medication. That's all."

"I know. I'm sorry, but you know how he is. It's hard to stop him sometimes."

"Yes. I know. We'll talk about it later," the man said.

Only Josie seemed to realize how distressed Bernard Reynolds was; only Josie seemed to hear the catch in the girl's throat. A lie of that magnitude was not easy to tell, and yet she had done it. Josie had the feeling that she had done it because her father – her dead father who had risked so much to bring Josie here – would have wanted her to. So Josie did what she had to do, too.

She left Ha Kuna House, taking her questions with her, already making plans to get her mother home to Hermosa. Bernard Reynolds moved to the doorway to stand beside Amelia Francis and watch them go. When Josie and Stephen were on the stairs he said:

"I wish you had consulted me about your father. I'd like to get some information on his living arrangements."

"But he's not a resident. I was allowed," Amelia answered.

"Technically, no, he isn't, but we cared for him long before you came to us. I can't help but worry." Bernard Reynolds turned toward her. He was so close it made Amelia nervous. "Tell me where he's staying and with whom, and I'll coordinate his care."

"You can just give me a prescription for his medicine." Amelia moved around him.

"Let me ask about that," Reynolds said. "It's an intricate compound."

"Okay." Amelia started down the hall but he called her back.

"Give Emily two doses tonight. She's had a very hard day."

"She's fine. She's not upset," Amelia objected.

"Give her two, Amelia," he insisted. "Please. It will make me feel better."

"Yes, sir."

Amelia hurried down stairs but before she went to the kitchen to make the lunch trays, she slipped into the sitting room and took her cell phone out of her pocket. She hoped she wasn't too late.

CHAPTER 12

"Neurocentrism" or the view that human experience and behavior can be best explained from the predominant or even exclusive perspective of the human brain is a delusion according to authors of the book **Brainwashed: the Seductive Appeal of Mindless Neuroscience***...the authors chide the premature application of brain science to commerce, psychiatry and ethics. Most neural real estate is zoned for mixed-use development...–* LA Times Book Review

ॐ

"You can't blame her, Josie. You can't blame her one little bit. I mean that, of course, in the most practical sense. The woman is daft."

"Don't say that, Stephen. Just don't," Josie warned.

They were back on the main road headed to Kaunakakai boat harbor where the *No Problem* was docked. Josie's head was back and her lashes lowered but her eyes weren't closed. She watched the road, taking no pleasure in the scenery. She was exhausted and her hand was beginning to hurt like the devil. Her thoughts were at once immovable objects refusing to be prodded into some sort of order and stream of consciousness washing away before she could grab hold.

Hours

That word flashed in her brain. The hours in her life that she had been alone. The hours she had spent searching for her mother. For Hannah. For herself.

Minutes

Minutes she spent with Ian Francis. The minutes looking at her mother who had no idea that they belonged to one another.

Seconds

Seconds locked in silent conversation with Amelia Francis.

Josie turned her head to look out the window, half listening to Stephen. She appreciated his good intentions but she wished he would just give it a rest. He didn't.

"I didn't mean daft daft. Not like a loony bird daft. I mean she's not right in the head because it's physiological. You think she was perfectly normal before she took off, but there may have been signs." He shook his head, one hand left the steering wheel and he poked his temple. "Alzheimer's. Insidious, if you ask me. She lives in an alternate reality because of her body, not because she's crazy. Certainly it's not because she disliked you or likes that girl any better. Believe me. I know. I've seen it. There's no rhyme or reason and that's what you're looking for. Rhyme and reason, my lady. Pshaw!"

His hands were back on the steering wheel. That was that. Stephen Kyle had spoken. He laid out the whole situation and then wrapped it back up quite nicely, ready to put it out for the trash man and be done with it. Josie swiveled her head and looked at him. He was a funny man. Generous, kind, and brash and she was lucky to have met him. She knew she would believe that eventually.

"I hate to point this out, but you couldn't know anything about me or what I'm looking for."

Josie's didn't want to fight with him. She was weary. Her hand hurt. Her head hurt. She wanted to be with Archer or Faye or Burt or Hannah. She wanted to be with someone who understood her. That's what she was trying to tell Stephen Kyle. Instead she challenged him and he rose to it.

"Hah, you don't know who you're dealing with! I am Keoloko, and I know a great deal about everything, including you." He chanced a glance her way, which was not much of a gamble without the rain. "You're a looker and you don't even know it. You're a bit of an adventuress, considering how far you've come, but the way you talk about your man and that girl you're looking for you've got the making of a fine wife and mum yourself. You're a brave girl. If you weren't, you would be hysterical having seen a man kill himself. You would have gone back to Hermosa Beach and taken to your bed. You're kinder than you let on; a bleeding heart, actually. You would have handed Hannah off to the dole and been done with her if you weren't. You're a virtuous woman otherwise you would have seduced me by now and enjoyed the pleasures of my intimate company. Don't know you! Cripes!"

Josie chuckled despite herself and sat up straighter, feeling better for his nonsense. "You are hard to resist."

"And your resistance makes you a unique woman."

Stephen made a turn and the harbor came into view. The sun was low and the light rippled over the water. The white boats were startling against the blue. Some had tall sails and others fly away bridges and satellite dishes.

There was a lot of money in the world, and a lot of beauty, and none of it mattered when a heart was broken. Stephen pulled into a parking space marked Keoloko, ratcheted the emergency brake, and contemplated the silhouette of Maui on the horizon.

"It's a rough shake, Josie. I know that," Stephen admitted. "My dad had Alzheimer's before they really knew much about it. He forgot everything but me. Funny that."

"At least he remembered you," she answered.

"It's not as fine as it may seem. He was so angry. That's what Alzheimer's does. Makes a man angry and scared and he expected me to fix it. He was angrier still when I couldn't."

"What did you do?"

Stephen's body answered the question before he voiced it. He was lost and disheartened for a moment. Keoloko was gone, replaced by a good son remembering a dying father.

"I endured the slings and arrows. Not a word of love or gratitude he had for me. When he passed, his death left quite a void. Him going that way wasn't exactly how I imagined he would end his days."

"Finding my mother wasn't how I imagined it would be, either." She laughed sadly at the understatement.

"I know what you imagined." He nudged her a little, held out a hand as if he were showing her the future. "You saw her across a room, tears come to her eyes, you take her in your arms, she tells you she's been looking for you all these years. She tells you it's a miracle."

"Something like that," Josie agreed. "But then I realize all she would have to do was Google me if she wanted to find me. She'd get a bunch of hits and send me an email."

"Ah, so you're someone. Lovely. But let me finish," Stephen chided. "The heaven's open, a chorus of angels sing, the sun shines, and you and your mum shop and lunch."

"Everything except shopping. I'm not much into that," she laughed.

"I met Sophia Loren once, you know."

"Really?" This was a ridiculous tangent but she was game.

"Yes, indeed, I did. It was a beautiful evening in Rome. We were in the same restaurant. I crossed her path and was so taken with her magnificent bosom that I inadvertently spilled my drink. Sadly, not on her bosom."

"And this has something to do with our current situation?" Josie asked.

"Please, woman," Stephen complained. "Anyway, Sophia turned sideways so that I could get by. Which I did as gracefully as my divine body would allow. I said my thank yous, naturally. Those glorious breasts of hers brushed my chest. I went back to my table and ordered another drink."

"The point being?"

"The point being, Josie, you simply must accept certain things. I will never have the pleasure of putting my hands on Ms. Loren's bosom, but I was blessed to see said bosom up close. You were blessed to have your mum for the years you did, she can't help you get the other years back. You may never know why she left, or why she's in that place, so be satisfied with the glorious moment of seeing her up close. Like seeing Sophia's bosom, you must not lament what could have been. Make the best of the situation, I say."

"What is the best in a situation like this?" Josie asked.

"Bullocks!" Stephen exclaimed. "How am I supposed to know? But we'll figure it out. You'll stay with me and the girls. Certainly, that will lift your spirits."

"No. I'll be fine. Just get me back to the hotel," Josie said. "But thanks for the offer."

"A bad decision, if I may say so. Support is what you need, and I am here to give it. Free of charge and happily."

"And why would you do that?" Josie asked.

"I do it because island life makes you batty and something as interesting as this is a wonderful diversion. I do it because there's a chance you might forget that man of yours and come to me for comfort in the dead of the night. I do it because I have a soft spot for an honorable quest. I do it because now you are a Keoloko girl and no one messes with them."

Stephen patted her knee and then threw open his door. He came around to her. The door creaked a bit when he opened it. Josie took his hand and stepped down. Even in flats she was taller than he was but it didn't seem that way to her. The longer she knew him, the taller he stood. Stephen put his arm around her waist and gave her a squeeze.

"All right, then. Come on. The water's going to get choppy, and I swear I cannot bear to be on that boat if there's more than a ripple. As soon as I drop the keys with the harbor master, we'll go home, pour a stiff toddy, and I'll let you spend the rest of the evening wailing and swearing and weeping before I take you to your hotel if that's what you want."

"I don't weep," she assured him.

"May I suggest weeping is a more practical way to express yourself than putting your fist through glass." He gave her one more squeeze then let her go as they walked toward the harbor master's office. He opened the door for her. "The girls are dancing for an engineering convention. They won't make much off those cheap bastards. You can gnash your teeth while they're gone that way no one will ever know. Or, we'll go to the show tonight and watch the girls. You'll be enchanted. I guarantee it."

Stephen dropped the keys, gave his thanks to the young man at the counter, and they were at the boat a minute later. Josie stepped from the dock to the deck while Stephen dealt with the tether. She wandered to the stern while she dialed Archer. As much as she appreciated Stephen Kyle's help, it was Archer she needed to talk to. His phone rang four times. He didn't answer. She left a message.

I found my mother.

Josie considered erasing it. There should have been some more eloquent way to make such a momentous announcement. Or maybe she should have kept it all business, reporting on the circumstances, offering a tightly worded strategy for the next hours and days but that was impossible. She had no strategy; she didn't know what would happen in the next minutes much less days. Josie also realized that the message was exactly right since those were the words that had run through her mind when Emily looked at her. It had been so simple, so satisfying, during that microsecond of recognition and relief. *I found my mother.* Rage was what happened the second after that.

"Josie. Josie! Come here and put out your good hand, woman."

Josie pocketed her phone and looked over the side. Stephen held the rope, ready to toss it. She caught it awkwardly and stowed it. He had hold of the chrome railing and was ready to swing onto the deck when the man from the office hailed them as he ran down the dock.

"Bloody hell. Now what?" Stephen stepped down. Josie put her hip against the railing as the man came up to her.

"Are you Josie Bates?"

"That's me."

"Got a message for you." He handed her a piece of paper up and left with a quick wave and an even quicker 'aloha'. Stephen got on the boat.

"Bad news?" he asked as he tried to look over her shoulder.

"It looks like we've got a date tonight," Josie said.

"Ah, a three way. Lovely of you to include me." Stephen moved about, still trying to get a look. "That note isn't from Reynolds is it? Wouldn't fancy a three way with Reynolds."

"Nope." She gave him the paper. "I hope you know where that place is because my newly found sister wants to bond."

CHAPTER 13

"Where are you?" – Josie

"Just across the Oregon border. Hardly a town, but there's a place that serves good coffee. I'm running down a guy who took in Linda a few years back." – Archer

"Like Linda tells the truth." – Josie

"There's always a first time. What about you and this girl?" – Archer

"I don't know. I'll call after we talk to her." — Josie

"What's this guy's name again? The one who's hanging around?" – Archer

"You mean the man who helped me find Emily? Stephen Kyle." – Josie

"Okay." – Archer

"He's helping, Archer." – Josie

"I'm not worried. What's he look like? Stop laughing, Jo." – Archer

❦

Stephen Kyle put on his Sunday best to keep their date with Amelia Francis. His head and face were freshly shaved, his nails were buffed and the faint scent of coconut and mango clung to him. A shark's tooth dangled from a gold chain around his throat. There was another slim chain on his wrist and he was decked out in a purple silk Tommy Bahama shirt emblazoned with yellow hula girls that set off his white shorts.

Josie had changed into a short t-shirt dress and traded her gold studs for hoops, but still wore the flip-flops Stephen had given her. She felt better for the two hours she'd spent at the hotel. Showered and rested, she had searched the Internet for mention of Ha Kuna House and found none. Finally, Josie rested because there was no sense trying to devise a strategy before she heard what Amelia Francis had to say. She caught a cab back to Stephen's house.

"Don't you look elegant," he crowed when she arrived. "Even the bandage on that hand seems chic."

"You don't look too bad yourself." Josie returned the compliment.

"I can already see the desire in your eyes and we haven't even had our evening cocktail. Do try not to lose your head, Josie."

"I'll try to restrain myself." She raised her voice when he went to close up the house. "I talked to Archer."

"And what is he making of all this?" Stephen called back.

"He was pretty surprised. He's going to stay where he is and run down the missing persons report for me on my mom. That will have an official description of her, times and dates. He's also going to get a copy of her birth certificate and mine. That should be enough for Reynolds and anyone else who's interested."

"Ah, Josie, men at your beck and call. Between the two of us we should be getting your mum back to you in no time." Stephen locked the last window and picked up his keys. "Malia! Aolani! Anuhea! Get your lovely rears in gear. Time to go. Chop. Chop."

The girls came through the living room, Aolani giggling, Malia self-contained as always, and Anuhea after that. They looked like beautiful birds with their flowers and sarongs. Anuhea took the keys to the van, gave Stephen a quick kiss on the cheek, and said:

"Someone called about the Tiki bobble heads. A whole bunch of them were broken."

"Thank you, dearest. I'll see to it. Now, off with you. Josie and I are going out on the town."

He watched long enough to see the van make the turn onto the main highway before he settled Josie in the Porsche.

"Let's see what's on the little blond girl's mind, shall we?"

He stepped on the gas and they flew through the black Hawaiian night. Josie had no idea what Amelia wanted but she knew one thing: this was probably going to be the last smooth road she traveled for a while so she sat back and enjoyed the ride.

༺᠀᠀༻

Eugene had thought to call the girl on Ian Francis' phone one more time. He had been thinking about that for the last three hours while he worked on policy statements, made budget notes so Senator Patriota would appear to be well versed should he be asked why the Foreign Relations Committee spent three times what other senate committees did on administrative expenses. Of course, Eugene's figures had nothing to do with reality since there was no reason that their spending should be so high. The trick was to make it all appear to be reasonable.

Eugene had moved that phone – Ian Francis' phone – from one side of his desk to the other. It bothered him like a bratty child would, sticking its tongue out, daring Eugene to pay attention.

He was grateful that Morgan had brought it to him. In fact, for a brief moment, Eugene was almost giddy with the thrill that Morgan had come to him, but now having the thing on his desk was making him nervous; in the same way the spotlight being turned on the NSA was making him uneasy; and the new rounds of declassification made him anxious.

Eugene glanced at the time. It wasn't late, but he was tired. He tidied his desk. He sent an email to the staff reminding them that punctuality was expected. He sent a private email to the intern who was taking just a bit of a liberty by being too familiar with Ambrose. The last thing he did was pick up that cell phone, consider it, and then open his top drawer. It would be best for him to forget about this darn thing. In fact, in the morning he would send it back to the medical examiner's office and have it placed with the body. No one would ever claim either the body or the phone. They would eventually be disposed of and Eugene would laugh at how he worried.

Yet before he could put it inside it rang.

Eugene dropped it.

The screen lit up.

It rang again.

Fingers shaking, heart racing, Eugene picked it up, pressed answer, put it to his ear, and heard:

"Daddy?"

❦

The restaurant Amelia directed them to was a small neighborhood place called The Blue Hawaiian even though the clapboard was painted green. At one time it had been a family home but now there were tables on the front porch and tables in what had been a big living room. The walls blossomed with three-by-five cards on which people had written whatever came to mind: phone numbers, stick figures on surfboards, alohas from Sacramento to Boston, France to Australia. It seemed as if someone from every state in the union and every country in the world had passed through The Blue Hawaiian or else the staff made this stuff up during down times.

Tonight was not one of them.

When Josie and Stephen arrived the joint was jumping. Every table was filled, pork, fish, chicken and rice platters were flying over the heads of diners and landing on tables with record speed and with incredible precision; the plates were piloted by waiters and waitresses in khaki shorts, white t-shirts and sandals. There was music but Josie was hard pressed to figure out where it was coming from and curious about who had chosen the playlist. The Blue Hawaiian reminded her of Burt's.

Josie and Stephen had arrived ten minutes early to familiarize themselves with the turf before Amelia showed up. When a half an hour went by and she still wasn't there, they ate dinner each with an eye on the door. At nine-thirty they moved to the bar, a patch of real estate that passed for a lounge by virtue of the fact that it had four stools and a television mounted on the wall. Things were quieting down as they came upon the ten o'clock hour.

"I don't think she's coming," Josie muttered.

"Then we shall hunt her down tomorrow, weather permitting," Stephen assured her.

"I think we're banned from Ha Kuna House, in case you've forgotten." Josie took a taste of her wine.

"No pity party, Ms. Bates. I won't have it. Besides, it's not an easy crossing sometimes to get from Molokai. Perhaps Miss Amelia missed the ferry."

He chucked her shoulder with his and got part of the smile he was looking for.

"I will admit it's a shame we don't have any way to contact her. It would have saved us a bit of time. We could have been doing some homework just to get the ball rolling. Still, I will admit to a bit more than normal curiosity about her given what you told me."

Josie set aside her wine. She'd had more to drink since meeting Stephen Kyle than she'd had in the last six months. Between these two days, her trek to Washington and back, she was getting sluggish. She needed to pick up a volleyball game, a run, to sleep in her own bed – preferably with Archer. Truth be told, what she really needed was to wipe the world away for a while was to be lost in lovemaking with Archer.

Stephen raised a finger and ordered another drink for himself. Josie swiveled around and planted her elbows on the bar. Stephen remained face-forward, keeping his eyes on both the door and the ladies.

"What kind of homework were you thinking?" Josie asked.

"We might do a quick look on who owns Ha Kuna House," he answered. "The only interest I usually take in my clients is in their credit report and the timeliness of their checks. In this case, it might be interesting to know a little more about the place. Reynolds obviously has someone he answers to."

"Or he's just checking with a lawyer," Josie speculated. "That's what I'd do."

"It is odd that he runs such a wonderful house for a handful of people," Stephen noted lazily.

"You can have anything if you're willing to a pay a price," Josie said. "But that would mean my mother has money, and if she has money, where did she get it? My father's military pension ended when he died. I would have known what we were paying out, especially after he got sick. I handled all the bills then."

"Do you think your mum might have found someone else? Some rich man who pays for her keep?"

Josie shrugged with seeming nonchalance, but something inside cracked a bit. The idea of infidelity had always been there, unspoken between her and her father yet Josie refused to believe it. She wanted her pain to have meaning; she wanted Emily's disappearance to be about something bigger than a man.

"Service like that doesn't come free. I should know, now shouldn't I?" Stephen raised a brow. Josie raised one right back.

"So either my dad was paying for this which means he knew where she was all along and didn't tell me, or some other guy's been footing the bill. I hate to break the news, Stephen, but neither of those options make me real happy."

"Did you ever get a feeling he knew where she was?" Stephen asked just as the bartender put a drink on the bar behind him. Stephen caught it up. "Do you want something?"

"Water," she said, continuing with her train of thought after he left to get it. "No. I'd see him looking at her picture sometimes. A man doesn't look at a picture the way he did if he knew where to go get her."

"But you never asked. Ever?" Stephen pressed.

"I was thirteen when she left and he was overseas. What was I going to say? Do you think mom was tired of being left alone with me? Or, how about, dad, was she messing around with someone?" Josie laughed. "Not exactly dinner talk."

"What work did your dad do then? I mean after he left service?"

Josie shrugged, "He had one more deployment. It was short. I don't think his heart was in it. After that he just quit. I went to school; he got a job at a local gun store. He took care of me. He was a good dad."

"You didn't find that odd?"

"The job at the gun store?"

"No, his silence. When you were a grown woman, you would think he'd share something. If you had grown up a silly cow perhaps not, but you were a lawyer and quite a successful one," Stephen pointed out.

"You checked me out," Josie teased.

"It was the least I could do," Stephen laughed. "I must say you've been involved in some interesting things. Come out the other end rather nicely. Well done."

"Thanks." She lifted her water glass in a mock toast then cocked her arm and put her chin in her other hand. "I suppose I should have asked my dad straight out. We weren't like that. We were military. Take a hit; suck it up."

"Heavens, you make the English look like blubbering fools. Your upper lip is so stiff as to be granite," Stephen barked. He took a drink, and added: "Must have been bloody hard for you both."

"It was what it was." There was a beat in which Josie lost herself and then she shared the moment. "I wish he could have seen her once more. I would know what to do if I could have seen how he reacted."

Stephen said, "If caring is what you feel then you take one road. If you don't care, you go another."

"And if I'm just curious? Is that valid?" Josie asked.

"If you were simply curious you wouldn't be sitting there with your hand wrapped up like a mummy."

"I suppose," she mumbled.

"You must have some things left from your father," Stephen said. "Why not look through them."

"Maybe," she shrugged.

"Well, that's what I would do soon as I got home," Stephen scoffed. "Never know what you'll find in the attic."

Behind her, Josie heard the scraping of chairs. She looked over her shoulder. A large table was finishing up dinner and people were hugging one another goodbye. One young man put his arms around a pretty girl and pulled her close for a kiss. They were in their own world; Josie was in the real one and it had nothing to do with walking down memory lane or trying to remember what was in her father's boxes.

"Reynolds didn't say Emily has Alzheimer's. Did you notice that? He said they care for people with memory disorders *like* Alzheimer's."

"And?"

"And, what if Emily's problem can be counteracted by medication or therapy?"

"You don't think they've explored every option? They're a nursing facility, after all," he pointed out.

"Amelia isn't a nurse. You said yourself that once your guys brought a doctor out from Maui. That means there isn't a doctor in residence or one who visits on a regular basis. Twenty-some years ago options to treat things like Alzheimer's were limited. So she ends up in this place and everyone thinks there's nothing they can do for her and that's it." Josie turned on her barstool, touching Stephen's arm as if she could pull him along the road with her. "Ha Kuna House is like a fancy holding pen."

"How are you going to determine what it is or is not, what your mum's medical situation is or is not, without the records that Reynolds won't let you see?"

Behind him, the bartender tapped his shoulder and offered Stephen a Blue Hawaiian. "Brah-dah, got an extra. On the house."

"Many thanks, my friend." Stephen plucked up the tiny umbrella and nipped the cherry off the end before offering Josie the pineapple. She dropped her hand and shook her head. He set it aside.

"I can't stand the stuff myself. Do you know how much pineapple I see on a daily basis? Literally tons. Pineapple pops, pineapple dipped in chocolate, pineapple to ship back home to the bloody folks, crushed pineapple, pineapple slices, whole pineapples. People who come to the islands can't get enough of it."

He finished his litany, sucked up his drink through a straw and when he came up for air he was back to Emily.

"And what does it matter what's wrong with your mum? Do you think you have all the time in the world? What you're talking about – therapy and such – would take time which I doubt you have."

"I would make it," Josie answered.

"Truly, now? You'd give up your home? You'd give your man an ultimatum – move with me to Molokai on the off chance I can get my mother to remember who I am? And what about the girl you came to find? What about her?"

Josie couldn't argue with him there. In the last months Hannah was all she thought about; in the last hours she had been forgotten and Josie was ashamed.

"So, you're finding blood a bit thicker than water, are you?" Stephen nudged.

"What did you do in your last life, Stephen? Work for the Spanish Inquisition?"

Josie's snipe was friendly as she turned on the stool. Their knees were touching. She leaned close to him. "You're a little Barnum & Bailey, a little Hugh Hefner, but you're not just a sideshow are you?"

"I am not, but I find it beneficial to be considered such at times," he answered. "I'd begun to think there was nothing for me any longer but warm breezes, swaying palm trees, and a passel of lovely women passing through my home. Not a hard life, mind you, just one that goes too easily. I like a bit of excitement, intellectual or otherwise."

"Still not answering the question," Josie insisted. "Were you some Fortune Five Hundred CEO? A scientist. An inventor?"

"Nothing quite so exotic," he chuckled. "I was a solicitor in England. Had my own firm and dealt with international clients. I made a tidy little sum and invested well. But the law ceased to interest me at a certain point."

"What point was that?" Josie sat back and leaned against the wall.

"The point where my wife threw me out and my government decided to tax me at seventy percent. You're not much better in the U.S. Government always has its hand out, doesn't it? Still, there are shelters. I've covered my arse. I can afford to be a bit eccentric. Even got my bar ticket here so I don't have to deal with any shysters."

He offered his glass in a toast and Josie met him in the middle with her glass of water.

"Here's to success," Josie said.

"In all things that matter," Stephen answered.

Josie smiled. Her butt hurt. She needed to stretch her legs. She was disappointed and tired but the evening was not wasted. Archer and Hannah would like this man as much as she did if they could meet him. But liking had its limits. She was about to call it a night when Stephen listed slightly, raised his drink, and gave a nod in the general direction of the front door.

"Your mum's extra daughter has arrived."

Bernard Reynolds knocked on the cottage door. Johnson opened it and skipped the pleasantries.

"On the phone now."

Reynolds walked in and shut the door behind him. It had been hours since Josie Bates and Stephen Kyle disrupted what had been a pleasant day, but Reynolds still resented their intrusion mightily. Johnson was no happier, but it was hard to tell. He was a guy who just took care of business. No muss, no fuss. Not that there had been much to do before this, but Bernard had always assumed this was how Johnson would react to a crisis.

Reynolds went to the kitchen, opened the refrigerator and took out a beer. He wandered back into the living room and settled himself on the couch to listen as Johnson offered a few affirmatives and hung up. He leaned back in his chair and laced his hands behind his head.

"Well?" Reynolds asked.

"I think they forgot about us. The broad I talked to acted like she'd never heard of the House."

"That was the whole point. Keep calm and keep quiet." Reynolds splayed his legs, grabbed a pillow and held it over his midsection. He lounged on the couch keeping his eyes tight on his buddy. You could never be too careful even when you trusted someone.

"So, what do they want us to do?"

"Wait and see," Johnson said.

"That's it? They aren't sending anyone out?"

"Nope. I'd say you lucked out, my friend." Johnson moved to the upholstered chair that faced the sofa. He put his feet up on the coffee table. "You know, I used to think this was an old folks home for Vets same as the last dork. Difference is, I'm a little more curious than most. That will teach you to leave sensitive material lying around. You never know who's going to be looking over your shoulder."

"Yeah, well, I'm glad you know all of it. I thought it would be such a cush job out here all by myself in the middle of Hawaii. It's hard when you don't have someone to confide in," Reynolds mumbled.

"You made some tough calls," Johnson said.

"Good enough for government work as they say," Bernard agreed, secretly pleased with what appeared to be praise from Johnson.

"And you'll retire well. That pension's nothing to sneeze at," Johnson pointed out.

"There is that." Reynolds hugged his pillow closer and took a drink of his beer. He sighed. He pointed his can at Johnson. "That woman is going to come back."

"Negative. She's not to be on the grounds," Johnson said. "The folks will talk to the lawyers. Tell her you'll get a restraining order if that's what it takes."

"Oh, that's subtle," Reynolds guffawed. "I'm glad you're not in the front office. I told her the truth. It's a matter of protecting Emily's rights. That will hold her for a while. It's Keoloko I'm concerned about. Maybe we should cancel the account. You know, take away that contact point. He's the one who brought her."

"I didn't ask them but for what it's worth, I wouldn't. We still need supplies and that's pretty much the only game in town right now. Besides, it would look too reactive."

Reynolds took a deep breath and blew out a little tune. He tossed the pillow aside, and put his fingers on his closed eyelids.

"I could never have imagined this. I had no idea there were relatives around. Fifteen years and everything rolls along." He dropped his hands and looked at Johnson. "Now this. It's just not fair."

"Shit happens, Reynolds."

"I could quit. Maybe that's what I'll do. Just quit. Maybe I should never have taken the job in the first place. I just didn't really think it through. The pitfalls. The personal liability."

"I hear you, man," Johnson answered thoughtfully.

"I took this job because it was honorable, know what I mean? We were doing what was best for those people."

"I don't even know why they kept 'em around in the first place," Johnson countered.

"What else were you going to do?" Bernard grumbled.

"Kill 'em," Johnson suggested.

Reynolds stared across the room at Johnson and Johnson stared right back. It was a long minute before a grin split his face and he threw back his head and laughed.

"Good one. You had me going, Johnson."

Reynolds laughed, too, and shook a finger. He resisted the urge to wipe the ring of sweat at his hairline. There were times he just didn't get Johnson's humor and there were times Johnson just made him nervous.

"I'm just sayn' that it wouldn't have made much sense not to do everything in my power to keep this place going. They would have had to find a different place, move everything, and get it set up. And the trauma it would cause those poor people? Not worth it. And what were we looking at? Another five years at most and they'd all be gone, right? That's what the last doctor said."

"How would I know?" Johnson was bored with the conversation. "I think it will blow over, though. Our folks will probably let Emily go and you keep your buddies in the house. It will all be like it was. You're a good man, Bernard."

"Thank you, Johnson. I appreciate that. And you're probably right." Reynolds took a look around, buying a minute that would hopefully calm his heart. Every few minutes it just beat like the dickens. "Did they say when they'd get back to us?"

"A few days. A week maybe." Johnson got up. He was a tall man, fit and powerfully built. When Reynolds was very drunk and he squinted his eyes he thought Johnson looked like Iron Man.

"Okay, so that's the plan. I can hold Emily's daughter off for a week. Probably more." Bernard hesitated, trying to decide if he should tell Johnson the rest. In the end, he had to. "There might be one more problem. Ian Francis didn't come back with Amelia. She left him with relatives. I get it, of course. Poor kid probably couldn't take it anymore. But if anyone finds out about the house from him then I am majorly screwed."

"And how are they gonna find out, Bernard?"

"I don't know," Reynolds mumbled. He put his hands in his pocket and refrained from telling Johnson that he just wanted someone else to worry with him. "I always felt bad about him. He was such a nice guy. But he brought it on himself, you know. There was no choice, really. I did what I had to do."

"Collateral damage, my friend," Johnson commiserated. "We all follow orders."

"Still, if he managed to put a cohesive thought together. Whew," Bernard mused. "I mean, whew, a lot of people would be unhappy."

"Yeah, well, he can't and nobody will find out unless you get squirrely." Johnson got up and walked to the door and opened it. "Just keep doing what you're doing. Everything will be fine."

"Yeah, but I keep thinking—"

"I think you should go to bed and get some sleep."

Johnson gave the door a little shake and Bernard left, walking off into the night. Johnson stood there long enough to hear the door of Reynolds' house open and close. He looked at his watch and then at the main house. In the next five minutes he heard the sound of car wheels on gravel. The night girl arrived, late as always. Pulling a pack of smokes and a lighter out of his pocket, Johnson leaned against the doorjamb, lit his cigarette and inhaled deeply. Like clockwork, the night girl's buddy showed up. Johnson didn't think the night girl did anything but sit on her butt and gossip with the other girl every night. Lazily, he wondered if Bernard knew about this. He didn't see how the man could miss it. Johnson could set his watch by them. Then again, it was Bernard he was thinking about. The man was also a creature of habit. Once he was in for the night, he had no interest in what went on in the house. Once he was in his office, he didn't see what was going on right outside his window.

Johnson took one last drag and was glad to have lingered. The air felt good, the cigarette helped him think. He would hate to see this gig go down, that was for sure. He had a nice little side business going that was damn lucrative. If he was reassigned there's no way he'd ever have it this good again.

Johnson flicked his butt onto the ground and went inside only to turn around and go out again. He found his cigarette butt, picked it up, went back inside, and flushed it down the toilet.

He was, after all, a caretaker.

CHAPTER 14

Last year, in October, the congressman Denis J. Kucinich introduced in the American Congress a bill, obliging the American president to get engaged in the negotiations aimed at the ban of space based weapons. In this bill the definition of a weapon system includes: any other unacknowledged or as yet undeveloped means inflicting death or injury on, or damaging or destroying, a person (or the biological life, bodily health, mental health, or physical and economic well-being of a person) through the use of land-based, sea-based, or space-based systems using radiation, electromagnetic, psychotronic, sonic, laser, or other energies directed at individual persons or targeted populations or the purpose of information war, mood management, or mind control of such persons or populations... – Psychotronic Weapons website

ॐ

Amelia Francis looked nervous, lost, exhausted, and brittle. In short, she looked exactly the same way she looked at Ha Kuna House. The only difference between this Amelia and that one was that she was holding a purse and not a broom. She held that purse close and across her body. No woman did that unless there was something important inside.

"Don't cut her too much slack," Stephen whispered while they watched Amelia look for them.

"Great minds think alike," Josie said under her breath.

"Or fools seldom differ," Stephen shot back. "Oh-oh, she's pegged us."

He gave Josie a poke just as the two women made eye contact. The blond woman's jaw set. She walked directly them and then past then with hardly a pause.

"There's a table outside in the back."

Josie and Stephen exchanged a look. Stephen left some money on the bar. The bartender slipped it off and into his pocket as he watched them go. In the kitchen one of the cooks tossed his head up slightly. Amelia gave a sober nod in return. She pushed through the screen door. Josie was next. The door bounced wide enough off her open palm for Stephen to get through. As he pulled up the rear he bellowed, "Ah."

The women paused and turned around. Amelia gave Stephen a withering look; Josie a curious one. He stared back all wide-eyed and innocent.

"Sorry. One never quite gets over the feel of the night air in Hawaii. Like a caress, don't you think?"

They obviously didn't. They turned their backs. He followed, disappointed not to have charmed them.

The backyard of the establishment was nothing but a patch of dirt carved out of the tropical forest. It was partially lit by a bare bulb over the small porch and there were three steps that led from the noisy kitchen. Amelia flipped a hand, indicating a metal table that had at one time been part of a patio set. It was rusted and dented. There was a hole in the middle where an umbrella should be but someone had stuffed it with flowers that were long dead. Amelia took the chair on the left and Josie chose the one across from her, checking to make sure the seat was intact before she sat down. Stephen, not liking the looks of the third chair, went scrounging in the dark. He came back carrying a short wooden bench and was barely settled when Amelia began talking to Josie.

"I didn't expect ever to see you again after Washington." Amelia's voice was lovely, beautifully modulated, and confrontational.

"I didn't know you wanted me to find you," Josie said.

"It doesn't matter. You're here and it's pretty obvious you were surprised to see Emily, so I guess he didn't tell you about her. I don't know what you know."

"I know that you saw me in that hotel room. I know you could have stuck around and talked to the police. I know you put me through a lot."

Josie heard her voice rising and tightening. Where she was headed wasn't going to do anyone any good, but Amelia didn't mind. She was ready for a fight.

"You aren't the only one who had a hard time. My dad killed himself and I couldn't even stay with him. I was afraid to talk to the police."

"There was nothing to be afraid of unless what you two were doing was illegal. What's in those bags? Drugs? If that's it, then what did it have to do with me?"

Amelia shut her down with a quick, "It's not like that."

"Fine. Let's start at the beginning. Was he really your father?"

Amelia nodded. "Yes."

"You have a funny way of showing you care. He died in the street and now he's in the morgue in Washington. He'll be cremated and left in a jar because you didn't have the decency to claim him."

"Josie," Stephen warned. "Let Amelia speak."

"She could have spoken in D.C. She could have spoken at Ha Kuna House," Josie retorted, hardly believing what she heard coming out of her mouth. She couldn't help her anger, but she should have been able to control it.

"Josie," he warned again, clearly seeing what Josie did not. The girl's indignation started at her very core, shellacking her narrow backbone with steel. If Amelia walked they would have no connection to Ha Kuna House.

"You're not very much like your mother, are you?" Amelia said.

"I wouldn't know, and neither would you," Josie responded.

"Ladies," Stephen held out a hand to each of them. "You've both had shocks in the last little while. One parent lost, one found. I think it would behoove you to get a few facts on the table. What do you say? Think that will work?"

Amelia's eyes slid his way and Josie's lowered. When they looked at one another again, Josie nodded, but Amelia had some ground rules.

"I want him to go away."

"He stays," Josie answered.

"No, he doesn't," Amelia insisted. "He works for Reynolds. I don't trust him. Neither should you."

"Ho-ho, young miss. I work for myself, not Reynolds."

"If you want my help you take his, too," Josie said. Amelia glanced at Stephen, unconvinced and unsure of what to do. Josie pressed her. "Don't imply Reynolds is dangerous if you're not going to back it up. I'm tired, I'm not happy, and I am going to move forward with or without you."

"I didn't say that Mr. Reynolds was dangerous, but my father was worried about him." Amelia backpedaled.

"Then go to his boss," Josie said.

"Before I talk about him, I want to know if you're sure my father is dead. Positively sure he's dead."

Josie checked with Stephen. He offered a slight shrug, unsure what to make of any of this either.

"Why is it even a question?" Josie asked.

"Because someone called me from his phone. I just thought that maybe I was wrong. Maybe he's still alive and he pushed the button but he forgot to talk. I called back and someone answered and–"

"I saw his body," Josie interrupted. "Whoever called you, it wasn't your father."

"Maybe the medical examiner had his phone and was trying to track down a next of kin," Stephen suggested.

Amelia shook her head.

"They would have said so. And it was really late in Washington. That scared me so bad I almost didn't come. How do I know people aren't watching us? How do I know that phone is even in Washington? It could be anywhere. Anyone could have it. They could be here right now."

"Exactly what are you afraid of? You've got to be specific or we can't help," Josie said.

"I'm afraid that someone tried to keep my dad quiet about what he knew."

"Amelia!" Josie threw up her hands. "We were the only two people in that hotel room. Me and him, and I didn't kill him."

"I didn't say you did. I mean, whatever was done to him made him jump. He said it was the powder that was making them all sick." She drew her purse closer. "If they do an autopsy then maybe they'll find out something."

"The cause of death was pretty clear, so it's doubtful anyone will do an autopsy," Josie answered. "Do you have any idea what that stuff is?"

"No." Amelia shook her head. "I asked Mr. Reynolds. I told him I wanted to know what my dad was taking. He just said it was special to each resident and had to be compounded. I never got a straight answer. If the residents don't get it, some of them get really agitated. Emily hears voices and see things."

Josie leaned forward. This table was their campfire and Amelia Francis was spinning scary tales in the dark.

"Your dad drew a picture of a woman bound to a chair. Did you ever see Emily tied down?"

"No, but it doesn't mean it never happened."

"Sounds like general psychosis." Stephen made his pronouncement with such authority the two women stopped talking. They waited for him to go on, but his eyes widened and he raised his palms. "It was only a comment. Isn't that what everyone says? Oh, she's off her meds. She's psychotic. You know."

Josie rolled her eyes, but Amelia was energized.

"Exactly. He stopped taking his medication and then he tried to take Emily's away. But Emily started having nightmares without it and the night girl went to Mr. Reynolds and complained because she was making more work. I don't think he ever figured out that my dad had stolen Emily's medicine, but after that he did spot checks for a while to make sure we were dosing correctly."

"Why didn't you just give this stuff to a doctor?" Josie asked.

"Dad thought everyone was working for Ha Kuna House. He said we couldn't trust anyone."

"Classic paranoia," Stephen interjected again but Amelia was done with him.

"This isn't funny." She snapped before turning on Josie. "My father needed your help. He gave you what he thought was important."

"How did he even know I was Emily's daughter? How did he know where I would be?"

"I gave him a computer to keep him busy while I worked. He saw your picture and some reports about those hearings you were going to. He started making plans and putting things in a bag and then in a suitcase and he'd do it all about twenty times. He wouldn't let me take your picture off the computer. I kind of got it. I saw the resemblance to Emily. Your last names were the same. When he insisted that you could save Emily, I just got kind of caught up in the whole thing. Before I knew it, I used up all my savings on plane tickets and made up this story about going to see relatives." Amelia shoulders slumped. She sighed. "It was so stupid. I don't know what I was thinking."

"But that was it? All he had was a picture on the computer? You're sure Emily didn't tell him about me? You're sure she didn't remember me?" Josie pressed.

"I don't know! I don't know!" Amelia pounded her fists lightly on the table, catching herself before she screamed or beat a hole through the rusty top. "If it makes you happy to hear that Emily told him about you, then she did."

"Okay. I'm sorry." Josie caught one of Amelia's wrists and held it tight. "Are you good?"

She nodded. "Yeah. Sure. Look, I've taken care of my dad for four years, but the last six months have been hell. I don't sleep. I kept watch because he said they were coming to get us. Not just the residents. He said all of us were going to die."

"And who was it that was going to do you in?" Stephen asked.

"The government," Amelia answered.

Stephen didn't laugh and neither did Josie. Stephen because he was intrigued, Josie because she was remembering Ambrose Patriota's warning about the fringe who would have you believe that they, and they alone, knew what evil lurks in the world.

"That's just not so, Amelia. The government had nothing to do with your father's death," Stephen assured her.

"Whatever was done to him drove him to suicide," Amelia answered.

"Then find out who prescribed the stuff and what it was supposed to cure." Stephen threw up his hands. "Good grief, I cannot believe there is no doctor to talk to the poor souls in that place."

"I've tried every which way from Sunday to find out where it comes from." Amelia drew in a breath and pulled her lips tight together as she calmed herself. "I would sit up with my dad while he ranted. I'd try to figure out how to get him to take the medicine. I put it in his drinks and he'd figure it out. Then he wouldn't drink anything for days. It was the same thing with food. Nothing could have been weirder than the life we were living, so why not go to Washington? Why not try to find you? Why not try to save Emily? It seemed so important at the time. He could make everything seem so important."

"Balls, woman, you make it sound as if we've stumbled upon the Island of Doctor Moreau." Stephen snorted. Josie cast him a look. She had heard Ian Francis' voice, she had looked into his eyes, and she had gotten caught up in his madness. Stephen, though, wasn't buying any of it. "Please, Josie, this is just ridiculous. I'll grant the man was sick, but this girl has bought into his paranoia. I shall call it what it is. Par – a – no – ia."

"Look. I liked the way things were." Amelia looked straight at Josie. "I know you were hurt to find out that Emily thinks I'm her daughter but that is her world. She thinks my dad is her husband. We were happy thinking that. I didn't want anything to change. Emily doesn't know it has changed."

The apology and protestations and laments of Amelia Francis drifted Josie's way on a Hawaiian breeze but all she heard was the sad truth. Under the table Stephen Kyle put his hand on Josie's knee and gave her a squeeze. She took no offense at Amelia's outburst or Stephen's touch. It was painful to realize her mother had chosen another family and harder still to acknowledge Stephen's sympathy.

"All right," Josie murmured.

"I never saw any harm in it. I didn't know you existed until a few weeks ago. Maybe calling me her daughter was her way of remembering she had one."

"I said, all right."

Josie shot up and walked away, stopping when she stood at the edge of the circle of light. Crossing her arms, she rocked a little on the cushion of her flip-flops. Behind her Stephen reassured Amelia that Josie would be fine. Josie knew that was debatable: Fine came in all forms. She might look fine, she may act fine, but she never would be truly fine. Only Archer would understand that the mountain of hurt and regret and pain that was breaking through the crust of her soul made her not fine. Like a good soldier reluctant to join the battle but dedicated to the cause, Josie went back to the table.

"Okay, let's hear it."

Half of Washington D.C. slept and the other half were awake and watching. The ones who were awake patrolled the streets, were glued to computer screens, and listened in on telephone conversations. When mischief was detected, the watchers called other people whose job it was to stop it. Sometimes, mischief made their jobs easier because it came directly to them. Usually it didn't appear late at night, but there was always the exception and that night the exception was Eugene Weller.

He had put on his overcoat and braved the bad weather to get to a small building on a side street in a middle class neighborhood where some of the watchers worked. He doubted more than a handful of people knew the building housed a very specific unit of the NSA.

On the stoop, he took off his hat – a fedora that he was particularly fond of wearing in the fall – but didn't unbutton his coat. He held his identification up to an almost impossible to detect camera eye embedded in the grout between two bricks. The lock was disengaged. He went in. A security guard sat at a table reading a magazine. Without a word, Eugene handed him his identification again and the man indicated a pad on his desk. Eugene pressed his thumb onto it.

"Do you know where to go?" the man asked.

"Yes."

Eugene took the stairs to the second floor. He was at home in the silence and emptiness. Only one of the desks on the second floor was occupied and it was there that a young man worked diligently. Eugene walked right up to him and stood by his side but the young man kept working. When he was ready to talk, he laced his hands behind his head, looked at Eugene and said:

"Yeah."

Eugene took Ian Francis' cell phone from the pocket of his coat.

"I would very much like to know who this phone belongs to, a print of the histories: text, email, phone records. I would like to know where it was purchased. I would be especially grateful if you can pinpoint specifically where the user has been for, say, the last year."

The young man took the phone. "Cheap."

"Can you?" Eugene asked.

"Give me twenty," he answered.

Eugene went to the small coffee room down the hall. Without unbuttoning his coat he put a printout in front of him and highlighted items pertinent to his report. When he was done he had highlighted seventy-five that interested him out of four hundred and eight. He had also spent exactly twenty minutes doing his chore. The young man came in with a printout and handed it to Eugene. He waited neither politely nor impolitely as Eugene perused it.

"Thank you."

"Anything else?" the young man asked.

"No," Eugene answered. "I'll take it from here."

The man melted away. He was like Eugene's friends in college. Once they had served their purpose they were forgotten.

CHAPTER 15

"You want a smoke?" – Resident of Cozy Motel
"No, thanks." – Archer
"Nice place here." – Resident of Cozy Motel
"A little woodsy for me." – Archer
"That's funny. Don't get many funny people up here." – Resident
of Cozy Motel
"What kind do they get up here?" – Archer
"People who keep to themselves." – Resident of Cozy Motel

⤙∽⤚

Lydia Patriota's party shoes were very pretty. That night
she wore gold satin pumps, the four-inch heels studded
with Swarovski crystals. Those shoes had cost a fortune
and had been all but hidden by the sweep of her chiffon
gown, but Ambrose didn't care. The fact that he was
sitting with her sharing a brandy, her shoes glittering
against the carpet, her long dress gathered between her
knees like a farm girl astride a bale of hay, made every
penny he spent on her worthwhile. There wasn't a man in
the world that wouldn't have paid a king's ransom for the
pleasure of watching her. In fact, seeing her dressed this
way was almost more titillating than seeing her naked and
Ambrose knew why. Coming from an evening such as
they had, the scent of the men she had danced with still
clung to her, the envy of the women she spoke with still

trailed her, the delight she took in it all still flushed her cheeks.

"Don't you ever get tired, Lydia?" Ambrose asked.

"Do you?"

"No, but I'd think you would be bored by all this now."

"Never." She sipped her brandy and he could see the curve of her lips through the bowl of the glass balloon. She reclined on the satin sofa, put her legs on the back of it, and crossed them, ankle over beautiful ankle. Her lips glistened as she licked off the liquor. The hand holding her glass dropped to her side.

"So, what did we learn tonight?" Ambrose rested his head on the back of his chair and closed his eyes.

This was how they ended every evening since they were first together: Lydia talking, Ambrose listening. He valued her instincts and her insight. Some might have thought this simply a habit, but habit was something one did thoughtlessly. He and Lydia had no habits.

"Where shall I start?" Lydia laughed her throaty laugh. "Senator Bidly? Mona Kluger? How about the waiter who is now in possession of the money clip that fell out of Ambassador Hargerfeld's pocket?"

"You are sharp eyed, Lydia," Ambrose chuckled. "Start with Mona."

"That twit? How she got elected I'll never know," Lydia scoffed. "All right. Her gown was off the rack, her hair reeked of cheap hairspray, and her jewels were paste."

"Lydia," Ambrose chided.

"Girl stuff, honey, otherwise Washington would be boring with all you men strutting around like peacocks. I'm telling you, you all look the same to me after awhile."

"I hope there's an exception," Ambrose didn't open his eyes. He liked to feel her voice melting as thick as liquid gold into his brain.

"Only you, darlin'. You are the right peacock." She chuckled. "Well, Mona says she's getting plenty of grief from the good folks at home about all sorts of things. They're not happy with the immigration stall; they're furious about this new insurance crap; they're still harping on the lack of jobs. She's got five cities in her district going bankrupt and everybody's wondering why they can't get bailed out."

"Because the world has gone to hell in a hand basket is why," Ambrose answered as he opened his eyes. "There is no money. Besides, her districts are of no importance."

"She knows that, but she's looking for something, anything. She hasn't got one thing to crow about during her campaign," Lydia pointed out.

"And?"

"And she's thinking if you could just throw her a little bone she would be ever so grateful."

Up came Lydia's hand. She took a drink but she was lying at an odd angle and the brandy spilled into the indentation at the base of her throat. She swiped at it with one finger. When that didn't do the job she used the silk chiffon of her gown as if it were an ordinary napkin. Ambrose was enchanted the way one might be when a particularly beautiful dancer falters on stage and goes on without embarrassment.

"What does she want?" Ambrose asked.

"She wants you to talk to Tom Critchfield and have him shoot some transportation bucks her way. It wouldn't have to be much. A hundred million."

"And in return I would get what?"

"Her undying support for your presidential run."

Lydia turned her head. That gorgeous, perfectly formed face of hers wore an expression more suited to a gambler with a good hand than a trophy wife.

"I don't need it," Ambrose reminded her.

"True," Lydia agreed, "but she's part of the women's caucus and you know they've been having second thoughts about you."

"I don't know why," Ambrose objected.

"Oh, honey, everyone on the hill knows Sylvia Dias's people have done everything but bought a bed and spread her legs for you and you haven't given her a second look. She's the only one who has any viability as a VP and you act like she's the last person you'd invite to the prom. And don't you think I know, honey, that you had Eugene leak a short list two weeks ago? Undisclosed source, my ass. There wasn't one woman on it even as a nod."

Lydia threw her legs over the side of the sofa, shot the rest of her brandy, put the glass on the table, and planted her feet.

"I don't know why you won't do it. Far be it from me to lobby for someone just because we are the same sex. Most women in politics are idiots, but it only makes sense to look at a one for the ticket. You'd make history with a woman VP and it's not like a woman could hurt you, Ambrose. Every damn poll shows you winning by a landslide. Why not bring a honey along for the ride?"

Ambrose laughed, "That is precisely why I will not choose a woman. I do not want to make history because of my running mate."

He pulled at his black bow tie until it was loose. No one wore a tuxedo like Ambrose Patriota and even at his age no one looked better discarding one, but his wife was not to be seduced.

"Sylvia Diaz is perfectly acceptable, but she's young. She'll have her time. There's someone else I want," Ambrose said.

"Blazes, sugar. You've decided?" Lydia's eyes widened and Ambrose was thrilled to have surprised her. "Come on, honey, who is it?"

"I will not divulge the name until I am positively sure and that includes talking with said person."

"Not even a pronoun to give me a hint. Now that is intriguing, Ambrose." Lydia slipped off her shoes. She wasn't wearing any stockings and Ambrose wondered if she was wearing under things. She got off the couch and her gown cascaded to the floor. She walked over to him and put a hand on his face. "I dare say I love a challenge. Let's see if I can't coax it out of you upstairs."

"It will do you no good." Ambrose took her hand and kissed her palm. "I will tell you this. Mona was going to get the money from transportation anyway. This way she'll think it's my doing. You call her in the next day and a half and breathlessly tell her that you think I'll be able to swing it for her. Will that keep you happy for a bit?"

"A day or two maybe." She withdrew her hand. "I love that people think I have that much sway over you."

"But you do, my dear. Yes, you do," Ambrose stood and reached for her. She melted into him.

"Just not enough when it comes to the big stuff like who will be your running mate." Lydia's beautiful brow furrowed but it was only because she was truly concerned for her husband. "You don't want to lose too many friends with a dark horse, Ambrose."

"In Washington friends are easily lost. It's alliances that are important. I'm confident in those," Ambrose reminded her. "You, my dear, are my only true friend."

"Honestly, Ambrose, if I could package you I'd be a rich woman."

"You are already a rich woman." He switched off the table lamp. His hand had just gone around her waist and they were headed upstairs to find out about her lingerie or lack thereof when the doorbell rang.

"A bit late," Ambrose groused and sent her up without him. "I'll take care of it."

The bell rang again, annoying Ambrose even more that whoever it was at this hour didn't have the decency to be patient. When he opened the door his irritation grew two-fold.

"Eugene?"

☙◦❧

"My dad taught college, but then he got offered the research job at Ha Kuna House so my parents moved here before I was born. My mom was a piece of work, so I just took off after high school. I finally came home and found my mom gone and dad pretty much living at Ha Kuna House. He was like the others, just wacko. My dad didn't deserve to be alone. He was always good to me so I stayed."

"Who paid for his placement?" Stephen asked.

"Mr. Reynolds told me it was part of his insurance and I should just leave him as long as he was happy. I didn't think he was, though. The whole place didn't seem happy. It seemed kind of – I don't know how to explain it – like I was always in some alternate reality."

"It's convenient that you got a job there," Josie noted.

"It was smart," she answered. "I didn't have anybody beating my door down wanting to hire me because I was a high school graduate. Dad still had title to the house near town. I thought he might get better if he lived with me. Dad and Emily spent their days together, Mr. Reynolds pretty much just kind of left everyone alone, and dad and I went home at night. Some days felt perfect and some were scary and some were boring. I didn't have anyone else. Do you understand?"

Josie understood the path Amelia had wandered down all too well. They both lived with their fathers while Emily stood between them. The woman was a placeholder in their lives, a point of reference.

"What a waste," Josie murmured. "It would have been so easy to bring Emily home."

Stephen cleared his throat. He was uncomfortable sitting with these ladies as they paddled down the River Styx. They needed to get ashore and find a point to all this.

"Amelia, sweetie, do you know who was responsible for Emily's commitment or anything specific about her condition? I think we'd be better served by knowing that."

"I don't," Amelia shook her head.

"You don't seem to know much, do you?" Josie noted.

"Listen, I used everything I had to get my dad to you: all my vacation time and all my money. I think about it now and it was bizarre; all that planning and secrecy just to give you some pathetic stuff. He rolled and unrolled that bag a hundred times. He said he knew they'd be looking for it. Stupid."

Amelia dropped her chin and let her head swing back and forth. Her voice cracked. Josie thought she looked like some nocturnal animal making its way through the dark looking for a place to hide. But when Amelia looked up that night creature was all teeth and claws, ready just in case she found something to dig into.

"You can't be all passive aggressive like it was our fault that you and your dad didn't know about Emily. For all I know your father put her in there. What do you think about that?"

"My dad wasn't even in the country when she disappeared," Josie objected.

"Doesn't matter now. Does it?"

"I'm not accusing you of anything," Josie countered.

"And I'm not apologizing for anything. My dad is dead and Emily is alive. You should be grateful."

Amelia grabbed her purse and took out an envelope. From inside the restaurant came the sounds of running water and dishes clattering. When Amelia spoke again, her voice was close to a whisper.

"There are only four people in residence now. Only Emily can still be engaged. There's me, and another full-time aide, and a caretaker who lives on site. There's Mr. Reynolds, of course. He lives in a larger house out back."

"One person on each shift to take care of four sick people?" Josie asked.

"It's a better ratio than most nursing homes," Amelia assured her.

"Who owns that place?" Stephen asked. "Reynolds?"

"My paycheck comes from a place called MPS. It's headquartered in Virginia."

Amelia slid the envelope into the middle of the table. Stephen picked it up. He took out the pages inside, perused them and handed them off to Josie. She scanned the top sheet and then counted quietly as she flipped through them.

"Twenty-five resident admission forms." Josie raised her brow and pursed her lips. "So?"

"There are twenty-five forms. Twenty-one of those people are dead. I didn't think anything of it, but my dad wouldn't let it go. He was obsessed with their deaths. He kept saying they were disappeared on purpose. He didn't say these people were killed. He didn't say they died. He said they were disappeared."

"But couldn't that sort of behavior be part of his illness?" Stephen asked.

"That's what I thought, but then I realized that in all the time I worked there I never saw a visitor. I never took a phone call for a resident. There were no letters. We never got new residents. Half the time Mr. Reynolds was at his house because there wasn't much to do in the main house.

"One day I was in the office when everyone was sleeping and I was bored out of my skull. I know I shouldn't have, but I went into the files. I figured if I knew something about the residents I could talk to them, maybe jog their memories. Those forms were all I found."

Suddenly, there was a bang from inside the restaurant. Three heads turned. Stephen stood up, straddling his little bench. Amelia put her hands on the arms of the chair as if she was ready to launch. Josie collected the papers and put them under the table just as the screen door flew open and the burly cook threw a skinny kid down the stairs. The kid yelled something then scrambled up only to fall again. They all held their breaths, anticipating that he would come their way. When he disappeared round the corner of the building, when the screen door slammed shut again, they relaxed. Josie brought out the papers and spread them in front of her.

"These aren't even proper admission forms." She pushed one back at Stephen. "There is no contact information, no social security numbers, no next of kin, no personal information of any kind, even about their medical history. There's just a name and date, time of admission, and a phone number."

"Did you ever call the number?" Stephen asked.

"No," Amelia admitted. "I didn't know who I would be talking to. It might be someone who would report me to Mr. Reynolds or sue me or worse."

"But you made copies," Josie said. "There had to be a reason you did that."

"At first I was just curious, but then I got spooked. No one was admitted between 1973 and 1987 except Emily. See? January, 1987 and after that no one."

"She disappeared in August of 1986. Where was she for those six months?" Josie wondered, before addressing Amelia directly. "Do you think she ran away with your dad?"

"No, my mom and dad were just married then," Amelia said. "And look, there's no admission form for my dad. There's no paperwork on him at all and he was living there for a long time," Amelia countered. "Even if they considered him an employee and took over his care out of gratitude, there should be something."

"Your dad is more than a little bit of a mystery, isn't he?" Stephen chuckled even though he was befuddled. "If what you say is true and the dates on these forms are correct, and we're assuming all these people were adults when they came to live at the house, that means by the late eighties they were all very old. Is it so odd that there would be deaths?"

"But when they passed away they were just gone," Amelia insisted. "I never heard about a funeral. There isn't a cemetery on the grounds. I never saw a mortuary car or a hearse. Once I asked where their belongings were in case anyone came looking and Mr. Reynolds said he sent everyone's things to storage. Don't you think that's weird?"

"We can't make a judgment if we don't know the operating procedures," Stephen said.

"My father couldn't bear the idea that Emily would simply disappear one day. That's what this is all about." She looked from Stephen to Josie, tired and ready to get on with things. "Look, I totally get that what we did seems nuts. I've asked myself a thousand times if I'm insane, too, but then I look at those papers. I didn't know most of those people but Emily is real, then you were real, so I figure my dad couldn't have been a total lunatic."

Once more the screen door opened but this time the cook called out to Amelia that they would be closing. She called back her thanks and told him they wanted nothing. After that, no one at the table spoke and no one contemplated Ian Francis' insane legacy more solemnly than Josie. She was thinking about Ambrose Patriota's contention that a portion of the citizenry lived in their own reality, causing harm, creating turmoil, living in shadows, and communing with spooks and ghouls who walked among us.

"I don't know what you expect me to do," Josie murmured.

"You owe him something." Amelia's words came out on a wistful sigh. "Without him, you never would have known about Emily."

"Amelia, your dad was a troubled man." Josie picked up the papers and tapped them on the table until they were neat and even again. She put them in front of Amelia. "I will always be grateful that he led me here. I will always be sad that your dad died without knowing I found Emily. Above all, I understand your dedication to him but you are going to waste your life chasing his demons."

"The way you wasted yours looking for Emily?" Amelia asked. "I mean, she could have been dead for all you knew. Were you ever going to give up?"

Josie shook her head. "I would have wondered about her until my dying day, but my life had moved on. Yours should, too."

"So my dad is gone like those other people? Is that okay with you? I mean what if it was Emily?"

"The girl has a point." Stephen looked at Josie and then gave Amelia a sympathetic smile.

"If something is wrong at Ha Kuna House wouldn't you want someone to save Emily if they could?" Amelia pressed.

Josie was not immune to her pleas. When she was younger, she had been so sure Emily was just around the corner. The years went on, the corner was never turned. Amelia was in the first throes of her crusade. Josie needed to put her energy into her own family. Emily was right in front of her. She could live without knowing what had happened all those years ago. What she needed was to get her mom home. That would be Josie's closure. Sadly, Amelia would have to find her own. Still, Josie knew there was something she could do to help. The question was what.

While Josie considered her options, Amelia took the papers and put them back in the envelope. When she was done, she looked up and Josie was reminded of the old woman in that Washington alley: homeless, alone, shocked to find herself sleeping in a heap of trash, stunned to find herself a piece of trash. That's when Josie made her decision.

"I think you should get back to Washington, claim your dad's body, and bury him. I'll pay for it all." She reached into her purse, took out a card and wrote her private number on it. "You can reach me here. I don't want you staying at The Robert Lee Hotel again. Send me the receipts for the trip, the mortuary, whatever you need. It's the least I can do, but that's all I can do."

Josie pushed back her chair. Stephen took his cue and stood up. Amelia still sat where she was, defeated, too tired to beg any longer. Josie put her hand on Amelia's shoulder, bent down, balanced on the balls of her feet, and looked Amelia in the eye.

"I'm going to be taking my mom home with me. No one will be able to hurt her."

"She'll always think I'm her daughter. That will never change," Amelia muttered.

"I will make it change."

Amelia blinked. She looked as if she could barely hold herself upright. Josie's hand dropped from Amelia's shoulder to her hand. Her fingers were cold and shaking.

"You need some rest. You need to put this in perspective," Josie offered.

"We're both daughters. I don't know that there's much more to say than that."

Josie took a deep breath and withdrew her hand. Amelia still clutched the envelope and Josie let her eyes rest on it. Twenty-five people. Twenty-one of them were dead. What was she supposed to do with that? Her plate was full: Hannah, Archer, her practice, and now Emily miraculously in the mix. Amelia was pushing it all aside and demanding space for her and her father. That this girl may be part and parcel of his insanity made it all the sadder.

"Go away from here, Amelia," Josie said as she stood up.

Stephen gave Amelia a kiss atop her head and then they both walked away leaving the girl to ponder her future at a rusted table in the middle of a patch of dirt surrounded by paradise. When they were almost at the car, Stephen asked:

"And what are you going to do, my girl?"

Josie took a few more steps, yanked open the car door and just before she got in and slammed it shut she said:

"I'm going to court. Want to come?"

෨෨෯

"This is unacceptable, Eugene. This is really unacceptable." Ambrose paced in front of Eugene Weller who, for the first time in his career, did not allow his gaze to follow the senator's every move. He sat on the couch like a dunce, mortified by his teacher's ridicule. He was sick to his stomach but the senator didn't let up. "This is nothing, Eugene, and you know that. You panicked because of a list of documents released to the archives."

"There are standing requests by the public for anything referring to those programs, Senator—" Eugene began but Ambrose silenced him.

"It is a small public, Eugene. Miniscule. The general public has far more to worry about than things that happened three decades ago."

"But the phone—" Eugene started once more only to stop as Ambrose threw up his hands.

"A dead man's cell phone that, I might point out, is in your possession. Put it in a drawer. Throw it away. Never think about it again. I don't know why you are fixated on this, but I promise you, if you keep this up, your concern will become a self-fulfilling prophecy."

Eugene twitched. He colored a less-than-pleasing shade of burgundy. Ambrose Patriota's exasperation made no sense. Eugene had meticulously created a timeline and presented multiple scenarios of the impact on Senator Patriota should this information find its way into the public domain, but the senator refused to even look at it.

"The phone was purchased in Hawaii. On Molokai. The woman who answered is Ian Francis's daughter. His daughter, sir."

"And my children have cellphones, Ambrose countered. "You cannot read any implied action into the fact that she answered it or that she called you back. You are the one poking at a hornet's nest, not her. She might be wondering why someone had her father's phone, called her, and did not speak. And, if she is in Hawaii, then she has already chosen not to pursue the matter of her father's death. That means she does not want to call attention to it anymore than we do. That also means that she probably has no idea what her father was up to. Perhaps now she's rethinking everything because of you."

"I realize that now. That was not wise." Eugene symbolically turned away from Ambrose, hunching his shoulders, baring his back. He deserved each stinging lash the senator wanted to lay upon him. "I was surprised and I reacted. I wanted to cover my bases so that none of this came back to you."

"Have you thought that this is not a part of my history that I wish to revisit? Have you?"

Ambrose shoved his hands deep in his pockets and rocked on the back of his heels. Lydia was probably fast asleep. The evening was ruined and he resented it, but he also knew that he was no better than Eugene. He was overreacting and needed to calm himself.

"Eugene, you have been very thorough and I appreciate that. I also appreciate the spirit in which all this has been undertaken, but this is only a problem if we make it one. What was done is done. Shred that information, go home, sleep, and come to work tomorrow with your mind refreshed. Look forward not backward, Eugene."

"You're correct, of course," Eugene muttered.

Ambrose sighed. He sat down next to Eugene. The boy was like a son constantly striving for favor and knowing he would always prove inadequate, or a dog eager to please but having no idea that the master had grown tired of the same old tricks. The older man put his hand on Eugene's narrow shoulder.

"What is this, Eugene? Really? Are you concerned that I won't need you after the election?"

"The thought never crossed my mind, senator." That Eugene was shocked was evident; that Ambrose didn't care was also evident.

"You are only helpful to me if you are level headed," Ambrose warned.

"Helpful?" Eugene repeated, hardly believing his ears.

"Now more than ever I need to you to be that, Eugene. And, if you become angry with me and think you can use this against me for your own purposes—"

"Never, sir," Eugene breathed, sickened that the man could think such a thing much less speak it.

Ambrose smiled the smile that Eugene so admired, the one that won over anyone who was graced by it. The senator patted the younger man's back, leaned just a bit closer, and lowered his voice to an intimacy Eugene had never heard before.

"Of course you wouldn't, but I had to ask. We think we know one another but it is easy to make assumptions of loyalty. Sometimes one must be clear."

Eugene looked at the hand on his shoulder. A few hours ago he would have taken it, kissed the ring on Patriota's finger in a show of fealty, but now he was off his stride. The conversation had taken a turn that was unfathomable. Then Ambrose squeezed his shoulder and the warmth of that gesture, the weight of his hand, finally worked its magic.

"Senator," Eugene began, "I–"

"What Eugene? What?" Ambrose's hand fell away and the expression of affection was replaced with one of pique.

"I should go." Eugene stood up. "I am sorry."

Ambrose stood, too, all traces of his impatience gone.

"That is good. Just remember, in politics a situation becomes a scandal only if fed by alarm. I think the fact that a man died is bothering you. Isn't that what prompted all this?"

Eugene nodded even though that was not how he read the situation at all. It was that Ian Francis had waved a flag before he died and Eugene knew it for what it was: a battle cry directed at Ambrose Patriota.

"Well, put it out of your mind. We have a presidency to win. We have great things to do. Do you understand?"

"I do," Eugene whispered.

"Good. Let's not talk of this anymore. Can we agree on that?"

Ambrose had somehow turned Eugene toward the door. It was open. Once again he was being handed his coat. Once again he was on the street looking at the closed door to the senator's house but now he was warm despite the wind and the chill. He had the confidence of the greatest statesman ever to walk the earth and he would prove to him that his faith was not misplaced.

Much later Eugene would realize that something was wrong. At that moment, though, the feeling of dread was so deep inside him that it could be mistaken for a bit of indigestion or overexertion. He went back to his apartment, undressed, and climbed into bed intending to sleep but he could not. He was not convinced, as Ambrose seemed to be, that Ian Francis had not opened up a can of worms. Eugene finally drifted off only to have his dreams haunted by facts, figures, and faces. It was fertile ground to grow the seed Ambrose had planted and the plant was blooming with tiny buds of discontent and disappointment in his senator.

In his home, Ambrose was also having thoughts about Eugene. He went to his office and made notes to pass along to Norma. She was such a lovely, efficient woman. Unlike Eugene, Norma followed directions without hysterical extrapolation of Ambrose's motives. When he was finished, Ambrose went upstairs, undressed, and got into bed alongside Lydia. He rolled on his side. She took his hand.

"What did Eugene want?" she mumbled.

"To be important," he said back.

CHAPTER 16

"Still here. Portland PD got back to me. There's nothing on Hannah or Sam Idle. I'll give it one more day, and if it doesn't pan out I'm heading home. Sorry on the missing persons. Still running it down, babe. Let me know how it goes in court. Going to get something to eat." – Voice message, Archer to Josie

෨෧

Stephen parked his car in front of the old courthouse in Wailuku, Maui. It was a charming, one story wooden structure distinguished from others of the same era by the two columns framing the doorway. The columns were fat and ornate and as out of place as a formal gown at a luau. In the old days the supports on the little courthouse must have looked intimidating to the Hawaiians; today they seemed dearly archaic in the shadow of the giant block of the high-rise hall of justice. It was the high-rise that was Stephen and Josie's destination.

In a nod to the seriousness of their business, Stephen had donned an exquisitely cut blue suit with only the faintest hint of a grey pin, a white shirt, and red silk tie. The jacket had been neatly hung in the back of the car for the short ride. He retrieved it and then reached for a briefcase fashioned from oxblood leather. Stephen pushed his sunglasses up his nose. His hairless head shone in the Hawaiian sunshine, his substantial figure looked almost sleek in his well-cut suit. He clearly relished dusting off the bar ticket he had earned when coming to live on the island. This was, he said, like getting back on a horse.

"You clean up nice." Josie gave him the once-over.

"I'll wear a tux to your wedding and you will see just how marvelous I can look. Then you'll leave your man at the altar and we'll run away to Bora-Bora for a honeymoon. It will be a luscious scandal."

"If you come to the wedding don't forget to bring the girls," Josie said. "Not that it wouldn't be entertaining to watch you dance."

"We will all dance at your wedding, including your mum. But first we have to spring her properly."

They set off at a clip, across the lawn, into the building, past the permanent demonstration site of the Ohana Council whose members fought for Hawaiian sovereignty, and up to the third floor where Judge Mohr waited for them. He was on the bench but off the clock. The judge was a small man with a big smile. He wore a polo shirt open at the neck and was engrossed in a magazine that he set aside the minute they arrived.

"Come in! You're punctual, Stephen."

The judge waved them in with one hand and reached for the robes on the back of his chair with the other.

"Ah, Your Honor, I wouldn't keep you waiting knowing how full your calendar must be." Stephen passed the bar and Josie followed him through. "I'd like to present my client, Your Honor. Ms. Josephine Bates."

"Aloha, Ms. Bates. Pity you've come to the islands on business. The weather is perfect today. No one should be inside after all this rain."

He had both arms in his robes and was dealing with the snaps that ran from chin to knee as he spoke. He flashed a grin but Josie wasn't sure if it was directed at her or simply an expression of pleasure that he had managed the snaps correctly.

"I'll bet you're trading well, Stephen. I hear we've set a record for tourists this month. We won't have a slice of pineapple left to us for Thanksgiving if this keeps up."

"I'll set aside a few for you and your family. Just tell me where to send them." Stephen put his briefcase on the plaintiff's table, and unbuckled the straps as Josie took her seat.

"If only," Judge Mohr sighed. "Even a gift of pineapple is unseemly between us. There are way too many rules, Stephen."

"That's what keeps a poor attorney in business and a judge busy. All of us running about, trying to figure out what the lawmakers meant when they wrote the blasted rules."

Josie tried not to fidget as she listened. If this had been Los Angeles, they would have been rushed through to make way for a hundred other attorneys cooling their heels as they waited for their time in front of the bench. Here, *bumbye* was the rule not the exception. The court would get to business when it got to it so she relaxed as the judge and Stephen exchanged news of Mohr's children, the expected height of the waves that day, and the health of Stephen's girls. The court clerk was called in. She also indulged in pleasantries with Stephen until, finally, he became Mr. Kyle and Judge Mohr morphed into the jurist he was. The hearing regarding the guardianship of Emily Baylor-Bates began with Stephen

Kyle doing what Josie would have done if only she were licensed to practice in the state.

"Your Honor has already read the filing, but for purposes of your housekeeping I would like to present you with a copy for your reference during these proceedings."

With a flourish, Stephen produced said paperwork and passed it along. Judge Mohr held it not quite at arm's length and gave it the once over.

"Everything is in order, Mr. Kyle. Many thanks." He set it aside in favor of a green folder, tattered around the edges and unimpressive in bulk. "You put my clerk through some hoops to find this. It isn't much, but at least we have a starting place."

"I apologize for the extra work, but I assure you that the guardianship of Emily Baylor-Bates is well worth it. My client, her daughter," Stephen waved at Josie with considerable pomp, "has spent almost twenty-seven years searching for her mother, and it is within this court's jurisdiction to reunite this family. Emily Bates is currently residing at the Ha Kuna House on Molokai, Judge."

"I am not familiar with the place," Judge Mohr said.

"I doubt there are many people on the islands who are. It is a privately run concern for people of certain limited mental capacity," Stephen answered.

"A nursing home?" the judge inquired.

"Of sorts, although there are no medical facilities on the premises. There a minimal staff of caretakers," Stephen answered.

"A care facility." The judge nodded.

"Whatever you wish to call it, Emily Bates has been a resident there in excess of fifteen years. This is known only because the current director informed us that she was a resident when he arrived. We believe the date of her commitment was January of 1987, but that is not corroborated with any certainty. We do not know who requested this action, or why commitment was deemed necessary, or why it appears that no effort was made to locate her family who were well and able to care for her all these years.

"We have faith that you will advise us on all points now that her file has been located. We will seek that the current order be voided and that Ms. Josephine Baylor-Bates, her daughter, be appointed guardian ad liteum. We further ask that all records, including, but not limited to, Emily Bates' medical records, be released to her daughter immediately and that she be provided with the name of any and all doctors including psychologists and psychiatrists who have attended Emily Bates. This is requested so that Ms. Josephine Bates can make a determination about her mother's ability to travel and what special care might be needed once guardianship is transferred."

"Thank you, Mr. Kyle. That is an excellent summary of your motion. Almost word for word what you have written to the court and the court has familiarized itself with." He turned his attention to Josie. "Are you a resident of the islands, Ms. Bates?"

"I am not, Your Honor. I live in Hermosa Beach, California."

"And what is your profession?" he asked.

"I'm an attorney. I have a small private practice," she said.

"Do you have a family? Children?"

"I am going to be married soon. It will be my first marriage. I have no biological children," Josie answered. "I have a ward who recently turned seventeen."

"She resides with you?" Judge Mohr asked even as he made notes. He looked up expectantly even though Josie hesitated only for a millisecond before answering: "Yes."

This was not a lie; it was only the simplest answer. There was no need to complicate things that were already complicated enough where Hannah was concerned.

"And now you wish to also be responsible for your mother. When was the last time you saw her?" he asked.

"When I was thirteen," she answered.

"Was there any contact between you all these years?"

"No, Judge," Josie said.

"Who did you live with after your mother's disappearance?"

"My father. He is deceased," Josie responded.

"And you had no indication about what might have happened to your mother? For instance, do you believe that her disappearance had to do with marital difficulties? Abuse of some kind, or possibly that another man was involved?"

"Definitely not to the first and second question, Your Honor. As to the third, not to my knowledge."

"So, in your recollection, your relationship with your mother was not strained all those years ago. You would characterize it as a good relationship?" he asked.

"I would, Judge," Josie answered. "Yes, a very good relationship."

"And do you plan to have the lady in question live with you?"

"I do."

"You are financially and emotionally able to care for her?" he asked.

"I am," Josie answered. "She won't lack for anything."

"Well, then. All this is well and good on the surface." He put his pen down. "Since you are an attorney, Ms. Bates, you understand that the court must consider many things before a ruling is made. Not the least of which is the current status of this woman and her history. Unfortunately, the record is not going to guide me in any significant way."

He opened the court file and pulled out a piece of paper.

"The only thing in this file is the order of guardianship making her a ward of Ha Kuna House. There is no indication that she has family, what her mental and/or physical conditions were at the time of her commitment, or who requested it. It is very possible she was lucid enough to request it herself which, of course, would throw a wrench into your petition. If Emily Bates wished to commit herself, then we would need her to testify that she now wishes to change her status and assign you guardianship. That would be very unusual indeed. As you can imagine, if the lady were coherent enough to understand these proceedings, wouldn't she prefer to be independent of a guardian? So, what we have here is a duly authorized order of guardianship signed in January of 1987. Where did you last see your mother?"

"At Fort Hood in Texas. We were stationed there. My father was in the service," Josie said

"Molokai is a long way from Texas," the judge noted. "Was she ill previous to that date?"

"Not that I know of, Your Honor."

"And how did you find her at Ha Kuna House? Well?"

"Well cared for," Josie answered.

"And her response to your appearance?" Judge Mohr probed.

"She didn't know me, Judge," Josie admitted. Beside her, Stephen moved. He raised one hand, one inelegant finger, and cleared his throat.

"The women had very little time together before the administrator felt it best that we leave, Judge. It was a rather upsetting discovery for Ms. Bates, as you can well imagine. Mr. Reynolds, the administrator, was concerned for the welfare of Emily Bates. He was to contact his superiors regarding the situation, but it's been a number of days since we first became aware of this situation and we have heard nothing. Our attempts to reach out to Mr. Reynolds for permission to see her again have been rebuffed. We have only been advised that the situation is being considered. This causes my client concern and puts Emily Bates in limbo."

"I see." Mohr said.

"And that, sadly, brings us to the court for a resolution. If you could please tell us who signed the order, we will be happy to work with that person," Stephen suggested.

"Judge Iona signed the order and that's the extent of our documents. Things were simpler back then, but there still should have been more here." Judge Mohr flipped open the green file. "Copies of the petition for instance and doctors' reports at the very least. We are simply going to have to muddle through and try to reconstruct events. It will be difficult given the amount of time that has passed, but we must proceed in the letter and spirit of the law."

"Perhaps, Your Honor would be kind enough to recuse yourself in favor of Judge Iona." Josie stood and addressed the court, surprising the judge and annoying Stephen.

"Judge Mohr, my apologies. Given the personal nature of this matter, I believe Ms. Bates finds it difficult to restrain herself despite the excellence of her representation."

Stephen clicked forward from the waist with a courtly bow. Whether the gesture was one of apology or designed to regain the spotlight was unclear.

"Understandable, Mr. Kyle," Judge Mohr assured him as he plucked up the one sheet of paper that was in the folder. "I would actually be quite happy to shoot this right along to Judge Iona, but last I heard she was retired and living in Vermont with her daughter. There is an initial that I imagine to be a doctor's, but that's really all the information I have. I will have to assume that this assessment was acceptable to Judge Iona, and that Ha Kuna House was deemed an appropriate venue. Do you have some reason to believe that it is not an acceptable place for the lady?"

"We have seen the facilities and everything seems to be in order," Stephen answered. "However, we are concerned about the lack of on-site medical assistance. Should weather turn, it would be impossible for Ha Kuna administrators to get doctors in from Maui or, if a specialist was needed, from the mainland. Mr. Reynolds was unwilling to provide even the slightest information regarding the condition of Emily Bates while we, who had only seen her for less than an hour, were aware that there are certainly mental difficulties. Ms. Bates is concerned there might be physical consequences to this condition. We do know that she is medicated twice a day, but we are not privy to what that medication is or what particular ailment it addresses."

Stephen skirted the issue of how they knew Emily was medicated twice a day, deeming this the improper time to bring up Amelia. There was a fine line between appropriate concerns and conspiracy theories.

"There are only two aides to care for four patients at the facility. Add to this that Emily Bates has been missing from her family for twenty-seven years, and I'm sure you will agree that there are medical issues afoot. No one would voluntarily remain away from a loving family as Emily Bates has. There had to be a concrete reason for this behavior which was aberrant based on all accounts."

"All accounts being those of Josephine Bates, your client, isn't that correct, Mr. Kyle?"

"Certainly correct, Your Honor, since we can imagine no better witness to the state of Emily Bates' mind before her disappearance than the daughter she doted on. As with children who the court seeks to return to the bosom of the family at all costs, so should it be when a child wishes to reclaim a parental relationship."

"That is very nice, Mr. Kyle. A wonderful speech." Stephen beamed at Mohr's compliment but the judge, while appreciative of the rhetoric, was not swayed by it. "But let's be real. Emily Bates does not know her daughter and cannot confirm any of this. That's a little bit of a problem isn't it, Counsel?"

"That is a thing of the moment, Judge. With time, we are certain the relationship will be re-established and recognized. Sadly, Mr. Reynolds has not only refused us information, he has barred us from the facility pending input from his superiors and, I am assuming, counsel of his own. Certainly this is an understandable initial step, but it is doubtful those people will know the circumstances of Emily Bates' commitment anymore than you can from the minimal information in that file. Retention of care is simply a matter of business for Ha Kuna House administrators; it is a matter of honor and love where her daughter is concerned. At the very least, as a first step and a show of good faith on Ha Kuna House's part, a release of her medical records is warranted."

"Actually, you are wrong. Retention is a legal matter considering the existing order," Mohr answered. "Still, I understand what you're saying, and I am not unsympathetic to your client's position. To your second point: release of medical records. That is also problematic. This court is reluctant to compound this confusion by directing a piecemeal release of records. All or nothing is in order. However, we are walking on shaky ground since there are privacy issues to consider. I'm not at all comfortable going there without more information."

"It's a Catch 22," Josie called out. "I need access to those records to prove her need and my standing, judge, but you want me to prove my case before I can access the records."

"Ms. Bates, please," Judge Mohr admonished.

"Emotions are running high, Your Honor," Stephen interjected. "But I will not apologize for that. What should be a joyous occasion is not because it appears Ha

Kuna House is concerned that we are litigious. We are not. We simply don't want to run in circles. Our hand was forced."

Judge Mohr pointed his finger at Stephen.

"Had Ha Kuna House packed up Emily Bates and sent her off with your client it would not speak well of their concern for her or their liability. I applaud them, Mr. Kyle. There is no information as to why Emily Bates was committed to their care. Conversely, I have no concrete evidence from Josephine Bates that would compel me to overturn this order. I'm sure that is clear to you. Now that we have that straightened out, the question becomes this: how will we proceed? The answer is, we will take baby steps to insure the appropriate outcome and protection of Emily Bates' privacy and person."

Mohr sat back, shook out the wide sleeves on his robes, and picked up a pen.

"First, a county social worker will be assigned to assess the situation and make recommendations as they pertain to the woman's current level of care. I will also ask for a referral of both physicians and psychologists who can conduct independent assessments of her physical and mental state. I will ask the social worker to also conduct a background on Ms. Bates.

"Simultaneously, Ha Kuna House will be requested to provide the court with a history and all records as pertain to Emily Baylor-Bates. I will then decide which ones can be made public so as not to run afoul of federal laws and regulations. I will, naturally, entertain any documentation that will support Ms. Josephine Bates' bid for guardianship. I don't want to be inundated with paper, Mr. Kyle. Make sure everything you send to this court is appropriate to the question at hand. That will include, but not be limited to, proof of familial association, affidavits of character from someone who knew the family and Ms. Bates as an individual, and any records from authorities regarding her disappearance, domestic disturbances, etcetera.

"Finally, I want a plan of action from your client regarding housing, medical care, and daily care. There will have to be oversight and, should Ms. Bates want to take her mother out of our jurisdiction, I want to know exactly where she is taking her along with all contact information. If anyone else were to come looking for her, I want the record of this proceeding to be complete."

Judge Mohr took a deep breath. That was all the time Stephen needed to take the floor again.

"In anticipation of the court's possible reluctance in this matter, I have prepared an *ex parte* custody application."

Judge Mohr let out a long, low breath that turned into a nod to his clerk who collected the paperwork and delivered it to the bench.

"An *ex parte* application is not to be taken lightly, Mr. Kyle. There can be consequences that are sometimes not in the best interest of the person in question. I do not see any supporting affidavit that Emily Bates is in danger of immediate and irreparable injury should the current situation continue."

"I can subpoena one of the aides at Ha Kuna House who feels sure that Emily Bates should be removed from the institution," Stephen said.

"Wouldn't we have saved a lot of time if you'd just brought her today?"

"She is rather a reluctant witness, Your Honor."

"But obviously concerned enough that she offered you some reason to believe that the removal of the senior Ms. Bates is urgent."

"The assumption is based on information the lady received from a third party who was intimately aware of Emily Bates' history."

"Then why don't we have an affidavit from that person?" Judge Mohr's sunny disposition was fading.

"Sadly, he is deceased." Stephen took a millisecond to appear to lament the witness' passing. He was bright enough in the next as he heartily advised the court, "I would suggest that since there is no clear record of Emily Bates' history, it is even more imperative that my client be allowed broad latitude in this matter. We are requesting generous access to her mother under an *ex parte* ruling until the court decides on permanent custody which, we have no doubt, will favor my client."

Stephen clasped his hands in front of him. Josie cut her eyes his way. He winked and the side of his mouth turned up ever so slightly. He was sober as a judge the moment the real one on the bench responded.

"Well, Mr. Kyle, as usual you are eloquent but you fail to persuade me that an *ex parte* custody order is warranted. I have no heart to tangle with a witness who not only is reluctant but who also is a step removed from the real issue. I agree, however, that Josephine Bates should be allowed visitation while social services conducts their investigation. If there is any chance that Emily Bates' memory can benefit by your client's presence, we should take it. Not only in the hopes of supporting your client's claims but of finding out if Emily Bates would have any objection to a change of guardianship. I think a reasonable amount of time will be three weeks for all reporting. Then give me another week to review the material and–"

"A month? Your Honor, I respectfully request that this matter be expedited," Josie called but Mohr was not swayed.

"A month, Ms. Bates." His next words were for her more than for the record. "I understand that rediscovering a parent is an amazing event and that you are eager to get on with rebuilding your relationship. However, given the minimal information I have and the fact that you are asking me to take your word that you are who you say you are, I will not make a hasty decision. It's not only that I am legally bound to defer to the ruling of Judge Iona, I do so because it is the right thing to do. There was a reason for Ha Kuna Houses' guardianship all those years ago. I hope we are able to determine what that reason was. I further hope that if I award you guardianship I will do so with complete faith that I have made the right decision. Is that a fair goal?"

"It is, judge." Stephen answered for both of them knowing that Josie was still disappointed. If she had been counsel, she would have counted this a victory. She was the client and deferral felt like defeat.

"*Mai ho`okaumaha* means don't worry in Hawaiian, Ms. Bates." Judge Mohr offered this as he sat back in his chair indicating that the proceedings were almost at an end. "I have a feeling you will have no trouble convincing me that you are legally and emotionally the best guardian for Emily Bates, but convince me you must."

"Yes, Your Honor," Josie answered.

"Very well then." Satisfied, the judge went about the final business. "Mr. Kyle. During Josephine's visitation, should she find anything untoward or questionable that warrants immediate attention, I will expect you to contact the court. I want no manufactured crisis. My clerk will notify social services today and they will assign a caseworker. He or she will arrange for the medical and psychiatric evaluations, interview you, and go to Ha Kuna House to assess both Emily Bates and the housing situation. Please provide this caseworker with a list of contacts in Ms. Bates' hometown so we can corroborate her good standing. I think we are done."

"Before we are dismissed, we would like to request a copy of the commitment order," Stephen asked.

"Susan?" Mohr held out the folder to his clerk. "If you would."

"And we would like a formal order for generous visitation for Ms. Bates in case Mr. Reynolds continues to be reluctant."

"Since Ms. Bates seems to be a reasonable woman, I will grant her visitation every other day but in the setting Mr. Reynolds deems wisest. This would include supervision if he thinks that is necessary. We'll let Mr. Reynolds cap the number of hours so that this does not disrupt his business or upset either Emily Bates or others in his care. However, I will require that access be allowed for at least three continuous hours. We will allow forty-eight hours for Mr. Reynolds to make necessary arrangements. Visitation can begin Sunday. Is that acceptable?"

The clerk returned with the Xerox just as Stephen answered:

"Yes. Completely."

The clerk was already on the phone, the judge was busy with paperwork and Josie and Stephen were about to leave when the judge had one more request.

"Mr. Kyle? Regarding Ms. Bates' ward. I'd like a full background on her, too. You can never be too careful."

CHAPTER 17

"When are you cutting out?" – Madge

"A day or two. I'll miss the hash browns." – Archer

"Wouldn't mind leaving myself. Not going to get rich here."
– Madge

"You're kind of off the beaten path." – Archer

"Tell me about it." – Madge

"I like the drawing of you back there." – Archer

"I traded some kid a burger for it. She's pretty good with a pencil."
– Madge

"I'd pay her to draw one of me for my fiancé." – Archer

"Why? She knows what you look like." – Madge

"It will remind her of when she liked me." – Archer

"Funny." – Madge

"What about the girl? Do you know where I can find her?"
– Archer

"She comes in now and again." – Madge

"I'm staying down at the Cozy Motel. Here's the number and something for your trouble. Let her know you've got a cash customer." – Archer

"Good lord, woman, will you stop looking at the phone like a lovesick puppy? The man is busy. He'll get back to you when you can."

Stephen Kyle was behind his desk, gold-rimmed granny glasses sitting on the tip of his nose as he made notes on a legal pad. He hadn't raised his eyes in the last two hours; not even when he admonished her. Why bother to look when he could feel her vibrating in the quiet house.

Anuhea, Aolani and Malia had finished their chores and flown the coop. The twins had gone surfing. Malia hadn't bothered to fill anyone in on her plans. Josie couldn't blame the girls. The addition of one more body had thrown off the rhythm of the place. Still, Stephen had been right to insist that Josie move in. The Grand Wailea was expensive and he had an office from which they could work.

"I'm not looking at the phone and the only thing I am anxious to hear is what he found out," Josie mumbled.

"Don't be absurd. I know love sick when I see it."

Stephen took off his glasses. He put his fingertips to his eyes and rubbed gently so as to "not to get all wrinkly like an old lech". Josie swung away from the computer.

"How hard can it be to put your hands on a missing person's report and some medical records?"

"Government isn't always accommodating and it is Saturday. Besides, even the army doesn't keep records in perpetuity," Stephen reminded her.

"The army keep records on everything and everyone forever," Josie assured him.

"Maybe records that relate to their warriors," Stephen countered. "Your mother was a spouse. Quite a different thing, if you ask me."

"You can find anything if you look hard enough. Archer will find it."

Josie ran over the notes she had input into a file, unhappy with the minimal information she'd been able to dredge from her own memory. She couldn't remember the name of the family that lived beside them that last awful year at Fort Hood. She thought of contacting her best school friend during that time but she wouldn't know anything about Josie's parents. The years in Hawaii before they moved to Ft. Hood were a blur. Her mother was like all the other army wives, exceptional because she was Josie's mother and Joseph's wife.

"You are as optimistic as you are selfish, Josie. You just want what you want, don't you?" Stephen laughed.

"Takes one to know one." Josie shot him a grin. "What about you? What have you got?"

"A confusing labyrinth of corporate crap, I fear," Stephen sighed. "I had a bloody hard time trying to track who owns that damn place. Ha Kuna House is a subsidiary of MPS, Incorporated, which is all well and good. MPS is a supplier of hospital goods and are, in turn, owned by another corporation that has a stake in the administrative operations of VA hospitals around the U.S. So, we have a slim connection to the military which might – if we stretch the thread thinner – somehow put your mother into an institution that had some contract with the armed services."

"Spouses aren't treated at the VA," Josie pointed out.

"As I said, a stretch by anyone's imagination." Stephen flipped to the next page on his notepad and read his notes. "MPS is a huge concern. They have distribution centers for medication and hard goods, they handle offsite administration and record keeping for more than a dozen private hospitals and seventeen hundred VA hospitals, clinics, community living centers, and domicillaries."

"Okay, then maybe there was some kind of exception and the Ha Kuna House is a domicillary. That would make total sense. I was just under the impression that kind of thing was for vets only."

"Me, also!" Stephen barked as if surprised he and Josie were on the same wavelength. "That's why I drilled down a bit. There is no domiciliary run by the VA in Molokai. There is one on Honolulu and some community outreach on some of the islands but not Maui or Molokai."

"Curious." Josie wriggled her fingers, urging him on.

"MPS's mother company is even larger and has R&D, operational development, medical device manufacturing, and educational materials. They have their thumbs in many pies."

He relaxed, tossed the notes and rested his crossed arms on his belly.

"Does it not seem odd to you that either of these concerns would own a place like Ha Kuna House? It wouldn't be more than a mosquito bite of an entry on their big balance sheet. Annoying to deal with I'd imagine, and doubtfully lucrative enough to pay for its own upkeep."

"At least we're in the right ballpark," Josie said. "It would make some sense that MPS would supply and/or own nursing homes."

"Ah, glad you brought that up." Stephen waggled a stubby finger her way. "I've checked the HCIAS directory for nursing homes and Ha Kuna House isn't listed. Granted, that agency has strict licensing parameters and since there are no registered nurses or physicians on staff, the facility might not qualify to be listed. If it is a domiciliary, elder care or some such, there is no state licensing that I know of for that. They have an EISN. It's on the paperwork they completed when doing business with Keoloko. I'll have my accountant run it down on Monday and try to find a business license and tax returns. Since they are a holding of a publicly traded corporation, we should be able to find them on an annual report. Ha Kuna House is like a bastard child. It exists and yet no one wants to claim it."

"It still comes back to money for me. Who is paying for it?" Josie flipped her pen and caught it.

"I know a lovely lady over at the Medicaid offices. She says there is an ongoing research grant from Health and Human Services that folds Ha Kuna House into the mix. I've given her the names of the four folks under Reynolds' care. She's going to see what she can find on those individuals. You know, Medicaid payments, perhaps social security information."

"Can we find out what the terms of the grant were?" Josie asked.

"I doubt it's top secret," Stephen chuckled.

"Then I suppose we can extrapolate that Ian Francis was a professor researching neurological problems and was possibly covered under this grant. The government isn't paying for a privately held facility but granting an award to an individual. Ian chose Ha Kuna House from which to do his research and that makes things legal."

"And he shared that amazing windfall with Reynolds or whoever was here before him? I doubt it. An individual grant wouldn't be enough to heat the place or pay an administrator and staff," Stephen reminded her.

"That we know of," Josie countered. "Anyway, lucky Ian to get a job when he was sane and a facility at his disposal when he went bonkers." She tossed the pen again and it seemed to rotate lazily before she caught it. "It would sure change things if Ian was dealing with something viral and not psychological. Maybe that's why this is all so secret. Think about it, Stephen. The guy was doing his research thing and then years later comes down with whatever ails the subjects he's supposed to be studying. If that's the case, then it makes sense that Ha Kuna House is so remote. Do you think we should be looking at the CDC?"

"You mean like the lepers? Wouldn't that be quite the irony to stumble on a new colony on Molokai? Only instead of people losing their ears and noses, they lose their minds. I shall want the rights to that museum. I'll make a bloody fortune."

Josie crumpled a piece of paper and threw it at him.

"Worse things could happen to a bloke," Stephen insisted. "Ha Kuna House is a kind of a proper place, don't you think? No one is in any pain. They are happily unaware that they are unaware. If I lived there I'd make me a fantasy that I was an Arab prince with a harem."

"That is your real world. And don't forget, Ian is dead and Amelia has inherited his obsession. Not a happy ending." Josie pointed out just as his phone rang. He was on and off in less than a minute.

"This is an interesting turn. Robert Cote is the name on the deed of Ha Kuna House. Land records, Josie. The land upon which the place is built is the stone no one would think of turning over. Copies of the records will be sent along. It was purchased for cash in 1986. It was a private transaction."

"That makes no sense." Josie swiveled back to her desk and found the copies of the original commitment papers Amelia had provided.

"Ben Farrah, 1964. Amy Sloan, 1972. Marcel Washington, 1966. Ha Kuna House was already established as far back as sixty-four. Why would someone buy it in eighty-six?"

"In Hawaii we buy the building, not the land. That building has been around since the late eighteen hundreds wouldn't you say? By nineteen eighty-six the lease would have come up. This man simply bought the house in eighty-six and owns the structure and the right to keep the damn place running."

"How much did he pay?" Josie asked.

"Fifty thousand to MPS Corporation," Stephen answered.

"Then why is Amelia still getting her paychecks from MPS?"

"Perhaps they needed to get it off their books. The plan would be to divest the smaller properties to individuals working under a separate business license but retain the administrative responsibilities." Stephen pushed himself up. "Would you like some coffee?"

"No, thanks." Josie tucked her phone in her back pocket and followed him as she kept the conversation going. "And why would they do that?"

"Depreciation was depleted, something like that. Perhaps they needed to show additional income, although what the man paid is a pittance. When we get to the bottom of this I promise, the owning and running of Ha Kuna House will be nothing stranger than some entry on a balance sheet."

"Except this isn't really relevant. We don't need to know who owns the place we need to find out who makes the decisions. Reynolds is going to have to divulge that in his report to the court, but I don't want to wait." When they got to the kitchen Josie stopped in front of the cabinet and Stephen shooed her away so he could get to the coffee cups. But she kept talking. "And think about this. In '86 there were twenty-five residents. Wouldn't the new owner have to notify the families of the change?"

"Not necessarily. I could easily sell Keoloko Enterprises or hand it over to my son – if I had one, of course – and the business would go on. He wouldn't necessarily have to advise the clients that it was transferred. They would still place orders and be billed by Keoloko."

"We're not talking pineapples. Each resident must have had an advocate of some kind. Ha Kuna House couldn't unilaterally make decisions for all of them."

Stephen shrugged, "What if, like your mum, they had no idea who their family was?"

"Twenty-five people all end up in one place without any personal information? Come on." Josie put her rear against the counter and crossed her arms as if to underscore the ridiculousness of that proposal.

"Of course there is some information, woman," Stephen scoffed. "Reynolds isn't an idiot nor is he a monster. It's not like he's got a little zoo over there. Social services will investigate and report to the court, the court will issue an order, and we will be given your mum's records. That's all we want – unless you've decided to help little Amelia investigate all those dead folks."

Josie shook her head. "No, but when we get to court I want to know everything so Ha Kuna House doesn't drive the narrative. If we could locate even one other family who wanted information that would give us leverage."

"Agreed." Stephen pulled a face. "Aolani made the coffee today. Poor girl. Quite challenged in the kitchen." Stephen added two teaspoons of sugar but still was not happy. "How are you coming on your statement about little Hannah?"

"It's coming along."

Both of them knew that Hannah's status as a runaway and the threat of possible violence should she return to Hermosa would not sit well with the court. Josie would leave it for as long as she could.

"There are no death records in Hawaii for any of the people who supposedly passed away at Ha Kuna House, by the way. I've looked up all but three," Josie changed the subject.

"That's disconcerting. Make a note to ask Amelia specifically which patients she asked Reynolds about," Stephen suggested.

Before Josie could answer her phone rang. She held up a finger. Stephen waited patiently but listened closely as she spoke. It did not sound like a good conversation.

"Has your man run off with another, then?" Stephen inquired when she hung up.

"No. He saw one of Hannah's drawings in the coffee shop near where he's staying," Josie answered. "He's going to hang around and see if she comes back in."

"That should be good news but your expression says otherwise."

Josie pocketed the phone again. "It seems my mother was never officially considered a missing person. No one filed a report."

"No one?" Stephen asked.

"No one," she answered. "Not even my father."

CHAPTER 18

Everything is possible, nothing is impossible. There are no limits. Whatever you can dream of can be yours. – The Secret

૭૦૬

"Don't look like that, my girl. The report might have been filed with civilian authorities." Stephen suggested.

Josie shook her head. "He checked with Kileen – that's the closest town to the base – and with Austin PD. Nothing."

"Perhaps he used the wrong date. You yourself said it took your dad three days to get back home. Who was the first person you told? Perhaps they reported it. Have your man check from that date and see if he comes up with anything."

"Archer covered his bases, Stephen," Josie snapped.

"All right, then."

Put in his place, Stephen left her to stew, trailing the smell of bad coffee after him. He was almost through the office door when he peeked behind to see if she was with him or going to wallow for a bit on her own.

She wasn't wallowing but she also wasn't ready to work. Josie had paused by the wall of glass in the living room and was looking out onto a day that had turned windy and cloudy. The waves would be blown out so the girls wouldn't be surfing. Nor would they be coming home. They would go into Lahaina to do whatever young girls without a care would do. The fact that they once had great cares caused Stephen to take a moment and think fondly of them. Josie was no different than his girls; she needed a soft place to land. Since Stephen believed he was a most brilliant man when it came to women, he knew enough not to interrupt Josie Bates' thoughts.

Hers were not so different from Stephen's. She was thinking the girls were simply versions of Hannah. Being around them made her long for Hannah and Archer and Max. Strangely, Josie did not long for her mother and it was that knowledge that grieved her. Outside, the trees bent to the wind, the clouds skated on it, the waves were brushed by it, and here she was, standing in the eye of a perfect-storm.

"Methinks you're not quite all here, my California friend." Josie heard Stephen but stayed silent. That didn't stop him. "Are you thinking about your dad?"

Josie shook her head, "I was thinking about Archer."

"Then there's more to your introspection than just needing a hug. Pity, if that's all it was then I am a fine stand-in."

"Contrary to evidence, I really don't like things to be complicated. That's why I love Archer. What you see is what you get." Josie smiled.

"Psh. Lawyers thrive on complication," Stephen laughed.

"Until the complication is personal and then we're wimps," she admitted. "I'm just not sure I want to know the truth."

"Can't fault you there, darling. It's appearing that the picture won't be pretty when we've got it all together."

"My gut tells me that report never existed." She looked over her shoulder and the light in the room cast shadows over her eyes making her look cat-like and mysterious. "If my father knew where my mother was and that's why he didn't report her missing that would make me a fool." Josie opened the glass door. The warm, moist breeze blew in. She threw her head back and breathed deeply. "A stupid, little girl of a fool who was lied to her whole life."

Outside, beyond the jungle of trees, the sea was serrated with the kind of waves Stephen Kyle hated to sail upon. Josie hated them because when you swam in water like that the waves stung you, and slapped at you, and the pain was unremitting, and exhaustion was inevitable. Josie's personal sea was now full of them and she wanted someone to pull her out of the water.

"It's hard to breathe, Stephen. I want go home and get married and live with Archer and find Hannah. I wouldn't think of my mother anymore because..." Josie paused. "Because I would be happy."

Reluctantly she closed the door, wandered to the center of the room, cupped her hands over the back of the sofa, and pushed up on to her toes as if to prove that standing taller would make her stronger.

"I miss Max, too."

"You are a collector of orphans," Stephen answered.

"We're two of a kind, Stephen."

She settled on the rolled arm of the sofa, one leg crooked and the other resting on the floor. When she spoke again she sounded tired, as if she had climbed one too many mountains and couldn't face the next one.

"I have a professional history I'm not so proud of. When I got to Hermosa Beach I was licking some pretty bad self-inflicted wounds. It took a lot to reconstruct a life in a place I love, with a man I love, and a dog, and the beach outside my house. Then Hannah came and it was all good." She chuckled. "Sounds like a commercial, doesn't it?"

"You've got everything but granny at the table," he agreed.

She bit her lip, taking a moment to choose exactly the right words. It wasn't Stephen's sympathy or absolution she wanted. Josie wasn't sure if she even wanted him to listen, she just needed to speak the truth and try it on for size.

"I'm forty years old and I'm tired of having issues with my parents. I think I'm done."

"Criminey! That's no good," Stephen blustered. "You're still in a bit of shock. Not to mention your hand. Don't forget that little bit."

Josie looked at the well-wrapped gauze, the neatly placed clips. She could feel the skin pulling tight beneath. It was healing. Healing always hurt.

"Curiosity is different than masochism. All I ever wanted was for her to tell me why she left. I'll never get the answer, so why bother with all this?"

The rain came again, pounding for only a minute on the flat roof. Josie spoke first when it let up.

"I have to ask myself if I want to be Emily's guardian because I'm arrogant and controlling or selfless and loving. Think about it. What will I really accomplish if the court sides with me?"

"You'll be able to care for her," Stephen suggested.

"The people at Ha Kuna House do that," Josie said. "What happens when I get her back to Hermosa Beach and the novelty wears off? I'd have to hire a day nurse so I could work. I'd have to care for her at night which would affect my relationship with Archer," Josie went on. "And let's talk about Hannah."

"Ah, yes, Hannah. The wayward, reckless woman-child."

Stephen tired of leaning against the doorjamb so he sidled to the bar, heaved himself on to a stool, slid open the door, and rattled the bottles. When he came up for air he had a bottle. A generous slug of his favorite scotch landed in his coffee. He was settled in the front row of the theater and so far the first act was quite intriguing. He couldn't wait for the second.

"I promised Hannah a home, not a rest home. Bringing Emily back would change everything. And there's Archer. Can you imagine four people in a small house?" Josie punctuated her frustration with a sound that was half laugh and half groan.

"Bigger houses can be had," Stephen suggested.

Josie would argue that her house was her home. Archer and Hannah were willing to make it theirs, but Emily couldn't make a choice. She would be moved and set down like a beautiful, uncomfortable piece of furniture, a perpetual guest who couldn't recognize her host. Yet, there was more to it than that.

"I don't know if I love my mother, Stephen."

He tilted his head but didn't respond. What was there to say to someone like Josie? Those beautiful blue eyes of hers were bigger for the shock of bangs hanging messily across her brow. Her wide-necked t-shirt fell off one shoulder revealing just a hint of a fragile collarbone. Her long legs were bronzed and smooth, her shorts sexier because they were worn with such casual disregard. She looked young and vulnerable until one looked closely and saw that age and experience were the details that made her beautiful and substantive. She was an Amazon without her shield and bow, and the arrows loosed by the foe had pierced a skin Josie did not know was so thin. If Stephen had been another kind of man he would have swooped her up into his arms and into his bed with promises that he could do the impossible; love away her pain. Pity he was a righteous man.

"That little confession calls for a bit of a different fortification." He reached under the bar again. Josie joined him as he poured two tumblers full of whiskey and slid one her way.

"If I took Emily with me I'd never know if she wanted to be with me. Maybe she was running away from me."

He drained his glass, and while he poured again he said: "You're afraid, my girl. That's the long and short of it."

"I am," she admitted and Stephen thought that was a courageous thing. He put his hand over hers.

"Give it a bit more effort, Josie. She's your mum." His hand slid away but Josie caught it and held it.

"And Hannah? What do I do about Hannah?"

"Your man's got that covered." Stephen lifted her hand and kissed it. Then he gave it a nice pat and said: "Come on. We've a lot of work to do."

Josie was about to tell him that she was done with it all, that she was tired of working on an unsolvable mystery, when something flashed in her brain. It was quick and unclear like a word on the tip of her tongue, so she scrambled after it before she lost even that much.

"Stephen. What's the name of the man who bought Ha Kuna House?"

"What?"

She clasped his hand tighter and gave it a shake. "You know, the guy who bought the place for fifty grand? You saw his name on the title."

"Robert Cote." He peeled his hand away from hers so he could refill his glass. "Why?"

"He's the guy who signed most of those forms Amelia gave us." Josie got off the bar. "Including my mother's. And guess what? I've seen it somewhere else."

Josie hurried toward the office. By the time Stephen got there, she was already rifling through the pile of paperwork and notes she had accumulated.

"Good grief, what are you doing, woman? I thought you were giving up?"

"Guess not."

She shot him a grin and went back to what she was doing. Finally, she whipped a sheet of paper out of the pile. Josie shoved the court order committing Emily Bates to Ha Kuna House at him. Stephen squinted. She pointed.

"Right here. Look on the back. It didn't register when I first saw it. I was more concerned with the order itself."

"Damn hard to read. Ink's faded. Ah, I've got it. ICE. In case of emergency. A phone number and initials. RC." Stephen read out loud and then pulled back. "I would say that is just too strange a coincidence. It's one thing to sign admission papers or buy a piece of property, but quite another to have the power to commit a person. Bit of a conflict of interest, wouldn't you say?"

"Let's find out, shall we?" Josie picked up the phone. "Read the number to me."

She dialed as fast as he read. The phone was answered on the fourth ring. Josie gave Stephen a thumb's up, but her smile faded when she heard:

"Department of Homeland Security, how may I direct your call?"

CHAPTER 19

"C or K on Cote? – Archer

"C. C-o-t-e." – Josie

"I'll check when I get home. Day after tomorrow I'm headed out."
– Archer

"No sign of her or Billy?" – Josie

"It was a long shot. People only need so many pictures. She's trading them for food so she's probably moved on where the pickings aren't so slim." – Archer

"I suppose." – Josie

"Sorry, babe. I don't have anywhere else to go with this." – Archer

"I know." – Josie

"I'm not giving up." – Archer

"I know." – Josie

"I love you." – Archer

"Back at you." – Josie

ல∞ல

The *No Problem* cut through the water with Josie at the helm and the absolutely gorgeous boat hand, Danny, kicking back, waiting for the wheel when she tired of fighting the waves. Stephen was below nursing an 'upside down tummy.' Josie had suggested that he stay on Maui but he was determined to be her moral support. He lasted all of ten minutes before the choppy sea got to him. She would have gone back, but she was late for her scheduled visit with the social worker and the ferry wouldn't get her to Molokai on time. With the sound of the wind too loud for her to hear Stephen's moans and laments, Josie let her thoughts wander to Mr. Robert Cote.

He was not employed by Homeland Security as she assumed. Rather, he was retired from the Department of Defense. The phone number had simply been taken over by Homeland Security as they expanded into the offices of the DOD. It took twenty minutes of talking and checking for the woman on the other end to make the connection, but eventually it was made. Sadly, Josie couldn't get the woman to tell her:

Mr. Cote's Department of Defense designation in 1986.

Where Mr. Cote resided.

Whether Mr. Cotes was alive.

Or, what connection Mr. Cote might have to Ha Kuna House.

Despite the lack of information, Josie was satisfied. She found her purpose once more. She put her self-doubt behind her and Emily's welfare at the forefront. Archer would start a background on Mr. Cote, Stephen would talk to the old timers on Molokai who might have known him, and Josie had already drafted a petition for Judge Mohr to include Robert Cote's employment records from Ha Kuna House, MPS, and the Department of Defense in his orders. Sadly, it would all take time and Josie was becoming impatient.

The boat kicked and bucked over a particularly large swell. Josie grasped the wheel tighter and shook off the spray. She loved days like this: A little wild, a little challenging. It was time for her to keep her eye on the prize: Molokai. Somewhere on that island, in that house, there were the answers to her questions. When she had them, Josie was sure she would be amazed she hadn't seen what it was all about sooner.

Josie pushed at the throttle. The *No Problem* hit the waves hard and fast and the boat fairly flew over the water. Danny was enjoying the ride. Below deck, Stephen Kyle moaned. If Josie had heard him, she would have pointed out that the only way to deal with misery was to endure until it was over.

In a Homeland Security cubicle, the woman who had fielded the call about Robert Cote the afternoon before, looked at the time, and thought twice about inputting her data regarding the conversation. It was twelve-thirty and she had promised to meet her lover for a lunchtime quickie. Still, Cote was on the list and she didn't want to be the bottleneck that clogged the system. Torn as she was, she opted to finish her work.

She clicked on the flag, and waited for the screen to come up. Her fingers flew over the keyboard. She filled in the time, the date, referenced Robert Cote, entered the name of the woman inquiring, and attached a link to the recording of the conversation. It was now twelve thirty-nine. Precious minutes. Still, if she hurried she just would make it and the word quickie would take on a whole new meaning.

She hit send.

Robert Cote was no longer her problem.

"Well, this has been a great meeting. Just great. I can't tell you how much I appreciate all of your information. Awesome, ladies."

Pilipa Foley, newly minted social worker for the State of Hawaii, was as fresh faced and eager as a kid on the first day of school. He was turned out in jeans, a shirt he had obviously pressed himself, and a tie. His briefcase was a canvas backpack. He filled out his standardized forms with painstaking precision, pleased as a puppy making it to the top of the stairs when he completed one.

"So, Emily? Emily?" Pilipa leaned forward and did everything but snap his fingers to get her attention. When she turned his way, when she smiled her empty smile, he grinned back brightly. "Emily. Are you happy here?"

Emily blinked. "Yes. My daughter has a lovely home."

Emily took Amelia's hand. Pilipa colored. Josie watched, no longer shocked or hurt by Emily's reality.

"That's Amelia. Do you know who this is? Emily? Do you know who this is?" Pilipa touched the older woman's knee with one hand and Josie's with the other.

"No," Emily answered.

"Are you sure you don't know her? Her name is Josie. Josephine Bates." he tried again.

"No. I–" Emily shook her head. "I don't – I don't think…No…"

Emily dropped her head, her fingers laced into a fist and that fist bounced off her lap. Josie smiled at Pilipa Foley to ease his embarrassment. After he had a few hundred heart-wrenching cases under his belt, he wouldn't think twice about something like this. Suddenly, Emily lifted her head and looked at Josie.

"You swim in the ocean."

Josie was startled. Amelia sat up straighter and the two women shared a glance. Amelia nudged her with a look.

Answer the woman.

"When I was a girl I swam with my mother in Hawaii," Josie said. "I got caught in a wave. My mother laughed."

"I'm sorry." Emily's hands were trembling. Josie didn't hesitate. She took them in her own hoping this breath of a memory and her touch would bring Emily back to her.

"Why are you sorry?" Josie asked.

"Your mother shouldn't laugh."

"It's okay," Josie whispered.

"Were you afraid?"

"Yes." Josie admitted. "But my mother wouldn't have let anything happen to me."

Josie wanted to say so much more. She wanted Emily to know that she was stronger for that day; it meant everything if Emily truly remembered it. If she had, the memory was now gone. She was looking at the front door.

"May I go for a walk?"

Pilipa shook off his surprise. He cleared his throat. "That's fine. That would be good if you want to take her, Ms. Bates."

"Me? Alone?"

"Yes, I need Ms. Francis for a few more minutes."

Josie was about to decline but changed her mind. If she couldn't take Emily for a simple walk, what was she going to do once they got back to Hermosa?

"Sure. Why not."

Amelia stood up, too. "Go out the front door and take the path to your right. She always went the other way with us."

Josie understood. They all tried so hard to get Emily to remember Josie and it was Ian who was granted that privilege.

"Okay. Let's go, mom." Emily didn't move.

"She doesn't remember she asked to go for a walk." Amelia nudged Emily up, turned her, and handed her off to Josie. "She'll go slow. You're going to have to judge whether or not you've gone too far. If she gets tired she'll just sit down. Or if she zones she'll just stand in one place. It will be hard getting her back, so you really have to be aware."

"I'll be careful. Thanks." The transfer was made but Amelia watched until the two women were through the front door.

Outside, Emily and Josie stood on the porch. Stopping and starting was exhausting and they had only gone across the room. Josie couldn't imagine how long it would take them to walk The Strand at home if this was how things went.

"Okay. We'll wait a minute," she said.

As she waited for a sign from Emily, Josie thought of Stephen. No doubt he had an unpleasant journey back to Maui on the *No Problem* with Danny at the wheel, but she was happy she had insisted that he go home. It was nice to have quiet time with Emily. She opened her mouth, ready to share the story of Stephen and his seasickness, but one look at her mom told her that would be a waste of breath. Instead, she said: "Let's walk now."

They went down the steps and Emily was surprisingly sure-footed. Josie laced her arm through Emily's, not to keep her from falling but to keep her from wandering away. She squeezed a little closer. The contact felt so right.

"I'm sorry you won't remember that we took this walk together, mom."

They walked on steadily. Emily remained silent so Josie made her own conversation.

"I'm sorry there's nothing I can do to make you remember me. I hope you would be proud of me. I think you would love Archer and Hannah. I think you would love me."

The wind blew. The trees and flowers trembled and then stilled. A raindrop fell.

"I'm sorry it's going to rain." Josie chuckled at the one-sided conversation. Then she stopped smiling. "I'm sorry about dad."

"I love Ian," Emily said.

"So I hear," Josie sighed.

Emily lifted her face to the breeze. Her hair ruffled and she looked beautiful. They walked down the path: a yard and then two. Another yard. Emily paused. They went further. Her step faltered. In the next few feet she stumbled. Josie caught her and Emily pulled her daughter closer, tighter.

"I got you," Josie assured her but something was wrong. Emily was pale. Her breathing was rapid. "Are you okay?"

"Okay." Emily repeated the word.

"Are you sick?"

"Sick."

Emily's face was moist with perspiration. She trembled. Not just her arm but her whole body. Her jaw locked. Josie took hold of her with both hands.

"Oh, no. I'm sorry. I'm sorry. It's too far," Josie babbled. "Come on. Turn around."

Josie tried to guide her, but Emily was rooted and wouldn't budge. It was like she was frozen in the face of an oncoming train, but there was nothing scary in this place; there was nothing but trees and plants and beautiful things.

"Emily. Please come with me," Josie pleaded. "Mom, I don't know what to do. Please help me."

Frantically, Josie looked for something out of place but concluded it had to be her. Had she said something? Done something? Is this what had happened all those years ago? Was it the daughter visiting some terror on the mother?

"Please—" Josie begged.

Just then Emily shuddered and her knees buckled. She started to fall. Above them the sun disappeared behind a cloud and shadow rolled over them. Josie tried to lower Emily but she was dead weight and collapsed on to the dirt and on to her knees. Her face went into her hands. Her body jerked and Josie – strong as she was – could not hold her, raise her, or comfort her. She sure as heck couldn't get her back to the house.

"I'll get help. Stay there. Stay there."

Josie shot off the ground and ran back the way they had come leaving her mother alone under an ever-darkening sky.

෴

Emily Bates knelt in the dirt with her face in her hands. If she didn't look, she was safe. If she didn't cry, she was safe. If she couldn't be seen she was safe, so Emily made herself a small thing in the big forest. Time past, but she didn't know how much. Fear paralyzed her, but she had no concept of what fear was.

So Emily didn't understand what was happening when a man got down on one knee in front of her. He took hold of her hands and tried to move them away from her face. He was strong but still it was difficult to move her. It was as if her hands were made of steel. That's what she believed. But if she was made of steel, he was made of something stronger because he forced her hands to her side.

She stared ahead but didn't see him. Emily heard the wind but not the snort of curiosity from the man. He couldn't believe she didn't react when he got close. Not that it mattered. He knew what to do.

He put one hand on her forehead and gently rubbed the space between her brows with his thumb. He cooed and rubbed. He was surprisingly patient. When the trembling subsided, he put her on her feet and turned her.

"Let's go."

At the sound of his voice Emily Bates began trembling all over again.

The man who caught the memo at DOD was extraordinarily efficient. He drilled down on Robert Cote, took a second to note the dates of service, and then forwarded the whole thing to interested parties including the secretary to the division chief. She in turn, coded it and sent it on to the next level.

And so the notice that someone inquired about Robert Cote snaked through the system. The information listed his last posting and all programs related to his service.

The message was split twelve times for there were twelve agencies that had either flagged his name or his posting. By the time it reached all twelve destinations, the man at the computer was on to the next bit of business.

His, he was sure, was the stupidest job in all of Washington.

※ ※

Josie burst through the front door of Ha Kuna House.

"Amelia! Amelia! Come quick. I'm sorry. I'm so sorry. She just started shaking and I couldn't get her to move..."

Amelia was out of her chair before Josie finished, clipping the taller woman's shoulder as she dashed toward the door. Josie spun around and went after. They ran down the path, Josie slipping on the now wet earth, slapping a palm frond out of her way as she tried to get her footing. Amelia turned back, but Josie waved her on.

"Keep going!"

But Amelia had stopped and as Josie righted herself she saw why. A man dressed in work boots, fatigues, and a white T-shirt was walking Emily toward them. He had a hold of her and for a second Josie flashed back to her parents walking arm in arm, quiet and content. But this wasn't her father and Emily wasn't reliving the past. She was gone again.

Away from Josie.

Away from everyone.

CHAPTER 20

"Came to say goodbye, Madge." – Archer
"Something for the road?" – Madge
"A burger should hold me." – Archer
"You got it. Hey. Look what the dog dragged in. Honey, this guy's been wanting to talk to you about that picture." – Madge

❧

Ambrose Patriota stood at the bank of microphones. Clustered behind him were seven of his brethren waiting their turn to address the escalating NSA scandal. There wasn't much to say, actually. Every government listened in on every other government, their own people, and their own lawmakers. Like business, government was only as successful as the leverage it wielded against its competitors. In the grand scheme of things, this was a tempest in a teapot fed by a malingering media who preferred the ease of a perceived scandal to investigating a real one. They were so easily pleased and played so Ambrose did what he did best: he said what the public needed to hear.

"I am distressed by the administration's lack of transparency regarding the NSA. However, I am not surprised. We have seen this time and time again. The administration says one thing and does quite another. The president of Brazil has cancelled her state visit in protest. The   foreign   relations   committee   will   make recommendations, but we cannot reverse an administration-sanctioned program. We can only register our protest and try to convince the president that his ways must change."

"Senator Patriota, if you're elected what specifically would you do differently?"

"Senator Patriota, can you address the ramifications for our foreign policy?"

"Senator Patriota, congress has threatened to subpoena your records, will that—"

Ambrose ignored all the questions and spoke to his purpose. No one, after all, expected specifics.

"Confidence in the United States has eroded to a dangerous point. The president says he is not to blame. The buck must stop somewhere, and if not with him then with who? I intend to work with the House in a cooperative manner, not only to find out who has ordered this egregious over-stepping but how high it goes."

When Ambrose was done he walked alone to his office, feeling absolutely naked when he entered it without Eugene. But there were others to notice him and his secretary was the first.

"Senator Hyashi called and would like to see you at four. It will work but that means you'll have to dispose of Mr. Zanga in forty-five minutes. He's due at 3:15."

"Save me from Mr. Zanga, Norma." Ambrose took off his jacket and hung it in the closet.

"No can do, sir. Kid glove time. He can bring a pretty penny to the war chest. While you take a few minutes to wish he wasn't coming, sign these letters. First, condolences to Mrs. Petrie on the death of her one hundred year old husband."

Ambrose signed.

"Two Eagle Scout congratulations."

Ambrose signed again.

"Five condolences to the families of those marines killed over in Afghanistan."

Ambrose signed, signed, and signed.

Norma collected them all. They would be in the afternoon mail and in two days they would be opened and treasured by the recipients. That's why Ambrose never allowed an automatic signature on letters commemorating personal events. Fundraising letters were another matter. No one treasured those. Today, though, he would have been happy for the robo-signature even on a death letter. The pen felt heavy.

"Mrs. Patriota wants to know if the sixteenth of next month is still good for the governors' dinner," Norma went on.

"Remind me who will be there?"

"Texas, Arizona, California, Ohio."

"A good line-up. Tell her yes. Tell her to make it very special. We want to keep them happy."

"Everyone is happy with you."

"So you say, Norma."

"Call backs on your left as usual. Think-about-its are on the top right and make-'em-sweat on the bottom right. Oh, and that report I gave you a few days ago? There's an update. Do you want me to re-print the whole thing or just the new activity?"

"Just the new activity is fine. Thank you, Norma. I appreciate it."

That was it. She had plenty to do on her own desk and the senator needed to attend to his, but he wasn't quite ready.

"Norma?"

"Yes, Senator?"

"Have you seen Eugene?"

"No, Senator, I haven't. Would you like me to track him down?"

"It's just unlike him to be absent so long," Ambrose mused.

"Maybe he's playing hooky."

"Do you think he might have?"

"There's a first time for everything, Senator." The woman shrugged.

"True, Norma, but it's Eugene we're talking about."

"You have a point there," she said. "Really. No trouble to find him for you."

"Thank you, Norma. Perhaps that's a good idea."

She left only to return ten minutes later and proved her worth. She had everything he wanted: the new print out and information on where Eugene had gone.

Ambrose thanked her for both. As she left, he was thinking that the boy was proving more interesting than Ambrose gave him credit for.

Ambrose added a few more numbers to his NSA request. It would be good to know who Eugene was talking to in his spare time. Finally, Ambrose called the US Attorney and had a long chat about the possible need for a wire tap or two.

☙❧

Woodrow Calister's brownstone was a far cry from Ambrose's beautifully appointed home with its Persian rugs and fine art. It was not visually stunning like Jerry Norn's glass penthouse. And it certainly wasn't a homey place like Mark Hyashi's in Virginia where his wife kept a family home identical to the one in their district. Woodrow Calister's place was comfortable, big enough for him to monitor the entire footprint easily, and well appointed enough to put off any female who might suggest it needed a woman's touch. But Woodrow Calister's place was special because it had a most unique library.

The darkly paneled room was more than just a private retreat: it was a safe room. Woodrow had personally installed the fire doors, the alarm system, and recording devices. He was quite proud of his handiwork because it reminded him of the good old days when he was a master electrician. A far higher calling, he thought, than that of politician. Right now, though, he was intrigued by the politics that had brought that evening's visitor to his doorstep. Eugene Weller sat on the edge of the leather sofa, knees together, briefcase at his feet.

"Are you sure you don't want water with this?" Woodrow asked.

"No. Thank you."

He handed Eugene his glass: two fingers of bourbon instead of his usual white wine. Woodrow's chair was opposite Eugene, and the lighting was recessed above him to create the appropriate shadows. Eugene was quite well illuminated. There wouldn't be a shadow to cross his face that Woodrow wouldn't see. Woodrow lit a cigarette.

"Does Ambrose even know you're here?"

"No. He does not," his voice caught. He felt as if he were betraying his senator and he had no idea why. What he was doing was insurance for Ambrose, protection in the form of a powerful ally. Still, Eugene felt a need to qualify his statement. "But, Senator, I hope you know I wouldn't be here if I didn't think this situation was critical."

"That is not a promising opening salvo," Woodrow noted. He flicked his ash and took a drink.

"I'm sorry. I don't mean to be overly dramatic. I have briefed Senator Patriota about this. He is unconcerned, but my concern is growing. Considering this might affect you if you were to be Senator Patriota's running mate, and that it involves the DOD and you chair the committee, I thought your counsel would be appropriate."

Eugene took a drink. He took another. The booze didn't warm him and Calister's silence did not reassure him. His decision to request this meeting was impulsive and now he realized it could also be risky. This meeting could be construed as insubordination.

"Eugene, please, I'm happy to help but I need to know what you're talking about before I know if I can do anything," Woodrow prodded. "Is Ambrose sick?"

"No. No. Nothing like that." Eugene shook his head vehemently. "This has to do with the disruption a few weeks ago during the hearing on Eastern European Organized Crime."

"Yes. I heard about it." Woodrow drank, too. "I didn't hear about any fallout."

Eugene cleared his throat.

"The most immediate fallout was that the man who was responsible for it killed himself later on that evening."

"And this is relevant because?" Woodrow was already not liking the sound of this.

"The man in question was part of a program under the Department of Defense's guidance in the eighties. It will be in your archives. You'll remember MKUltra?"

"This guy was a part of that?" Woodrow became noticeably engaged as he snuffed out his cigarette.

"No, sir. Ian Francis was a researcher following up on the aftermath of that and ancillary programs. CHATTER respondents and, in one case, Artichoke. He was intimately involved in the final phase, charged with the concluding research and wrapping it all up."

"And?"

"And," Eugene breathed. "Instead of completing his work it became necessary to absorb him into the program. At that point there were still fifteen residents, ten had passed on, funding needs were not increasing, the subjects and protocols were too old to be of value, and so the determination was made not to replace him."

"That all sounds appropriate." Woodrow took a drink. "Do you know who made these decisions?"

Eugene read off a short list of project managers and one undersecretary.

"What about the secretary himself at the time these decisions were made?"

"I haven't inquired," Eugene said. "I thought it better not to enlarge the inquiry at this time. As Senator Patriota's chief of staff, this might be construed as overstepping my bounds internally. If this matter does enter the mainstream, I don't want it to appear that the senator was hands-on."

"I assume you've come with some plan should this become a matter of public interest," Woodrow said.

"If there were a call for a full blown investigation before the convention, I was thinking your department could investigate but put it on the back burner. That would possibly mitigate the impact to the campaign. Let it play out without any real inquiry and bury it."

"Good thinking, Eugene." Woodrow took a drink. "But I still don't understand why you're concerned now and what it might have to do with Ambrose. It seems to be a problem for the DOD."

"Projections were that the project would officially wrap up completely in 2020, but when Ian Francis disrupted the hearing and threw around the project names, I followed up. That's when I ran across this."

Eugene set aside his drink, retrieved his report and handed it over. The big man snapped open a pair of glasses and perused the information, turning a page forward and one back, taking it in, giving no indication that he was alarmed by what he was reading. Eugene forced himself not to fidget while Woodrow Calister read.

"I'd like to familiarize myself with the details tonight. I am vaguely aware of Michael Horn. The lower courts showed some interest in his suit, but it's been stalled for years. I think the clock will play out on that part of it."

"I'm not concerned with the courts but rather with what's happening on his website and with his phone records," Eugene said. "Ian Francis' suicide was noticed. I thought I had squelched it but a small piece appeared in

The Post and that led to renewed activity on Michael Horn's part.

"Still, it's not just him making noise. Josie Bates — Senator Patriota's witness – is in Hawaii. She's been at the facility. A few days ago she logged a call to DOD about Robert Cote. You'll see he was the one who administered the program for a time."

"And did she get ahold of him?" Woodrow asked.

"No, he's retired and protected." Eugene answered. "The fly in the ointment is her mother. She is in residence."

"Oh, for God's sake," Woodrow muttered and dropped his head into his upraised hand.

"We didn't know that when she was invited to testify on the Eastern European problem – not that it would have made a difference. It was the mention of her in *The Post* article that caught Michael Horn's interest. We know he's called her Hermosa Beach office multiple times but so far we have no record of him calling Bates' cell."

"Wonderful." Woodrow rolled his eyes.

"The current administrator of Ha Kuna House naturally blocked access to her mother and notified the project director. You may want to touch base there and offer some assistance."

"Why isn't he letting her see the woman? I doubt she's in any shape to do any harm and denial will look suspicious," Woodrow complained.

"It's not just visitation. Bates has gone to court. She wants guardianship transferred. The judge is moving slowly which gives us time to consider our options. He's asked the house for records on the commitment and her care."

"Don't have the government contest it. Cut the woman loose and this all goes away. She can't be in any condition to compromise anyone at this point. Bates will be happy and forget about the facility."

"The problem is that no one knows what will happen if the mother is in an uncontrolled environment." Eugene finished his drink. "I've met Josie Bates. She is going to want answers. If she gets them, history becomes a current event and Senator Patriota gets dragged into the mess. I don't think that's the way you want to start a campaign."

"You have a point there," Woodrow muttered.

The two men retreated into their own thoughts both considering the fragility of power and how it could be rendered impotent by inconsequential people: an attorney from California, a businessman from Cleveland, a woman without memory, and even a dead man.

But Eugene had one thought that Woodrow Calister did not. Eugene thought that as the guardian of the gate he was actually in a position to do more harm than any of them. If he were a different man he could be the one to ruin Ambrose, not save him.

శ్రీఈ

Josie knocked on the cottage door. When Johnson opened it he looked her straight in the eye. That was unusual because most men liked to start at her feet and work their way up. She stuck out her hand.

"I'm Josie Bates, Emily's daughter."

"I know."

His legs were planted wide and his hands grasped the door on either side. He looked like a spider waiting for something tasty to fly too close to his web. He took his time before gripping her hand.

"Johnson."

"The caretaker," Josie matched his grip and then shook his hand to keep this friendly. "Amelia told me after we got my mom upstairs. It was kind of crazy out there, so I didn't have a chance to thank you for bringing her back."

"Sure," he said.

Josie wasn't put off by his lack of hospitality. She was sure this man found foe more often than friend on his doorstep.

"Could I come in for a second?" she asked.

"I wasn't expecting company."

"I won't take up too much of your time."

Johnson considered her, decided she was more interesting than whatever else he had to do, and slung himself back. There was barely enough room to pass. Josie never cared for that particular male game: blocking an entrance so a woman had to turn to face him to get where she was going, her back up against a wall, his lips suggestively close, having to endure the intimidation of someone bigger and stronger than she was. Josie was as tall as Johnson so that changed things. He had to step back when she walked straight on. Josie thought she heard him laugh when he closed the door.

The place was more like a generous studio rather than a cottage. There was a kitchen, a bathroom, and in the big living room a desk and table. She did a double take on the table and the disassembled handguns spread out over newspaper.

"So, your mom was kind of out of it. How's she doing?" he asked.

Josie pivoted smoothly. She smiled and ignored the elephant in the room in favor of the rhinoceros.

"She hasn't spoken. Something scared her out there."

"I was the only one out there. I don't think I'm that scary. Do you?"

Josie ignored the question. "Even when she talks, she doesn't say much anyway, but Amelia seems to be worried."

"None of them talk much," Johnson responded. "Do you want to sit down?"

"For a minute. I've got to catch the ferry back to Maui." Josie sat on the sofa, the table with the guns still in her peripheral vision. "I guess I was hoping that she might tell me something – anything – about the situation she's in. It doesn't look like that's going to happen, so I thought I'd ask you a few questions."

"I won't have the answers."

"Anything will help," Josie assured him. "How long have you worked here?"

"Six years."

"So, you've seen a lot of people come and go?"

"Not that many." Johnson sat opposite her, his arms on his knees, his hands hanging between them. The muscles on his shoulders were so pronounced he seemed to have no neck. This was not a man who would give up anything easily but he could probably take whatever he wanted.

"But there used to be a lot of people here," Josie insisted. "They were old. They passed away. Do you remember any of them? Maybe you talked to some of their relatives?"

"I work on the grounds. I don't get involved in anything else."

"Still, six years is a long time. You must have seen someone or something," Josie persisted.

"Nope," he answered. "Anything else?"

Since this wasn't a courtroom, and he wasn't a witness, and there was no reason to circle around him for the record, Josie decided not to waste any more time.

"Look, here's the deal. I want to take Emily home with me. Reynolds isn't giving me anything. I don't know how my mother got here, I don't really know what this place is, and there are a lot of things that don't add up."

"Such as?"

"Such as who pays the bills? Who pays you?"

"I get cash," Johnson said and Josie was amused. It would have been fun to have him on the stand.

"That's unusual, don't you think?"

"Money is money." He shrugged.

"Did you know Ian Francis?" she asked.

"Sure did. Nice guy when he wasn't drooling."

"Did you know him before he got sick?"

"I saw him," Johnson answered.

"What would it take to get you to remember anything about the place you've been working at for six years?" Josie asked, ready to meet his demands.

"Lady, you don't have anything I need," Johnson laughed.

"When were you discharged?" Josie shot back, hoping a sharp turn would change things.

"What makes you think I was?" Johnson went right along with her, the curve doing nothing to throw him off. In fact, he seemed to be having a good time and that made her even more curious.

"Okay." She got to her feet. "I don't know what's up with the stonewall, but I'll get around it. If Reynolds were smart he wouldn't contest the guardianship. You think he'd be happy to have Emily off his hands."

"Not for me to say," Johnson stood up, too. He stuck his hands in the pockets of his fatigues. He wore combat boots. You could put him on any U.S. base anywhere in the world and he'd fit in. But out here in paradise he was a duck out of water. Josie started for the door and he followed behind offering some advice.

"If you take her walking again you may want to steer her clear of that road. It could get kind of dangerous out there. A misstep on those cliffs wouldn't be pretty."

Josie looked over her shoulder. She paused and nodded toward the table. "Maybe it's not the cliffs she has to worry about. It looks like you're doing a little more than gardening out there."

"You never know when you'll find a snake," Johnson drawled.

"There are no snakes in Hawaii," Josie answered.

"Do tell. I guess I don't have to go snake hunting anymore."

"I guess not." Josie grinned but the smile never made it to her eyes. She put out her hand. "I didn't get your first name."

He took it. Again, his was a vice-like grip. No shake, no sign that this was a friendly gesture and every indication that this was a power struggle.

"Peter. Peter Johnson."

"I'll be here every few days, Peter, until we get the guardianship question settled. If you think of anything that you'd be willing to share, I am happy to make it worth your while."

"Sure thing."

Josie saw herself out. She could feel him watching her until she got into her car but his interest felt mild, not malicious. Maybe the guy was what he said he was: a caretaker with a macho streak. Maybe he was an ex-con. Maybe a Vet. It wouldn't be too hard to find out. She fastened her seat belt, started the car and drove down the long road that led back to the main highway. Josie didn't turn on the radio. She wanted to live a little while with the hinky feeling she was getting from Ha Kuna House.

Behind her, Johnson sat down at the dining room table and resumed his chore. He pushed the cotton mop onto the cleaning rod and the cleaning rod through the bore of both guns until the cotton came out white. He lubricated the action, reassembled his hardware, and used the luster cloth until his weapons shined. He put one gun in the top drawer of the desk then strapped a shoulder holster on for the other one. He was headed off to check his garden. If he came across anyone there, they were stepping where they didn't belong and deserved exactly what they got – and that included Josie Bates.

CHAPTER 21

"I'm at the hospital, Jo." – Archer

"Are you all right?" – Josie

"I thought it was Hannah. It was the girl she was hanging with and I spooked her. She got onto the bed of a truck." – Archer

"And?" – Josie

"The driver took off. She flew out. They've got her in an induced coma." – Archer

"Go back to your hotel. Get some sleep." – Josie

"She's critical, Jo." – Archer

"It's not your fault." – Josie

"It feels like it. I'll stay here until she wakes up. What about you?" – Archer

"I'm fine. Don't worry about me." – Josie

"Jo? About your dad's discharge. You had the wrong date." – Archer

"Okay, so I was off a couple of days." – Josie

"Years, Jo. He resigned int'82 not '86. Jo? You there?" – Archer

Bernard Reynolds cast Johnson a look but didn't bother to say 'get your feet off my desk'. Nor did he say 'don't smoke in here'. He definitely didn't say 'go back to the cottage because you're giving me the creeps'. Instead, he sat down and started fiddling with papers hoping that Johnson would get the hint that he didn't want company. He didn't get it, not even when Bernard tapped his pen and cradled his head on his upturned palm as if he was concentrating. When Johnson didn't move, Bernard put down the pen, crossed his arms on the desk and asked:

"Do you want something or are you just passing time?"

"I have some news."

A Cheshire Cat grin split a face that didn't deserve it and Bernard was annoyed.

Between Emily, Josie Bates, visits by some wet-behind-the-ears social worker, guardianship hearings, and the silence from his superiors, Bernard was getting incredibly nervous and Johnson was no help.

Johnson took another drag of his cigarette, threw his head back and forged his lips into a perfect O as he blew a smoke ring. He flicked his ash into a coffee cup he had swiped from Bernard's desk.

"What?" Bernard snapped.

"First, I got a question," Johnson said. "Did you file the status report this quarter?"

"Of course I did," Bernard answered.

"Bummer." Johnson mused and then asked: "Did you sign Ian's name to it?"

"Yes," Bernard said.

"Double bummer."

Johnson took another drag and this time he blew a smoke ring in a smoke ring. Bernard didn't notice. He was staring at the tire-like treads on the soles of Johnson's heavy boots. Finally, he couldn't take it anymore.

"Do you mind?" Bernard pushed at Johnson's feet.

The other man dropped them to the ground, leaned close to the desk and said: "Ian Francis is dead."

The color drained from Bernard's face, his shoulders slumped, and the muscles in his stomach pulled so tight he almost cried out.

"I don't believe you. Who told you that?" he whispered.

"I got a memo asking for clarification on the House," Johnson said.

"Why didn't they send it to me?"

"Because you are the House, buddy. They want me to check up on you," Johnson reminded him.

"Oh, no. Oh, no," Bernard moaned.

"Yep. He was in D.C. of all places. The cops checked up on Ian when they confiscated his pass after he raised the roof at a hearing. The Department of Defense still showed Ian actively assigned to Ha Kuna House. Then he commits suicide and the cops pass that along. Some computer puts two and two together because your last report went in after the guy jumped. Now they're asking the million-dollar question: how could Ian Francis file resident status reports, if Ian Francis killed himself? Bad timing, Bernard. Really bad."

"Ian killed himself?"

Bernard turned a shade paler than a ghost. He had no real affection for Ian Francis so news of his death didn't upset him but Amelia's lie and his own stupidity did.

He reached for his in-box and found a stack of communiqués. They came in like clockwork but he answered when he felt like it because no one on the east coast paid attention. He flipped through them, looking for something with Ian's name on it. There it was. Sent weeks ago. A memorandum asking him to advise. Bernard fell back in his chair.

"Oh God. Oh, God," he moaned again as he tossed the request toward Johnson.

"Guess that's why they came to me. You don't answer your mail," Johnson drawled.

"How did it happen? Ian I mean," Bernard asked.

"He jumped out of a hotel window. But that's not the best part. He met up with your favorite lady there. Josie Bates. He scared the shit out of her from what I hear, but he must have told her something because she's here."

"No. Nobody is that good an actress. She didn't know about Emily. She was looking for someone else – a girl. Ian didn't tell her anything about this house. Ian couldn't have told her anything."

Bernard's brain was going a mile a minute, pinging from anger at Josie Bates for darkening his doorstep to Amelia for being a lying little bitch, and Ian for being a nut case with enough brains left to get himself all the way to Washington in the first place. Johnson had a simpler outlook.

"It doesn't matter how Bates got here; it matters that she did. Ian's dead, so we can chalk him off the list of worries. It's Amelia I'm not too sure about."

"I know. I know. I can't believe she made up that story about relatives taking him in," Bernard said.

"I can't believe you didn't run it down," Johnson pointed out.

"I meant to. I won't stand for it. I'm going to find out what she's up to right now." Bernard grabbed the telephone but Johnson was quick to get out of his chair and slap his hand back down.

"You're not going to do anything," he growled. "We've got to figure this out from our end. The dude is dead and you're putting through updates on the residents under his signature. They could haul you in for fraud and a zillion other things. You're going to be looking at a lot of time, and it's not going to be in a place as pretty as Molokai."

"Who would prosecute? They wouldn't dare," Bernard objected. "Nobody would risk the public exposure."

"Hell, there's some crusader out there who would love to tie you to a stake. Me, I'm just a hired hand," Johnson reminded him. "It's on your shoulders, but I want to help you. So let's just think."

Johnson took his seat slowly, ready to spring in case Bernard Reynolds needed some extra convincing. He didn't. He was envisioning his federal trial, his conviction, his incarceration. Johnson, was envisioning how they were going to get out of this mess. He didn't necessarily need Bernard Reynolds to keep his little enterprise going but it made things a whole lot easier. The last thing either of them needed was an investigation. Thankfully, Bernard was coming around.

"You're right. Okay. You're right." Bernard took a deep breath. "Who contacted you?"

"It was a computer generated checklist asking me to confirm sender's viability," Johnson said.

"That's good. It was just kicked off and some clerk forwarded it," Bernard said.

"But it's not going to stay that way if they go back through the records. You've been faking Ian's reports for years. How many quarterlies does that add up to? A whole, helluva lot, Bernard. Taking it all off the table is the easiest solution."

"What do you mean take it off the table? What does that mean?" Bernard demanded.

"Shut the place down, Bernard. Just shut it down. Those goons in Washington don't care what happens to you and some of them would probably be happier not to have to deal with this anymore. You'll be doing everyone a favor."

"You're right. You're right." Bernard sat back in his chair, miserable, not quite comprehending what Johnson was suggesting, but agreeing anyway.

"Give it some thought. Come on over tonight and we'll talk about it."

Johnson rapped Bernard's desk and took his leave. Bernard watched him walk across the open area and took note of the beautiful grounds, the well kept paths, the jungle beyond. He couldn't imagine what it would be like to lose all this. Still, he knew it had to come to an end someday. He just didn't expect it to end this way.

�’ᴁᴈ’

Lydia Patriota looked out one window of the limousine while Ambrose looked out the other. He was silent; she was worried. Something was on his mind, which was all well and good, but the fact that he hadn't shared his concern with her was something new.

She smoothed the skirt of her dress. She crossed her legs. She looked at her husband just as the car turned and the oncoming headlights illuminated his face. He was such a handsome man.

"Lydia, is there anything you did when you were young that you are ashamed of," he asked.

"I am young, Ambrose," she laughed.

"True. Then let me ask you this, is there a transgression that you would not want known to the public."

Lydia swiveled in order to look directly at her husband. "If there's something you want to ask me, honey, then ask me because there is nothing I am ashamed to tell you."

Ambrose laughed, "No, nothing like that. Infidelity is not the question."

"Then what is it?"

"If you were young and did something and it came back to haunt you years later, if it really was nothing in the grand scheme of things but someone wanted to make it important, how would you handle it?"

"Could I just kill whoever was so damn interested in what I did when I was a kid?" she asked.

"Not an option, Lydia."

"All right then. I suppose I'd say 'sorry, I was young'. If that didn't work then I'd spin the hell out of it until everyone was so dizzy they didn't know what they were looking at."

Ambrose smiled. She was so wise. He said: "You look particularly lovely tonight, my dear."

He kissed his wife and counted himself a lucky man. Lydia kissed him back and then looked out the window again. Now, she was really worried.

⤜⤏

Josie swayed with the pitch and roll as the Molokai ferry made its way across the blustery ocean. Her head rested against the wall, her arms were crossed, and her feet planted on the worn floor inside the cabin she shared with a few other travelers. This time Stephen made no attempt to accompany her and she was glad. He could spend his time hunting down a chemist to look at the medicine packets and she would have some time to think.

Josie thought about Judge Mohr's understanding of Hannah's predicament, his concern for Emily's state of mind since her episode in the jungle, and his admiration for the plan Josie had given him for Emily's care when she got to Hermosa Beach. She couldn't have asked for a better judge. She only wished her petition had remained her biggest problem. It wasn't.

The boat pitched. The woman next to Josie gasped and put her hand to her heart. Josie gave her a quick smile that she hoped was reassuring, rolled her head against the wall, and looked at the other unhappy passengers. Deciding the quarters were too close, Josie minced her way out to the deck and fell onto one of the benches just in time for a rollercoaster drop. She breathed deeply and turned her face into the needles of spray instead of away from it. Molokai rose from the sea, its lush mountains veiled in the mist. Alone on the deck, she couldn't keep her thoughts from going back to the fly in the ointment: her father.

Upstanding, trustworthy, the brave warrior and selfless father was also a liar if Archer was right about his discharge. And if he lied about his service, logic dictated that he lied about Emily. Even if it was by omission, that was a vile thing to do. She understood why he wouldn't want to visit some horror on a child but Josie was a grown woman and a lawyer when he passed. She would not have been devastated by a deathbed revelation.

It was the knowledge of her father's deception that made Josie reconsider the situation she found herself in. She no longer wanted to give up and go home because now there were amends to be made. Maybe not on behalf of her father, but because she had spent so many years placing blame at her mother's feet. For that, Josie was truly sorry and she would make it up to Emily. Toward that end, she braved the unfriendly sea to keep her visitation appointment. She was determined not to give Judge Mohr or Bernard Reynolds any reason to question her commitment to her mother.

Suddenly, the boat lurched. A wave slammed against the side and every plank shuddered. Josie grabbed onto the cabinet next to her. When the boat started rolling again, she put the hood of her windbreaker up and pulled the drawstrings to close the neck. A few minutes later, the boat entered the harbor. Josie was first off the ferry and inside the Keoloko car when she finally figured out what to do. The idea hit her like a brick. It was so simple Josie couldn't believe she hadn't thought of it before.

She had questions and they all had to do with the government: Who worked for what agency? What about the discrepancies of her father's service records? Who really owned the real estate in the middle of a national park? Why did a Department of Defense employee have anything to do with Ha Kuna house? Why was a Canadian scientist employed by the United States government for decades? The list went on and on. The government was an unwieldy beast with a thick bureaucratic skin that seemed impenetrable, but there were people who could cut through it for her.

Josie whipped out her phone, ran through her list of contacts, and pressed the one she wanted. She was so excited by her epiphany she could hardly contain herself. When her call was answered, she said: "Josie Bates calling for Eugene Weller."

෧ඁ෩

Eugene Weller's conversation with Josie Bates had been surreal. Her call came out of the blue and the sound of her voice unnerved him. She had, of course, been top of mind but only as a concept, just one tab in an ever-expanding file, a name associated with phone numbers in daily reports. She was the grit in his oyster. He had never expected to speak with her again, certainly never expected that she would feel comfortable calling him directly, and definitely certain she wouldn't feel entitled to a favor.

It had been five minutes since he bade the woman goodbye and he was still paralyzed. His right hand lay atop the telephone, his left was still flat on his desk, his spine was rigid, and his neck muscles so tight he was starting to get a headache.

He sniffed, raising one nostril and then the other. He opened his mouth and stretched it wide and long until his jaw muscles popped. Then he shook himself like a wet dog. He felt the blood starting to flow. Finally, Eugene took his hand off the phone, put his long fingers to his temples and pressed the soft little indentation in his skull. He raised both arms, landed his elbows on the desk and was just about to grasp his pounding head in his upturned palms when he heard the knock, saw the door fly open, and Ann's compact and competent self walk in.

"Dammit. I told you to wait until I give you permission to come in here."

Ann stopped cold. Her eyes were the size of saucers, her lips frozen around the first word she had intended to speak. In all the years she had worked for Ambrose Patriota – and by default Eugene Weller – she had never heard the man raise his voice. When Eugene was unhappy he drawled, he snipped, he degraded, he insulted, but he never, ever screamed. Thank goodness he had never done it before since he sounded like a nine-year-old girl when he did.

Eugene swallowed hard. He rotated his neck and raised a hand, flipping his fingers to indicate she may enter. "Sorry. I'm sorry. Come in."

"Senator Patriota's proposed schedule for pre-convention activities."

She approached cautiously and slid this on to his desk. When he didn't move, she put the next one under his nose.

"Mrs. Patriota would like you to arrange for a VIP tour of the capitol including lunch in the Senate dining room. I've listed her guests, their personal contributions, connections, and available dates for the tour."

Ann held her breath.

Nothing.

Her mouth went dry; her brain went into overdrive.

Maybe Eugene was dying.

Maybe he was being indicted.

Maybe Senator Patriota was dying or being indicted.

Maybe Eugene had been fired.

Maybe he got laid.

Maybe he tried to get laid and couldn't manage to…

Ann pushed that image straight out of her mind and got on with work.

"Eyes only from NSA."

She put an envelope in Eugene's line of sight. His lashes fluttered. His torqued lips ratcheted tighter. There was a beat, a breath. He was about to manage a thank you but Ann had fled.

He picked up the eyes-only, opened the seal, and gave it his full attention: phone numbers, times, dates, names, and so much more. Michael Horn, Amelia Francis, Bernard Reynolds. And there were other names and numbers: the law firm in Hermosa Beach, a man whose number indicated he was roaming out of area into the northwest. And there was Josie Bates making a nuisance of herself with the DOD, the VA, Fort Hood, Ha Kuna House, the Maui courthouse, and the personal number of Stephen Kyle who ran Keoloko Enterprises. NSA was doing an exceptional job. All of this information was cross-referenced by date and time, duration of calls and in some cases notations on the outcome of the conversations. The picture was coming into focus for Josie Bates, Eugene was sure, but it was sharper for him. The net Bates was throwing was wide and uncontrollable. She wanted simplification but that could only happen with his help and he wasn't about to give it. He dialed Woodrow Calister's very private number. It was answered on the second ring.

"I received a call from our friend in Hawaii. She would like me to expedite a number of requests under the Freedom of Information Act," Eugene said. "I think it's time we have a meeting with Ambrose."

"No. We protect him at all costs. Do you understand, Eugene? Plausible deniability where Ambrose is concerned. That's what we want. I'll look into it. I'll take care of it all."

CHAPTER 22

"The girl's name is Sandy Macintosh. She's a runaway. Pick up if you're there. Okay. I'll fill you in later. Hope everything is going well with Emily. Love you." – Voice mail, Archer to Josie

ಲಾಡಿ

Amelia slipped into Emily's room, closing the door quietly behind her even though there was no one in the house who could possibly be disturbed. Amelia nodded to Josie but looked at Emily as she crossed the room. The older woman was ready for bed dressed in a pink nightgown, her short hair brushed to the side, her pale skin pearly in the shadows. Silently she gazed at nothing, thought of nothing, and felt nothing as far as Josie and Amelia could tell.

In the distance there was a flash of lightning. Josie counted the seconds until she heard thunder, a crash and then a roll under the onslaught of rain. She thought of Stephen Kyle, snug in his house with the girls and his special scotch to keep him warm. She thought of Archer in his motel cabin in Oregon. She thought of Faye cuddled up with Max. Josie had tried to call them all but the phone wasn't working and neither were the lights. They flickered, went out, and popped back on again as Amelia slid onto the cot she had set up for Josie. They sat side-by-side across from Emily.

"He's still over at Johnson's place. I don't know what to do. We should have permission for you to stay."

"I doubt he'd throw me out in this weather," Josie said. "Don't worry about it."

"What if I get fired?"

"You don't want to stay here, do you?" Josie asked.

"No, but I want to leave on my own terms," Amelia answered.

"Let's not worry about something that hasn't happened. Reynolds won't even know I'm here."

"True. I stayed lots of times when I couldn't get dad home. I don't think Mr. Reynolds even knew about it. If he did, he didn't care."

"The weather will be better in the morning, I'll be out of here before he even gets up," Josie assured her.

"Okay," Amelia sighed. "Have you heard anything from that man you called?"

"Eugene Weller?" Josie shook her head. "No, it's too soon."

"You didn't mention me, did you?"

"No," Josie said.

The lights popped again. The rain fell harder. Josie thought this must be what it felt like to be Emily: always in the dark, memories of Ian coming and going like the rain. Amelia was more practical. She said:

"You should see how this is done."

"What?"

"Putting your mom to bed. If you're going to take her home with you, you better know how things are done," Amelia answered.

"I don't know if she'll be going home with me," Josie reminded her.

"She will." The lights went back on. Amelia was looking at Josie, her narrow face pinched, her lips pursed and her shadowed eyes looking wearier than ever before. "Come on. Get up. She can't do it on her own."

Amelia got Emily off the bed and the ritual began: gentle direction and encouragement, small steps, pauses. A toothbrush, a hairbrush, more encouragement, sit down, feet up, lay down, cover her with a quilt. A prayer.

"I don't pray," Josie said.

"When you live with someone like your mom long enough you will." Josie glanced at Amelia. The young woman was looking fondly at Emily. This was no complaint on her part, but a notation that sometimes a caregiver needed a higher power to make it through. "She'll fall asleep in a while. It comes on very fast. She doesn't wake up at night. She's not like Ian. You'll be able to sleep at home."

Amelia went to the switch near the door and turned off the light. When she returned, she stood with Josie. Emily's eyes were still open. They glittered. Her hand moved.

"Take it. Give her a pat," Amelia directed.

Josie did, but hers wasn't the hand Emily wanted. Her hand went limp before she raised it again. This time Amelia took her hand, kissed it, and put it under the covers.

"She'll come around." Amelia's voice was tight. Josie had nothing to add. She knew that Amelia was just preparing herself for losing Emily. "Try to get some sleep."

"You, too. Goodnight," Josie said but she was talking to Amelia Francis' back. "Amelia?"

"Yes?" The woman paused looking ghostly in the intermittent light from the lamps that swung on the posts outside.

"Thank you for everything."

"Sure," Amelia said.

"Sleep well," Josie answered and meant it.

❧❧

"Okay, Bernard. It's time. Bernard!"

"What? Yeah? I'm okay. I'm set. Let's do this." Bernard Reynolds jerked up, kicking over the bottle of booze and spilling it on the cottage floor. "I'm sorry. Johnson, it's a mess. I'll clean it up."

"Don't be an ass." Johnson said with disgust.

They'd been at it through the early evening and into the night, drinking and planning, planning and drinking. The guy couldn't hold his liquor and was proving to be more of a wuss than Johnson could ever have imagined. He waffled, he wailed, he could think of a hundred unintended consequences but couldn't see the one important intended one – that his butt would be saved. What he didn't know was that Johnson's would, too. If Reynolds wasn't up to the task then Johnson would have to do it on his terms. That wouldn't be good either. There would be way too much to explain if they did it his way so it had to be Reynolds.

"I'm not being an ass. I'm ready. Really. All set to go." Bernard stood up and pushed his hair back. He tucked his shirt into this pants and then pulled it out again. "I'm set. Let's go."

"Good. Put your jacket on. It's still storming out there."

Finding himself a little wobbly, Bernard excused himself and went to the can. When he came back his face was ruddy as if he had scrubbed it hard.

"You solid, Bernard?" Johnson tossed the man's jacket at him. Bernard caught it and put it on while Johnson talked and checked his gun.

"All set," Bernard said.

"Okay. You've got everything you need in the office, right? Enough of that medicine?"

"Yes," Bernard said.

"And you're sure it's the right amount?" Johnson pressed.

"I'm not a doctor, Johnson." Bernard complained. Johnson shot him a look and Bernard backtracked. "Yes, I'm sure this will do it. And I'm sure you won't need that. Just leave it here, Johnson."

Johnson held up his gun, "No can do. I never go out without it. Besides, you want me to have your back, don't you?"

Bernard didn't point out that there was no one interested in his back at the moment. He also did not think now was the time to reiterate that he really, really, really was having second thoughts about this whole thing. Even if the powers that be came after him, there were ten valid arguments to be made for his ongoing deception. Protection of the program and Bernard's superiors was not the least of them. Certainly that would not only be understandable but forgivable. Still, Johnson was a single-minded sort of fellow and a stickler for detail. He threw open the door. Bernard hesitated but finally went for it only to stop when he came abreast of Johnson.

"She's not here," Bernard said.

"Who?" Johnson asked.

"The night girl. Her car's not here and it's late."

"The storm probably hung her up. All the better. Amelia will catch it all in the morning."

"I can't believe Amelia left and didn't wait for her," Bernard said.

"Well, since her car isn't here either, I guess she cut out," Johnson drawled. "Doesn't matter anyway. There's nothing to do at night."

"But that wasn't the plan," Bernard complained.

"It doesn't matter who finds them. It matters that they're found. You report it and the operation is done. They'll have this place cleared out before the fax is dry. They aren't going to put anything else in here for a while so we can hang out. That's the plan, Bernard. That's what we agreed on." Johnson gave the man a little shove.

"Okay. Okay." Bernard pulled his jacket collar up.

Johnson took Bernard's arm and together they ran across the yard, splashing through the mud, their pants wet almost to the knees. They went through the back door and Johnson stopped.

"Take your shoes off," Johnson directed.

"What?"

"If anyone wants to check this out, then we can't have mud all over the place. It's got to look natural."

Bernard thought that was the smartest thing Johnson had said all day; he also thought it was a bit frightening that Johnson was thinking ahead like that. Bernard removed his shoes and put them neatly by the desk in his office. Johnson did the same and then waited while Bernard opened the closet, turned on the overhead light, and took out a box.

"Is that it?"

"Yes."

"Okay, let's go," Johnson said.

Bernard hesitated, holding the box in front of him like a kid disappointed in a Christmas present. Johnson retraced his steps. Bernard looked at him. He opened his mouth but the look on Johnson's face told him all he needed to know. The big man wanted this wrapped up and he wasn't going to take no for an answer.

The night girl was upset and scared. She was more scared than she was upset because the road seemed to disappear and reappear with no particular rhyme or reason. Even though she knew she wasn't near the cliffs, now and again she would throw the steering wheel one way or the other believing that she was just about to sail over the edge of one. She wondered where her friend was. Maybe she was already safe at Ha Kuna House. Or maybe she was smart and had stayed home all together.

The night girl sobbed. She sat in her car crying, her hands on the wheel, trying to decide if she should go forward or back. She decided to go forward since it was six of one and half a dozen of the other. She stepped on the gas. The mud was too deep, and her tires too old to gain traction.

"Oh God! Oh God!"

The night girl muttered and wept and wept and muttered as she stared into the Hawaiian darkness, cringed under the wrath of the Hawaiian storm, and wondered if she was going to die of fright.

CHAPTER 23

Scientists in Edinburgh announced that they have completed a mind-meld. Not exactly a Star Trek Vulcan move but they do confirm that they have successfully connected the mind of a man and a mouse. The man was able to move the mouse's tail just by thinking about it. How's that for a dose of Sci-Fi? – KFI talk radio

෨෧

It was almost midnight when Amelia threw off her blanket and swung her legs over the side of the couch. Palms down on the worn fabric, feet solidly on the floor, her chin rested on her chest, and her blond hair fell over her eyes. Those eyes of hers stared through the golden strands and into the darkness, pixilating everything in the room into fields of gray and sparkles of white. As it is with people who work in shadowy places, Amelia saw more than a normal human being would; as with those who work with the sick, she heard more than most people ever could; as with people who are often alone, Amelia could sense when things were amiss and something was amiss in Ha Kuna House.

Amelia stood up, listening again for the sound that had disturbed her uneasy sleep. It was not the old lady calling out. It was not Mr. Traini snoring. It was not Emily, agitated and wanting Amelia's hand to hold. It was not the night girl and her friend giggling. It was not a crack of lightning although that's what she thought it was at first. But it was something because Amelia's nerves were on fire like Fourth of July sparklers. She knelt with one leg on the sofa, her other foot still on the ground, her arms crossed on the back of the couch so that she could look out the tiny dormer window. The rain still fell in sheets, but the wind had died down. Amelia pressed her forehead against the glass and strained to see the grounds. There was nothing out there.

She stood up again, her eyes sweeping the room, landing on the small chair with the broken arm, the boxes Keoloko had delivered a day earlier, the broken padlock hanging from the small closet door that led to an open space under the eaves. Amelia knew that there was a loose board right in front of her so, when she finally did move, she avoided it.

She cracked the door and saw the one to Emily's suite was still shut. She went to the top of the stairs and looked over. The landing was empty. She slid down the steps and stayed close to the wall. On the second landing, she looked over again and that's when she saw the night girl's legs. Another step and she saw the night girl's friend lying beside her. Amelia knew they were dead. It wasn't the blood on the floor, it wasn't the fact that the night girl's eyes were open and unblinking or that her leg didn't twitch. Amelia just instantly knew that they were dead. Whoever had killed them was in the house because she heard an angry voice tumbling down the hall from the kitchen. The voices weren't loud enough to identify, but she knew one belonged to a man.

Amelia didn't run or cry out or panic but she imagined she would soon. Until then her instincts guided her. She retraced her steps, keeping her eyes on the open spaces below. On the second floor she crept into Mr. Traini's room. He would be the easiest to secure. If she got him into his wheelchair she could get him into the closet. That would be little protection, but it was the best she could do.

"Mr. Traini." Amelia eased back his sheets and leaned close to his ear so that he could hear her whispers. "Wake up Mr. Traini. Listen. You must listen…"

Amelia pulled back. Her fingers were trembling when she touched his pulse point on his neck. As soon as she determined there was none, Amelia Francis' grabbed the railing around the bed and doubled over, forcing herself not to throw up.

⌇

Johnson and Reynolds faced off in the kitchen. Bernard was the color of ice. It wasn't because he was appalled that he had just given the residents a little too much of their medicine – that didn't really feel like murder – but because of what Johnson had done. Johnson was an animal. He didn't look any different for having shot two young women as they came through the front door, wet and grateful that they were safe at last. Now that was murder and the sight of that was enough to make the color drain from Bernard Reynolds' face forever.

"Are you crazy? Are you crazy?" Bernard had said that about twenty times and Johnson was getting tired of hearing it.

"Hey! Hey! What was I supposed to do?"

"Just..." Bernard sputtered. His hands were flapping like wings "Just nothing. I mean, for God's sake, you killed them in cold blood."

"You killed the other people."

"They were half dead," Bernard wailed. "We needed the night girl to find them. We agreed. She would find them and assume they all just passed away in their sleep. It's not like it would have been unexpected." Bernard paced. He threw up his hands. "What were we thinking? It was a stupid plan. Now there are two girls with bullets in them. We can't do this. It was wrong from the start. We have to call someone. I'm not going to be running for the rest of my life. I won't, Johnson. It will be fine. If we turn ourselves in now and explain...Look...Here's how it is."

Bernard bumped around his desk, knocking things over in the dark, opening drawers until he found his flashlight. His hands were shaking so badly the darn light danced all over the place. He babbled as he fell into his chair and pulled the phone toward him.

"Here's what we say. We say they surprised you. It was self-defense. You are security and it was storming. Totally understandable on a night like this. And the other three? Natural causes. That's how we explain that. I mean, since we didn't get to Emily no one is going to think that we were...we were..."

Bernard juggled with the receiver. It flew out of his hands but he caught it and held it to his chest. Johnson stepped forward and put his hands on the desk.

"Say it Bernard. No one would think we were going to exterminate them. Is that what people won't think?"

"Well, yes."

"You're an idiot."

"No, I'm not. And I'm the authority here. You seem to have forgotten that. Good grief, Johnson, how did I ever let you talk me into this? This was crazy from the beginning. What were you thinking? What were you…"

Bernard Reynolds never finished his question. Johnson didn't want to explain again what he was thinking so he put both of them out of their misery with a well-placed shot between Bernard Reynolds' eyes.

❧

"Wake up."

Josie bucked and cried. Her cries were muffled by a hand over her mouth, and her body was pinned by someone lying on top of her pushing the breath out of her. Her panic was almost unbearable until she realized it was Amelia who was doing these things. Josie blinked but she couldn't see Amelia's eyes. They were nothing but two black holes in her pale and narrow face. Her breath was hot and her shushing urgent.

"Be quiet," she hissed, sliding off only when Josie nodded.

Amelia gestured toward Emily. Then she pointed downstairs, put her finger to her lips, and began her pantomime all over again. Understanding what needed to be done but not why, Josie put on her sweat pants. When she went for her shoes, Amelia shook her head hard. Josie swept them up as Amelia motioned for her to listen at the door. Josie did as she was directed, but heard nothing. She glanced over her shoulder to see that Amelia had Emily sitting up.

She put her ear back to the door.

Once again, she looked over her shoulder.

Amelia and Emily were ready to go. Josie reached for the doorknob but Amelia frantically pointed toward the room where Josie had first seen Emily. Josie shook her head vehemently. It was a dead end. Amelia ignored her and half dragged Emily with her into the rocking chair room.

Having no choice, Josie went after them only to turn and lunge for her purse. Slinging it across her body, she dashed into the room in time to see Emily and Amelia disappear through a panel in the wall. Josie ducked through. Her last thought was the hope that she wasn't following a woman as insane as her father. The opening was half her height and when the panel shut and the darkness enveloped the three women, Josie cried out.

She could not hear the wind. She could not see outside. She could not orient herself. She could not bear pitch black or silence or enclosed spaces. It was the mountains, the mountains all over again, and Archer was not coming for her because Archer did not know where she was. Just when Josie was sure that she would perish, a warm hand took hers and a silken whisper followed.

"Don't be afraid. Come with me."

And with that, another panel opened and there was just enough grey light for Josie to see that Amelia was urging them down a rickety stairwell but it was Emily who held Josie's hand so that she would not be afraid in the dark.

CHAPTER 24

Scopolamine known as hyoscine and Brugmansia is a tropane alkaloid. It has become increasingly popular as a date rape drug, because unlike other date rape drugs that knock the victim out, this drug leaves the victim in a state of compliancy, in an awake zombie state, where their mind is totally controlled so they can participate in the rape, then remember nothing at all. It is that very result that made the drug so appealing to the CIA. – Wikipedia

✤

The Speaker of the House, a lobbyist for the airline industry, and a civil rights activist were dining at Seasons, table 53. Woodrow Calister and Ambrose Patriota had the slightly preferable table 54. Before they got down to business, they talked about Lydia and her exceptional fundraising capabilities. They talked about the young doctor who was awarded the grant to further her studies of mind management. They talked about football and they talked about the menu. Ambrose praised the new chef; Woodrow lamented the chic portions. They talked about the problems in the Middle East.

They did not talk about Eugene Weller, Ha Kuna House or the targeted requests of Josie Bates for information. They did not discuss Michael Horn or certain declassified documents that were now available regarding CHATTER, Artichoke, and Marigold. Woodrow and Ambrose did not talk about these things because to protect Ambrose's presidency was to protect Woodrow's own destiny.

Woodrow did not enjoy keeping secrets from his friend because he was a very decent man. But he was also a decision maker and once decisions were made he owned them. These things made Woodrow an excellent senator and would make him an exceptional vice president.

Sadly, he was never going to get to test his mettle. He was not going to be on the ticket. Ambrose told him so between the arugula salad with heart of palm and the seared salmon accompanied by asparagus quenelles. Thoughts of collective peace and prosperity, decency and practicality were forgotten as Woodrow Calister experienced an unprecedented fury and embraced a ruthless selfishness.

"I am disappointed. I am surprised and disappointed."

"I know, my friend."

Ambrose interpreted Woodrow's even tone as acceptance. The older man motioned to the waiter for coffee. Only Ambrose thanked him when he brought it. When he was gone, the two men remained silent as they added their sugar and cream and stirred their coffee with silver spoons.

"Who will it be, Ambrose? Who could fill the spot better than me?" Woodrow demanded.

"Jerry Norn," Ambrose answered and the knife in Woodrow's gut pulled up and laid him bare. "I considered Mark, but Lydia and I both agree that it should be Jerry."

"I hate to point this out, but Lydia is your damn wife and since when is she the authority on who is best for the country?" Woodrow's chin clicked to one side and then the other as if grinding down the hard edges of the words he was about to say. "I'm better on paper than Jerry and I'm a better man in the real world, Ambrose. Quite frankly, this is a bullshit decision."

"I know how it looks right now, Woodrow," Ambrose said. "I don't often give nod to politics, but this time I'm afraid I must."

Ambrose sat back. He touched the sides of the delicate china cup with the tip of his elegant fingers. In the soft lighting of the restaurant Ambrose knew he looked his best, he only wished he felt it. This was not a pleasant conversation. He, too, was disappointed on so many levels but this decision was necessary.

"You have performed admirably for this country, my friend. You have made the hard calls. You hold people's lives in your hands and yet the public will never know you for the true patriot you are. If I were to put you on the ticket and there were questions that couldn't be answered about those calls, your candidacy would be detrimental to the campaign."

"I'm not head of the CIA, Ambrose. I head up a committee," Woodrow pointed out.

"You might as well be a spymaster. Do you want to be questioned about what you know of our Middle East operations, or what happened to the president of–"

"That would make better press than trying to explain why the vice president of the United States can't keep it in his pants. With me you'd at least be having an honest discussion of how this country is governed." Woodrow picked up his coffee. He couldn't look at Ambrose. He muttered in his disgust, "My God, Ambrose, is that the kind of above-board ticket you want? Jerry's candidacy is tawdry."

"And controllable," Ambrose reminded him.

"Then why not Mark? Hyashi would be better than Jerry."

"We already have the Asian vote and good relations with Japan." Ambrose dismissed the idea.

"I'm not talking about his ethnicity. I'm talking about a good man with a solid family life," Woodrow shot back.

"Not an exciting ticket." Ambrose waved away the suggestion. "And I'm not sure he's committed to my vision. Oh, he may be fascinated by the possibility of consciousness and manipulation, but I see him waver. I see his worry."

"At least he's thinking, Ambrose. That's more than I can say for Jerry."

"You sell our colleague short," Ambrose chuckled. "Jerry's mind never stops looking for profitable opportunity. Not just money, Woodrow, but opportunities to make this country greater than it has ever been before. Unlike you or I, Jerry's currency is love. The more he gets, the more he gives. Everyone responds to him. Women are wooed, men want to have a beer with him, old folk see their wayward sons and grandsons in him. The public loves a bad boy, Woodrow, and we, sadly, are far too boring together. No, this is the perfect ticket: Jerry's energy and my gravitas. It's the stuff that captures the imagination."

"That's what you're all about, isn't it, Ambrose? You want to screw with people's minds to get what you want. I imagine Mark is right to be concerned. You are a sick bastard."

"The science of politics is quite different from the science that will deliver the world from the consequences of its own misguided thinking," Ambrose answered. "Besides, I might need you for something more important. I'm waiting to see how it plays out."

"There isn't anything more important, so don't patronize me."

Woodrow pushed aside the coffee. He leaned over the table and lowered his voice even though no one would have dared come close now that the conversation had intensified.

"Four of our troops were killed testing Medusa. Did you know that, Ambrose? They were killed testing a weapon that shot sound waves into their brains. This was a weapon that our research assured us was non-lethal."

"I am sorry to hear that." Ambrose sat back. "But you can't deny that testing was necessary. Better to disable the mind than to shed blood if it's for a good and noble cause. The mind is the thing we must conquer. The mind is—"

"Save it Ambrose." Woodrow stood up abruptly, "If I were you I wouldn't be worrying so much about people's brains, I'd be worried about who's watching your back."

Woodrow Calister walked out of the restaurant leaving Ambrose Patriota to ponder that Woodrow was almost prescient. For, indeed, Ambrose Patriota knew exactly who was watching his back and who wasn't.

❧

Johnson had put his boots back on and now walked the house without worrying about the noise or the mess he was making. Emily Bates was the only one left in the house and she was as good as dead. But when Johnson got to Emily's room and saw the empty bed he was on his guard. He did a quarter turn and stepped back to look into the adjoining room. She was not in the rocking chair. The bathroom was dark.

Keeping his weapon steady he sidestepped to the bed and put his hand on the mattress. The sheets were warm. He backed up a step and touched the cot. It was cool, but canvas did not retain body heat in the same way that cotton sheets did. He had no way of telling if someone had lain on it ten minutes or ten hours ago. Then again, he had never been in this room so he didn't know if this was standard operating procedure because Emily was ambulatory. Maybe the night girl had the cot ready in case her party friend didn't show. Maybe Amelia used it during the day. Not that it mattered. Nobody was using it now.

The wind cracked and howled again, the rain beat against the glass of the tall window where he had often looked up to see the beautiful, mindless woman staring out at nothing. It bugged him that she'd given him the slip, but he wasn't overly concerned. She wouldn't last long out there. Even if she did, what in the heck could she tell anyone? She was an idiot, as good as deaf, blind, and dumb. Johnson walked to the window. His gun now dangled from his hand. The night girl's car and her friend's were watery images on the drive.

He started back through the house, still bothered that Emily was nowhere to be found. He hated loose ends. By the time he got to the back door, Johnson had worked himself into a good snit worthy of Bernard Reynolds.

❧❧❧

The staircase was built into a pocket of space between the inside and outside wall. What Josie had assumed were windows to the interior of the house were really additions to the façade at the back of the house.

"What is this place?" Josie whispered.

"The servants used it in the old days," Amelia answered. "Come on, Emily. Just a little more."

"Who else knows it's here?" Josie asked.

"It doesn't matter." They wound down and down until they reached the ground floor and stopped between two doors.

"Kitchen." Amelia nodded toward one door but opened the other. Warm, wet air blew in and Josie pulled Emily close, shielding her with her body. Amelia didn't wait, she ran the minute she called out: "Come on. Go now."

Josie started after her but Emily pulled back. Josie tightened her grip on Emily's arm. This time she wasn't going to be caught off guard; this time Josie would be the strong one.

"She said go."

Josie forced her mother outside. Head down, they rushed after Amelia, Emily awkward and stumbling, but keeping up better than Josie would have thought possible. They were almost across the backyard and into the forest when Emily fell. Josie screamed for Amelia. By some miracle she heard and rushed back. Together they picked up Emily and ran again, throwing themselves into the forest, cutting a parallel path to the road Emily and Josie had taken a week earlier.

Amelia threw herself into a thicket and pulled Emily and Josie with her. Huddled together, they stared ahead, waiting. Suddenly, Amelia lunged forward and grabbed the vines and branches and pulled them tighter to create a natural hutch. She sat back and put her arm around Emily.

"The night girl and her friend are dead. Mr. Traini, too. Maybe Mr. Reynolds." Amelia whispered. "Everyone I'm pretty sure."

"Who did it?" Josie asked.

Amelia shook her head. She pushed her wet hair out of her eyes and then pushed Emily's short hair back as she spoke.

"Whoever it was, they were still in the house. I heard a man."

"We shouldn't stay here," Josie warned.

The rain was coming through the canopy of plants and tree branches. She didn't mind for herself or Amelia, but she had no idea if Emily was strong enough to stay as they were.

"I don't know where to go," Amelia answered.

The words were barely out of her mouth when Emily bolted, scrambling up, fighting through the plants, all arms and legs, and grunts. Josie caught her gown but she twisted and turned until she was free. The younger women fought their way out and into the rain. Tenting their hands over their eyes, they squinted against the needles of water.

"There!" Josie sprinted ahead with Amelia on their heels.

All three women crashed through the forest, Emily too far ahead to be caught. She fought through the low hanging branches, pounded across the ground cover, slipped on the muddy bare patches of ground, slashed at the vines with frantic hands. She was suddenly strong, all motion, a physical force to be reckoned with. More than that, though, Emily Bates seemed to have a purpose. Something spawned her flight, something drove her to keep a step ahead of her daughter, and something deep in her brain guided her forward on a true path. Suddenly, Josie realized they were getting close to the cliffs.

"Mom!" she screamed, but she had lost sight of Emily.

When she reached the place where she had last seen her mother Josie fell to her knees, bent over, and slammed her fists into the ground, but Amelia was sharper eyed.

"Get up. Get up. Look at this." Amelia hunkered down a few feet away, pushing aside plants. "She's in there."

"Where?" Josie crawled to Amelia and got onto her haunches. At first all she saw were plants and vines but then her eyes adjusted.

"A cave?"

"Something else," Amelia said.

They peered at a corridor high enough and wide enough for two men to walk through. At one time it had been paved but the concrete was now cracked and broken. A dry breeze blew up toward them so whatever was in there, it was sheltered. Josie found her cell phone. There were no bars to connect her to the outside world but she had a flashlight app. She held it up and led the way. Ten yards down they stopped in front of a heavy wooden door hanging on rusting iron hinges. In the middle of it was an opening hatched with iron bars.

"What is this?" Amelia whispered.

Josie shook her head and ran the light over it, top to bottom and side to side. Amelia moved up against Josie's shoulder.

"Emily?" Amelia called.

There was no answer. Instead, carried on the cool, dry air of the bunker they heard:

"Marigolds. Marigolds, Ian. Yes, we are."

CHAPTER 25

Restricted Environmental Stimulation Therapy (REST)
There are two basic methods of restricted environmental stimulation
therapy (REST): chamber REST and flotation REST.

❧❧

Josie couldn't imagine anything blacker than pitch and yet this place was. It was blacker than the sea that had embraced Billy Zuni, darker than the cement outbuilding where she had been a prisoner, darker than her child's heart after her mother's desertion. This place, Josie was sure, was darker than hell and it wasn't because it was buried in the ground, it was because this place was evil.

They were in a high domed, concrete room. An old, tin light fixture hung from the ceiling but it looked like it hadn't been used in years. Josie pulled the chain. It didn't work. A sweep of the place with her flashlight illuminated boxes, tables, and equipment stacked around the perimeter. Emily Bates sat in a high backed wooden chair carrying on her conversation with Ian Francis, long dead and lying on a slab in a morgue, forgotten by everyone but her. Amelia let go of Josie. Intrigued by the place, she pirouetted just outside the halo of Josie's beam. Suddenly, Emily stopped singing and Josie swung the phone her way. Her mother's hands hung limply over the chair arms as she watched Amelia. That's when Josie noticed the restraints. Ian's carefully drawn picture was now a reality.

"It's a storeroom." Amelia stopped turning and went for a box. "Mr. Reynolds didn't lie. They did put everything in storage."

"It looks like more than that." Josie turned from Emily and held the light up so Amelia could read the labels.

"James. 1967. Sterling. 1972. These are the names on dad's list."

Amelia opened up a box and took out some small vials, a large jar half filled with white powder, and some ancient blister packs. She held them up like a handful of treasure for Josie to see.

"Medication. I guess it's what was left over from the people who died."

"I suppose," Josie muttered. She joined in and opened another box. "Files. All sorts of them. This one is Traini. He was in the army."

Amelia opened another one. "More pills in this one. I need more light."

Josie turned the phone her way but caught Emily in the shaft. Her head hung low and she was shivering.

"Hold on. I think we need some blankets. Do you have anything over there we can use?"

Amelia found one under the stored table and tossed it to Josie who wrapped it around Emily.

"She's freezing," she muttered

"At least it's dry in here. She'll be better soon."

Amelia went back to the boxes. She pulled one out, opened it, and came up with wicked looking syringes.

"No wonder Emily doesn't like needles. This is her box."

Josie walked over to take a look. The vials were marked E. Bates and they also were printed with a number. If there was a box of medication then there had to be a box of files just like the others.

"Amelia, hold this." Josie pushed the phone into Amelia's hands. "Shine it over here."

Heaving and grunting, Josie pulled box after box down from their stacks, reading the labels as they landed with a thud.

"Ha Kuna House files. Resident files. Here's one that looks like it had something to do with your dad's research." Josie pulled again. "Here, I have the year Emily was admitted."

Sitting cross-legged on the ground she opened it as Amelia came up behind her, holding the light high. Josie flipped out a file and set it aside. She found another and muttered:

"Supply logs. Building permits to add the caretaker's house." Josie dug in again and came up with a diary. She tossed it Amelia's way while she took out a calendar. "Robert Cote's."

"He was the director before Mr. Reynolds."

Amelia joined her, setting the flashlight on one of the boxes so they could both read. Behind them, Emily began to hum but Josie paid no attention.

"I'm going back to the house."

"Why? For what?" Amelia caught her arm and pulled at her but Josie wouldn't be swayed.

"We need Emily's medicine. We can't give her this stuff. Who knows how long it's been here. We don't know how long we'll be here or what will happen to her if she doesn't get it. Where do you keep it?"

"In her bathroom. There's a week's worth. There should be more in Mr. Reynolds' office, but I'm not sure where." Amelia's eyes filled with tears. "Don't leave me alone with Emily. What if something happens? What if you don't–"

Josie swooped down and took Amelia by the shoulders. "This isn't Washington. She isn't your father. I'll be back. I will."

Josie went back the way they had come, swallowed up in the dark before Amelia could talk her out of it. Behind her Amelia shined the light on Emily and that's when she saw the battery on Josie's phone was dying.

৵৽৻৽

Drenched, confused, and fearful, Josie watched the house from the edge of the tropical forest. She saw nothing and could only hope that whoever had been in there left once they finished their grisly task. Josie wanted to go back to Emily and Amelia but she couldn't, she wouldn't. It wasn't just the need for the medicine that drove her on; it was her desperate need to understand all this. If there was something in that place that could not only explain her mother's disappearance and her father's betrayal, she wanted it.

Crouching in a runner's stance, Josie decided that if she was going to go, the time was now. Intellectual commitment, though, was far different from physical action and she fell back more than once. Finally, calling on every ounce of fortitude she possessed, Josie counted to three, pushed off and sprinted toward the house. She kept low even when she slipped through the back door.

Josie paused, listened, and heard nothing except the sound of her own ragged breathing. She bit her bottom lip and realized that she had lied to Amelia. She did pray. That very second she was praying that the sound of her breathing didn't reverberate through the old house; she was praying that she would see Archer and Hannah again; she was praying that this night would end soon.

Josie pushed away from the wall and threw herself into Reynolds' office. One look at him sitting behind his desk, a neat shot between his eyes, told Josie that he knew who had done this. Unless she stumbled over Johnson's body, she had to assume he was the shooter. Like a bull, Josie breathed hard through her nose. As she worked, she thanked God that the light was minimal so that she didn't have to stare at Bernard Reynolds' sightless eyes. In seconds Josie had ripped the office apart: dumping drawers, pulling open cabinets, and rummaging through his desk after she gathered the courage to push Reynolds' chair away.

There wasn't much but Josie took what she could carry: the calendar, a stack of papers, a small address book. She stuffed these things into a bag she found in the closet. She would sort it all out later. Then she noticed the trashcan and went back to grab the crumpled papers inside. She plucked them out, smoothed them as best she could, and then held one up to the window as she tried to make out what was written on it.

❧∞☙

Johnson dumped his gear in the trunk of his car. Positive he hadn't left anything in the cottage, he sat on the edge of the trunk and finished off the bottle of Johnny Walker he and Reynolds had been drinking earlier. It was probably the best drink of his life because if he hadn't taken it he wouldn't have been looking at the back of the main house and through Bernard's office window.

"Well, well, Ms. Emily. Look at you. Got all the way downstairs by yourself."

He chuckled at his good luck, tossed the empty bottle into the car trunk, and took out the one last thing he needed to tie up a loose end.

Josie went past the girls' bodies, slid across the floor, grabbed the bannister and flung herself onto the stairs. She took two at a time. On the second floor, she pushed open all the doors to see if there was anyone inside who might have been overlooked and been left alive. Most of the rooms were empty, their beds stripped to the mattresses, their owners long gone, and no new resident expected. Finally, she opened a door and saw Mr. Traini, hurried to the bed, and put her fingers on the pulse point. He was gone but there was no wound. He seemed to be asleep. Quickly, she ran her hands over the bed, down the side of the body and found what she wanted: an empty powder bag and then another. She tossed them in the bag she carried.

Josie went back down the hall, found one more body and two more plastic bags. She took the short flight of stairs to the third floor and did the same. Room after room was empty except for the one next to the room where Amelia had been sleeping. Josie paused in the doorway of that room. The sense of urgency deserted her. Slowly, she walked to the bed where the old woman lay.

Josie had expected no less but seeing this nameless woman dead only doors down from where her mother slept moved her as nothing else had. It could so easily have been Emily.

Josie put her bag down and took the sheets in both hands. She smoothed them over the lady's chest, tucking them in around her. She stroked her hair, cotton soft, more white than grey.

"I'm so sorry," Josie whispered. She picked up her bag. It was time to get Emily's medicine and be done with all this but before she could leave the room she heard:

"Emily? Emily, sweetheart, where are you? Come on now."

༚

Peter Johnson's voice traveled upward in such a fashion that Josie knew he was in the foyer, at the bottom of the stairs, his face raised to see if Emily would come at his call. Her mind raced forward and backward, trying to figure out what was going on. There was only one explanation. He had seen her – crossing the open space, rooting around Reynolds' office, stealing up the stairs – and mistaken her for her mother. Now he was after her and he had a gun but that didn't mean he had the advantage. Let him think that Emily was wandering mindlessly through the house. He would be off his guard, confused when he couldn't find her, and that would give Josie enough time to get out of the house and back to the cave. When morning came she would try her phone again. If she couldn't summon help that way, she would walk the miles to the harbor and get it. All she had to do was survive until then.

She crept to the door of the old woman's room and listened. The rain was loud but Johnson's heavy boots on the uncarpeted stairs were louder still. He was on the second floor, walking up and down the hall.

Four steps.

Silence.

Three steps.

Silence.

Four Steps. Silence.

He was looking into the empty rooms the same way Josie had but wasn't stopping long enough to check the bodies. He already knew those people were dead.

He started up the stairs that would take him to the third floor, her floor. His foot hit the landing. There were three doors on her side of the hall and she was number two. Her head whipped right and left. She couldn't see into the darkest corner of the room but that didn't mean Johnson wouldn't see her cowering there. He might notice a glint of skin or note an unintentional flinch of anticipation. Hiding in plain sight was not an option. Knowing she had no other choice, Josie went back to the bed, put her bag on the far side, and crawled in beside the corpse. She shuddered, bit her lip, and pulled herself close. Her knees were bent so that her body was exactly the same length as the dead woman. If Johnson didn't look too closely, if he didn't touch the bed, he would pass her by. Just as she crooked her knee and got her head further under the covers, the man pushed the door open wide. Josie held her breath. She closed her eyes and clutched the dead woman's nightgown. She didn't want to die alone.

A second later Johnson moved on. Looking into the small room where Amelia had slept on the couch. Josie raised her head and listened. She could hear him roaming around Emily's room, working himself into a lather. She heard a crash. It had to be the rocking chair going through the window. Josie listened to him curse and call out for Emily and then she heard him coming back down the hall. He came slower, his steps not as pronounced as they had been on the way up. Josie ducked her head just as he came parallel with the door to her room. She hoped he didn't see her move and she prayed the smell of fear wouldn't catch his attention.

She needn't have worried. The only thing either of them could smell now was gasoline.

❧

"Stephen! Stephen! Wake up. Wake up!"

Stephen Kyle reached out, took Malia by the waist, and pulled her into him. She landed atop his round belly with a *humph*. Her Brooklyn came out faster than water from a spigot and she pushed herself off.

"Stephen, it's me!" Malia slapped his chest that was covered for sleep in a Keoloko T-shirt emblazoned with *Whales do it on Hump Day.* "Come on, get up."

"Malia, love. I was dreaming of a goddess and there you were." Stephen mumbled. He pushed himself up in his big fine bed, the covers falling to his lap. He rubbed the top of his head as if the friction would bring him to his senses. "Are you all right? Crimey, Malia, it's barely light out. Oh wait! It's still dark out. Stupid me."

"Stop complaining," Malia ordered. "Turn on the TV, Stephen."

Befuddled with sleep, Stephen wasn't fast enough so Malia crawled over him, grabbed the remote, and pointed it at a flat screen sprouting from an antique trunk at the foot of the bed. He turned his eyes away with an 'oomph' of protest at the glare.

"Isn't that where Josie is?" Malia demanded.

Stephen cracked an eye then bolted upright. He snatched the remote from Malia as the other girls came to sit on the bed and watch the pictures an early morning hiker had taken, and the local news had run, of Molokai on fire. Well, only a very small part of Molokai – the part where Ha Kuna House was.

CHAPTER 26

"Hello. Hello? Is this Josie's man? If this is his phone, call Stephen Kyle. I am a friend of hers. I have some bad news...My number..." – Voice Message, Stephen Kyle to Archer

"This is Aolani. Stephen can't talk right now because he's upset. Our number is 808-478-5482. You can talk to any of us. Just call us back soon." – Voice message, Aolani to Archer

Aolani sat cross-legged on the bed, the phone still in her hand, her eyes wet with tears as she patted Stephen's broad back. Anuhea had her head in his lap and while he stroked her long dark hair. She pulled Kleenex out of little square box and handed them around to anyone who sniffled. Malia was sitting on the floor, her back up against the foot of the bed. She was the only one who didn't cry, but no one doubted she sorrowed.

"We need to go over, Stephen. We need to go now."

"Ah, Malia, I don't think it would help anything. The authorities have it well in hand," Stephen said, accepting yet another Kleenex. "We'd be in the way."

"You can't just leave Josie there," Malia insisted.

"The newsman said they found bodies. I can't claim her. We have to leave that to her man. He'll get back to us–"

"No," Anuhea sat up and pushed her long, long hair away from her face. "Malia's right. We should go."

"*'Ike aku, 'ike mai, kokua aku kokua mai; pela iho la ka nohana 'ohana.*" Aolani dipped her head and looked at Stephen. She widened her eyes, pressing him to the right decision.

"Yes, yes. You are correct. Family first. Go on now, girls. Get dressed. We'll go find Josie." Stephen shooed them away. He gave a great sigh and turned to look at the gardens beyond his window. "Or what's left of her.

Woodrow Calister rolled over in his bed, half asleep but only half. He hadn't slept well since Ambrose had dropped his bombshell. Life had gone on. No one had known of his distress. What kind of politician would he have been if he was that transparent? And as the days went on, he started to think that Ambrose was reconsidering. Jerry had not been named, there had been no meetings between the two men that Woodrow knew of, and certainly Jerry would have crowed about it if there were. Lydia was still making sounds as if she believed Woodrow was the favored son. So Woodrow kept his counsel just in case this was a test. He answered the phone half thinking that it would be Ambrose calling to tell him he had passed. It wasn't. Woodrow sat up and turned on the light as he listened to his briefing. He hung up and dialed Eugene Weller. Eugene picked up and sounded as if he were wide-awake.

"There's been a fire in Hawaii."

"Bad?" Eugene asked.

"Yes. It's all gone."

"Is there anything to do?" Eugene asked.

"I've taken care of it. Everything should be wrapped up by morning."

"Thank you, Senator."

"I think we can rest easy," Woodrow said.

He hung up, turned on his side, and smiled. It didn't matter what call Ambrose made. Woodrow Calister was pleased that the man would be safe. He was pleased, because Ambrose was his friend. He must never forget that. There were so few to be had in Washington.

꙳

Malia had been at the helm of the *No Problem*, sailing it across the still turbulent sea under a bright sun. The storm from the night before had left the island sparkling and vibrant and Molokai never looked more beautiful. Sadly, Stephen couldn't admire it. He was hanging over the side of the boat looking nearly as green as the island.

Aolani and Anuhea, sat in the deck chairs with their feet up, silently watching the horizon, lost in their own thoughts until the boat pulled up to the dock. When it did, Aolani jumped down and caught the rope that Anuhea threw. When the boat was secure, Malia put her arms around Stephen who fell into them.

"I wish that God would take me. Throw me overboard. To the sharks," he moaned.

"We're docked, Stephen. Five minutes and you'll be okay. Breathe deep."

Malia got him on his feet and Aolani helped him down. He crashed onto the dock. Anuhea hovered, Malia jumped down. If he fell backward it would take all three to get him up again, but he didn't. The twins took his arms, one on each side while Malia went on ahead.

"There's only the truck, Stephen." She called this over her shoulder.

"I want the big car, Malia," he grumbled and the girls looked at one another.

"Josie must have it, Stephen," Anuhea said.

"Ah. All right then." Stephen lumbered down the dock and climbed into the passenger seat of the blue truck. He put his head back but already the color was coming to his round cheeks. "One of you will have to drive the other one back when we find it. Are there an extra set of keys in the Harbor Master's office?"

"I don't think so, Stephen," Aolani muttered.

"I think you're right, my love. Perhaps someone will have found them. Josie's purse. Perhaps, they'll have found something." His voice trailed away. He rolled down the window and looked out as Malia started the engine.

She drove toward Ha Kuna House while Stephen gulped air and tried to imagine that the wind was blowing raindrops off the trees onto his cheeks and not tears out of his eyes.

అ∽

Stephen stood outside the fire department perimeter trying to engage anyone who passed his way. The men who did, though, had no interest in talking. That didn't surprise Stephen. Not only was their task grim, they were not locals. These blokes wore white jumpsuits to sift through the ash and rubble of what had once been a beautiful house. Actually, though, they weren't sifting at all – they were carting away everything including the ash that had been watered down and cooled to a paste.

In the distance, Stephen heard the thump of helicopter rotors. More than likely it was only a local tour taking in the spectacular view of the cliffs, but it gave him the chills to hear it as he was looking at such horrible scene on the ground.

Two large unmarked trucks were onsite, their loading bays open. One was already packed neatly with square boxes five across and three high. He estimated it could hold rows at least ten deep and that meant a whole lot of Ha Kuna House ash was packed inside. In the other truck large debris filled the space. It was all wrapped in plastic and labeled with yellow tags. Stephen was reminded of an airline crash where the bits and pieces of a plane were collected and later would be laid out and reconstructed to try and figure out what made the bloody thing fall out of the sky. He had the oddest feeling, though, that these pieces of Ha Kuna house would never again see the light of day. He wandered toward that truck to see if he might catch a glimpse of whatever was written on one of the tags when someone finally decided it was time to have a chat with him.

"Sir! Sir. Stop there." A tall man strode toward him, his hand out.

"Hello, there," Stephen called as the man stopped between Stephen and the truck.

"Is there something I can help you with?" he asked and the way he said it proved he was not a personable sort.

"A friend of mine. Josie Bates. She was staying here last night. She is a very tall lady, so perhaps you've found...well, perhaps you've found something of hers. Perhaps she was injured and already sent on to hospital," Stephen suggested.

"If you haven't heard from her you probably won't. My condolences." The man turned away, but Stephen wasn't done.

"Wait, man! You can't leave it at that. I would think there are other families needing information, too. Mr. Reynolds. Where is he? I'll talk to him."

"Mr. Reynolds was in his office last night. There were four residents and an aide. I'm afraid they are all deceased." The man's eyes never left Stephen's and while Stephen would have been happy to contest such a bold thing, the man in white had no time for games. "I will have to ask you to leave the premises, sir."

"Of course. Yes, I see that it would be for the best."

Stephen stepped back and made as if he intended to go. Behind him, the man was satisfied and went back to his job. He didn't notice that Stephen was walking slowly, considering that something was not right. Six people dead in the house was a tragedy, but...

Six...

Six...

Stephen stopped. The number was wrong. There had to be more than six people in that house if Josie had stayed the night. Josie, four residents, and one night aide. Certainly shouldn't the man have said seven deceased if Reynolds was also gone?

Stephen swung toward the two cars in the drive. Both were covered with ash but untouched by the fire. Neither belonged to Keoloko Enterprises. The residents couldn't drive. There was only one night aide. Perhaps this was Reynolds' car and yet Stephen thought not. He motioned to Aolani. She came at his call, her tiny feet dragging, her beautiful young face sorrowful.

"Aolani, my sweet. You must do something." He took her around the shoulders and turned her away from the white-suited trolls climbing over the ash and heaps of charred wood. He whispered: "Darling girl, do you think you might pop over to the red car without anyone seeing you and take a look at the registration?"

"I can try."

"Go on with you. I'll stand in front. No one will see past me now, will they?"

Despite the circumstances, Aolani giggled as she walked away. She was in and out of the car in seconds.

"It belongs to Kate Damon," She said when she came back to him.

"That's my little burglar. Did you manage an address?"

"On Ena Street."

"You are a smart girl, Aolani. Where are the others?" Stephen craned his neck. It did not escape his notice that the man who had spoken to him earlier was watching them.

"They went to find flowers. Aloha for Josie and her *makuahine*. So sad to die young, but it's good to die with her mother."

"Ah, you have a heart of gold, Aolani. Go help them, will you? I'll be back in a moment."

Aolani went off and Stephen didn't even take time to admire the sway of her hips under her long cotton dress. He walked the opposite way, on the path he and Josie had taken on their first visit, keeping his ears sharp and his eyes open just in case the blokes in white were snooping about that far afield.

He saw the cars before he even reached the turn out. One was the SUV Josie had taken the day before. He looked in the other and confirmed the pitiful excuse for a vehicle belonged to Amelia. Stephen looked at his phone. The little bars were nonexistent. He would like to talk to Molokai's fire chief. He wanted to know who the men collecting ash and bones and teeth at Ha Kuna House were. He wanted to know why the local fire patrol was not assisting. Mostly, Stephen wanted to know where Amelia and Josie had gotten themselves off to. More to the point: why hadn't they shown themselves when the cavalry rode in?

Knowing he could not get the answers to these questions while he looked at the lovely, sad faces of his girls, Stephen bundled them on to the ferry and sent them home. They begged him to come with, but he pleaded a need to mourn privately – as well as to see if there were any Keoloko goods to be salvaged. When they were gone, he treated himself to a cocktail or two. Finally, judging that the men in white were gone, he went back to the Ha Kuna House property. Sure enough, the men were gone and they had left the place as clean as mum's kitchen after Christmas dinner.

Stephen walked the perimeter as he punched a number into his phone, kicked with his sandals at the graded earth, and thought it odd that not even a piece of one of the hospital beds, a porcelain toilette, or the behemoth refrigerator he had known to be in the kitchen was left.

"Ah," he said when the phone was answered. "Chief. Stephen Kyle here. Fine, thank you. But you have had quite a night. The fire—"

He was interrupted, listened, and then took it upon himself to interrupt back.

"Of course. Federal land. I didn't realize the feds had fire marshals at the ready. Quite a team? Oh yes, I think so. Certainly professional. I saw them at work until I was sent on my way. Spic and span here."

Stephen listened again and then laughed from the belly, talking as he walked toward the caretaker's cottage.

"Oh, of course. I wouldn't want me contaminating the scene either. I fear contaminating anything I touch, quite honestly. I imagine your men had already—"

Stephen did more pausing than talking. He had never known the fire chief to be so verbose. He listened as he tried the door to the cottage. It was open and empty. He walked toward Reynolds' house as he kept up his side of the conversation.

"So you say? They needed no help. Happy days, the federal government finally accomplishes something. Good to know."

They both had a laugh over that and then lamented the tragedy once more. The chief wished him aloha and Stephen wished him aloha back. The chief went back to his work and Stephen tried the doors of Reynolds' place. It, too, was open so Stephen invited himself in. The house was pristine, as if the cleaning lady had just been in and done her level best. Stephen wandered through the place, opening closets and drawers willy-nilly. There was nothing there. Not even a book or a pencil, not a sweater or a towel. The men in white, he imagined, had taken it all. Poor Reynolds. Fifteen years in the place and someone wanted to make it seem that he never existed.

Tiring of finding nothing, Stephen went back outside and continued on his walk. He took the path that led to the cliffs, dialing Josie's number as he went, getting only her voice mail. Molokai was fixing herself up after a rough roll in the hay with Mother Nature. The sun was out; the plants were lifting their flowers and leaves as the water evaporated. The ground was still muddy underfoot but not running with water. Something buzzed past Stephen's ear and he swiped at it. His eyes scanned the jungle. He listened harder than he had ever listened in his life, but all was quiet.

Stephen trudged on, looking for all the things one sees in a movie or reads about in books: the bit of fabric hanging on a branch, footprints on the ground, a tangle of hair on a thorn, stones piled in the shape of an arrow. Stephen tired and he became cranky that he had not thought to at least have one more drink while he waited out the Ha Kuna cleaning crew. He raised his voice.

"Josie! Josie Bates! Show yourself!"

Stephen waited. His eyes narrowed as if that would help him see that which he was beginning to think did not exist. He put his hands on his hips and planted his feet and pushed out his chest. His magnificent stomach stretched his buttons to bursting; the tail of his lime green shirt fluttered in the breeze and, if there had been anyone to see, they would have been privy to a hint of pale paunch.

"Josie! I haven't got all day. Chop, chop," he boomed.

The seconds ticked by. Perhaps he must acknowledge that Josie and her mum had perished and accept the mystery of it.

"Josie! Jo—"

He tilted his head, cleared his throat and put his chubby fingers to his eyes. Surely, this was nothing more than a wayward cinder in his eye that was causing him grief and the last little whiff of smoke that had gotten into his throat and cut off his speech. Stephen took one deep breath and decided to call one more time in his best, biggest, English voice and then he would be done.

Before he could cry out yet again, the bushes shivered, the leaves rustled, and a branch broke. Covered in dirt, and mud, and ash, her short hair singed to nothing on one side of her head, Josie Bates shouldered her way through the forest and into the clearing. She stopped when she saw him, her body sagged, and the bag she was carrying dropped to the ground. Her eyes softened, her burned lips titled upward. Behind her, Amelia hovered with her arm around the ever beautiful, perpetually vacant Emily Bates, but Stephen only had eyes for Josie.

"By God, I have found me an Amazon," he whispered before those errant cinders found their way to his eyes once more.

CHAPTER 27

"He was waiting for information on Sandy MacIntosh. She was hurt in a truck accident." – Josie

"Was he a relative?" – Oregon Community Hospital Nurse

"No. His name is Archer. A big man. Quiet." – Josie

"I'm sorry. I'm just coming off the night shift. I'll leave a message for the next shift. They might know. Can you call back?" – Oregon Community Hospital Nurse

"Who should I ask for?" – Josie

"I'm not sure who's going to be on. Sorry. I've got to run. Call back after ten." – Oregon Community Hospital Nurse.

"But is she awake? Is she talking? Look, who can I talk to…" – Josie to no one

❧

Josie sat on the sand with her back up against the low wall that separated Hermosa Beach's Strand from the beach. The hood of her sweatshirt was pulled up and the strings tightened beneath her chin. The shirt didn't match her sweatpants which were her oldest and warmest. Underneath she wore a long sleeved t-shirt but it was Max lying across her legs and gathered into her arms that kept her warmest of all.

She had been sitting this way for twenty-minutes, thinking of nothing and worrying about nothing. There could be no bigger shock than finding her mother, no bigger terror than facing a wall of flames and surviving.

There could be no horror worse than what she had found in that cave. So she wouldn't worry about anything, not even Archer and Hannah and Billy. She would trust that they would keep themselves safe and get home to her as soon as they could. But she couldn't sit this way until they did. There was still so much to do.

"Come on, Max."

She kissed the top of his head, stood up, dusted the sand off her butt, and took one more look at the large, low moon hanging over the Pacific. They went around the wall since Max's jumping days were over. No one else was out except Mrs. Fenwick's cat. The Horowitz children ran through their living room past the picture window and Josie heard Marjorie Horowitz's muffled voice calling after them. Not much had really changed since she left a month earlier for Washington and yet everything had. She certainly had.

She was wary, wondering who was watching her even now that she was home. But there was no one lingering where they shouldn't be, no car parked out of place, and nothing in her house that had been disturbed. She was thankful for that especially. The house was now a bit cramped but other than that it was perfect.

She paused and considered her place while she waited for Max to take a detour and sniff out something irresistible on the sidewalk. The outside lights illuminated the front step and the patio off her bedroom as they had been every night while she was gone. Tonight, though the bedrooms on either end of the house were lit while the bare picture window looking into the living room was dark. That's the way Josie would keep it. Until this was over, she didn't want anyone looking in on her from the outside.

When Max joined her, she opened the gate and it swung noiselessly on its hinges. At the front door she swiped the hood from her head, let Max go first, and hung up his pink leash on its hook. The homecoming had worn him out so he went to his bed while Josie followed the sounds of women's voices. Faye brightened as Josie walked in.

"We were just going to send out a search party, weren't we Amelia?"

"I was thinking of sleeping on the beach but Max wanted to come back." Josie gave the older woman's arm a squeeze.

"I can't get used to you not having hair."

"I have hair. It's just shorter," Josie objected.

"Shaved. Are you sure you don't want a doctor to look at the burns."

"They aren't that bad," Josie insisted. Amelia was tucking Emily into bed so Josie deflected Faye's concern in her by asking: "How's she doing?"

"Good. Really good." Amelia stepped away and put her hands on her hips "It's only been a couple of days without that medicine. I guess it's too early to tell if there will be much change without it."

"She's lucky it didn't kill her. Scopolamine in all four of those packets. With the doses those patients were getting it's amazing they weren't dead long ago."

No one in the room could argue with that. The lab Stephen contracted with reported an alarming cocktail of drugs that Amelia had been giving the residents. An unintended consequence of their curiosity was that the lab wanted to know where the stuff had come from since the legality of the concoction was in question. Josie wasn't ready to share that information yet.

"She's lovely, Josie." Faye interrupted Josie's thoughts. "I still can't believe she's here."

"Me either," Josie murmured.

Emily looked even more beautiful because she was lying amidst the riot of colors and exotic appointments that Hannah had so lovingly arranged and reluctantly left behind. It was nice to have this room occupied again.

"Are you going to be okay on the roll away?" Josie asked Amelia.

"Sure. I'll probably be awake half the night anyway."

"I hope not. You all need to rest," Faye said as she left the room. Amelia followed, only to pause at the draped easel.

"Do you mind?" Josie shook her head. Amelia lifted the sheet and looked at the last painting Hannah had done. The woman who was a combination of Josie and Hannah looked back at them with clear, wise eyes. "She looks like Emily."

"I guess she does. Kind of prophetic," Josie answered.

"Kind of weird. I hope Hannah comes home soon. You'll have your whole family here." It did not escape Josie's notice that Amelia sounded melancholy. That was understandable. Seeing the home Josie had waiting for Emily underscored how alone she was in the world. Amelia shrugged a little as she said: "I didn't know what I was giving any of them."

"I know. It's okay," Josie answered.

Amelia lowered the sheet, turned off the light and followed Josie into the dining room where Faye was setting out coffee. The overhead had been dimmed, the room looked cozy, and Stephen Kyle was regaling Faye with the story of their escape from the island of Molokai as he organized the paperwork in manageable piles.

"I can tell you, I thought Josie was a goner for sure. Bright girl, that. Getting out of the house the way she did."

"And what way was that?" Faye asked.

"Here she is. She can tell you herself."

"I wish it was that heroic," Josie laughed. "It was pure reaction. Self-preservation. Johnson lit the gasoline and it just erupted. That woman's body protected me to a point but my head was up. I fell off the bed when I got burned. There was nowhere to go but back against the wall. It was so dark and I hadn't noticed there was a closet. I just wanted to get away from the heat so I went in but it turned out it was connected to the one in that room where Amelia had been sleeping."

"You were lucky that lock was broken on my side or you never would have gotten out," Amelia said.

"That's the truth. The hall was engulfed so I couldn't go down the main staircase. I went through your room and across to Emily's. Luckily he hadn't done such a good job there. I was able to make it down the back stairs and get back to Amelia and Emily."

"Looking the worse for wear, I can tell you," Stephen added. "I've been patching her up since I met her."

"And then we came right home," Josie said. "I had no idea how we were going to manage that since Emily had no identification. I couldn't get her on a plane."

"That was never a worry," Stephen insisted. "I told Josie I knew everyone on Maui, including a lovely reclusive gentleman with a private airplane. A private plane only needs a flight plan. No security, you see. Did I tell you that we listed the passengers as Aolani, Anuhea, and Malia? I don't think Josie found it amusing, but I certainly did."

"A brilliant ploy," Faye agreed even as she cast Josie an amused look.

"Ah, Josie. Amelia. Finally, I've found the perfect woman. Faye agrees I'm brilliant. Now, if only she liked Scotch."

"No one is perfect," Josie said as she pulled out a chair.

Amelia sat opposite Stephen at one end of the table and Faye to Stephen's left. They stared at the crumpled papers and dirty files that had been taken from the cave, the notebooks that Amelia had gathered quickly before they left the island, and the things Ian Francis had thrust into Josie Bates' hand that started the journey.

"So," Faye murmured.

"So," Josie echoed. "I guess I'll start at the beginning."

She picked up the plastic bag imprinted with the image of The Robert Lee and took out the lock of hair and the notepaper with the manic writing.

"I think this is a lock of mom's hair and then there is this."

Josie got up and brought Ian's notes to Faye.

Rememberrememberemembermk
Poor thingpoorgirl isamarigold.
Ultraartichokechatter!Marigold.
195319751982SWGBS1986EB.

"Once I found Emily, I forgot about this stuff. But given what we found in the cave, this makes sense now. Emily and all the residents were victims of a government run program. Look here." Josie leaned over to point at the notes. "The end of the first line is MK. Ian wanted me to remember what MK was. I didn't know what that meant then, but I do now.

"The second line seems to be about Emily. We assume Marigold is the name of the program at Ha Kuna House.

"Next line down actually a history of covert government programs.

"The final line refers to the dates relevant to the start of each program."

"I've run down most of them. There were thousands of people involved in those operations back in the day," Stephen added.

"Before we left, we did some quick research. Artichoke and CHATTER were the code words for early programs dealing in mind control. Artichoke was the navy, isn't that right, Stephen?"

"Right. The big program was called MKUltra and that was sanctioned in 1953," Stephen answered. "Hospitals, universities, research facilities and individual scientists from the United States and Canada, even England, were all taking part although it's been proven that many did not realize the insidiousness of the thing. The United States even employed Nazi scientists in the early days because they had experience with human experimentation in the camps. I think we can safely surmise that your father, Amelia, was an unwitting victim even in his capacity as a researcher."

"I know he was. I've read enough in his journals now to see that he was slowly putting it all together," Amelia said.

"I imagine we'll find records giving instructions that he be neutralized or whatever they call it," Stephen surmised. "What easier way to keep him silent than to do to him what was done to the residents. These drugs could be administered without the knowledge of the victim. That's what I find so frightening. That one could be plucked up and made to disappear that way is almost unfathomable."

"But it was easy," Josie said as she reclaimed her chair. "The army used their own enlisted people as subjects. They branched out to mental patients and transients. These people were specifically chosen because they had no family or community ties. There was no informed consent. They were subjected to experimental drugs and later physical torture. Sleep deprivation. Rape. Electrocution. I can't imagine how horrible it must have been for them."

"What's truly amazing is that they kept meticulous records of how these people were dosed, the different medications, the length of sleep deprivation and their reactions. When they passed away, they simply boxed up the records and stored them," Stephen added.

"We may never have everything, but I'm betting there's enough in that cave to sink a whole bunch of people. Reynolds for one, but he's already dead," Josie said. "I still think it's amazing Emily led us there. The chair she was sitting in had restraints, so did the tables. We found an electroshock machine. We have to assume she was tortured."

"You know that's probably why she collapsed the day you took her for a walk, don't you?" Amelia said. "She thought you were taking her there."

"I know that now," Josie answered. "But when we needed a safe place, she must have known that cave would be the last place Johnson would look."

"So were the people in the house still being tortured?" Faye asked.

"No, I would have known. I think we were just watching them until they died." Amelia looked around the table and saw that Stephen and Josie were nodding.

"MKUltra was publicly exposed in the seventies," Josie added. "They thought they destroyed all the documents but some survived. There were hearings and trials and a lot of outrage."

"Everyone involved was prosecuted," Stephen said. "I suppose the general public thought that was that."

Josie pointed to the notes again. "1986 with EB right after it. We're assuming that's Ian's reference to Emily's admission. We don't know what the third date is or whose initials they are but Ian was trying to put this into some kind of context for me. He just couldn't communicate well enough to tell me straight out."

Faye picked up some of the papers and looked at them, "It's like a horror movie. I didn't think things like this happened here."

"It wasn't just these. There were many more," Stephen said. "Project Paperclip. One called Midnight Climax where subjects were drugged and taken to government run brothels in San Francisco. I surmise Ian was trying to tell Josie that Marigold was also an offshoot of MKUltra. I haven't been able to find anything on it in the public domain like the others. I assume that is because it is still a current program."

"But to what end?" Faye insisted.

"Control," Stephen suggested.

"Curiosity," Amelia offered.

"Because they could," Josie answered and then asked Faye: "Do you have the information Michael Horn sent?"

"Here you go." Faye handed it over and Josie spoke while she laid it out.

"This man is continuing a lawsuit initiated by his grandfather who was a victim of MKUltra. His grandfather committed suicide before it got to the courts. Horn must have known about Ian's work because when he saw the notice of Ian's death in the paper that made mention of me he started calling. I'm sure he thought I had information for him. If I had called him, it would have saved us a lot of grief. I'll read this complaint tonight, and then contact him when we're a little clearer on what we have."

"So, if I extrapolate that this is something the government doesn't want anyone to know about, then maybe someone in government ordered Ha Kuna House razed." Faye raised a brow. Hearing the thought spoken out loud was sobering but even Faye wasn't convinced. "But you're still alive. Emily is here."

"The body count was correct. There was an extra girl in the house and Emily was with us. That meant that there were still five people in the house plus Reynolds. No one knew Amelia or I had spent the night. Everyone just assumed we were where we were supposed to be: Amelia at her house, me on Maui, and Emily in her room."

"And I received notification through the court as attorney of record for Josie that Emily was dead. Case closed. Josie has no legal standing and therefore could not claim her mother's body. They referred me to a contact at MPS if she's interested in follow-up. But I guarantee you that by the time anyone inquires about the remains, they will be gone. All neat and tidy," Stephen said.

"Whoever is responsible for this was wise enough to know that killing a handful of people the world forgot about was preferable to doing anything to me. That would have raised questions," Josie added.

"Oh, that reminds me," Faye said. "I ran Peter Johnson like you asked. He is not a nice fellow."

"Is he in the service?"

"Not anymore. He was dishonorably discharged. Drug trafficking. He has been employed by Blacknight Security. I don't know if they placed him at Ha Kuna House though."

"A mercenary?" Stephen breathed.

Josie answered. "Maybe the feds should look around the place. Hawaii's notorious for its pot farms and that house was sitting on forty acres. Maybe that's what he was taking care of."

"Which adds another dimension to the tragic fire," Stephen suggested.

"If that's what he was doing. It's not our concern unless he shows up on my doorstep," Josie said.

"God help him if he does," Stephen said.

"But I still want to know how Emily got there," Faye insisted.

"I think my father put her there. I don't know why. I don't know how he pulled it off, but the evidence doesn't look good." Josie put her hands on the table and pushed back.

"What are you going to do now?" Faye asked.

"I'm going to get some air."

༄༅

Michael Horn put on his favorite sweater and over that a sweatshirt that had seen better days. He had on his fleece lined sweatpants. He pulled on his gloves and a watch cap. He left the television playing as was his habit. Not that it would deter the people who concerned him, but the sound of it always gave him the feeling that things were normal when he opened the door again. So the TV stayed on when Mark went out for his evening run.

On the porch, he jogged in place and gave himself an energetic hug. It was going to be a horrendously cold winter considering the end of fall was already freezing. He looked around the neighborhood. The Meisen's lights were on. Mrs. Garfield's upstairs lights shined. In the early dark, the houses looked a million miles away. That was too bad. He wouldn't mind waving at a neighbor now and again or lingering over the fence for a chat. That's what he got for being able to afford a place with acreage.

Inside, the phone rang but he decided if he didn't leave right then he'd simply go inside and fix himself a bowl of soup and call it a day. He tapped down the steps, saw his breath in the air and thought he should consider moving to a smaller place. Then he picked up speed and fell into a nice rhythm and, as always happened, he found himself smiling. Running made him feel free of responsibility and worry. The crisp air carried the sound of his running shoes hitting the pavement. He paid no attention to the car that approached him, illuminated his face, and sped past leaving him in the dark again.

He should have paid attention to the car that came from behind. That one didn't pass. That one plowed into him, tossing him high in the air. He landed in the field near a windbreak of cypress.

The last thing he heard was a woman screaming at someone to send an ambulance; the last thing he saw was his grandfather walking across the field toward him.

CHAPTER 28

Mind control (also known as brainwashing, coercive persuasion, thought control, or thought reform) refers to a process in which a group or individual "systematically uses unethically manipulative methods to persuade others to conform to the wishes of the manipulator(s), often to the detriment of the person being manipulated". The term has been applied to any tactic, psychological or otherwise, which can be seen as subverting an individual's sense of control over their own thinking, behavior, emotions or decision making. – Wikipedia

ॐ

While the others slept, Josie went to the hall closet and took down the box that contained everything her father thought was important. The tape across the seams was yellow and brittle and the box was deep, wide, and unwieldy. Until now it had simply been something that moved with her and been stored because she knew what was in it.

She put it on the floor and opened it up. Inside, she found his uniform and a Dodger's baseball hat. There were twelve love letters from him to Emily and Emily to him, but Josie could only stomach two given what she knew. In a manila envelope, she found what she had been looking for. Joseph Bates' honorable discharge dated 1982, four years earlier than she'd been led to believe. No one had made a mistake. Archer hadn't misheard. Here was the proof that her father lied for years. She tossed it aside and dug in again.

She found a coffee cup from Lake Tahoe, a reminder of her parents' honeymoon. The handle had been broken and her father used it to hold his pens. There was an empty bottle of perfume. Josie held it to her nose and smelled the slightest scent of Shalimar.

She found pictures of Emily, each more beautiful than the last: a wedding photograph, Emily in a bathing suit holding a fancy drink, Emily in a hat in front of church, pregnant with one hand resting on her stomach. Emily and Josie standing in front of the house in Texas. Josie lingered over that one. Her mother's arm was around her shoulders as if protecting her. Josie was tall and gangly even then, smiling, and having no idea that she shouldn't be. Josie would keep the ones of her mother and her, but not the wedding picture. Everything her father had owned was going out in the trash, and she would never think about him again.

Josie kept the holster that had held her father's service revolver, the one that was now in the drawer of her bedside table. She would sell the holster with the gun. It had no meaning for her any longer. Her father didn't really protect her when she was young, his gun wouldn't protect her now. There was no magic and she always thought there had been.

There was another envelope filled with her report cards, a picture of her in her volleyball uniform just after she heard she won a scholarship, and a picture of the two of them at her law school graduation. Her father had been so handsome, so disciplined, so smart and supportive. Now she added actor and deceiver to his list of credits. The question was why?

She took an old-fashioned photo album out of the box, sat on the hall floor with her back up against the wall, and balanced it on her outstretched legs. There were pictures of her father as a boy. Josie had barely known her grandparents on either side so the pictures meant little to her.

Finally, Josie grabbed her father's dress uniform jacket and searched the pockets. She found his dog tags, a set of keys, a coin and she found something she didn't expect: a small blue velvet box. In the dim light coming from the kitchen, in the silent house, Josie felt incredibly alone the minute she touched it. She wanted to put it back and forget she ever saw it. Instead, Josie flipped the top, took one look at what was inside and closed it again. Her head fell back against the wall. Her hand dropped to her lap.

"Damn," she whispered.

Here it was, the last nail in her father's coffin. Inside the box were her parents' wedding rings. Not just her father's but her mother's, too. Josie had spent so many years accusing her mother, convicting her of desertion without evidence and in absentia, and the guilty party was the one with who stayed behind. All those years and he could have put an end to Josie's grief.

Too tired and too sad to move, Josie thought she would sit that way until dawn but suddenly she was alert. She heard something inside the house that wasn't right. It could have been the house settling, or Max moving with his dreams, but the danger of Molokai was fresh in her mind and she was on her guard. Slowly, she got to her feet.

Emily and Amelia were at one end of the house and would be of no help if somehow trouble had followed them. Stephen was sleeping on the couch in the den that was close to her bedroom. To reach him and her gun, Josie would have to go through the living room, a big and open space that would leave her vulnerable.

Knowing she had no choice, Josie stepped into the kitchen. She went past the kitchen window. The backyard was no more than a patch of cement, two flowerbeds and bougainvillea clinging to the wall so there was nowhere for anyone to hide. No one was out there.

At the end of the counter, she drew a knife from the block, scooted around the refrigerator, and put her back up against the wall so that she could see the entire living room. Carefully, she edged into the middle of the room and crouched near the sofa for protection but there was no need for caution. There wasn't an intruder in her house; there was a ghost.

Emily stood in the dining room looking like a child with the pants of her white pajamas covering her feet and the sleeves of the top reaching to her fingertips. Josie walked across the hard wood and up the three steps that led to the entry and the dining room beyond. Max didn't move. Emily didn't either. Josie put the knife on the table.

Standing shoulder to shoulder with her mother, she looked at what had caught Emily's attention: the hula girl plates hanging on the wall. When Josie was little her mother told her they were precious because they reminded her of a happy time. When Josie was older, those plates had saved her life. She could still see the cracks where she had pieced one plate back together after it had fallen off the wall during her struggle with Linda

Rayburn. She had ripped into Hannah's mother with one broken piece because there was no choice. Josie had glued the shards back together because that plate symbolized her life and heart: both were almost broken, both were now pieced back together, and both were stronger for all of it. Standing there with Emily, Josie knew she had been wrong to attach so much meaning to them. These were just cheap plates that her mother had fancied when she was whole. Nothing more and nothing less.

"Come on, it's late."

Josie took her mother's arm, but Emily didn't move. She turned her head and smiled a glorious smile. She said: "Do they belong to you?"

Josie was too tired to get her hopes up that Emily was remembering but she smiled back nonetheless.

"Yes. I used to love them."

"I love them, too," Emily whispered.

Josie turned Emily so that they faced one another in the dark. In her hand was the velvet box. She took the thin gold wedding band out and then tossed the box on the dining room table. Josie took her mother's right hand, pushed up the long pajama sleeve, and put the ring on her mother's finger. It was the only thing that had been taken from Emily that she could get back, but Josie would be damned if she would put it on Emily's left hand.

"This belongs to you," she said.

Gently, murmuring the way she heard Amelia do, Josie walked her mother to Hannah's room and put her to bed. Amelia slept and that did Josie's heart good. She closed the door behind her. Her house was peaceful but she knew that a thousand miles from Molokai was not safe because they were also a thousand miles from Washington, D.C. That, Josie knew, was where all this was heading.

Needing to sleep, needing to clear her mind, Josie went back to the hall wishing Archer was with her. Not to tell her what to do, but to be her sounding board, her confessor, her advisor. If he had no counsel, she wished he was there to make love to her. But he was gone; doing what few men would do for the woman in their lives. He was putting his own on hold for her.

Back in the hall, Josie got on to her knees and repacked her father's box, but when she lifted the old album an envelope slipped out and fluttered to the floor. She picked it up and sat back on her heels to examine the pale blue onion paper emblazoned with bars of U.S.A. red. It was an old airmail envelope addressed to her father. The sender was Father C. Ridge. Turning it over, she took out the sheet of paper and unfolded it. She read it once. She read it twice.

Don't worry about God. Forgive yourself.

Josie looked at the envelope again. The postmark was Berlin. She got off the floor and went to the kitchen to rummage through the drawers. Finally, she found a small magnifying glass. Flipping on the light over the sink, she peered at the barely legible date stamp: 1992.

She put the letter back in the envelope and the envelope in her pocket. God might have forgiven Joseph Bates, he might have even forgiven himself, but since God wasn't going to smite anyone for her father's sin and her mother's trial, Josie figured it was up to her. When she went about it, though, she wanted to have as much ammunition as possible because she didn't want to leave anyone who was responsible for this standing.

CHAPTER 29

"I got a handle on the guy who was driving the truck." – Archer

"Take the sheriff with you." – Josie

"Jo, I don't need anyone looking over my shoulder. Let me get the lay of the land first." –Archer

"Okay. I trust you. I miss you." – Josie

"But you're not going to wait for me to get back to finish this thing with your mom." – Archer

"I've got to do it now." – Josie

"Just thought you might need a hand to hold." – Archer

"Not this time. I've got to do this on my own. – Josie

"That's what I was afraid of." – Archer

"We're almost there. Take care, babe." – Josie

"You, too." – Archer

❧

Josie's Jeep flew past the acres that comprised Camp Pendleton. No buildings could be seen from the highway, but there were troops in the high grass practicing maneuvers. For the most part, though, the base appeared to be nothing more than miles and miles of beautiful, untouched acres of California beachfront. The base, though, was not her destination.

Father C. Ridge no longer served and that came as no surprise. This information had not been hard to come by. Josie placed yet one more call to the Veterans Administration. This time a heartfelt story about a dying father who wanted to get in touch with the priest got her the information she wanted. Ridge's final posting was at Camp Pendleton and when he was discharged he didn't go far. He was now the pastor of the Good Shepherd Church in Oceanside.

She turned the Jeep away from the ocean and wound her way up the hill through well-kept neighborhoods of ranch houses and two story homes. Every third house was identical and pleasant. The neighborhood was uncluttered: no one painted their garage purple, or hung gargoyles from the eaves, or put surfboards on their front porches. It was a perfect place for a family, just not a family like Josie's.

At the top of the hill she ran into a dead end and made a right into the parking lot of a church. The Jeep was only one of three cars in a lot that could accommodate a hundred. Gardens flanked the church building, birds twittered, sprinklers chuckled as they spit water five feet onto a perfect lawn, hesitated, and turned to spray again. Josie got out, stashed her sunglasses, and pulled open the big church door. She found herself in a bright, airy nave. In front of her, rising to a towering peak, was a window that looked out onto the ocean two miles away. The glass was seamless, a marvel of engineering. If anything could make a person believe in God it would be this view: iridescent blue water and cerulean sky, white wisps of clouds, an underscore of black shingles and red tile rooftops.

The pews and kneelers were built from blond wood and there was no barrier between the nave and the sanctuary. Josie's shoes were soft soled so it wasn't until she was almost on top of the women cleaning the altar that they noticed her.

"Hello," the tall woman said, her smile glorious in the house of the lord. "You must be the woman Father Ridge is expecting."

"Right through there." The shorter one pointed to a door before Josie could answer.

Josie said her thanks, breathed in the smell of Pledge and Windex as she passed the altar, opened the sacristy door, and found a white haired man repairing a torn vestment.

"Father Ridge?"

He looked up; he smiled.

"You are the spitting image of your mother."

❧

Father Christopher Ridge was eighty-three years old and had lost his faith in many things but not God. He was, however, beginning to have doubts that God was a white-haired, bearded guy. In fact, he was thinking that maybe Joan Osborne had it right; perhaps God was one of us.

And would Josie like something to drink?

And, yes, he learned to sew quite handily when he was in the army so he mended his own vestments. He could also cook and liked to watch reruns of Monk.

Josie found all this out in the space of ten minutes after they had settled in, taking two small chairs near a round table by the window. When he was finished telling her these things, Josie handed him the letter.

"Do, you remember writing this?"

"I do. I wasn't sure what would prompt you to come, or how you would find me, but I've been prepared for many years. Your father asked me to give you this." He pushed a slim book toward her. "He wasn't a man of many words, but I knew he agonized over whether you were strong enough to know these things. I don't think he had any need to worry."

"I don't want to read that," Josie pushed it away "All I want is to know what that letter means."

"Then I suggest you read this. That's what he wanted. If you do that, then I will answer your questions. I suppose it boils down to how curious you are." Father Ridge pushed the book back at her. "Or outraged, depending on what you think you know already."

He went back to his worktable and picked up his needle. She doubted he would be surprised to see her walk out. She doubted he'd be surprised if she stayed. He was a man who accepted things. Before she could make her decision, he said:

"I have always been sorry about your mother."

Then he sighed and started stitching. Josie picked up the small book. Twenty minutes later she sat with one hand to her mouth, the other still holding the book that lay in her lap, and her eyes fixed on the horizon where a golden sun was drowning itself in the sea.

"Are you all right?" Father Ridge touched her shoulder. "Would you like a drink?"

"No. Thanks." She put the diary back on the table, and crossed her arms atop it.

"I'll have one." He fetched a small glass of port and then sat across from her.

"I don't know what to say," Josie began. "What I already knew was surreal. But this? This seems almost impossible."

"It isn't," Father Ridge said. "The Department of Defense recruited your father because he was a trusted officer and passionate about protecting his men in battle. There was no better person to speak for this program than a man like him. He thought he was doing something honorable."

"But he recruited those soldiers for human experiments. The people I saw were shells. They couldn't think. They couldn't communicate. Did he really think that was better than shooting them in the head?"

"It wasn't like that, Josie. The briefing he received was not truthful. He was given a set of parameters that he shared with recruits. He believed they would be subjected to sleep deprivation, hypnosis, and climate extreme experiments. This was nothing more than what they might encounter as prisoners of war. He had no idea about the drugs or the physical abuse. Don't forget, he wasn't the only recruiter. There were two others. They all worked the bases, identified the prospects, signed them up, and sent them on. I have to assume they were also duped, but I can only speak to what your father knew."

"But we lived on a base, he collected his pension. How could that be?"

"Every country has covert operations. The army cooperated with the defense department and made it happen. It was simply assumed your father was deployed overseas and on rotation like everyone else. That meant he could be away from home for long periods of time."

"Then he rocked the boat and it wasn't so simple anymore," Josie said.

"Your father became suspicious when he was denied requested reports on some of his recruits. One thing led to another and he put the pieces together. Your father went to his superiors and threatened to go public if they didn't shut the program down. Instead, they decided to shut him down. He never found out how they convinced your mother to leave the house that night, but once she was part of the program they had the leverage they needed.

"Your father was frantic when he found out. He assaulted a superior officer and at least one of the other recruiters. He called the newspapers. He went to the police."

"No, he didn't," Josie insisted. "There was no missing persons report."

"There was," the priest assured her. "But everywhere he went, the government wiped away his imprint. Paperwork disappeared, people he talked to were reassigned or intimidated."

"If he was causing that much trouble, why wasn't he court martialed or jailed?" Josie asked.

"He was no longer with the army so a court martial was out and jailing him would give him a pulpit. Whoever he was reporting to made it clear that it was very easy to make him disappear completely. There was no mistaking the threat, Josie. If he stayed silent, you would both be safe."

"Me? They threatened a kid?"

"It was implied. Neither one of us believed they would hurt you, but given what they had done to your mother he couldn't risk it." Father Ridge shook his head. "Still, he tried once more. He promised not to pursue the matter if he could see your mother one more time. He had such elaborate plans to save Emily. He was going to bring her home and the three of you would go away and be safe. He was like Rambo."

Christopher Ridge tried to smile but the sad memories outweighed the fond ones and he failed miserably.

"Josie, your father had never seen the actual human devastation this program wreaked until he saw your mother. Emily had no memory of him or you. The only saving grace was a doctor he met. He was kind, but he was frank. Emily would never again be able to live in the real world. Your father felt he had no choice but to leave her where she was. This man gave him her wedding ring. I know that much."

"Ian? Ian Francis. Was that the name of the doctor?" Josie asked.

"I don't know, I'm sorry," Father Ridge answered.

"It must have been him. That's how Ian knew about me. My father told him, not my mother. She never remembered me, but he did."

Josie closed her eyes and thought back over the last weeks. She saw Ian Francis' face and her father's. They both loved the same woman and both risked everything to protect Emily's daughter. She had been so wrong about so many things. Josie opened her eyes again, seeing more clearly than she had for a long while.

"Why didn't you do something?"

"What your father told me was a confession. He was very specific. If you read the diary then I could speak freely." The priest picked up his glass and finished his port. He looked toward the ocean. "I often wondered if I would have been as brave as he was. I was fearful of people who could do such things. These were people you did not cross."

"And that was why all those people were wards of Ha Kuna House," Josie said. "The administrators could legally make decisions about their care and no one would question it. My mother was the exception, but they made sure my father wouldn't make trouble. Not knowing if she was alive or dead, he couldn't risk telling me before he died."

Christopher Ridge looked back at her. He folded his hands on the table. He had aged in the last minutes and looked every minute of eighty-three years.

"I think he felt most terrible that people thought your mother had deserted your family. He loved her so much. He loved you even more. I even think he loved his country, just not the people who ran it. Not after that."

Josie took a deep breath and blew it out through her pursed lips. She said:

"He should have told me."

"There was nothing you could have done. You were a little girl."

Josie picked up the diary.

"I'm not a little girl anymore, Father."

CHAPTER 30

"Josie, my girl, It's me." – Stephen
"I can't talk. I'll be late." – Josie
"Don't hang up. You have to know." – Stephen
"What?" – Josie
"Someone wiped the history in my computer. It's as if Keoloko never did business with Ha Kuna House. Scary, stuff, my girl."
– Stephen
"Lord." – Josie
"I suppose he could help, but I'm more efficient. I have hard copy. Never did fancy a paperless society. The point is that they can do it. Be careful. Bring your glorious body back in one piece." – Stephen
"Yeah, and you watch your back, too." – Josie
"Be an Amazon." – Stephen

అఌఅఌ

Josie walked into the Russell Building entering off Constitution Avenue. She wore the same coat she had worn weeks earlier, the same boots, and the same gloves but now she carried her lawyer's satchel. It was a big, black box of a thing that looked like a traveling file cabinet. The exhibits inside were not going to be used in defense of a client, but rather an indictment of a government run amok.

Her purse went through the metal detector and her briefcase was searched. When everything was handed back, she followed directions to the elevator that would take her to the third floor and Ambrose Patriota's office. Before she went in, Josie stepped aside and took her phone out of her purse. She dialed Archer.

"Pick up," she whispered. "Please, pick up."

When he didn't, Josie leaned against the wall and took a minute. She felt like she was going in to court prepped but not prepared, passionate but already the underdog. She laughed at the fleeting thought that it would be nice to have Stephen Kyle with her. He would get Senator Patriota's attention. Then again, Josie imagined she already had that – or at least she had Eugene Weller's. There was no going back, no calling for reinforcements, so Josie hitched her case and opened the door.

"Ms. Bates." A handsome middle-aged woman hailed her before the door closed. "I'm Norma, the senator's secretary."

"I don't remember you from the last time I was here," Josie said.

"I'm his personal secretary. We had staff to take care of you during the hearings. I understand the Senator has carved out a half on hour for you. You must have made quite an impression when he last saw you."

"I don't think so," Josie answered, "but I hope I will this time."

"Then follow me. I know he's waiting."

They didn't have far to go and yet it felt like Josie was walking the green mile. Josie caught the eye of an aide who was speaking on the phone. He seemed to look through her. At another desk, two young women were engaged in serious debate about the order of a presentation book. This could have been any office in any city in any state but it wasn't. This was the office of the man who could help Josie get justice for her parents, Ian Francis, and all the people who were harmed by what the government had done.

"Here you are." Norma held open the door to Ambrose Patriota's office.

"Thank you," Josie murmured and stepped inside.

The senator sat behind the desk dressed in a dark grey suit, an eggshell colored shirt, and a salmon colored tie. His arm was on his desk and Josie noted the glint of light off his gold cuff links. He was listening intently to Eugene Weller who looked exactly the same as he had weeks ago. He was the forgettable man in a well-cut suit. But when they looked at her, Eugene Weller took on the appearance of a man alight with purpose.

"Ms. Bates." Senator Patriota rose but made her come to him.

"Senator. I appreciate you taking time to see me." Josie shook his hand when she got close enough.

"Not at all."

He gestured toward a chair that was just far enough away from the desk to make a visitor feel slightly unwelcome. Josie pulled the it closer.

"Mr. Weller." Josie gave him a nod as she put down her briefcase.

"Ms. Bates."

"Well," Ambrose began. "I won't insult you with small talk. I understand that you have something grave you wish to share with me."

"I do," Josie said. "The last time we talked, you told me that people like Ian Francis needed someone to speak for them. You joked that, perhaps, he should have hired a lawyer if he wanted to be heard.

"Senator, I am a lawyer. I am speaking for Ian Francis and for my mother and my father. I want to tell you about a conspiracy and crimes committed on those three citizens and other–"

"I already know, Ms. Bates." Ambrose interrupted her as if they had met on the street and he had no time to gossip.

"You know about Ha Kuna House?"

"I do," the senator said. "Eugene?"

The younger man produced a thick file. He placed it on Patriota's desk and stepped back. The senator opened it and looked at the first piece of paper.

"I have a most disturbing overview of an operation that, unfortunately, is the last vestige of a terrible time in our history. CHATTER, Artichoke, MKUltra." He shook his head as he lamented the history. "So many more horrendously executed programs. Our government should be ashamed."

"The government should be held accountable," Josie corrected.

"I understand your mother was one of the unfortunate victims," Ambrose went on. "I am distressed to hear that. Eugene's research, unfortunately, came too late to help her. I have been briefed about the fire. My sincere condolences."

"Yes, there was a fire," Josie said even as she realized he was only going through the motions. He was looking right at her and not seeing the healing burns on her lips, her shorn hair, and the hand that was still red and swollen. "Senator. Look at me."

"I beg your pardon?"

"I need you to pay attention to me," Josie insisted. "First, the history of this project it is not unfortunate, it is appalling. Second, my mother is safe and well."

Eugene's eyes flickered to Patriota who registered no surprise. For Josie, though, Eugene Weller's reaction told her all she needed to know. They had been following the events more closely than she imagined.

"We have a report that six bodies were recovered," Ambrose said. "Isn't that true Eugene?"

"Yes, sir, but the bodies haven't been identified. It was assumed they were the residents."

"Where are the bodies?" Josie asked.

"I don't have that information," Eugene answered.

"I'm sure you'll follow up on that Eugene," Ambrose said. "But it won't be of interest to you, Ms. Bates, since your mother is well."

"You're talking about this like it was a fender bender and we're exchanging insurance information. At least twenty-five U.S. citizens were unwittingly used for experimentation. I don't know how they ended up in Ha Kuna House or why, but I think this is something that deserves to be investigated."

"Certainly it deserves looking into, but not by me. I will, however, pass along this information to Senator Calister. His committee interfaces with the DOD and I think that is the appropriate place to start. Don't you Eug–"

Ambrose never finished his thought. Josie was on her feet, her hand slamming down on his very expensive desk.

"Don't you dare pass this off. Don't you dare," she snapped.

Eugene Weller fell back a step before recovering from his shock and lunging for the phone. He picked it up.

"Securi–" he began but Ambrose stopped him.

"No, Eugene. That's not necessary."

For a minute Josie thought Eugene wasn't going to do as he was told. Finally, he put down the receiver.

"Sit down, Josie. I may call you Josie, may I not?" Ambrose asked.

"I don't think so, Senator." The only thing that landed in the chair was her briefcase. She opened the latches as she spoke. "When I was here before you told me that there was no need to advocate for Ian Francis. You dismissed him as an insane person. Well, Senator, Ian Francis was only crazy because people in this town, in this government, made him that way. They took his life and my mother's as sure as if you executed them. Collateral damage was me and my father and Ian Francis' daughter."

Josie took a deep breath and grasped the first section of files. She pulled them out and put them in front of Patriota.

"I don't want to be referred. I don't want Eugene here being tasked to look into things. I want someone with the power to make this right and that is you. You want to be president? Then act presidential. Find out what Marigold is and how far it reaches, make reparations, and make whoever is responsible pay."

"Senator, please, let me get security," Eugene pleaded.

"No. No need. I will give Ms. Bates the answers she wants." He gestured toward the chair again. "Now, sit down."

Josie was like a live wire in a puddle of water, dancing, sparking, dangerous because she couldn't control her ire. She should have waited for Archer. She should have brought Stephen. She should have held back until she could speak as a lawyer and not a daughter. But she was here now so all the choices were hers. Patriota nodded again. She moved her briefcase and sat.

"Eugene, I wonder if you might leave us."

"I don't think that's wise, Senator," Eugene objected.

Josie looked at him. Her blue eyes were like ice and her jaw was made of stone and he was afraid to leave her with Ambrose Patriota. Still, he had no choice.

"Where is your mother, now?" Ambrose asked when the door closed and Eugene was gone.

"That isn't your concern yet. Not until there are hearings," Josie answered.

"There won't be hearings, Ms. Bates." When Josie didn't respond, his curiosity got the best of him. "Do you want to know why?"

"It seems you want to tell me."

"There is only one reason and that is because they would be futile. Everyone who was responsible for what happened to your mother is dead or of no consequence. Who would we punish? Who would we apologize to?"

"You know about Marigold, don't you? What is it?" Josie asked.

"Marigold was the name assigned to the project to care for those people who were affected by some of our more ambitious attempts to understand the human mind. MKUltra and CHATTER subjects were among them. The people who participated were well cared for and given the best of everything. If you saw the house in

Hawaii, you know that. Sadly, we were never able to reverse the effects of their treatments but we did not abandon them."

"Participated?" Josie breathed. "These people didn't participate. They were kidnapped and assaulted. The government is not excused when their actions are egregious just because they offer a bed to the tortured."

"The government has paid a high price for MKUltra," Ambrose argued, unhappy that she wasn't pacified. "We lost the confidence of our citizens even though we had their best interests at heart. Certainly we can be misguided, but that doesn't mean there wasn't good to come from all these things. We learned so much about the mind and our soldiers benefited. Because of these programs, we learned to create weapons that attack the brain and not the body."

"You destroyed lives," Josie countered.

"Do not make us out to be barbarians. We cared for those we hurt."

"That's what Ha Kuna House was? The government's way of making up? You should have just finished the job you started and killed them. It would have been kinder. It sure as heck would have been cheaper."

A tremor of shock and surprise ran through Ambrose Patriota. It was the first real emotion Josie had seen from the man.

"You don't mean that. You can't mean that."

"You kept twenty-five people hidden away and waited for them to die. Why not put them out of their misery?"

"Because this is America. We don't kill indiscriminately. We care for our own."

"I can't believe it," Josie breathed. "Are you listening to yourself? You really believe the government is the priority."

"No, not the government. The country and all it embodies. The goodness, the ethic, and the morality that is synonymous with America. It is what I, and all those who came before me, protect. There are always those who must sacrifice for that. Our warriors, ambassadors, our citizens—"

"You're crazier than Ian Francis was. Do you hear yourself? These people didn't sacrifice, they were ripped away from their families," Josie argued.

"They had no families." This time it was Patriota's hand that came down hard on the desk, his eyes that flashed. "Their lives had purpose because of what was done to them. What we found out helped our soldiers survive prison camps and interminable deployments and…"

"My mother had family." Josie was half out of her chair and fighting back. "Someone has to pay. I want the records opened. I want to know how many facilities like Ha Kuna House are viable. I want autopsies on the people who died in that fire. I want to understand what was done to these people."

She pushed the files toward him.

"These are meticulous records. Nazi Germany kept records of their 'experiments' as if it was something to be proud of and so did this government. Read these, Senator, and then tell me how humane these programs were."

"Do you want me to be ashamed? If that's all you want, sit down and I will read them now."

"I want more than that. I want you to go public. If you won't, I will go to every media outlet and release these documents."

"And I have the power to stop you. You realize that, don't you? I have the pulpit, Josie, not you. I have the power, not you."

"And I have the passion. And I have my mother. People will look at her—"

"They will look at her the same way they looked at Ian Francis. She is just a sad, crazy person."

Josie drew up and stood tall. She lowered her voice.

"There is a man named Michael Horn. His grandfather was a victim. The Supreme Court is poised to hear his case."

"That case will never be heard." Ambrose said.

"You're not that powerful," Josie scoffed.

"No, but God is. Mr. Horn died two days ago. A hit and run while he was jogging." Ambrose chuckled at her expression. He knew what she was thinking. "No. No spy games. The road was dark. A woman hit him. Fate intervened. No one will pick up Michael Horn's cause, and he will not be one of your soldiers."

Ambrose stood up and went around his chair. He rested his arms on the high back, relaxing now he had the upper hand.

"Josie, there is no one who remembers or cares about these things. Ha Kuna House is gone. I doubt your basketful of files will add up to an indictment. You don't want to be Michael Horn and spend fifteen years of your life working through the court system looking for some sort of justice. Go back to your business. There is no pound of flesh to be had; at least none that will satisfy you."

Josie listened to Ambrose Patriota's smooth voice, his concern for her life, his logical arguments, but her gaze was fixed on the wall behind him where pictures of a prestigious life were displayed. There was only one picture that interested her; the one of Ambrose Patriota, young and in uniform, his eyes hidden by the black bill of his hat.

She had known him before.

She had seen him before.

She had been younger then and looking up at a man taller than she was.

Josie got out of her chair and walked behind him. Patriota swiveled around to watch as Josie took the picture off the wall. She looked from the picture to him and smiled grimly.

"I know whose pound of flesh I want. It's yours."

Josie tossed the picture onto his desk as she walked back to where her briefcase was. She talked while she swept her files back in to her case.

"The night my mother disappeared she was talking to a man in uniform. I saw them but they didn't see me." Josie snapped her case shut and looked at him. "You were in our living room. You were the one who convinced her to leave. What did you tell her? Why did you take her?"

"Eugene was correct to be worried about you. I must give him credit. I had to be reminded about your mother and father and I have no idea what I told her. It was so long ago. I was so ambitious back then. My superiors were very pleased with how I solved the problem of your father. It seemed a little thing at the time. It was a little thing. "

Josie stood up straight. She felt lightheaded. She had not really expected an answer; she had not been prepared for an admission. Her jaw twitched. Her gut clenched. The great man thought her mother was a footnote, a little thing, her father was of no consequence and both of them were stepping-stone in his career. Now, facing off with Josie, he was once again convinced of his superiority. She, too, was a little thing.

He shouldn't have been so cocky.

"This little thing has come back to bite you, Senator." Josie said. "I intend to destroy you. I don't care it if takes days or months or years. I will not let my mother and father be forgotten, I will not let the country be served by a man who does not see its citizens as worthy of his attention or protection. I swear that I will not end up dead on the roadside like Michael Horn or mindless like my mother. I promise, I will finish what my father started. "

Josie turned to leave but Ambrose called to her before she reached the door.

"Those files are the property of the United States Government, Ms. Bates."

Josie paused. Her lips tipped up and she considered Ambrose Patriota with a lazy gaze. She hefted the case, unhinged the latches and dumped the contents on the floor.

"They're all yours."

"Think about what you are doing. What was done is done. It is history," Ambrose warned.

"We learn from history." Josie ambled toward him until she was close enough to put him on his guard. "I will make a deal, Senator. Step aside. Do not stand for nomination. You will retire when your term is over and disappear. No speaking engagements, no books. Do that, and I will back off. "

"You can't stop everything you find distasteful. That is the way of the world, Josie."

"I can try, Ambrose," she said as she turned to leave. Before she opened the door, she had one more thing to say. "I've changed my mind. You've got two weeks."

CHAPTER 31

"I can barely hear you. Jo? You there?" – Archer
"Archer? You're breaking up?" – Josie
"I'll be home...Okay?" – Archer
"Archer?" – Josie

⤝⤞

Burt washed glasses. Josie sat at the counter and Max was lying at her feet. The television flickered and the joint wasn't quite jumping. It was that odd afternoon time when people tried to sneak out of work early on a Friday and only half of them made it. In another few hours Burt's by the Beach would be too busy for Josie's taste. These days she wanted to be home. Still, it was the perfect place to meet for the big event.

"What do you hear from Amelia?" Burt asked.

"Stephen has them all settled," Josie answered.

"That Stephen was a piece of work. I'd like to have some gorgeous girls to go home to." Burt held up a glass, gave it one last wipe, and put it on the shelf behind him. "What about Emily?"

Josie crossed her arms on the counter and smiled. "She's happy to be home."

"That was a tough call for you, huh? I mean sending her back."

"Not really. I expected it to be, but Hawaii is her home, Amelia is her daughter." Josie pick up a paper napkin and started folding it into ever-smaller squares as she talked. "Once I heard a judge talk about her husband's Alzheimer's. He was in a home and he had a new girlfriend. The interviewer asked the judge if that was upsetting to her. She said it was a joyous thing because her husband had found love in his reality. She still visited him every week, but he thought she was a friend. I'll be satisfied if Emily remembers me when I visit."

"And she's in good hands," Burt pointed out. "I liked Amelia. I'm glad she isn't going to be alone."

"Me, too. It worked for everyone. I can afford to pay her for Emily's care, Emily has a home, and they both share memories of Ian."

"Did you get him when you were in Washington? I'd want someone to get me," Burt picked up another glass and started wiping.

"I did. We'll scatter his ashes when Archer and I go over in June." Josie reached down to pet Max who raised his head into the caress. "In the end, Ian Francis was the hero. He must have been so frightened when he made that trip and walked into that building. I wish I could have thanked him."

When she sat up again, Burt was looking worried. He said: "You really, doing okay? I mean really?"

"I am, thanks." Josie patted his hand. "Hannah's not home, but Archer is."

Burt nodded to the window. "Yeah, but it looks like he picked up a chick on his way over. You better watch yourself."

Josie swiveled on the stool just as Archer and Faye came through the door. Archer nodded at Burt and kissed Josie.

"Sorry we're late," he said.

"You're not. We have another two minutes."

"I don't know if I'm ready for this news conference," Faye said. "I'm going to need a drink."

Burt made a Bloody Mary for Faye and put out two beers for Josie and Archer. A couple came in and he pointed them to the back of the restaurant. He hurried away with menus but he was back just as the five o'clock news opened on a shot of Senator Ambrose Patriota standing at a podium and surrounded by colleagues.

"Turn it up, Burt," Archer directed and all four of them fell silent as the senator began to speak.

"I have a statement to make. I realize it is late in the day but I did not believe this should wait."

"That's bull," Archer muttered. "He knows any announcement on Friday is buried."

"Shh." Josie nudged him to silence. She wanted to hear every word.

"It has been brought to my attention that a federal facility located on the island of Molokai in Hawaii was recently destroyed by fire. After investigation, it was determined that this facility was overseen by the Department of Defense. Its purpose was to house the last victims of government run programs that conducted controlled experiments on human subjects. These programs were a horrendous chapter in our history and the last of the active programs was shut down in 1990."

Patriota squared his shoulders and paused. The sound of cameras clicking could be heard. He touched his lips as if trying to keep them from trembling. He was a very good politician because, when he looked at the camera, Josie could swear she saw tears in his eyes.

"I come before you ashamed to admit that many years ago, when I was a young Army officer, I took part in the recruitment of my fellow soldiers for these programs. They were then subjected to torture and drug experiments. I was not involved in the running of those experiments. My job was to simply make contact with members of the military and recruit them."

"And kidnap their wives," Archer muttered.

"For these actions as a young officer, under orders from my superiors, I am deeply sorry…"

"Here it comes, Jo. He's going to step down," Faye whispered.

Archer pressed against Josie, enfolding her in his arms.

"No, something else is going on," Josie murmured.

"I do not know what the future will bring," Patriota went on. "But I do know that our citizens are precious. Our goal should be to protect each of them from enemies outside our borders, not become the enemy within.

"I am no longer an army officer and I am no longer young, nor am I inconsequential. I am a United States senator with the moral charge to right wrongs when I find them. As such, I cannot let this pass without a complete investigation of the fire at Ha Kuna House. To that end, I am asking the Justice Department to look into the matter after hearing recorded conversations between the high-ranking officials at Department of Defense and Senator Woodrow Calister. Senator Calister not only had knowledge of the covert program called Marigold as recently as fourteen days ago, but he was personally involved in a decision to shut down the facility. Only days after one of his telephone conversations with others in the government, the facility was burned to the ground resulting in the deaths of six United States citizens. I will be calling for a full investigation..."

Josie shook her head. The man was the ultimate politician.

"He's good," she said. "He confesses to talking in church and then passes the blame for the mortal sin. Patriota will get a slap on the wrist and Calister will be sent to political hell."

"What do you want to do now?" Archer asked.

Josie slid off the stool and picked up Max's leash. Archer put his arm around her.

"I want to go home. Night Faye. Burt." Josie leaned in and gave Faye a kiss.

"I'm sorry," the older woman said.

"Don't be. Patriota may think he's won, but this is just the first skirmish," she assured them.

"Hang in, Josie," Burt called as he watched them go. He looked at Faye and raised a brow. "It ain't over 'till it's over, is it Faye?"

"Not where Josie's concerned," she answered.

⇨⇦

Inside his very comfortable home, Woodrow Calister sat in his very special room, watched the television, and smoked. In a few hours he would be angry, a few hours after that he might feel like ending it all, but right now as he watched Ambrose turn to the very beautiful Lydia on camera and the very beautiful Lydia kiss him as if he were a most courageous man, Woodrow Calister could only admire Ambrose Patriota. He was a brilliant man and Woodrow was only a smart one.

He stood up, switched off the television, and refilled his drink. He was just about to taste it when he started to laugh. Finally, he understood what Ambrose had meant when he said he needed Woodrow for something more important than the vice-presidency. Woodrow was Ambrose's sacrifice to the god of politics; Woodrow had been thrown under the bus to save the presidency.

Woodrow raised his glass to a master.

Eugene answered questions from the press, spoke of Ambrose's exhaustion, his shock that a project like Marigold still existed, and reinforced the message of Senator Patriota's youth and the miniscule part he played in the whole affair. Eugene promised to keep them apprised of the timing of the hearings that would, he assured the press, be forthcoming.

When he was finished, he went back to his office and tidied up. He saw messages from Jerry Norn and Mark Hyashi but he would deal with them in the morning. All in all, things had gone very well. It did not occur to Eugene to lament Woodrow Calister's fate, it only occurred to him that he had been right all along: Ambrose Patriota deserved Eugene's undying loyalty.

Once outside Burt's, Josie and Archer ambled down The Strand, keeping pace with Max. When Josie nuzzled closer, Archer stopped and cradled her.

"I'll need to call Stephen and Amelia," Josie said as she snuggled into him. "They won't be surprised, but they'll be sad. Still, everyone is safe and I guess that's what matters."

"It's bitter sweet, Jo," Archer noted.

"Sure is. But one day it's going to be all sweet. I know where there is a cave with a whole lot of interesting things in it." She tipped up her head and smiled. "I have a friend who has a truck and can move all those interesting things right into a Keoloko warehouse until we need them."

"I had a feeling you weren't going to leave it alone."

Archer pulled Josie into him. She rested her head on his chest as Max settled at their feet.

"I'm glad you're home," she said.

"I'm sorry it's just me," he answered. "When that girl came around she had nothing. She hadn't seen Hannah in weeks."

"Then this homecoming is bitter sweet, too." Josie whispered. "Mostly sweet."

Just as she stepped back and put her arms around Archer's neck, just as her lips met his, just as she was feeling safe at home, Josie's phone rang. She pulled back but kept her eyes on her lover as she answered it.

"Hello."

In the next second Josie Bates tensed. Archer tightened his embrace and her eyes locked with his as she said:

"Hannah?"

<<<<>>>

Thrillers by Rebecca Forster

The Best-Selling Witness Series

Hostile Witness (#1)
Silent Witness (#2)
Privileged Witness (#3)
Expert Witness (#4)
Eyewitness (#5)
Forgotten Witness (#6)
Dark Witness (#7)

Before Her Eyes
The Mentor
Character Witness
Beyond Malice
Keeping Counsel
(USA Today Best Seller)

To contact me and to see all my books, visit me at:

RebeccaForster.com

Printed in Great Britain
by Amazon.co.uk, Ltd.,
Marston Gate.